ROOTS OF MURDER

ROOTS OF MURDER

A Novel of Suspense

R. JEAN REID

MIDNIGHT INK
WOODBURY, MINNESOTA

First Edition
First Printing, 2016

Book format by Teresa Pojar
Cover design by Lisa Novak
Cover image by iStockphoto.com/4672611/©spxChrome

Midnight Ink, an imprint of Llewellyn Worldwide Ltd.

Library of Congress Cataloging-in-Publication Data
Names: Reid, R. Jean, author.
Title: Roots of murder : a novel of suspense / R. Jean Reid.
Description: First Edition. | Woodbury, Minnesota : Midnight Ink, [2016]
Identifiers: LCCN 2016007448 (print) | LCCN 2016016637 (ebook) | ISBN
    9780738748771 (paperback) | ISBN 9780738749709 (ebook)
Subjects: LCSH: Murder—Fiction. | Drunk driving—Fiction. | GSAFD: Mystery
    fiction.
Classification: LCC PS3568.E3617 R66 2016 (print) | LCC PS3568.E3617 (ebook)
    DDC 813/.54—dc23
LC record available at https://lccn.loc.gov/2016007448

Midnight Ink
Llewellyn Worldwide Ltd.
2143 Wooddale Drive
Woodbury, MN 55125-2989
www.midnightinkbooks.com

Printed in the United States of America

To the Saints and Sinners Sazerac Gang.
Your insanity keeps me sane.

PROLOGUE

November, 1963

Dunwood's knots were sloppy, like the shirttail hanging out of his pants. Making no attempt to cover up what she was doing, Hattie Jacobs untied one, pulled the rope taut, and retied the knot. She could feel his eyes on her. He had said, "For you, a special deal—I give you a break on my usual charge." Hattie understood him; she'd been married, now widowed, with four children as evidence she knew what to do with men. Dunwood had looked her up and down after he said it, even going so far as to lick his lips. Hattie had coolly replied, "I don't need any special deals, Mr. Dunwood. I just want a fair price to get my belongings to New Orleans."

Hattie retied another knot. She then looped the rope in front of the wardrobe so it wouldn't shift. It was pressed against the couch where her kids would be for the long drive. Dunwood was supposed to help with the loading, but he had lazed his way through it, trying to flirt with the widow, and, when she ignored him, working his charms on Daisy, who at thirteen was both inexperienced in male attention and too well trained in being polite to her elders, so she giggled at his tired jokes.

Daniel, Jr., with anger still scowling his face, had pushed himself at a brutal pace, hauling and carrying, not waiting for Dunwood or Emmett to help with the heavier pieces, just dragging them himself. Emmett, two years younger than Daniel, had been the calm one, loading the truck carefully, putting the couch up against the cab. Rosa had stayed in the kitchen, methodically wrapping dishes in old newspaper and putting them in boxes, then labeling each box carefully. Daisy had flitted from task to task, distracted by Dunwood and her temperament.

Hattie had sold a lot of her things, but the truck was still full. It didn't seem much, though—one truckload for all the years she'd spend on this farm. She'd married Daniel when she was seventeen; this had been her life since then. All her children had been born here, in the back bedroom, the one closest to the well.

"You gonna ride up in the cab with me, Miss Hattie?" Dunwood asked with his lazy smile.

"I'm going to check the house one more time," Hattie told him. She had checked it, Emmett had checked it, Daisy had checked it, carrying out the old doll she'd abandoned to the attic when she'd turned twelve; now she was holding it as if it would give her some of her childhood back.

Hattie briskly walked through the rooms, her mind in the present; one last check that everything was packed. There would be time for memories later, when the rooms weren't such a palpable presence of all that was held within them.

Hattie left the house.

Dunwood had climbed into the cab and was starting the motor.

Hattie made a decision. "Daniel, ride up front with us. Emmett, Daisy, and Rosa, y'all get in back."

Emmett helped his sisters in, at twelve already becoming the man of the house. Rosa barely took his hand, scrambling in, probably bruising a place on her thigh as she did. She was ten and still enough of a tomboy not to take help from a brother. Daisy let Emmett carefully guide her. He even held her doll while she settled herself. Hattie couldn't remember any other time when the boys had touched the girls' toys, save for an occasional tease.

She abruptly turned from the sight of her youngest son carefully holding that doll. She couldn't, she wouldn't, cry. She motioned Daniel to get in first and briefly enjoyed the scowl that flitted across Dunwood's face as he realized he wasn't going to have Hattie all alone in the cab.

Hattie slid in beside her son. It would be a long ride in this slow truck, three or four hours depending on traffic. Hattie had been to New Orleans twice before, riding the highway along the beaches where she and her children couldn't swim, then into the swamp and bayous that separated Mississippi from Louisiana.

Dunwood let out the clutch and the truck pulled forward with a jerk. Hattie had intended to stare straight ahead, but in the last moment, she turned back to look at the place that had been her life for twenty years. The fields were a sleek and glossy green, the old oak spreading its majestic branches over the lawn as if embracing the land. The house was small, a faded white with green trim. In the center of the yard was the scorched place, a raw burn against the green grass.

Hattie turned her gaze ahead; she wouldn't look back a second time.

ONE

"HAS THE NEWS PICKED up since yesterday or would you be interested in old bones in the woods?"

It took Nell a moment to recognize her caller. "Kate?" she verified.

"Yeah, sorry, bad signal and low battery. I'm two miles past the Moss Road turnoff, out in the fringes of the state park."

"What kind of bones?" Nell asked.

"Human. Been here a long time. Some hunter will finally come home."

Nell glanced out her window. It was a beautiful day. A look at her desk revealed only mounds of paper. She quickly got directions from Kate, not wanting her battery to die.

Yesterday when she'd picked up Josh from his bicycle maintenance class, while waiting for him to organize his tools, Nell had chatted with Kate Ryan, who now ran the bike shop. Nell didn't know Kate very well; most of what she'd learned was secondhand from Josh, and then only what he thought was exciting, like Kate used to be a forest ranger and had once arrested someone in the backwoods, marching him out in a four-hour hike. Kate had moved here almost a year before to care for her Uncle Toby, who'd recently died from cancer. Until a few months ago he'd usually come to the shop with Kate, although at the end he had done little more than sit and watch as she ran everything.

We should be friends, Nell had thought, but their conversation was still mostly confined to idle chatter, the weather, the next bike class. They had each said, "I'm so sorry for your loss" but hadn't moved beyond that. Yesterday Nell had commented it was such a slow news week she was almost tempted to run a blank front page with the headline "Nothing Happened."

Kate promised if anything interesting transpired, Nell would be the first to know. "Bones in the woods" did indeed qualify as interesting in a town like Pelican Bay.

Nell put on the old running shoes she kept in the office—Kate had warned her that she would have a half-mile walk in the woods—and then got her usual equipment: camera, notebook, and pens.

Neither of the paper's two cub reporters, Jacko or Carrie, was about. Lucky for them or Nell would have assigned them to look into dusty missing persons files to see if they could match likely names to the bones.

Just as Nell was at the door, Pam, the receptionist/secretary/ whatever's needed, said to her, "There's a call for you." The tone of Pam's voice told Nell this wasn't a call she wanted to take.

"Who is it?"

"Tanya Jones."

"I'm not in," Nell said shortly, almost adding, I'll never be in for that bitch. But she kept a thin veneer of professionalism and avoided cursing in front of her staff.

As the door slammed behind her, Nell realized anger had leaked into her actions. She strode across the town square, taking the long route to get to the parking lot, hoping the physical motion would calm her fury.

Tanya Jones was calling Nell to ask for mercy. Tanya's husband, Junior Jones, or J.J. to his drinking buddies, was the man who had made Nell a widow with two children. His truck had weaved into the wrong lane, over the speed limit. Thom and Nell had been on their way home.

Tanya was trying to keep J.J. from going to jail, and she seemed to think if she pleaded hard enough Nell would drop the charges. Nell had been barely polite the first time Tanya called, coolly cutting into Tanya's crying about losing her husband, her kids their father, the paycheck to pay for the diapers, to tell her that if her husband was really concerned about his kids he wouldn't have been driving blind drunk. With that Nell had softly put the phone down. But Tanya kept calling back, as if this was all she could think to do. Tanya hadn't the wit to see that not only was this not working, but saying "he was just having a little fun, only a few drinks and he makes one mistake, it's not like he was trying to kill anyone," while an excuse to use with their friends, didn't appease the new widow.

They had gone there together because it was late, and rainy. Neither said it, but Nell was a better driver, less distracted than Thom. Nor did they say it wouldn't do for her, a woman, to go alone. At times she fought those assumptions, but not that night. She preferred being with Thom than alone. A moonshine bust in the far, rural part of the county. The sheriff had called, offered to let them— Thom—take pictures if they hurried.

It had been late, after midnight, by the time they headed home on the dark, winding road, a tangle of trees guarding either side.

J.J. came careening around a curve, far over the line, slamming his heavier truck into their car, spinning it into the trees on the side of the road. Thom, in the passenger seat, was trapped between metal and jagged branches, solid wood. Nell remembered a sudden moment of terror, the scream of metal, her scream for Thom and the answering silence until she slid into a fog of pain and shock.

She woke in the hospital. In the cacophony of machines, people talking, TVs blaring, there was another silence. No one would answer her questions about Thom until the far-too-young police officer came and stood in her doorway. Even he didn't need to speak; his presence gave the news.

The sheriff had suggested Nell not view the body, they could do identification from dental records. She had ignored him and left the hospital for the morgue. The horrific image stayed with her, but she had to know, had to see Thom one final time. Looking at his battered and bruised corpse told Nell he was gone, never coming home.

J.J., in his much bigger and heavier truck, had stumbled away from the wreck. He tried to hide, pulling the license plate off the back, but he left the registration in the glove box. His black truck had a Confederate flag and a skull-and-crossbones on the back window, and that starred X cross and leering skull were jarring enough details for Nell to remember despite her bruised daze. They had picked him up half an hour later with blood still dripping out of his nose. He claimed the .2 alcohol level was from chugging bourbon since the accident "for medicinal purposes." He also claimed he hadn't seen another car, that his truck had blown a tire and skidded off the road. Then he "remembered" the other car, but swore the other people had been fine, talked to him and everything.

Nell talked to no one in the minutes after the accident, only screamed into the silence. She remembered nothing human until waking in the hospital, only the huge truck with its skull face. The last time Thom had talked to anyone had been in those few moments before … before it all dissolved into terror.

Tomorrow would be a month. The days were fragile. A phone call would shatter the calm she willed for herself—and walled around herself. The widow had to go on, care for her two children, run the paper Thom's grandfather had founded.

Get in your car and drive to the woods, Nell told herself; look at some old bones and a long-ago tragedy. That was what she did, thankful that Kate gave directions like a woman, descriptions instead of numbers. "Turn left where Moss Road crosses the highway, there's an old abandoned store there; follow Moss Road, keep a look-out for a lot with two ugly trailers on it."

Nell found herself bumping down a dirt road. Kate's directions here had been to stay on this road long enough "to get the car good and dusty, then look for an uprooted oak tree. Park around there and look for the purple bandanna tied to a tree to mark the trail. Follow the trail until you run into me and the bones. You should see my bike pulled to the side about fifteen feet in."

The oak tree was as promised, one limb protruding halfway into the road. After parking her car safely past the oak, and Doc Davies' car, Nell got out, just as the good doctor came puffing down the trail. Doc was the coroner, a genial general practitioner, who seemed to prefer the dead to dealing with managed health care. He was in his late sixties, with a round body and round face, eyes circled by round glasses and his head circled by a ring of white hair so sparse it did nothing to alleviate the roundness of his skull. Nell had met him on numerous social occasions; he liked to be out and about with a good glass of bourbon and a big, fat—dare she think—round cigar.

"Hello, Doctor Davies," Nell called out.

8

"Oh? Nell?" He squinted through his round glasses at her. "None of this Doctor Davies stuff. Call me David."

David Davies. Either his mother had a sharp sense of irony or a lack of imagination; Nell wasn't sure which.

"Even old, clearly dead bones require paperwork," he said conversationally as he leaned against his car.

"So what do you do with old bones in the woods?" Nell asked him.

"You dig them up, try to identify them, and then bury them again." He paused to catch his breath, his face now red from the hike. "I'm leaving the messy digging to Kate. She knows a lot more about old bones than I do." The coroner may have had many redeeming qualities, but the only one Nell came into contact with was his cheerful willingness to admit what he didn't know.

"She gave me a call. Thought I might be interested in the story," Nell said, to give him a chance to grab a few more breaths. Something else to learn about Kate—how she knew enough about recovering skeletons for Doctor Davies to let her do it. This was the kind of story the *Pelican Bay Crier* did well. Not just the name of the person, but who was he? How long was he lost? What happened to his family after he hadn't come home? Or if those questions had no answers, what happened to bones discovered in the woods? How many died similar lonely deaths?

"It's good to see you up and about," Doc said.

Nell took that to mean the bruises had faded. Her stitches were out, the cut on her eyebrow now just a thin red line. "It's a beautiful day," she answered.

"I'm so sorry about Thom. What a horrible loss for you and all of us." His words were practiced, easy. He had said them over and over again through the years.

Nell felt a flare of anger at his adept sympathy.

Then David Davies exhibited another redeeming quality—he seemed to notice. "It's a beautiful day to be in the woods. Unless you're a cigar man like myself and prefer slippers to hiking boots." He took a labored breath to illustrate his point.

Just as quickly, Nell felt ashamed. Don't be angry at the people who are trying to be kind, be angry at those who aren't. "I just had to get out. Too much paperwork at the office and it's supposed to rain tomorrow."

"A good choice, dear." With that, Doc Davies heaved himself into his car, a round Volkswagen. Maybe that was another redeeming quality, Nell thought as she watched him drive off—a man who matched his car.

She found the purple bandanna hanging from a sapling pine tree. It was good to be out of the office. Too many memories hung in those rooms. Dolan Ferguson, the paper's business manager, had tactfully suggested Nell change her office around. He hadn't said the words "move Thom's desk"—the desk that used to be Thom's—"out, rearrange the space so it doesn't look as if it's waiting for him to return." They shared—had shared—the office, her desk on one side and his on the other, facing each other with a space between wide enough for people to come in and talk. Or be caught in the crossfire, as Thom said. Maybe it wasn't just for her, Nell suddenly thought, awareness breaking the numbness of grief. Dolan had started working for Thom's father, had seen the boy grow into the man and into the Editor-in-Chief. Jacko and Carrie were the newest staff members and even they had been there for close to a year. They were probably wondering what the Widow McGraw would do. Could she run the paper by herself? Sell it to outsiders?

Nell had stayed away for a whole week with Thom's death and funeral, keeping her bruised face—and the guilt on it that she'd survived with only those bruises, a mild concussion, and some stitches—hidden. The next week she had come in to take care of the most necessary things, then found she needed the routine, and last week she'd come back full time. But she hadn't thought beyond the next day, the next week. Brushing a spider web out of her face, Nell realized that she would have to start thinking about the future; was this what she wanted for herself, to be running a paper in a small city on the Gulf of Mexico?

Thom should have been the one to survive. One of her first groggy memories was seeing the implacable fury on her mother-in-law's face as she stood at the foot of Nell's bed. She never said, never even hinted with words, but it was there. Two sons lost—one gone at an early age, drowned in a tide his eight-year-old body was not strong enough to fight. Now Thom, the one grown to manhood, and all she had left was her quisling daughter-in-law. A half-century of Southern politeness couldn't keep her rage completely hidden.

"I don't have to decide today," she said out loud. "Tomorrow … some tomorrow." But for today, the paper was here and would be her life. "At least I have something to put on the front page."

The path was muddy from the recent rains, although the day was brilliant with sunshine. Nell felt a faint stirring of excitement, of being on a story, the feeling that had caused her to choose journalism. Nell McGraw, intrepid girl reporter, bushwhacking through the forest in search of ancient bones. Mixed in with the excitement was also a faint stirring of relief—in the past month, she'd begun to think she would never feel anything again except alternating grief and fury.

One of the muddy patches revealed a recent mark of a boot print, assuring Nell that she had indeed turned at the right purple bandanna. The next sign of humanity was the sound of someone whistling. If I was alone in the woods with a skeleton, I'd whistle, Nell thought. Something to keep me company besides bleached bones.

"Hey, Kate," she called.

"Friend or foe?" Kate called back.

Nell followed the path around a large live oak, then spotted Kate about ten yards away. She realized Kate was probably in her early to mid thirties; she'd thought of her as younger. Maybe it was so often seeing her on a bike instead of driving, as if those were signifiers of youth and age. Kate was taller than Nell by several inches, with wheat-blond hair that had a few strands of gray to prove she didn't dye it.

"Friend, I hope," she answered.

"Friend, indeed. Come take a look at what I stumbled over."

As Nell approached, Kate crossed behind a large pine tree that had been a victim of lightning some time ago. It had recently split in half, one of the dead halves fallen, caught only by the encasing vines. Kate pointed to the skull revealed by the disturbed ground under the dead tree.

"He's been here a good long time," Kate said.

"How can you tell that?"

"I studied anthropology in grad school, including a few courses in forensics. This fellow has gone to bone, no cartilage or flesh left. Doesn't seem to be any cloth from clothing. Plus I'm guessing the tree grew over the grave, and that tree had a few decades of life before the lightning hit it."

"Are you sure it's a he?"

"No, just assuming. My first guess was this was a hunter who wasn't careful about the safety on his gun."

"What's your second guess?"

For an answer, Kate picked up two bones. "Doc Davies told me I might as well pull this fellow from the ground; he's clearly dead. These are the femurs, the thigh bones." She lifted the bones to chest height and held them together.

"Two of them. Aren't there supposed to be two?"

"Not two left ones," Kate said. "It's been a while since I've done much with bones and I could be wrong, but ..." She trailed off.

Nell stated the obvious. "Two left ones mean two dead people. Two careless hunters?"

"In one place, at one time? Could happen, but it's stretching probability fairly thin. Two guys get into an argument, they both have guns, one shoots, then the other one fires back and they both kill each other."

"So we have a very old drunken brawl," Nell said.

"Maybe, but why would they be on top of each other like this? They're both shot, they're both dying, they've killed each other, why cuddle up?"

"Maybe animals moved them." But she caught the other woman's unease.

"Animals might have scattered them, but we're again stretching the laws of chance to think two raccoons buried them on top of each other."

"Have you called the sheriff?"

"Oh, yeah, I was a good little girl, called him before I called you. But he's tied up with some jackknifed eighteen-wheeler spilling chemicals out on I-10. He said these old bones could sit a while longer." Then she added, "Of course, that was when I thought it was some stupid hunter. Guess I should call him and the doc again."

"Good thing you brought a cell phone."

"And a tree with easy enough branches to climb so I can get a signal," Kate muttered as she headed for the live oak with convenient branches.

Nell began taking pictures, starting at the spot where she'd first seen Kate. These shots might be for more than the front page. As she came back again, she heard the end of Kate's conversation.

"Sheriff Hickson, I used to be a forest ranger, so I know a few things about law enforcement, plus I studied forensic anthropology for a few years. I might be as expert as you can get before the rains come." There were a few more "uh-huhs," and then she punched the phone off.

"He's still at the accident scene," she said. "Two rubberneckers going the opposite way wrecked into each other and now both sides of the interstate are blocked, with one fatality, and Doc Davies is there, too. Do we do the right thing and call the chief of police?"

"So he can tell us it's not his jurisdiction?" Nell asked. The police took care of the town of Pelican Bay, and the sheriff covered the rest of Tchula County. Wiz Brown, the acting chief of police, had started with the department at eighteen and was now counting down hour by hour until he could retire in a few months. Seniority alone had propelled him into the chief's post when his predecessor had decided to have sex with a prostitute and not pay. The lady of the night had taken revenge by handcuffing the former chief to the bumper of his patrol car and relieving him of his pants. She had also taken the key to the handcuffs and called the media, allowing them plenty of time to take photos before a locksmith was summoned. Nell had published a shot on the front page, one of the most tasteful of the bunch with just a bare cheek showing. The ink wasn't dry on the chief's resignation letter—demanded by the aldermen in a rare show of actual decision-making—before he was beyond the town limits. So now Wiz Brown was in charge, and his vision for his term seemed to be to do as little as possible. He had refused to investigate a vandalism call because he claimed it had happened five yards beyond the city limits.

Thom had been content to let Whiz be. "He'll be out as soon as the aldermen find someone permanent. Why get riled up over a toppled mailbox?" But Nell had been annoyed enough to find the surveyor's map for Pelican Bay and wrote a story about the police not answering a call that turned out to be within the city limits.

Kate started to beckon Nell up to her branch, then seemed to remember that Acting Chief Brown was not likely to respond favorably to a request from Nell McGraw. It had been her byline on the story. Kate dialed the number.

Nell didn't even pretend to move away.

Kate was on what appeared to be hold for several minutes. Then a few "yeses" followed by, "Well, yes, it is way beyond the town limits, but this may be murder."

Nell watched the expression on the woman's face, Kate's growing irritation as she listened.

"I *have* called the sheriff. He's out on I-10 with the chemical spill," Kate said.

Nell was now jotting notes.

"In other words, Chief Brown, you're not coming out here to investigate what may be a murder scene?" Kate said bluntly.

Clearly the chief wasn't close enough to retirement to leave that bald statement without putting a spin on it, as Kate spent another few minutes listening to whatever his excuses were.

Finally she said, "I'm sure you're very busy, and you're right that these bones have been here a long time." Her expression told Nell that she wasn't agreeing with Whiz, merely parroting what he said so she could get off the phone. For that was what she did.

To Nell, she said, "Thunderstorms are predicted for tomorrow, so I'm going to dig some more now. Those two femurs mean there definitely are two skeletons."

"Can I help?"

"If you want. And I also think we should treat this as a murder site. Be very careful and don't disturb anything if you don't have to. Also, it's a good idea to take a lot of pictures."

Kate borrowed Nell's writing pad to make a sketch of the scene. Nell finished her photographing. They'd decided to get a good photographic overview, then a shot of everything that came out of the ground.

Nell acknowledged that Chief Brown's laziness was to her liking. This was an interesting story, certainly better than covering a sewage and water board meeting. Suddenly she felt like she'd run away from her current life of sitting in the paper's office, trying to plow through paperwork that seemed to have no meaning, trying not to stare at the empty desk across the room. Of going through the motions of being a mother, trying to keep the anger out of what should be a minor discussion with Lizzie about doing dishes. Of trying not to stare too directly into the aching loneliness that came at night when the motions of the day stopped. Today was the first time since Thom's death that she was out of the office and following a story. Lizzie and Josh were in school, and when they got out they could either go to their grandmother's (not likely, Nell knew, but where they were officially supposed to go) or hang out at home squabbling over who got to use the computer. They would survive without her. For the moment, she was in the woods on a beautiful day, with a story that would engage her and keep her from thinking about phone calls from Tanya Jones or running the paper and staying in Pelican Bay. She could dig old bones hidden in the woods and find out who these people were and why they died in this lonely place.

TWO

Nell and Kate had been digging for almost three hours. It was hard, exhausting work, and in the last hour Nell found herself lagging behind the younger woman. She was mollified to see Kate straighten up, rubbing her back the way Nell had a few moments ago, and then join her and the water bottle. Kate had brought several with her and they were on the last one.

"Can I ask the obvious question?" Nell said, as Kate sat down on the log next to her. "Why do you take bike trips equipped with digging tools?"

"To dig. There's something that might be an old Civil War trench around here, possibly a training ground for the local boys to fire their muskets. Some kids have been hacking at it with shovels. I made the mistake of letting on I have an MA in anthropology and the park ranger suggested I put it to work and excavate the site. I've been coming out here on my days off when the weather is good."

"Have you worked with human bones before?"

"I did some of my graduate work with a forensic professor. It was interesting as long as the bodies were of a certain vintage."

"Like our current company?"

"These are too young. I prefer bones dead long before I was born. If they cross my life … it means I might have known the person. Too close for me."

"'There but for Fortune,'" Nell quoted.

"How this person ended up in these woods could have been my path. But with the ancient bones, that was never a life open to me." Kate paused for a moment, then asked, "Does it bother you? Maybe I shouldn't have called you, maybe you wouldn't want to be out here where somebody died."

Nell paused before answering. "There is no place it wouldn't bother me. But what's in these woods is not my tragedy. It's a story. I'm a reporter—what I do is write stories."

They were silent, then Nell asked softly, "How is he … how does Josh seem to you?"

Kate didn't answer immediately, as if thinking. "Quiet. More subdued than before."

"Sad?"

"No, more bewildered. Sad will come. Like everything is out of place and he doesn't know where it belongs yet."

"I feel like he's trying to make up for Thom being gone," Nell said. "He does his chores with no prompting. He's started to do things that Thom did, like carrying out the heavy garbage." She had a flash of her son, the garbage can almost to his chin, pushing and heaving it down the driveway. She'd rushed to help him. She wondered what other things he was taking on when she wasn't there to notice. "But he can't be Thom, can't make up for …" Nell felt her guilt speaking, her hands on the wheel of the car.

Kate placed her fingers on Nell's forearm. She said, "No, he can't. And neither can you."

For a moment, Nell couldn't talk; then got out, "That obvious?"

"No, I'm just remarkably astute," Kate replied, giving Nell's arm a comforting squeeze.

"Lizzie, on the other hand … she's flung herself into being a teenager with a vengeance. If I had to tell her two times to do the dishes before, now it's four times."

"So, which is harder to deal with?"

"Lizzie, of course. She's angry—she has a right to be—and taking it out on everyone and everything."

"Family is the closest. She's been in the bike shop a few times with Josh, and she's always well behaved and polite."

"Well, at least she can maintain in public," Nell said, a hint of exasperation slipping through. On the day she'd helped Josh with the large trash, she'd had to make Lizzie come down from her room just before bed to finish the dishes.

"Maybe she wants to make sure you love her," Kate offered.

"Giving it the acid test, that's for sure." Nell gave Kate a rueful smile and added, "Oh, I've read the books. I know she's acting out from grief and it's her way of dealing, that I need to be calm and reasonable and perfectly mature."

"Easier said than done."

"Much easier. I'll let you know if I ever accomplish it."

Kate looked at her. "Nell, I don't know you that well, but I can't see you and Lizzie in a screaming match. No one is perfect, but I'll bet you win the mature contest every time."

"That, yeah. I'd be in trouble if I didn't."

"It's hard. But you'll come through it okay." Kate gave Nell's arm a final press, then got up, took another swig of the water, and went back to digging. Nell followed her lead, albeit at a slower pace; a good swig of water and then back to her assigned task of carefully brushing off the dirt and red clay from the bones.

After half an hour, Nell had to stand up and stretch her back again. Forty, I'm only forty, she told herself. My mother was two years before my birth at this age. Of course, her mother had let Maggie, her oldest sister, do most of raising her. Maggie was fourteen years older than Nell and had died of ovarian cancer the day after Nell turned twenty. She took another swallow of water, careful to leave a decent amount for Kate.

She surveyed the grisly results of their work. A good portion of a human skeleton lay spread out in a flat area. Most of the small bones were missing, so it lacked hands and feet, making the sight all the more macabre. Kate hadn't said much as the pile grew, as if she was waiting for the evidence to accumulate to prove herself right or wrong about this being two bodies.

Suddenly, Kate said, "Nell, come over here."

As Nell joined her, Kate pointed at the ground. Embedded in the earth was a skull. A second skull, proof that this unmarked grave held more than one body.

"Get a picture of the bullet hole," Kate said as Nell aimed the camera at their newest find.

"What bullet hole?" Nell only saw the skull, discolored, with dirt clinging to it. Kate pointed to a small round hole at the base of it.

Kate was silent while Nell took several pictures. Then she stated, "This is murder. No hunter could accidentally shoot himself in the back of the head."

"Two bodies, one definitely murdered. What have we stumbled over?"

"I don't know. I'm guessing there'll be little evidence save for the skeletons themselves. But I'm not sure I want to be testifying in court about what I found."

"You think it will come to that?" Nell asked. This was an old murder, and old murders were unlikely to be solved.

"I hope it comes to that." Kate shook her head as if clearing it, then said, "When in doubt, call the experts. I'm going to see if I can get my grad professor on the phone to see what she recommends."

"Mind if I keep digging?"

"Be my guest. Better to get him or her out before the rain."

Nell put down her camera and took over Kate's digging tools. She left the skull where it was and moved further down to see if she could find the rest of the skeleton. Starting where the hips might be, she carefully began loosening the soil.

She half listened to Kate explain what they had found. "Given that the first skeleton was relatively intact, I'm guessing they were buried, not just left here in the woods," Kate was saying. Then she described the discoloration of the bones. Nell surmised that might be a way of guessing the age. I hope Kate just recharged her phone, Nell found herself thinking. So far, she'd resisted the lure of communication everywhere. Partly because she didn't want to even consider answering a phone in places like the ladies' room, and the cell phone provided by the paper had sufficed. She used it mostly for work—which is where it was, snug in the charging station on Thom's desk. That solution had neatly avoided whether to get her kids phones—a situation Lizzie was less than pleased with.

Her trowel brushed against something in the dirt. Carefully, she excavated what she'd found. Part of a bone emerged from the dirt, then another one beside it. As she turned away more soil, the bones began to look like those of a forearm. Maybe I'll get a hand this time, make him look more human, Nell thought. Then her trowel scraped metal.

With her fingers, she burrowed into the earth to find the metal piece. Whatever it was, it was heavy and solid. Then, in growing horror, she realized it was a length of heavy chain and lay at the wrists of the body.

Her fingers resting against both the chain and the bone, Nell felt a sudden shiver of revelation. This had been a person, these bones covered by flesh as living and breathing as she was now. And this person had died a brutal death, their bones hidden in a place they were never meant to be found.

"Kate!" she suddenly called out. The other woman, still holding the cell phone to her ear, came over. Nell simply held up the few links she'd unburied.

"Oh, fuck," Kate said, then added a hasty "sorry," although Nell didn't know if it was for her or the professor on the phone. "One of the bodies appears to have its wrists bound with chain," Kate reported. Then she went back up the tree and spent a long time listening.

Nell gently let the chain fall back into the grave, then retrieved her camera. She took several shots as Kate finished her conversation.

"Okay," Kate said as she clicked her cell phone off and jumped down. "This is what Rebecca suggested. She was my grad advisor at the University of California. She's going to call a colleague at LSU and see if they would be willing to work this. I told her about the predicted rains and she said hightail it into town and buy a bunch of painter's tarps—the cheap plastic ones—then come back here and cover up anything and everything that might be part of this scene. Her assessment—and I agree with her—is chained arms and a bullet hole at the base of the skull aren't from a crime of passion."

"Agreed," Nell said. "This was cold-blooded murder. Meant to be hidden forever. We have about three hours of daylight left."

They both gathered their things, then Kate said, "It doesn't feel right … just leaving her here." She gestured to the partially assembled skeleton.

"Her?"

"Maybe. The hips seem to be a woman's."

"Oh, good Lord," Nell let out, then wished she'd said "fuck" like Kate. The years of child rearing made her seem more clean-minded than she truly was. "It seems even more evil, that a woman was killed this way."

"More evil? Or just closer to who we are?" Kate asked.

They packed up and headed down the trail, Kate walking in front of Nell.

They got Kate's bike wedged into the back of Nell's car, the effort aided immensely by Kate's knowledge of bikes and her ability to quickly remove the front wheel, the seat, and the pedals and turn the handlebars in a less dangerous direction.

As they neared town, Kate said, "You can drop me off. I can get my truck and go back out. There's no need for you to continue mucking about in the woods."

"You're going to dump me? Not on your life," Nell said. "Besides, for an exclusive, the *Pelican Bay Crier* can expense account the plastic, a couple gallons of designer water, and your phone bill for all those calls."

"Can't turn down an offer that generous," Kate said. A look of relief flicked across her face, as if she didn't want to go back out to the woods, with its buried secrets, alone.

Kate had a practical bent that suited Nell; they went in separate directions to accomplish their chores. Kate got the bravery points by venturing to the local sprawl mart during its after-school peak of madness. Nell was left to the relative comfort of the hardware store.

There were two men behind the counter, one a young high school-age kid who obviously considered a middle-age woman of no interest. The other man was old enough to be his father, and his son had evidently inherited his disinterest in women. They continued talking about the upcoming football game.

Nell started to tell them there were bodies to be covered up today while the football game wasn't until Friday. But she stopped. Someone had marched two people deep into the woods, murdered them, and hidden the bodies. Just because the murder happened a long time ago didn't mean those who'd wanted the silence weren't still about.

Nell headed to the painting supplies. The older man started to follow her, then two black teenage boys entered the store. He left her alone and followed them.

Nell suddenly wished she had a few illegal bones in her body—not to mention the skill and balls to shoplift. She'd obviously been assigned to the annoying-but-safe-woman category, while the two boys had been tried and found guilty. Nell quickly found the plastic sheets and noted that even if she were to fall into a life of crime—and what better cover than a middle-aged widow?—shoplifting bulky plastic tarps was not the best place to begin.

The high school boy did manage to tear himself away from the sports channel long enough to take her money. The two other boys joined her in line, carrying masking tape and markers and also talking about the upcoming football game.

Nell's next stop was a pay phone; she blessed the change in her pocket and cursed the work phone still at work. Lizzie answered on the first millisecond of the ring.

"You won't believe what happened in school today," she exclaimed into the receiver.

Somehow Nell suspected she was not the intended recipient of this juicy tidbit.

"What won't I believe?"

"Mom? What are you doing calling here?"

"I thought it might be nice to call home and let my darling children know I'm working on a story and might be out for a while longer." With a quick glance at her car to ascertain Kate was still shopping, Nell inquired, "Just what won't I believe happened in school?"

"Oh. That's nothing. Do you want to talk to Josh?"

Nell tried to quell the rising annoyance. Her mother had had no time for evasive answers. Had Nell tried Lizzie's end of the conversation, she would have been met with an "I asked you a question. Answer it now, Naomi Nelligan!" She would then thump her cane or whatever magazine she was holding to emphasize her point. Nell was the youngest of eight, and her seven other siblings swore by the time she came along, their mother had mellowed and she'd had it so much easier. Maybe it was easier, or maybe her mother had used up her mothering on the seven others and had little time or energy for the final and unexpected daughter. But the memories gave Nell little help in handling her own on-the verge-of-adolescence daughter with her mood swings and secrets.

"No, I don't want to talk to Josh. I want you to tell me what happened in school today."

"Ah, Mom, just the usual stuff. I got a B+ on my math homework.

"That *is* pretty unbelievable. Why do I suspect that wasn't what you were so breathlessly going to tell Janet?"

"Mom!" Lizzie let out an exasperated whine, making the word two syllables. "It's nothing, okay? Why do you have to always question everything I do?"

It's probably nothing, Nell told herself; someone broke off the three-week-long, love-of-their-life relationship to date someone else. Nothing for moms to be involved in.

"We'll talk when I get home," she said, not quite willing to let Lizzie win the point. Was that good mothering or just damn stubbornness? "I'll probably be a few hours more, so try ... try to keep things calm." In the past, she'd said "try to stay alive," but that wasn't funny anymore.

Nell saw Kate come out of the store with a surge of mothers and children. She said a hasty goodbye—clearly Lizzie was waiting for a more important call—and headed to her car.

Kate had been to the camping section and gotten stakes, a long roll of heavy twine, a large plastic storage container, and enough water to replace all they'd already swallowed twice over.

"Sale," she said as she loaded the jugs in the trunk.

"Good idea, although it's a struggle to get my kids to drink water unless it's disguised as lemonade."

"At least it's not Scotch with it."

"Yet. How much does the Crier owe you?"

Kate handed her the receipt. "I'll pay for the water."

Nell glanced at the amount. "Don't worry, it was on sale. Did you ... mention what we're doing?"

"To the thongs of just-out-of-school kids?"

Nell pulled out of the lot and headed back out of town. "I did some thinking while wandering the hardware store. Just because the murders happened years ago doesn't mean it's over."

"'The past is prologue.' But aren't you going to put this on the front page of the paper?"

"Eventually. I haven't decided whether to run it this week or not. Might be better to know more. We're a weekly paper—it's not like we can win the breaking news contest."

"Do you think someone from here murdered those people?"

"Someone buried the bodies here. How could a stranger know where to go?"

Kate's cell phone rang.

As she drove, Nell listened to Kate's side of the conversation. It was Rebecca, Kate's graduate professor, calling back. Her colleague from LSU was interested in studying the remains, but probably couldn't get to Pelican Bay until a few days later.

The oak tree hadn't moved, nor had the purple bandana. Nell parked the car, Kate ended her conversation, and they got out.

The sun had gone, and clouds heralding the soon-to-come rain had appeared.

Kate packed the supplies into a canvas tote bag, leaving, Nell noticed, the lighter stuff for her. Kate slung the bag over one shoulder, then tucked the plastic storage container under one arm.

"What's that for?" Nell asked as they started down the trail.

"Jane Bone. It might be a good idea to take the skeleton we've mostly unearthed with us. Sheriff Hickson or Chief Brown—not likely, I know—should get out here and secure the site sooner than later, but I can't see that happening today and I don't want to leave the bones out overnight."

"What do we do with them?"

"Got room in your refrigerator?" Kate said.

"Josh would love bones in the fridge. Lizzie would hate it and swear that I was trying to ruin her life."

"Guess it's the morgue, then, and Josh gets to settle for pictures."

The encroaching clouds darkened the day. The unmarked graves in the bright daylight had been unsettling; the gray gloom made Nell feel that at any minute, deep organ music would begin. She and Kate worked quickly, covering the ground with the tarps, staking the corners and weighing them down with rocks and tree branches. Kate carefully packed Jane Bone into the storage container as Nell took a final round of pictures, proof of how they had secured the site. Animals would be more than happy to gnaw on the old bones. But Nell felt a prickle that it wasn't animals they had to worry about.

THREE

Nell made the rounds, dropped off Jane Bone with the amazed morgue staff. She and Kate had said little, merely alluded to a long-ago lost hunter. She wondered if they were both spooked by the bullet hole and chains, or taking reasonable precautions. After that, Nell dropped off Kate, and only now, with the gray of the day dissolving into night, was she heading home.

"Shit," she said out loud as she turned into her driveway. "Shit," she repeated because she knew how much it would annoy the person whose car blocked hers.

Her mother-in-law's big boat of an auto was parked there. Mrs. Thomas Upton McGraw, Sr.—Mrs. Thomas, Sr. as Nell thought of her—had busted Nell. Kids home alone, no parental supervision.

If she hadn't been sure at least one of the three waiting pairs of ears had heard her, Nell would have seriously considered heading back to the office. Not that it would have changed anything, but she was dirty, and tired, and wanting something to eat and a long, soaking bath.

She had gotten along well with her father-in-law, and he and Thom had been enough padding between Nell and Mrs. Thomas, Sr. for them to have a congenial relationship. Four years ago, when Thom's father died, the tension had increased. Nell's version was that Mrs. Thomas was lonely and wanted more attention from Thom and her grandkids. That had led to times when Nell was left without a husband, or stuck doing double parent duty. Of course, it didn't help that she never felt approved of by Mrs. Thomas. The McGraws were an old family. Nell was the daughter of a large blue-collar Midwestern family, her parents the first generation born in America.

With Thom's death, their fragile cordiality had shattered. When he had been alive, leaving Josh and Lizzie for a few hours while they worked late had never been an issue. The children were old enough to know better than to play with matches or stick their fingers in electric sockets, and not yet at the age where they might sneak out to buy drugs or have sex on the couch. They could be more or less counted on to do nothing more troublesome than forget to do their chores.

But with Thom gone, Mrs. Thomas had huffed and puffed about not leaving the children alone. When Nell was exasperated, as she was now, she called it controlling, meddlesome, and a few other choice words. On more charitable days, she saw it as a way for Mrs. Thomas to be needed and connected to her grandchildren without admitting any of that to Nell or herself.

But tonight—after Nell let out some of those choice words— there was nothing to do but go inside.

"Mom, you're home," Josh greeted her.

"Nell, where have you been?" Mrs. Thomas asked, giving her dirty clothes a look. "Certainly not at the office."

31

"Hello, Mother. Hi, Josh. Where's Lizzie? No, not at the office," Nell said slowly, not sure how much she wanted to say. Her mother-in-law wasn't the reporter her husband and son had been—they would have quickly understood digging old bones in the woods for a story. Instead Mrs. Thomas, Sr. would see a single mother by herself (or almost, with only another woman for protection) in a place where people were murdered, and, most grievous of all, leaving her children home alone.

"I drove by, saw the lights on and that your car wasn't here, so I checked in."

"Lizzie's in her room on the phone," Josh answered. He was taking on Thom's role of mediating between them, Nell noted. Lizzie, on the other hand, was decidedly isolationist; she wanted to be nowhere near the battlefield.

"Lizzie is fourteen, Josh twelve. They're old enough to be by themselves for a few hours," Nell told her mother-in-law in as calm and nonconfrontational a voice as she could.

"I'm not so sure," Mrs. Thomas replied, using the same coolly nonconfrontational tone Nell had used; Nell noted that it was pretty annoying coming from the other direction. "Times have changed since you grew up. Even towns like Pelican Bay have their dangers."

"Mother," Nell said, the coolness slipping from her voice, "I can't follow them around twenty-four hours a day. Even when Thom was alive, there was no guarantee we could keep any and every bad thing from happening. Lizzie broke her leg with you, me, Thom, and Thomas all there."

"Still, Nell, I don't see why you can't bother to call me when you know you have to be late. Or just stick to a regular schedule, like Thom and Thomas used to do."

Nell could remember no such regular schedule, certainly not for Thom. He was often out at all hours, usually with his father. Between Thom and Nell, they managed to be home on a somewhat regular basis, but it was unreasonable for Mrs. Thomas to expect Nell to manage that and run the paper at the same time.

She was too tired to prevent the words from coming out. "If Thom kept such a regular schedule, we wouldn't have been on Post Road after midnight." And I wouldn't be a widow and we wouldn't be standing here arguing like this, she silently added.

"Mom," Josh said softly, taking her hand.

"Nell! You shouldn't say such things in front of … " Mrs. Thomas trailed off.

"I think they know," Nell retorted. Then she caught herself. This would solve nothing. She needed to find a way to de-escalate before it became really nasty. "Mother, I appreciate your concern, but I can't do the things two people did. I do call, I do check up on them; Josh and Lizzie knew I would be late." She thought of ratting on her children, telling Mrs. Thomas they knew they could go to her place—Lizzie showed remarkable enough facility on the telephone that she could call her grandmother—but that Josh and Lizzie didn't want to go. However, even to avoid an argument, Nell couldn't be that venal. Whatever the petty satisfaction, it wouldn't make things better to tell Mrs. Thomas that her grandchildren preferred the dangers of being home alone to her company.

"I know we're all going through a hard time." Mrs. Thomas regained her cool politeness. "But I do wish you wouldn't leave them home alone, especially when I can be over here so quickly."

Agree, then do it your way, had been one of Thom's mottoes. Nell saw no reason not to apply it to her mother-in-law. "I will try to make sure that the kids are either with you or some other adult if things come up." She wondered if TV would count as having adults around.

Lizzie finally came out of her room. In teenage obviousness, she rolled her eyes at the thought of having to call her grandmother to babysit if Nell wasn't here. Nell pretended not to see.

"However, I really wasn't coming over here to check on you," Mrs. Thomas continued. Lizzie rolled her eyes again, even more obviously to make sure that Nell saw. "I wanted to know if you've been getting phone calls from"—she looked down at a piece of paper in her hands—"Tanya Jones."

"She's calling you?"

"You know who she is?"

"Yes, don't you?"

"The name is … a little too familiar to me," Mrs. Thomas said slowly. "What have you said to her?"

So I have to reveal all my dealings while you keep yours to yourself, Nell thought. Maybe it was how women survived in the South thirty years ago—never reveal an opinion until it was safe.

"I've told her to … " Nell searched for a polite way to say it. "That I will do everything I can to see her husband in prison."

Mrs. Thomas slowly nodded, still maddeningly not revealing her thoughts. "Mrs. Jones told me that her husband has had time to think things over in the jail—she said they just couldn't afford the bail, it was set so high and that it must be nice to be friends with a judge—that he was reading the Bible and had seen the error of his ways."

"Nice to know he's seeing errors. To me she said he made one mistake and he shouldn't have to suffer years in jail for one minute of mistake." They were standing in the kitchen; much as she wanted to sit, Nell was reluctant to do so as it might inspire Mrs. Thomas to do the same and extend her visit. But she was curious about Tanya and her new approach. Curious and angry.

"I gather she thought that appealing to the Christian in me might be her best argument," Mrs. Thomas said.

"And did you find it 'appealing'?" Nell asked.

"Perhaps if J.J. Jones has finally found God in jail, then that's where he should stay. The outside didn't seem to be leading him down a righteous path. But she didn't quite stop with his jailhouse conversion. She also mentioned that his brothers aren't happy about him being locked up. She said"—Mrs. Thomas again consulted the paper—"that they were really upset about not having their little brother to help at the garage and she didn't know what they might do."

"They threatened us?" Nell almost shouted. Josh, still holding her hand, squeezed it.

"Not us. You. She said … " Mrs. Thomas glanced at the paper but read nothing off it; she was avoiding looking directly at Nell. "She said they've always protected their little brother, and, as angry as they are, she wouldn't want to be you." With that, Mrs. Thomas looked again at Nell. "Tempting as vengeance is, can you pursue it if there's danger?" She gave a bare nod of her head towards Josh and Lizzie.

Nell was silent, her outrage unspeakable—at least in words she could use in front of Mrs. Thomas, Josh, and Lizzie. Finally she said, "How dare she? A hint of a threat and I'm supposed to back down? Let him get away with his drunken murder?"

"What do you gain and what do you lose?" Mrs. Thomas asked, the same words, the same cadence, that had so often come out of Thom's mouth.

Seeing the echo of her dead husband in his mother took Nell to the hollow place where anger and grief seemed unquenchable. She burst out, "I lose my self-respect, I lose my chance to live in a moral world, I lose the rule of law if it can be overcome by a whisper, I lose ... " She faltered. I lose Thom's memory if it can be so easily sold away. She didn't say that to Mrs. Thomas. Nell continued, her voice harsh with fury: "What do I gain? The illusion of safety. Let's make the streets safe for drunk drivers. It can be Josh or Lizzie next time. Besides, it's the state vs. Jones, not Nell McGraw vs. Jones." But she was the state's star witness. If she decided not to cooperate, the case would be hard to prove.

No one spoke. Finally Nell broke the silence. "I'm not angry at you, Mother. I know that you've just been tapped as the messenger. But I am angry at ... " At everything, certainly at Thom's death and the shallow people who didn't want their mistakes to interrupt their lives, but also at living a life that was Thom's dream, having to raise their two children alone, the implacable changes that had slammed into her life.

"I understand, but I thought you should know," Mrs. Thomas said in the cool voice of hers that never let Nell know what she was really thinking.

"I do want to know. Tell me if she calls again. But it doesn't change things," Nell answered firmly.

There seemed little else to say. Mrs. Thomas picked up her purse and with a hug and a kiss from Josh and Lizzie, and a brief, stiff hug for Nell, she left.

Lizzie revealed the real reason for coming out of her room. "Mom, what's for supper? I'm starving."

"Mary's Pizza," Nell answered. That would make Josh and Lizzie happy and it would get her out of cooking. It would also give her a chance to soak in the tub while waiting for the food to arrive.

While Josh and Lizzie were in the kitchen making the momentous decision of which toppings to get, Nell slipped behind the bar in the den and poured herself a generous dollop of Scotch. She put the drink in the bathroom before heading back to the kitchen to give Lizzie the money for the pizza. She told them to be vigilant for the sound of approaching food.

We now worry so much about each other, Nell thought as she started the bath running. She added water from the tap to the Scotch, then took a long swallow. One week after Thom had died, and four days after the funeral, she'd drunk herself into oblivion. It had been a moment of sheer self-absorbed self-pity. She'd thought Josh and Lizzie were safely in bed and sat in the living room, refilling her drink time and again, attempting to slip into a void that didn't have sharp knives everywhere she turned: the desk in the corner with invitations replied to for events they would never attend together, a bed that seemed too empty and the groggy moments when she reached for him, the sailboat-pattern dishes he had liked so much—all the little details and moments that had been their life together were still so present in this house. In that lonely hour, Nell couldn't bear to look at them. So she'd refilled her glass again. But Josh and Lizzie weren't asleep enough to ignore her dropping the glass on the kitchen floor. They'd come running out of their rooms, too keenly aware that people close to them could get hurt to ignore the harsh shattering of glass. Nell was too drunk to hide it even from her children.

Lizzie had simply wailed, "Mom, I can't believe you've done this!" and stormed back to her room. Josh had silently cleaned up the mess even while Nell told him to leave it until morning.

The next day, Nell had simply said, "I'm sorry, I just fell apart. It won't happen again."

Now they worried about one another. Too much? What was too much worry? Josh and Lizzie would worry if they saw Nell take a drink. She would worry about them worrying. Mom was all they had left and if Mom couldn't function … She took another sip, then stripped off her dirty clothes and stepped into the tub, with the Scotch carefully placed on the floor. Sometimes it felt like the days were made of these fragile moments—her mother-in-law stopping by, wanting to take a drink after a long day. These should be small moments in an average day, but now they had long shadows.

Nell took the final sip as she heard the doorbell ring. She quickly got out of the tub, rinsed the glass, and brushed her teeth, then threw on clean sweatpants and a sweatshirt before joining her kids for supper.

Halfway through the pizza, Lizzie looked sharply at Nell. "Mom, are you okay?" she asked.

"Fine," Nell answered. "Just tired." The Scotch had mellowed her out, she realized, enough that Lizzie noticed.

"You sure?"

"I'm sure," Nell answered, a testiness creeping into her voice. "Just tired," she said with a ring of finality.

"Okay, whatever," Lizzie answered.

Josh started talking about a TV show he'd recently seen about shipwrecks in the Gulf. Nell was too tired to do more than listen, trying to nod attentively, but couldn't do what she should do, which was not leave her young son the burden of being family peacemaker. When Josh paused in his story, Lizzie stood up and asked if she could finish eating while watching TV. Nell nodded, adding that Josh could also go and watch. It had been one of the family rules, that they would eat together.

That night Nell's sleep was troubled with thoughts of old bones hidden in the woods and new threats from a drunk and his family. And the scrutiny of her children.

FOUR

THEY WOKE TO A downpour. Nell had mercy on her children and drove them to school instead of sending them on the bus. After watching long enough to ensure they didn't melt in the dash inside, she headed to the office of the *Pelican Bay Crier*.

Pelican Bay was an old Mississippi Gulf Coast town, and its center was clustered around a green square—or rectangle, really—with the requisite statues of Civil War generals. Confederate, of course. The old county courthouse, long past its use and now containing high-end retail shops of the quaint sort, sat at one end; the sprawling new city hall complex occupied the other. The Crier building was situated halfway between, on one of the long sides of the rectangle. Other buildings clustered nearby, mostly professional offices for law and accounting. The library sat across the square.

It was a very picturesque setting, although what it gained in beauty, it lost in practicality. There was a narrow one-lane road around the square, with deliberately high curbs to ensure that no cars dared to park on the green. Since it wouldn't do to have a parking lot marring this pristine scene, parking spaces were tucked off in inconvenient places. The ones the Crier staff used were hidden behind city hall, convenient for the workers there but a long walk for everyone else. Nell could cut through city hall, but that still left her half a long side away from the Crier's front door.

By the time she reached the ten steps leading up to the paper's massive oak door, her feet were soaked. Given that most of her staff worked newspaper hours, not school hours, she was the first one in. Fumbling to unlock the door only gave the rain one last chance at her.

Nell flipped on lights as she hastily tossed her umbrella in the stand. It dripped copiously, as if saying "see, I did keep a lot of water off you." A quick glance at her appointment book told her this would be a busy day. The mayoral election was coming up, so despite her lament to Kate about slow news, there were many events vying for the front page. It just didn't feel like news because the election was almost a done deal. Hubert Pickings, the current mayor, had little chance of losing. The talents and abilities of Mayor Pickings sorely tempted Nell to write an editorial about the benefits of term limits.

She also wanted to follow up on the bones. Two skeletons meant two missing people. Someone somewhere had wondered what happened to them, reported their disappearance. The Crier's archives—conveniently located downstairs—seemed a good place to start.

Thom's grandfather had either had the foresight or the luck to buy a bigger building than was needed for the first few decades of the paper's life. One of the older structures in Pelican Bay, it had been the city hall in the early 1900s. When the city hall outgrew the space after the second world war and moved to its new digs, Thom's grandfather had bought the building. And because the town square was built on the highest ground, there was enough elevation for basements, which was unusual for this part of the Gulf coast. The Crier had a large one, which served as its "morgue." The basement also contained a space, still called the darkroom, for the computers and printers the staff used for photos.

The size and location of the Crier building worked well. Reporters had quick access not only to the paper's archives, but to city hall and all it contained: the mayor's office, the offices of the aldermen, the rest of the usual administrative offices, and the police station. The modern courthouse, less conveniently, was situated on the outskirts of town.

Nell knew it would help things to have a better idea of how long the bones had been buried, but she wasn't going to wait until the expert from LSU arrived. She picked up the phone to call Kate but realized it was not yet eight thirty and the bike store didn't open until ten. She guessed Kate's home number was the same one her uncle had had, but her request wasn't urgent enough to disturb Kate's morning. Plus, Nell had to admit, much as she'd enjoyed—no, needed—the field trip yesterday, she still felt too consumed by grief to reach out for new friends. Calling Kate at home was too close to offering a friendship she didn't feel up to pursuing.

She sat at her desk, but her vision was caught by the shaft of gray light cutting across Thom's desk. I have to do something about it, Nell thought. In the past weeks she had opened the drawers and started to sort through them, but it was too hard to simply place the memories in boxes or throw them out.

Nell swiveled so his desk was firmly out of her sight. She started making up a list of assignments. Jacko was a digging-in-old-records hound. That was the easy choice. He was young, barely out of college, still with the dewy skin of a boy turning to a man and the eagerness of one who had not yet stumbled and fallen hard. He was also slight, about Nell's height, with blond hair and blue eyes, the kind of looks that would turn him into a teen heartthrob if he sang or acted.

The bone story was hers, but he would be a great assistant on the research end. Carrie she would send off to campaign events. Carrie was pretty and young, and well aware of it. Her hair was streaked with blond highlights, making it more than just brown. She tended to wear clothes that emphasized her cleavage and small waist. She'd looked great on paper, but she was turning out to be Nell's problem child while Jacko was the find. Carrie could be good but she was high maintenance, needing a lot of direction and feedback.

Jacko's assignment was easy. Nell could just tell him to find anything that might relate to two people missing years ago.

For Carrie, she couldn't just say, "Go cover the most interesting of the campaign events." She would have to suggest to Carrie where to go, what to look for, and even hint at questions.

Nell glanced over the list of events. What would have been the easy one, a picnic in the square, seemed unlikely given the downpour. That was too bad, because candidate E. Everett Evens was a lively character. He was running on what Nell called the Gone-With-the-Wind platform. He wanted to restore the good old days; not that he specifically named slavery or lynching or women being unable to vote, but those seemed the eras he harkened back to. He could be counted on to say things like, "Back then we didn't have teenage pregnancy, homosexuality didn't exist, the races knew their place, and women were happy doing their Godly duty of raising children and taking care of their men." She wondered if he would take the rain as a sign of whom God intended to vote for.

Another candidate, Marcus Fletcher, was speaking to the local chapter of the NAACP that night. His campaign had been low-key, as if he recognized that, no matter what his qualifications, Pelican Bay being sixty-four percent white made it unlikely a black man would win the mayor's race. That was a story waiting to be written,

Nell thought; not about one man's political ambitions but the whole fabric of how the races in this town interacted, what had changed since the civil rights movement. And what hadn't. Nell remembered the hardware store manager's treatment of the two black boys. That was out in the open; what happened in hidden places?

Like the woods. Nell suddenly remembered reading about the search for Chaney, Schwerner, and Goodman, the three civil rights workers killed in northern Mississippi. The searchers had found a number of other bodies in the woods: the black men—and women—whose lives were considered cheap and easy to throw away.

Nell suddenly shivered. That could tear this town apart. If that was what had happened to them, if they had died from that hatred.

Nell turned her attention to the more mundane and safe thoughts of where she would send Carrie. Somehow the local NAACP meeting didn't sound like the best place. I'll go, Nell decided. The paper didn't need to mirror the narrow-mindedness of the town.

This decision would also mollify Carrie, as that left her covering the only real candidate, Hubert Pickings, the current mayor. Nell considered him a drab, humorless man with an IQ lower than his belt size. Although he had quite a pot belly, that still didn't give him the intelligence to govern a real town. The best that could be said was nothing disastrous had happened in the last four years.

First on the schedule was the mayor giving a scouting troop an award for cleaning up part of the beach. It was at the Legion Hall and had the kind of buffet dinner he liked to linger at. Kids and no questions from the press was about the perfect event for him. Carrie could handle that. Nell hastily scribbling some question ideas that Carrie might be able to flirt her way into asking. She didn't think Pickings would really answer them, but her hope was he would say something inane enough to put on the front page. His cronies would accuse her of being a biased liberal intent of furthering her agenda. If being liberal was telling the truth, then they were right. Thom's father had said that even-handedness was pissing off everyone.

She put checks next to some of the other events on his schedule—not even Carrie deserved to have to go to them all—that also seemed good ones to cover. She'd have to trust Carrie would follow through.

Nell heard the front door open, a heavy thump as if something had been tossed into the center of the room, then the door slamming shut. She sat for a moment but heard no footsteps.

Cautiously peering out of her office door, she saw no one in the main room. Then she spotted it. In the middle of the floor was a rock with a note tied to it. What, Nell thought, am I stuck in a nineteenth century melodrama? At least they were polite enough to toss it in the front door instead of breaking a window. She slowly walked to the rock, still listening for any sound of their return.

Seeing and hearing no one, Nell picked up the stone. The note was wet, indicating that the perpetrator hadn't been prepared to deal with the elements. It was smeared but still legible. *"Free J.J.,"* it read, then added, "*next time mite not be a rock*." The writing was crude and the rock thrower not only hadn't thought about the rain, but he didn't possess a good dictionary either.

The door opened again. Nell hoisted the rock, poised to throw it if need be.

Dolan, the paper's business manager, entered. "Goodness!" he exclaimed at seeing Nell standing in the middle of the room ready to throw a stone at him. "And I thought that Mr. Thomas had some unique ways of communicating with the staff."

Nell quickly lowered the rock. "Sorry. Someone just came and left this for me. I was worried they might be coming back." She handed the note to Dolan.

He glanced at it, then said, "Going to give it to the police?"

"You think Acting Chief Brown will consider this his jurisdiction?"

"He just might, especially if you show him a map," Dolan answered dryly.

"Only a stone's throw from the police station." In a more serious tone, Nell said, "Will it do any good? They didn't break the window, so no vandalism. Of course, I know it has to be one of the Jones brothers, but how to prove it?"

"No, Chief Brown won't do anything official—you'd have to be dead for that—but maybe if someone talks to the Jones boys, they might think twice about pulling this kind of stunt again."

"Under the table, man to man, so to speak?" Nell said acerbically. "The duty of the good ole boy network to protect widows and children?"

Dolan looked stung by her retort. And why shouldn't he?

Just then Jacko, Pam, and Ina Claire came in the door, their three umbrellas entwined to offer maximum protection.

"I'm sorry, Dolan," Nell said softly. "Too much ... stress."

Dolan nodded but without really looking at her. Any reply he might have made was lost in the onslaught of complaints about the rain.

No one commented on the rock Nell still held in her hand. She turned and went back to her office. Through the open door, Nell watched her staff: Pam at the front reception desk, Jacko at the cubicle behind her. Dolan had his office in front, and Ina Claire, who managed the classifieds, had a small office next to his.

They're uneasy with me, Nell recognized. How can you not say something to a woman standing in the middle of the room holding a wet rock? Unless you're so unsure of how to approach her that you can't think of what to say. It was another empty place that Thom had left. He had been jovial, friendly, the one easy to talk to. He could also dither and dawdle and wasn't good at making decisions; that had been Nell's strength. Thom took the staff out the back door and across the street for coffee or bought the drinks after work. Nell would tag along, let Thom tell a few stories, listen to a few, create the camaraderie needed to work together; then it was Nell's job to say it was time to get back to work or to go home. When she'd returned—was it only two weeks ago?—she'd fallen back into the things she usually did. Nell could see the stories, see all the follow-through needed, think of the hard questions, the good ones. Thom usually led at staff meetings, handing out the assignments Nell had thought up. Her father-in-law had once said Thom did all the people work and Nell did all the real work. If he had a wife like Nell, he added, he would have turned the paper into a daily that everyone in the Southeast had to pay attention to. Nell had smiled at his wistful comment and didn't point out he could have had a wife like her. He'd chosen not to.

In the month since Thom's death, Nell had little interaction with the staff other than what was necessary. She hadn't recognized the distance and unease she was creating. If she was going to run this paper, she was going to have to learn to be at least adequate at the things Thom did. He would have known what to say about the rock. How could she expect her staff to talk to her if she didn't talk to them? Still she sat at the desk, paralyzed at the thought of going back out and … ? Taking on Thom's role? Despite how stiff and awkward she would appear?

But she had to do something. They needed to know her plans for the paper—even if she wasn't quite sure yet. She needed to remember to hand out the compliments and praise when it was deserved. Thom would say, "Nell and I think that you wrote a great story" or "Nell and I really appreciate the extra time you put in" so she didn't have to.

Nell wasn't good at compliments; neither the words nor the thought came easily to her. When Nell had made valedictorian of her high school class, her mother had merely said, "It's not like there were that many smart kids there." Her father, in a rare counter to her mother, had replied, "Still, she did a good job. Only valedictorian in this family." He was the one who had filled out the paperwork for her to go to college. Her mother didn't think a girl needed college, but she'd just said that and let it go, as if she couldn't be bothered to make much of a fight over her last daughter.

Why would the staff stay on, to work for a morose, silent woman, Nell questioned. She needed to go talk to Jacko about his assignment. Carrie still wasn't here. Thom and Carrie had gotten along well, with just enough hints of flirtatiousness to not arouse the suspicions of the wife or of the rest of the staff.

Nell had commented on it once to Thom. He had laughed, wrapped his arms around her, cupped her breasts, and said, "Why go out for ground round when you've got filet mignon at home?"

Nell had to admit he had a knack for saying the right thing at the right time. After that comment, and the ardent things he'd said in the night, she was able to see that the flirting came mostly from Carrie and Thom skillfully handled her crush on him to get good work out of her, while promising nothing more than being an office mentor.

From the moment he was gone, Nell missed the daily touches, a shoulder rub, sitting next to each other on the couch, thighs resting against one another—those myriad of ways that two people who were as intimate as they were touched. Now she was starting to miss the passion they'd shared, starting to feel the ache in her body for their lovemaking.

This is not something to be thinking about in the office, Nell admonished herself.

A crash and a muttered "Damn it" from the outer office interrupted her.

"You can probably glue it together," Dolan was saying to Jacko. "Wood glue's pretty powerful these days."

Jacko had tried to open his top desk drawer and, as it was wont to do, it came apart, the front piece still in his hand, one side on the floor and the bottom teetering half in and half out. The desk was an old battered one, but it seemed to have come with the building.

"Why don't you get rid of that and take the one in my office?" Nell heard herself saying. "Take anything that's … useful and just put the rest in a box."

"Nell, are you sure you want to do that?" Dolan asked. "Don't you think you might want to …"

"I can't," she burst out. "I've tried and I can't. Take the desk; it's not doing any good sitting empty. Just put … Thom's stuff in a box. I'll sort it later." She added softly, "It'll be easier for me; I can't do it right now." That admission let the other words come out. "I'm not Thom. There were a lot of things he did very well, that I'm not going to be good at. I'm not great at … social stuff. You must be wondering what's going to happen to the Crier. I'm still … trying to sort things out … But I intend to keep the paper going, at least long enough to see if Josh or Lizzie wants to take it over." Nell didn't know she intended to do that until she said the words, but it began to feel like a viable path. "This has been a … hard place to work in the last month.

I can't promise there won't be some difficult times ahead. But I'm dedicated to keeping what Thom and his father and his father before him have built." She looked at the expectant eyes focused on her—Jacko and Dolan, Pam at her reception desk, Ina Claire who had come out of her office. "I know in the past I would sit in that office and Thom would come out and tell you things. It may take me a while to adjust to that being my duty. Please feel you can come into my office. Please know you can ask me questions. Please … help me keep the Crier going." Nell again surveyed the expectant faces.

Dolan broke the silence. "Nell, we don't expect you to be Thom. Just run the paper and we'll support you."

"Hey, boss lady," Jacko said. "I'm in it for the long run. I'm learning a lot more about reporting that I ever did at Baby Gator U."

Unexpectedly, Ina Claire, who had been running the classifieds since they were written in stone, gave Nell a hug. "Don't you worry, dear, we all care about the paper too," she said as she let go.

"Anything I can do, just let me know," Pam added. "Even if I have to tell Tanya Jones to … " She stopped, unsure if she should use the curse words.

"To go to hell," Nell finished for her. "Speaking of, that rock I was holding was a present from one of J.J.'s brothers. *Allegedly* his brother," she added, her newspaper training surfacing. "With a note attached, warning me away. I don't think they're up to more than just harassment and petty threats, but be on guard." She turned to look directly at Dolan. "I'd appreciate it if you'd use whatever connections you have to help keep things calm."

"That I'll do," he said with a smile that recognized her statement for the apology it was.

"Okay, that's my Thom imitation, now I turn back into Nell and tell us to go back to work."

Jacko gave her a mock salute, Dolan a nod with a smile still on his face. Ina Claire reached out and squeezed her hand, and Pam said, "Yes, ma'am, madam boss lady."

"And as to work, I've got a project for you," she said to Jacko. She told him about the bones in the woods. Dolan and Ina Claire remained in hearing range and Pam's desk was never out of hearing range, so they all listened in too.

Dolan was the first to comment. "Two missing people? I don't remember anything like that."

"We don't know how long those bones have been there," Nell said. "They might be older even than you are."

"My dear young lady, nothing is older than I am."

"Except for me," Ina Claire chimed in, reminding Dolan that at seventy-six she was the most senior staff member. "This coast has enough crimes. The gambling in the forties, and now it's back; smuggling, drugs, alcohol. Back when this was a dry area there was a lot of rum running, the girls to service all the military boys that come through these parts." Ina Claire was usually a quiet person, save for her incessant phone work for the classifieds. The most Nell heard out of her was, "Now, how do you spell that?" But every once in a while the most amazing things would come out of her mouth.

She had left out one. "What about racial trouble?" Nell asked.

"They can tell, can't they?" Jacko asked. "If the bodies were black or white?"

"I don't know. I can ask Kate."

"The color that their skin once was won't prove anything," Ina Claire said. Then she added another of her unlikely thoughts. "It's the reaction of those who put them there that will tell you the tale."

Nell started to ask for clarification, but then two phones started ringing, including the line reserved for paying classifieds, and the moment was gone.

"Should I just dig, or do you have any suggestions?" Jacko asked Nell.

"Seems to me our morgue might be a good place to start, so head downstairs. After that, police or court records. Anything that seems reasonable. I'll give Kate a call and see if she has any guesses on the age of the bones. That might help."

"I can call Marion over at the library and see if she has any ideas."

"You can, although it might be good to be low key about this. Someone didn't want those bodies found. That someone may still be around."

It was now that Carrie chose to arrive at work. As she divested herself of her raincoat and umbrella, she caught sight of Nell and hastily muttered, "Sorry I'm late, the car wouldn't start."

"Whatever," Nell muttered in return. "I've got election events I need you to cover." She gave Carrie a moment to settle in as she retrieved the assignment sheet from her desk.

Carrie glanced at it, then commented. "I get prune face?"

"It's either that or waiting in the square to see if Everett has some comment on God raining on his picnic."

They were interrupted by the entrance of three people. Nell recognized one, Lambert Gautier. He was the head of one of the leading local advertising agencies and he specialized in politics. With him were a man and a woman, both dressed in the serious and sober fashions of those seeking office, safely dry under the golf umbrella he was carrying.

At least we're far enough along that I can't guess which one is the candidate, Nell thought. Carrie, in reaction to the man, sat up straighter, leaning forward enough to display her cleavage. It didn't even seem thought-out to Nell, just her instinctual reaction to a handsome man. Nell had to admit that he was handsome; tall, full head of dark brown hair with a hint of gray at the temples. The woman was equally attractive, also tall, also with thick brown hair; either no gray or it had been artfully colored away.

Lambert wasted no time; he put out his hand and crossed to Nell. "Mrs. McGraw. We've just come from filing for office and I thought I might run my candidate by the local paper so we could get a chance to do a meet and greet." He gave her hand a hearty pump.

"And who is the candidate?" Nell inquired, knowing if it were the woman, Lambert would have said that up front.

"Aaron Dupree, I'd like you to meet Nell McGraw," Lambert said, his one hand now on Nell's forearm and the other reaching out and grasping Aaron Dupree's shoulder as he brought them together.

"Mr. Dupree, how do you do?" Nell said. His handshake didn't have the false heartiness of Lambert's. He had somehow perfected a warm, dry handshake with the right amount of firmness.

"Mrs. McGraw, I'm pleased to meet you. One of the ways I've kept connected to Pelican Bay was by my parents sending me copies of the Crier. I've been reading you for a while."

"Aaron moved back here about six months ago, to help take over his father's business."

Lambert didn't explain who his father was and Nell needed none. Andre Dupree was the man who had built the Back Bay Country Club and the posh and pricey real estate that surrounded it. Andre Dupree had a very thick file; he had been mayor back in the seventies. Thom had met Aaron since he had moved back, but Nell had not been with him. Thom had repeated what he'd heard, that Aaron had moved away as a young man, to California where he got his law degree. Rumor was he moved back because his father had a stroke and he wanted to help his mother care for his father as well as their estate. Or because of his sister's recent divorce from a husband rumored to be abusive and he wanted to help raise his two little nieces. There was also a rumor that he'd come back because of his own recent divorce. Those rumors mentioned how it might be to hide his assets in with his family's and out of the divorce settlement.

Nell had been in the newspaper business long enough to know how useful and misleading rumors could be.

Lambert continued his spiel. "Aaron always intended to come back to Pelican Bay and follow in his father's footsteps, and he felt that now was the right time."

"You've been back here for six months?" Nell asked, although she knew the answer.

"Yes," Aaron said, cutting off Lambert. "I thought I'd wait until the next election before considering running. Six months seems a little quick to be trying to take over." He gave Nell a boyish grin. She kept her face neutral and left enough of a silence that he filled it. "Then I talked things over with my family and we decided that four more years of the current administration wouldn't be the best thing for Pelican Bay. It was their encouragement that made me decide to run."

Nell merely nodded, although she couldn't disagree with his assessment of Hubert Pickings and was secretly relieved the mayor's race was no longer a done deal. Not talking was one of her reporter's tricks. It worked especially well with people who were talkers; they couldn't stand the silence and filled it, often with things they wished they hadn't said. Thom had called it hunting, that she knew exactly when to be silent, like a lion watching a gazelle.

Lambert took up the talking. "So, I … we know it's kind of late to enter the race, but the only choice was to wait another four years or do it now. It's going to take a lot of work to catch up to the current mayor, but we felt that we had to take on the challenge."

Knowing he could well go on with this blather, Nell cut in. "Come on, Lambert, you know having the son of a former mayor charging in at the last second to enter the race will generate a ton of publicity. It's Hubert Pickings who'll have to scramble."

Lambert's face showed the debate going on; did he go the slick route and insist they were the underdog or admit that Aaron's splashy entrance would indeed create the kind of obstacle that Hubert Pickings had shown no ability to overcome? He finally gave a rueful grin and said, "Well now, there might be some truth to that." He was clearly used to dealing with the more politic Thom and not the blunt Nell. "But you know Thom and I used to talk a lot and we both agreed that with politics you just never can tell."

"Thom's not here," Nell retorted, angry at him for using Thom's putative views to bolster his, and angry at herself for the grief and anger that slipped in a moment of banal banter.

"Yes, ma'am," Lambert said, "and I'm sorry for your ..."

Nell abruptly cut him off. "We haven't been introduced," she said to the woman.

"How do you do?" she said, offering Nell her hand. "I'm Desiree Hunter, the voice of reality in the Dupree campaign, which is why I've been silent." Her hand was also dry, and her handshake firm for a woman. She seemed to sense that this was not the time to offer condolences to the recent widow. "I must also confess to being one of the strongest voices urging Aaron to run. Off the record, I've reached my quota of being able to say 'Mayor' Pickings. Another four years is far beyond my capacity."

"Too bad that's off the record," Nell said. "It's the best quote I've heard so far today."

"We'll have coffee after the election and I'll tell you what I really think."

Nell smiled at her.

Her introduction led to the introduction of all the staff. Nell listened politely as Dolan explained the running of the paper to Aaron Dupree, who was either genuinely interested or doing an excellent job of pretending. He was even clearly trying to remember the names of all the staff who weren't present: Alessandra Charles, who did the ad sales and worked mostly from home; Harry who did the fishing and boating columns; Stan, who did the movie reviews; the various stringers from along the coast; even the interns from the local college.

Carrie was hovering near, her eyes on Aaron. This was a candidate she would be happy to cover.

Desiree Hunter took papers from a portfolio she was carrying. "Here's the usual stuff," she said as she handed them to Nell. "Background, goals Aaron would like to accomplish if he's elected, a few perfectly posed pictures. The schedule for upcoming events."

"So do you think he's going to have an uphill battle to defeat Hubert?" Nell asked softly.

"I think Aaron's the best man for the job. I think the people of Pelican Bay are smart enough to realize that." Something in her voice made Nell realize she was more than just someone hired to do the job. A girlfriend? There was an unexpected partisan pride.

Dolan had finished his explanation and Carrie was saying, "I'm the reporter covering these elections, Aaron, so you'll be seeing a lot of me."

"We're doing the Angela show on Channel Four," Lambert interjected. "Gotta get moving."

Aaron made it a point to shake Nell's hand again. Desiree smiled at her and waved as they left.

The second the door closed behind them, Carrie turned to Nell and said, "Why don't I follow the new candidate?"

"I don't think they'll like you hanging around the Angela show," Nell answered as she perused the schedule that Desiree Hunter had given her. Carrie read over her shoulder.

"Can't I do him at the middle school? He's easy on the eyes," Carrie said, her finger stabbing a point on the paper.

"No, I think I'll do that," Nell answered.

"Oh, I see." The young woman managed an honest-to-goodness pout. "Keep the handsome ones for yourself," she muttered.

"Carrie!" Jacko cut in. "Out of line, girlfriend. She just broke up with her boyfriend and she's taking it out on every one," he added.

Nell was tempted to spit back that she had just been widowed, not merely finished with another in a long line of boyfriends. Instead she said, "I'm going to the school because that's Lizzie's class. It gives me a chance to see my daughter."

Carrie had no reply for that. Instead she busied herself at her desk.

Nell retreated to her office. Carrie had occasionally pouted with Thom, but he was always able to cajole her into doing things, even covering the odious sewage and water board meetings. I would have seen this coming, had I thought I needed to look for it, Nell mused. Whether through instinct or calculation, the young woman realized she had an advantage. With Thom gone, the paper was shorthanded. Right now the *Pelican Bay Crier*—and Nell—needed Carrie. As long as she managed the basics, decent coverage of things like Hubert's photo op, she would help keep things going.

Nell looked at her watch. The bike shop should be open by now.

A voice that sounded enough like Kate Ryan's answered, so Nell plunged ahead with her question. "Any guess how old those bones might be?" There was a moment of silence, so Nell thought perhaps a few more details might be needed. "This is Nell McGraw from the Crier."

"Sorry, I've been out in the woods digging bones with so many women it's hard to remember." Definitely Kate. "My very rusty and not-well-educated guess is somewhere from thirty to seventy years old. There are tests they can do that will get it closer. I know that's probably not much of a help right now."

"It'll keep us out of the Civil War archives."

"We can safely eliminate that. It wasn't a minie ball that made the bullet hole."

"Is it possible to identify the gun?" Nell asked.

"To tell the difference between a musket and an AK-47? Sure. But unless a bullet is still rattling around in the skull, we may not get much closer than that."

"Okay, not to hold you to it, but to give us a starting point, if you were going to guess how old these bones were, what would you say?"

"Definitely don't hold me to it, and if I'm way wrong, I don't want to hear it. I'd say about forty to fifty years. I'm guessing that more from the tree than the bones. That tree was mature, probably around fifty years."

"Any way of telling the race or ethnicity?"

"Yes. That's not too hard, actually."

"Any guess about Jane Bone?"

Kate was silent for a moment. "Would it help?"

"It might."

"It's hard to know without doing accurate measures and comparing them against the standard scales."

"I won't hold you to it," Nell reaffirmed.

"African-American on Jane. Couldn't see enough of the other one to guess."

"So Jane Bone might be an African-American woman who was killed about fifty years ago?"

"Might be. Don't hold—"

"—you to it." Nell's reply overlapped her. "You realize what this might mean?"

"Another thing: she was probably young, maybe twenties. She would be an old woman now, but she could still be alive today."

"Whoever did this wanted those bodies hidden. Maybe better to have left them buried for another fifty years, until we're beyond guilt and blame."

"How do we get beyond guilt and blame if we leave the bodies buried and hidden? Even justice late is better than none," Kate answered.

"You're right, of course. I should be thinking of this as a newspaper woman—it's a great story." Nell was also thinking of the rock this morning. Even on calm days, the Crier got its share of what she and Thom had called the loony tunes letters. Reigniting a racial conflagration might bring more than just letters. But I'm putting the cart way before the horse, Nell reminded herself. Kate could be wrong; or even if she was right, it could end up being a lovers' quarrel, the husband/lover killing his wife/girlfriend and her lover.

"I did talk to Sheriff Hickson this morning. I'm going to lead him and his men out there as soon as the rain lets up," Kate told her.

Nell could think of no other or better description for Sheriff Hickson than Good Ole Boy to the max, complete with beer belly and drawl. He was a big man, tall, towering even, made bigger by the weight that he'd put on over the years; his sparse gray hair, only a few stands left of the black it had once been, was slicked back in perfect order and usually hidden under a hat. His face, tanned and rough from years in the sun, was turning jowly, skin pulled by gravity and too many beers in smoky bars. He'd been sheriff in Tchula County for the last fifteen years and wasn't even opposed in the upcoming election. He wouldn't have been her first choice, but there seemed to be no first, second, or third choices in law enforcement, only the portly sheriff and the lethargic police chief. Nell did a quick calculation; Sheriff Hickson was in his early sixties, which would have made him about Lizzie's age fifty years ago. Young enough to be safe?

"Did you tell him about the bullet hole and chain?"

"Yeah, I thought I'd better mention it."

"How did he take it?"

"Did he seem guilty?" Kate asked, catching Nell's meaning. "No, more harried and stressed. He seemed relieved I'd already snagged a forensic expert to come take a look. I thought of that, too," Kate added. "Anyone old enough to be a killer when those people were killed becomes a suspect. Particularly someone who grew up here and knows the woods."

"I guess any murder you run into makes you paranoid. But it's not like you or I have any evidence. We just stumbled over old bones."

"That's what I keep telling myself. Call me if I can do anything else for you," Kate said, and then to someone in the bike store, "Let me know if you need help with anything."

"Thanks, Kate, I will." Nell hung up.

She did paperwork for a while, noticing Jacko had gone downstairs and Carrie had slipped out, although without a camera. There would be no pictures of Hubert Pickings with mashed potatoes dribbled down his tie on the front page.

Lacking that, Nell thought about just what to put on the front page, debating whether or not to mention the bones or to wait until a later issue. Of course, Aaron Dupree's announcement would be the lead. Then she decided to engage in what Thom had called her "shit-stirring reporting." There were a few hours before Candidate Dupree did his political stumping at Lizzie's school; Nell grabbed her umbrella and headed back to her car to drive out to the county courthouse.

The city limits, where the courthouse was located, marked the edge of what was now considered old Pelican Bay. Since the county jail was housed with the courts, this area had never become upscale and was mostly a polyglot of businesses, from lawyers to antique shops. But the location was central and the parking was easy, and, despite the jail, the presence of the sheriff's office there kept crime low.

Alberta Bonier was used to Nell and her diving into various records stored in the courthouse. Nell had to admit that she was much happier in a musty basement pouring over old records than doing the meet-and-greet thing.

The land now belonged to the state park, but who had owned it fifty years ago? After some searching, Nell finally found the records relating to that piece of property. In 1985, Hubert Horace Pickings had donated it to the park. Over twenty years before, his father Hubert Horatio Pickings had bought the property from Elbert Woodling. Looking at the deed of transfer, Nell was struck by the signatures. Hubert Senior's resembled his son's egotistical flourish. But Elbert Woodling hadn't signed it; his name had a shaky X next to it and a note in what looked like a woman's handwriting, neat and even: *"This mark serves as Elbert's agreement to the sale."* Elbert sold his property for three thousand dollars. Even for fifty years ago, that seemed low. Nell again compared the property listed on the deed with the tract in the state park. Only part of it was the land that Hubert Pickings, the elder, had bought from Elbert Woodling. Nell put the paper down and tried to remember what was on the other side of the park.

When that didn't work, she tried another tack. Hubert had money; how did his family get that money?

That was it, Nell remembered; and another reason she didn't like Hubert Pickings. The land they'd kept had become one of the most polluted spots in Tchula County. There had been a paper mill and cardboard factory, built on the Tchula River. In the early sixties? It had been torn down shortly after she'd moved here with Thom, the year she was pregnant with Lizzie. The owners had gone bankrupt and left a foul, ugly edifice and the mess it made in the river. Pickings had played dumb, claiming he'd just leased the land and had no idea they were making such a mess.

Nell smiled grimly. It's so nice when fate hands you the right facts at the right time. Shit-stirring reporting, indeed. A mashed potato tie couldn't compete with this. The bones would lead to the property and the property would lead to a rehash of the pollution scandal. And the scandal would lead to an announcement that there was a viable alternative to voting for Hubert Pickings.

She looked at her watch. Time to head for Lizzie's school. Nell glanced again at the deed. Elbert. The unnamed clerk had called him Elbert, not Mr. Woodling. Maybe they knew each other; this would have been such a small town back then. Or maybe he was black and she was white and a white woman would refer to a black man by his first name, even in something as formal as a property transfer. Nell wished she had more time to compare the sale price to other prices from the time.

The rain was still ensuring that no political picnics would take place today and perhaps not tomorrow. Nell wondered about the old bones still in the woods. At least one skeleton was safe and dry in the morgue.

Pulling up to the high school, Nell decided to pretend she didn't realize the spaces close to the covered walkway were reserved for teachers. An older man, long past retirement age, was stationed at the door. However, he didn't apprehend Nell for her nefarious parking, merely nodded his head in greeting.

She headed for the auditorium. Halfway there, a swirl of students engulfed her and out of it a voice cried, "Mom? What are you doing here?"

Nell turned, sighted her daughter, and veered to her. "I'm here to cover Aaron Dupree's campaign." They continued walking with the flow. Lizzie, to Nell's astonishment, didn't seem perturbed to be seen with her mother. Or maybe I'm overreacting, Nell thought. She was also relieved to notice that, despite her gentle and not-so-gentle hints about dress and hair, Lizzie wasn't even in the running in the outlandish competition.

"Want to ask Candidate Dupree a question for me?"

"Yeah, sure," Lizzie replied. "As long as it's not too out."

Nell considered, for a brief moment, a question about race relations in Pelican Bay, but that was too freighted a question to pass on to her daughter. "Ask whether he plans to involve youth in his administration, and if so, how."

That seemed to pass the "too out" test, as Lizzie said, "Okay, that's a good question."

"Where do the boring adults sit?" Nell asked her daughter as they entered.

"In the front, with Mr. Simmons," Lizzie answered, accompanied with her usual eye roll. Nell had to agree with her, not that she said that. Nell's experience of Mr. Simmons was that he was slow, even ponderous, in making decisions; could only see numbers, not how things affected people; and was far too easily swayed by whichever faction make the most noise. "But you can sit with us, if you want," Lizzie added.

Nell said, "You sure you want to be seen with your aged mother?"

"Ah, Mom, you're not that old. You're not a boring adult yet. You don't need to sit with them." Lizzie led the way to where her friends were sitting.

Nell wondered if that was how Lizzie really felt, or just an artifact from the previous evening of no motherly interference in choosing pizza toppings. I'm not being fair to her, Nell thought, assuming she's going to be an annoying adolescent. To the friends Nell didn't know, Lizzie introduced her as, "This is my mom. She's covering this for the *Pelican Bay Crier*." Lizzie seemed almost proud.

Nell was reassured to note most of Lizzie's friends were not the most fashion-forward of the middle school; the most shocking thing she could see was a pierced eyebrow. She decided to not worry about what she couldn't see.

As with most assemblies, it took a while for people to settle down; the process little-aided by Mr. Simmons reedy pleading of "Okay, children, find your seats."

It began with what Nell considered the usual drone: announcements, the trite clichés about how this was the best school in the world with the best middle school football team in the South, the slide into religion with a moment of "Let us pray" without actually adding "to Jesus," although that was clearly the intent. Then Mr. Simmons, demonstrating his mathematical ability and little else, did a long introduction, winding past civic duty and the importance of voting, not noting the irony in extolling voting to teenagers three to five years from the privilege.

Aaron Dupree sat slightly behind him, his face a calm mask even though he had to know Mr. Simmons was putting his audience to sleep. At least by the time these students could indeed vote, they might have forgotten this particular campaign stop.

Nell looked from his carefully controlled mask to the audience. Segregation might have ended years ago, but integration was still just a word. For the most part, the black students and the white students sat apart.

Nell noted with chagrin that although Lizzie's friends sitting around them included several Asian girls and one either Hispanic or Arabic, no blacks sat with them. Maybe I'm making too much of this, one random seating in one assembly, Nell thought. Or maybe it's something I haven't looked hard enough at, leaving the patterns and assumptions neatly in place.

When she'd first moved to Pelican Bay, she was married to Thom and so had fallen into his social milieu. She realized it was mostly white, with a few acquaintances of other races. Had she passed that on to her daughter, that unquestioning acceptance? Her thoughts were interrupted by weak applause. Mr. Simmons had finally finished his introduction.

Aaron Dupree was polite, but he quickly grabbed the microphone from Mr. Simmons. He also had the sense not to stay planted behind the lectern, but instead moved about the stage, using all the space the microphone cord allowed.

Nell had to admit he was a polished performer. He started off with a joke, followed with a brief and uplifting riff on his vision for Pelican Bay, then moved to the importance of education, following with how important young people were and ending with his sincere belief that Pelican Bay had the best football team. The applause after his speech was much less tepid than for Mr. Simmons'.

He opened the floor for questions.

The first few questions were about his days as a football player for Pelican Bay High. His answers had an 'ah, shucks, it was fun,' quality while still working in that they had won the state championship his senior year.

Carrie was right, Nell admitted; Aaron Dupree was a handsome man. The well-cut suit he wore accented his broad shoulders and trim waist, a physique that could be the envy of some of the current football players.

"Are you married?" one of the girls asked. Then she blushed and giggled, which caused a wave of titters in the audience.

"No, I'm not," he answered. "But I do hope someday to get there." He gave a quick glance to a woman who was also seated on the stage with him. Nell craned her head to be able to see more than the woman's knees. It was Desiree Hunter. If she was his intended, he had made a good choice, she thought.

Nell made a note to find out if this was a fiancé or just a girlfriend.

Then came Lizzie's turn. "Do you have plans to involve youth in your administration and if so, in what capacity?" Her voice was clear and strong, no fumbling over the words. Nell felt a surge of pride in her daughter.

"I would love to involve youth. I think we too often keep young people away from the adult world. I plan to work with the schools to have a program of internships so you can see what goes on in the mayor's office, at the police station, the library. I'd also like to work with local businesses to create a similar set of internships. For example, we have one of the best local papers in the state right here in Pelican Bay. That would be a great way to find out what the world of journalism is all about."

No, Nell silently answered, college is as young as I care to go. But she had to acknowledge his skillful answer. He had paid enough attention to notice she was here and had found a way to flatter without being unctuous.

He looked directly enough at her to catch her eye. Blue eyes, very blue, she noted. Nell held his glance for a moment, then Lizzie asked her follow-up question. "What's your time table for implementing this program?"

Nell was almost relieved to turn to look at her daughter. She was long out of practice in—in what? Had he been mildly flirting? Or was that just a symptom of her loneliness, to read into a practiced politician's sincere glance, a hint of interest?

He answered Lizzie's question. "Ideally in the first six months I'm in office, but I can't promise the aldermen will let me do everything as soon as I want to."

There were a few more questions, then Mr. Simmons managed to grab the mic back and tell the "children" it was time to go back to class. The children milled around the auditorium, their only major movement to the soft drink machine in the hallway.

Nell made her way to the candidate, with Lizzie following. Somehow Nell couldn't see Lizzie interning at the paper—even if she wanted to be a reporter; she didn't think the paper or her sanity could survive a teenage daughter constantly on the premises. But it wouldn't hurt her daughter to get a glimpse of just what it was her mother did. Nell tried to think of questions that would be both intelligent and impress her teenager.

Aaron Dupree had been buttonholed by Mr. Simmons, so he quickly turned when he spied Lizzie and Nell approaching.

"That was a very good question," he said to Lizzie, offering her an adult handshake. As Nell suspected, Lizzie didn't burst out and say, "Oh, my mom thought of that." Instead, she answered, "A lot of us kids want to make a difference, but sometimes it's hard to find a way to do anything."

"If I'm elected mayor, that will change. What is your name? Would you like to be a youth advisor on my transition team?"

Nell suspected he well knew her name. He might not have memorized all the children of Pelican Bay, but there was enough of a resemblance between them, he could easily guess that Lizzie was her daughter. His glance took in Nell, hovering just behind Lizzie.

"I'm Elizabeth McGraw, and I'd love to," she gushed. Then Lizzie—Elizabeth—remembered her manners, in a fashion. "Oh, this is my mom."

Aaron Dupree's hand was already out when he said, "Mrs. McGraw, I'm pleased to see you again so soon."

"Hello, Mr. Dupree." His look was as direct as it had been from across the stage. Nell glanced down at her notebook as if a question was there. "Are you going to raise our taxes to accomplish this program?"

"Not at all," he answered. "I'm going to count on the civic pride and duty of the people of our city. I'm hoping if I set the example with all the city functions, others will follow suit."

If her daughter hadn't been standing next to her, Nell might have asked him if he flirted with all the women reporters. But that was too adult for her darling daughter. She still wasn't sure if he was flirting or if she was just reading it in.

"Do you really plan to have student interns on the sewage and water board?"

"Ah, you've been to some of the meetings," he said with a quick smile. "Perhaps we should do everything in moderation."

Mr. Simmons took this moment to interrupt. "Young lady, you should be on your way to class," he told Lizzie, in a tone that seemed meant to curtail her moment of attention.

"She'll go in a moment," Aaron Dupree said. "Right now I've got to get her signed up for my transition team. Changing of governments only happens every four years and it may be a while before she gets another chance."

Again, Nell had to admire his style, and she silently praised him for preventing her from telling Simmons what she thought of his pedantry in a manner not suitable before her delicate—well, not, but mothers still had to set some standards—daughter.

Lizzie was happily agreeing to anything Aaron Dupree suggested. Fortunately, his only suggestion was for her to write down her name and contact info. Nell decided he didn't look like a white slaver, so she pulled out one of her business cards and handed it to Lizzie to write on the back.

With that, Lizzie happily skipped back to class—via the soft drink machine in the hallway.

"You have a great daughter," Dupree told her. "And I can only tell you're old enough to be her mother when I'm within two feet of you. Your hair color exactly matches hers."

"I'm impressed with your skillful use of flattery, Mr. Dupree," Nell said. "Perhaps I'm an economical mother and buy hair color in bulk."

"Call me Aaron. And, Mrs. McGraw, within two feet of you I can spy just a few gray hairs. That rules out economical hair dye."

Nell appreciated that he offered his first name without automatically going to hers. It was possible he didn't know it, but so far his political skill argued that he would damn well know the name of the Editor-in-Chief of the local paper.

Desiree joined them. "Aaron, darling, we've got to get over to the television studio," she said. To Nell she added, "Time to make some TV ads and they charge by the second."

"Of course. I understand the realities of politics and I hardly thought an appearance at my daughter's school would be a proper grill-the-candidate time," Nell assured her.

Aaron said, "Truly her brother's keeper. Nothing like having your sister as your ex-officio campaign manager. Really keeps you on schedule."

Ah, Nell thought, his sister. She kept her face neutral. At least, she hoped she did.

"'Campaign manager' is also a polite euphemism for chief cook and bottle washer," Desiree interjected.

"We shall certainly have to set up a time for you to do a proper grilling," Aaron said to Nell. He again shook her hand, lingering just a touch beyond the usual hearty shake of a politician, and then he and his sister left.

Nell hung back, letting them get a good distance away before she headed out.

The evidence of both her intellect and her instincts said he definitely had been flirting. It seemed important that Nell knew Desiree was his sister. That he knew more about her than their brief meetings suggested was probable. He claimed to have read the Crier, which meant he'd read her articles and editorials. It was an open secret she did most of the editorial writing and Thom's job was to smooth whatever feathers might have been ruffled. Though Nell liked to think she lived an opaque life, just like most people, she also acknowledged that Pelican Bay was on the smaller side of ponds and the person who ran the local paper was, by default, a big fish.

Nell considered her looks to be in the "no broken mirrors" range—pleasant, but nothing that would turn heads. Thom had insisted he'd watched her every time he saw her on campus and almost had an orgasm when they'd ended up in class together. She'd laughed off his flattery. After seventeen years of marriage, she still had laughed off his insistence she was good-looking. "Be real," Nell would answer. "You married me for my brains, ambition, and bust size."

Vivien had been the beauty in the family. Maggie was the oldest daughter, the second mother who took care of them all; Vivien the cheerleader, the beauty queen; and Nell had been, simply, the last daughter, smart because that was all that was left her. She still remembered her mother's voice: "You'll never be the beauty your sister is, so you might as well study."

The stab in her heart was still bitter at the memory of graduation, giving her valedictorian speech, with only Maggie and Frank, the brother closest to her in age, sitting in the audience. The rest had chosen to cheer Vivien on as she competed for whatever cheap tiara she was going after, Miss Hog Jowls of Indiana. It wasn't that Vivien was mean or demanded attention, but she seemed to live in a world that existed between her and the mirror and the stage. Their mother egged her on, as if Vivien's beauty was the best reflection any of her children could give her.

Nell glanced at her image in the window as she walked down the deserted hallway. Maybe I wasn't bad looking at twenty-five, but at forty? All those years spent next to Vivien's beauty had seeped into the mirror. The blurred image in the dusty school window was more blank than ugly. Filling in with memory, Nell saw a woman above average height at five-eight, her hair swept up in a chignon that was easy and quick. It was still the light chestnut color it always had been. Her mother called it dirty blond, as if blond was so clearly better than brown, even dirty was preferable. Her eyes were blue-gray, only the bare beginnings of laugh lines. She didn't have Vivien's jutting cheekbones or Maggie's wide smile, but her face was regular with a strong chin and the hint of dimples. Maggie told her she needed those dimples otherwise her face was too serious, with the eyes, brow and forehead of someone who read books, and studied.

Is this what Aaron Dupree found attractive? Then she hastily walked on. Even with her intellect and instincts saying that, if only for a brief flirt, yes, he did, she still found it unreal.

She and Thom met on a class project. They were both getting their masters in journalism at Columbia. They found they worked well together. Thom claimed that he was smitten the first time she edited him, but Nell remembered a more measured courtship, their togetherness while studying slowly and tentatively turning into romance. When Thom had first asked Nell up to his room, for something clearly more than books, she had turned him down. Not because she didn't want to, but because serious Naomi Nelligan couldn't imagine dashing and handsome Thom McGraw wanting more that a quick fling with her. He had asked again, and again, and finally asked, "If I marry you, will you sleep with me?"

Nell had cynically replied, "Already got the divorce lawyer hired?" Only then did she see the hope—and the subsequent hurt in his eyes. That she could hurt him gave her the courage to say yes.

No, I'm not very good at playing the sexual game, Nell thought as she left the school, hurrying to her car through the rain. She'd had a few lovers before Thom. Starting with, of course, the boyfriend she had dutifully dated in high school. But when she'd gone off to college she'd easily left him behind. They had done little beyond heavy kissing, which had suited Nell. He'd later written her that he was gay and hoped that she wasn't scarred for life. She had resisted the temptation to write him back saying, no, no scars, only disappointment in his kissing. The first person that Nell actually had kissed had been Sally, a girlfriend of hers; they were supposedly practicing for the real thing. But Sally was a much better kisser than most of the boys she dated. For a while she was worried that Sally's expert tongue had ruined her for the sloppy thrusts of boys. There were even a few occasions when she wished Sally would write her a letter saying she was gay.

She had finally lost, or rather thrown away, her virginity, at a frat party. She had simply picked the candidate that seemed both willing and reasonably sane. It wasn't painful like she was afraid it might be, but no fireworks went off either. Her first passionate affair had been with one of her professors. He was separated from his wife and they had two children. Nell could look back and see it clearly now—he was using her to fill his loneliness and to enjoy that exquisite attention from a young woman newly in love. He was a skilled lover, ensuring that her pleasure equaled his, teaching her ways to touch and explore.

He had been a bastard ending it, telling her he loved her and yet making excuse after excuse for not being able to see her save in class. She finally heard through the campus grapevine that he was back living with his wife. Nell got an A in the class even though she hadn't bothered going to the final exam.

She hadn't learned her lesson and repeated the same pattern on her first job, having an affair with the news editor while he was separated from his wife. It, too, had ended, but he at least was decent enough to sit down with her and tell her, and even admit he had been wrong; he was older and should have known better.

The end of that affair was what prompted her to apply to graduate school and get out of the Midwest.

Driving back to the office, Nell reflected that even before Thom, her experience hadn't been extensive. Not bad, though, for the one who wasn't beautiful. Another bitter wash came over her.

With Thom, whatever early awkwardness they'd had was made up for with ardor. Until Lizzie announced herself, they'd had quite a randy time in bed. "I'm a married woman, I get to be promiscuous with my husband," Nell had often told Thom while doing something like unzipping his pants.

This is not a safe topic to think about, Nell admonished herself as she pulled into the parking lot. That ease and knowing touch was gone. In a flash of anger, she pounded her fist against the steering wheel. With the pouring rain to cover her, she yelled out, "Goddamn it! Five minutes … and you'd still be here."

Now she was single, alone, and one man with one glance seemed impossible to handle. She and Thom had once or twice talked about what they would do if something happened to one of them. Go on living, find someone else to love. Occasional flowers on the gravestone is all you owe me, they had told each other. Those words had been easily said in the comfort and belief that it would never come to be.

"Find someone else to love. How the fuck do I do that?" Nell asked the pouring rain. As her anger ebbed, she admitted she felt a mark of attention to Aaron Dupree, not just appreciation for a handsome man. Safely in her car, she felt the slight tingle of possibility and attraction. He was a handsome man, he seemed interested. She was lonely.

I've barely been a widow a month, Mr. Dupree, she thought. But then she wondered if she was saying that to him or to herself.

FIVE

AFTER RETURNING TO THE Crier, Nell withdrew to her office, afraid her recent anger would be too palpable. Or, worse, her coworkers might read the lust that had flitted through her head. She used the energy to tackle stacks of paperwork. When that energy started to flag, she had to just look at the two phone messages from Tanya Jones to renew it. Just as she was approaching closing time, the end of her stack of paperwork, and her anger, Sheriff Clureman Hickson came knocking on her office door.

"Miz McGraw, I have a story for you," he boomed, even though she was close enough to see the gray in his nose hair.

He had often come to Thom with story ideas, most close to thinly disguised promotions of Sheriff Clureman Hickson. Thom usually managed to find some story angle in it, minimizing the sheriff's starring role although leaving enough to appease him. Nell left those for Thom to write. She couldn't help pointing out that the deadly snake the sheriff (with the able help of his deputies) managed to catch on someplace like the very doorstep of the Orphans & Small Dogs Home looked more like a garter snake than a water moccasin. Thom would take the copy and say that there were some times when it might be better not to check the facts.

Now the sheriff was back with another of his story ideas. Somehow she didn't think Sheriff Hickson would see the humor if she suggested channeling Thom.

He took her expressionless face for interest and continued. "Yes, ma'am, blood is thicker than water." With that pronouncement, he flipped open an oversized piece of paper that Nell recognized as a genealogy chart. His massive pudgy finger stabbed at the top of the sheet. "Turns out I'm descended from Alred Ellington, the master of the Fair Haven Plantation. He's my great-great-grandfather. Didn't know I came from such worthy stock, did you?"

The sheriff didn't wait for an answer, as if suspecting that Yankee Nell might not think slave owners worth much.

"His eldest son produced two family lines. One of them led to me, and the other led to a newly discovered cousin of mine." Here he consulted another piece of paper for her name. "Beatrice Carver. Seems that Miz Carver has done quite well for herself—I'm guessing it was her husband—and she did this chart and wants to connect with her family. This next Saturday, at noon, she's coming to town to donate the funds to buy a new highway patrol car, one with all the bells and whistles. Now what do you think of that story?"

I'm going to have to start wearing a bracelet with WWTD— What Would Thom Do—on it, Nell thought. Okay, she quickly told herself, for a small town like Pelican Bay, a long-lost relative coming to town could be a reasonable story.

"When did you get this news?" As she asked the question, Nell grabbed a notepad and took enough notes to look like she was taking this seriously. She went through the list: who was his cousin, where did his cousin live, why had she looked up the family, and what made her decide to donate an entire car? She was tempted to ask if it came with snake-catching equipment.

Nell dutifully wrote down his answers and promised that she would be outside the courthouse, with camera, at precisely noon.

Then she decided that this shouldn't be a one-sided visit. "Any thoughts about the bones found in the woods?"

He paused for a moment, then answered. "Damn fool hunter."

"Two damn fools?" Nell asked. "One with chains on the wrists?"

The sheriff gave her a sharp look. "Where'd you get that?"

"From the ground. I went out with Kate Ryan the day she found the bones."

"Don't put nothin' like that in the paper," he lectured her.

"Why not?" Nell guessed it was the usual police thing—keep details out only the killer knew—but she still wanted to hear it from Sheriff Hickson.

"You want to panic the town? All we need is rumors of chained killin' in the woods."

"Do you really think Pelican Bay will fall into a frenzy at the idea of two murders that happened decades ago?" Nell shot back at him.

"You still don't need to go puttin' it in the paper," he insisted.

"For how long?"

"How long what?"

"How long do I keep it out of the paper?" Nell repeated. "Do you really think that no one else is going to pick up this story?"

"Look, I know it's sad and too bad 'bout whatever happened to them, but those people are history. We'll dig 'em up only to then bury them again."

"Even if they were murdered?" Nell answered.

"Miz McGraw, be real. They been in that ground long enough for a big tree to grow over 'em. What evidence we gonna find? And even if we find something, what are the chances whoever did it isn't also already in the ground?"

"If that's the case, then what's the harm with telling the story?"

The sheriff let out a long sigh. Nell gathered he didn't appreciate logical women. He sighed again before answering. "Okay, Miz Mc-Graw, you can write your story, but you might just give us enough time to make sure nothing comes out of the ground that's gonna bite us in the butt."

Nell didn't let on that she was still debating whether to hold the story for next week's paper. It might depend on what else was discovered. And if the sheriff thought that she was genteel enough to be thrown off by the word "butt," he was much mistaken. Nell had learned to curse at a Catholic girls' school and there was nothing like a plaid polyester skirt and a nun with a ruler to expand the vocabulary. "I'll think about it. I plan to be there when the forensic anthropologist continues the dig. With camera ready, just in case there is any butt-biting."

The sheriff didn't see any humor in her comment. He shook his head and said, "Just don't forget the story about my long-lost cousin." With that he turned to go.

Nell decided he wasn't going to get off so easily. "Oh, Sheriff? Tanya Jones called Mrs. Thomas, Sr. and 'suggested' the Jones boys aren't happy about their brother being in jail. And if that didn't change, they might do something about it."

The sheriff turned back to face her. "They threatened Mrs. Thomas?"

"Used her as a messenger. The threat was aimed at me."

He seemed to be mulling this over, as if a threat to Mrs. Thomas was serious but Nell had fallen into the "looking to be bitten in the butt" category. "Tanya say just what they planned?" he finally asked.

"No, the opposite, she didn't know what they might do. And she wouldn't want to be me."

The sheriff mulled this additional information for a moment, then said, "You gonna go after Junior, aren't you?"

"Are you saying that I should capitulate to his brothers' threats?"

"No, ma'am." The sheriff had enough sense to recognize the undertone of fury in Nell's voice, even if he didn't seem sure what capitulate meant. "Not at all. Just that … Junior's been in the hoosegow now for 'bout a month. Tanya's gonna be struggling to take care of those kids."

"Perhaps there's where the Brothers Jones could do something constructive," Nell said coldly. "Assist with raising their nephews and nieces while Junior pays his debt to society."

"Now, Miz McGraw, I ain't sayin' that Junior don't deserve what he gets …"

Nell cut in. "Good. I'd hate to have the Sheriff of Tchula County say that a drunk driver with two previous arrests doesn't deserve to go to jail after he finally kills someone."

"But I am sayin' a little mercy might go a long way. Seems that Junior has finally learned his lesson and …"

He said something more but Nell didn't hear it, a blind fury coursing through her. "Fuck your mercy!" she suddenly shouted at him. "Your wife, your child. If they were the ones left dead on the roadside, how much mercy would you have? Don't you goddamn ask me to have mercy! Junior will get out of jail someday. Thom will still be in his grave."

"Now, Miz McGraw," the sheriff said. "I understand that you're upset."

"Don't you dare patronize me. I am not 'upset.' I'm fucking furious!"

78

"Now, Miz McGraw," he tried again.

She cut him off. "Junior had two previous arrests to learn his lesson. I doubt he has learned much more than he doesn't like being in jail."

The sheriff sighed again. He didn't like emotional women either, particularly ones whose emotion was anger instead of something more feminine. "It's not that you and I disagree. If it was my wife … jail would be too good for him. But the Jones boys, well, Junior learned his drinking from them and it worries me what they might do. You got two kids."

"Are you telling me that the law enforcement of Tchula County and Pelican Bay is helpless before the Jones brothers?" Even the sheriff couldn't miss the sarcasm in Nell's voice.

"No, Miz McGraw, not at all. But, well, Whiz ain't the most active police chief we've had, and even if he was, we're just lawmen, not guardian angels. Arrestin' them after the fact might not be much of a help."

"Isn't there a law against making threats?"

"Yes, ma'am, there is. But it's Tanya making a claim they threatened and Miz Thomas is the only witness. They deny it, Tanya ain't exactly gonna be a friendly witness."

"So they get away with it?" Nell demanded heatedly, angry at both him and the fact that what he was saying made sense. "And someone threw a rock in the door this morning, with a threatening note. I suppose they get away with that, too?"

"Did they do it? Yeah, who else. Can I prove it enough to do more than put them in jail for a few hours? I doubt it. Those boys are snakes and you don't want riled snakes."

"Nor do you," Nell acerbically added.

"I got a jail full of 'em," he reminded her. "I'll talk to those boys out on the porch, so all the neighbors hear. Tell 'em they won't like jail and that's where they'll end up if anything happens to you. That's the best I can do."

Nell suddenly felt exhausted, the anger gone, emptiness where it had been. She just wanted him out of her office. "Then I'll have to settle for the best you can do."

"You call both me and Whiz if they try anything." With that, the sheriff escaped.

Her office door had been open the whole time, so Nell knew, unless her staff had deliberately blocked up their ears, they heard everything. At least now they know I can say "fuck," Nell thought. It was as close as she could get to a positive thought.

SIX

"You don't have to dump me with Grandmom. I'm going over to Susan's for homework," Lizzie informed Nell when she said she had to go out after supper. Nell considered asking if Susan—and more importantly, Susan's mother—actually knew of Lizzie's impending arrival. But the convenience of it overwhelmed her morals. She just nodded in agreement.

"Kate's doing inventory at the bike shop this evening. I told her if it was okay with you, I'd come by and help." Josh wasn't a good enough soldier to face Mrs. Thomas, Sr. alone.

Nell again warred with her morals. Kate being the source of a good story compelled her to ask, "Do you think Kate needs your help?"

"It's counting and piling. I've helped her before."

That was close enough for Nell's conscience. "I'll pick you up after my meeting. So be prepared to turn into pumpkins at around nine."

That got the usual protest from Lizzie that they would be only halfway done, and the usual response from Nell that perhaps they should do homework first and gossip second. Nell quelled further protest by suggesting Lizzie might find it more conducive to study at her grandmother's.

After supper, she hustled them into the car and dropped Josh at the bike shop. She stayed long enough to give Kate at least a millisecond to protest. Kate just waved and Nell drove on to Lizzie's destination.

With her children safely deposited, Nell glanced at the address for Marcus Fletcher's talk.

It was a poor section of town. Nell noticed several houses that looked abandoned. Others were kept up, but the cars were older models, the lawn only what grew in the small space between the porch and sidewalk. She took another turn onto a street that some yesteryear had been a strip of stores and businesses. The shape of the building told their history: the door cut into the corner, the wide windows for merchandise, now with curtains on the inside and steel bars on the outside. Only two businesses seemed to still be viable, one a small grocery store on the corner garishly festooned with signs for cigarettes and beer. The other place was named Don's Hideout. It had similar beer and cigarette signs and the dim interior suggested a bar. In the middle of the block was what might have once been a municipal building, perhaps a school in the days of segregation or some other remnant of separate but not equal. Its door was open and the lights inside welcoming compared to the gaudy store and murky bar. There were enough men in suits standing outside to tell Nell this was the place. Something about political rallies was all the same, from the smell of frying chicken to the cooing babies offered as props to the men and, increasingly, women in suits with hands outstretched.

Nell found parking on the store-side of the street, then walked back across to the hall. One of the men standing out front asked as she approached, "Ma'am, may I help you?"

It was then Nell realized she was the only white woman. When she was young and had worked in Chicago and Fort Wayne, she'd preferred the multicultural neighborhood she lived in to the white suburb her brothers suggested for her. Then she'd moved here, and found that multiculturalism didn't extend to even decent bagels. It's easy to forget how separate things are, Nell chastised herself, when you're the one separated into the good neighborhood.

"This is where Marcus Fletcher is speaking?" she asked the man. She didn't sense hostility, just mild puzzlement.

"Yes, ma'am, this is. We don't usually get much of a crowd for these speeches now. It doesn't count if it's not on television." He turned slightly so that the light spilling from the doorway illuminated his features. He was an older man, something his erect carriage hadn't hinted at without the light to show the gray in his hair and the lines on his face.

"I'm Nell McGraw, with the *Pelican Bay Crier*. I'm of the contrary view that if it's not in the paper, it's not real." Nell offered him her hand.

His hand was firm and warm, with enough pressure to let her know he was still a vigorous man. "Welcome, Mrs. McGraw, to our gathering. We're pleased to have you here."

"I hope you'll still be pleased after I give the candidate the usual merciless media grilling," Nell answered. "The tough questions like what's he going to do about alligators in the sewer. And improving the school system, the tax structure."

"A daunting list, madam. I do hope you don't ask our candidate any tough foreign policy questions. He should have been boning up on his overseas capitols last night but went to his granddaughter's birthday party instead."

"But the people of Pelican Bay have a right to know where he stands on the situation in Uzbekistan. Surely you're not suggesting that I go easy on him on such a burning question?"

"Being a former member of the press corps myself, not to mention the candidate's press secretary, I would never suggest that you compromise your standards."

Life has unexpected graces, Nell thought. Here on this run-down street, with a man she didn't know, she had fallen into an easy and enlivening banter. But into that grace came the blade. She and Thom used to banter with this same easy flow. Nell faltered and didn't answer.

The silence stretched until he said, "My wife and I used to talk like that. She's been gone ten years and I still miss her terribly." Quietly he added, "I'm sorry for your loss."

"Is it so obvious?" Nell answered, her voice hoarse.

"No, not at all. I read the paper."

She hadn't written the story; she didn't even know who did. Jacko, she guessed. But of course Thom's death—murder, really—had been front page. Pictures of him growing up in Pelican Bay, leading to the discreet shot of the mother and widow, both in black. Nell remembered vaguely thinking it was a good photo—and a wrenching one for her. They were photographed from the back, a nimbus of sun breaking through the clouds of the day, Josh and Lizzie bracketed between the older silver-haired woman and the younger chestnut-haired one, with the sweep of the cemetery receding into rows of tombstones that finally blurred into the horizon.

Nell took a long breath and let it out before speaking. "Thank you. It's ... hard."

His only answer was to reach out and squeeze her hand.

"Mr. Fletcher is very lucky to have you as his press secretary." She gave his hand an extra press of thanks, then let go as other people moved by them to enter the hall.

"But I'm not so lucky. Mr. Fletcher just works me to death."

"Ah, so I should ask Mr. Fletcher his views on labor laws?"

"Best be careful, young lady; you know how politicians are. Once he gets started, you may be here all night."

"Care to become my 'high administration source who insists on anonymity'?"

"Are you asking that I become disloyal to my chosen political star?"

"No, of course not, but the threat of another Deep Throat may be all that keeps our elected officials honest."

Another clump of people entered the hall, leaving them the only ones still outside, save for two men by the bar. A glance at them suggested that they were doing a drug deal, the quick change of something in the hands. He noticed it too and motioned her inside.

The hall was sparsely furnished, with mismatched metal folding chairs, a small stage made of a few two-by-fours and plywood painted black. The walls either were institutional beige or a white that had faded over the years.

The man she had been talking to was clearly well known; other people came to claim his attention. He excused himself and added that he hoped she would enjoy the show.

Nell glanced around the room. She recognized a few other people: Harold Reed, the assistant DA who was rumored to be the legal brains behind the elected DA Buddy Guy's enviable conviction rate; Tamacia ... Nell couldn't pull up her last name, but she worked over in City Hall, one of the secretaries the mayor ignored and Nell had learned to cultivate.

Harold nodded slightly at her; he was with two other men Nell recognized as lawyers. She didn't know Harold very well, only from a few carefully scripted press conferences, the ones Buddy Guy didn't see enough political capitol in to handle himself.

Tamacia waved her over. "Nell, what are you doing here?" Tamacia was open and friendly and hadn't yet learned the finer points of political caution. Unlike the gentleman at the door, she saw no need to hide her surprise that the white editor of the local newspaper was at their event. "How'd you even find this place?"

"An old newspaper trick. Can't cover a story unless you can get to it, so they taught us to read maps."

"You're here to report on this?" Tamacia's tone was friendly, but underneath was a thread of suspicion.

"Who's going to be the next mayor of Pelican Bay may not be the lead in the *New York Times*, but it's a rather important story here."

"You're really going to report on what Marcus has to say?"

Nell answered, "If I can give a few column inches to Everett Evens and his 'wish I was in the land of cotton' campaign, it certainly seems I should give some to Mr. Fletcher."

Tamacia hooted and then said, "Don't tell Hubert I'm here. He'll think I'm plotting a slave rebellion."

"Reporters never reveal their sources, and you're one of my best in City Hall," Nell told her. "Has the mayor heard about the new candidate?"

"The phones were blazing today. Haven't seen Mr. Mayor sweating so much since that day the air conditioning went out in August." Then, in a lower tone, she added, "He can't bribe or blackmail Aaron Dupree, so my chances for a new boss look good."

Nell started to ask a follow-up, but one of the men took the stage and his amplified voice filled the space. He wasn't a great speaker, but was reasonably funny and that made up for the rambling length of his welcome. Nell's attention drifted in and out. Finally he got to the point of his speech, introducing the candidate. "Ladies and gentlemen and you two guys in the back, I want to introduce you to a great friend of mine, someone who probably needs no introduction, but I'm going to give him one anyway because I have to have a reason for standing up here jawing at you. I don't need to tell you the usual stuff: son of a sharecropper, had an uncle who was lynched, first in his family to go to college."

Nell was taking notes, wishing she'd had the time to actually research the candidate. Suddenly she wondered how well the *Pelican Bay Crier* had covered this side of town. How much would the paper's morgue contain on Marcus Fletcher?

The introduction continued. "And most of you know his record in the civil—or not so civil—rights days. That's when he got his nose broken. Good thing it wasn't a pretty one to begin with. Most of us grew up reading his rantings and ravings in the *Coast Advocate*. Like Ida B. Wells, he wasn't afraid to write about lynching and cross burnings. Most of us found out how right he was, that his rantings and ravings were those of a sane man fighting for freedom and justice." He covered all the highlights of Marcus Fletcher's life: his devoted wife, four children, one killed in Vietnam; named all the grandchildren; mentioned his banjo playing, even suggesting the very instrument was off to the side of the stage. Finally he ended with, "And here he is, the next mayor of Pelican Bay, or at least the most qualified."

The older gentleman who'd spoken so easily to Nell at the door walked to the dais. He looked directly at her for a second, smiled, then made eye contact with the rest of the audience.

Press secretary *and* candidate, Nell thought to herself. And cagey enough to not quickly tip his hand. Most candidates, even long-shot ones, would have taken advantage of having a one-on-one chat with the editor of the local paper. He had instead studied her.

His speech lasted no longer than the introduction had. There was the usual thanking of those who worked on his campaign, and then he said, "I have a simple platform, and it's not my own words or even my ideas. They come from men, men who owned slaves, a few hundred years ago. We are all created equal, and we all have the right to life, liberty, and the pursuit of happiness. Let's be real, folks. This isn't a campaign about winning. It's about having a voice."

Like Aaron Dupree, he talked about the importance of education, but his remarks focused on those struggling with poverty and hardship, and carried the knowledge that education was one of the few routes out. He was an articulate man, and Nell had to rate his speech as even better than Dupree's. But without real hope of winning—Nell tasted the gall that it was only the color of his skin that made the real difference—Marcus Fletcher could afford to be eloquent and bold.

After the speech, Nell waited for him to finish talking to those who came up to him. Finally, when he was shaking the last hand, Nell approached.

"Mr. Press Secretary, is it possible to talk to the candidate now?" she asked.

"I do believe that the candidate is ready for you, Mrs. McGraw."

"Thank you, Mr. Press Secretary, you've been most helpful. Now, Mr. Candidate, what impact do you hope running for mayor will have?"

"The short answer? To make sure the people of Pelican Bay know they don't have to travel far to view poverty and the effects of racism. The not-so-short answer, which I'll give to you since you're a newspaper and not a TV sound-bite machine, is to get the spotlight on a few things and maybe make them a little better."

"And which few things would those be?"

"Street repair. It takes twice as long to get anything fixed in this part of town than it does in the richer part of town. No, that's not just talk; for the last year, we've been keeping track and have a very boring report full of numbers on the average time for repair on Rail Street as opposed to Jackson Avenue. Then there are the schools. Seventy percent of students in the vocational tech classes are African-American. Six percent of students in the high honors track are. We're a little over thirty percent of the population here in Tchula County."

"How do you think we got here?" Nell followed up.

"What happens to a child, day after day, year after year, if you treat him or her like they're just not quite as good, not quite as smart?"

"Are you accusing the school system of institutional racism?"

He looked at her for a long minute, gauging both her question and his answer. "I'm accusing the school system of not doing enough to overcome the ingrained racism that has seeped into our souls. Institutional racism? We've had black candidates running for some office or other here in Tchula County ever since Fannie Lou Hammer dared take on the Democratic Convention." He glanced to her to see if she knew what he was talking about.

"The 1964 Democratic Convention in Atlantic City and the challenge to the all white delegation," Nell supplied.

"The Mississippi Freedom Democratic Party, MFDP." He said the initials with practiced ease, as if they and the memories around them had come to rest in a deep, resonant part of his mind. "That was a time." He paused as if remembering, then continued. "In all those years and all those candidates, how many of them did the *Pelican Bay Crier* cover?"

Nell could say that she wasn't sure and would have to do research. But she didn't. Thom was an intelligent and liberal man and his father had been an intelligent and liberal man. And Nell couldn't rattle off names and stories the paper had run on even the political yearnings of the black residents of the town. Marcus Fletcher had made his point with a sharp—and accurate—edge.

Finally she answered. "I think it's obvious we could do a … better job."

He nodded, seeming to know she had skipped a few of the easy and cheap answers and had had the grace not to deny the history of her paper. "You know, back in the sixties I thought things would be so different by now. That it would be the content of our character that would matter."

"Things are changing."

"They're always changing. Used to think I might live long enough to see them changed."

Most of the lights flicked off; the chairs had been put away. Only a few people were lingering at the refreshment table and the lights seemed to be their cue to linger elsewhere.

"Maybe my children and your grandchildren," Nell said softly.

"Maybe," he answered as they walked by unspoken agreement to the door.

They said nothing until they were outside. If they couldn't talk of the future, maybe they could talk of the past.

"Last weekend a pine tree was felled by the recent storms, out in what is now the state park," Nell said. "It uprooted and exposed two human skeletons."

He looked at her sharply. For a moment he saw her, then saw something else. But he said nothing.

"I'd like to find out who those people are and what happened to them. One was a young African-American female. One of them was shot in the back of the head."

Still he said nothing.

"You ran a newspaper, Mr. Fletcher. Did you ever do a story about two people who disappeared around fifty years ago?"

"I did a lot of stories. A lot of people disappeared."

His answer told Nell two things—he knew something, and he didn't trust her enough to tell her.

"I've been doing research," she told him. "The land belonged to the Pickings family, part of a parcel they bought in the early sixties from someone named Elbert Woodling. They made a lot of money off that land, leased it to the paper mill, sold other pieces when the interstate came through."

"Did they now?" His question was opaque, simply telling her to go on.

"I'll have to do more research, but the buying price seemed very low, even for the time. Even a family as limited in intelligence as the Pickings could have made money when they got the land that cheap."

"Are you planning to write a story?"

"The story of long-ago murders should get front page, don't you think? Especially when the bodies are found on property the sitting Mayor donated with the stipulation it remain wild."

Marcus Fletcher was silent for a moment. Then he said, "Very interesting. But Mrs. McGraw, there are a lot of old men like me still around. I think it's a very intriguing story, but others won't see it that way."

His words were a warning, not a threat. "True, Mr. Fletcher, but few of them will be as vibrant and fit as you are. Bigots in nursing homes don't worry me too much."

"Just remember, those bigots have sons and daughters raised with different wishes and expectations than you and I have for our children." He had walked Nell to her car and now opened the door for her.

"Are you suggesting I not write the story?" Nell asked as she got in.

He thought for a moment before answering. "I would like to see that story come to light, and the bitter truth is, you can write it in a way that I never could. But the past is stone and won't change. Your present and future can be harmed. I both encourage you and warn you. If it's the encouragement that holds, you might want to talk to a woman by the name of Penny March. She's elderly now, in the Whispering Pines home." With that he shut the car door for her.

Nell rolled down the window. "No more clues about the two bodies in the woods?"

He straightened up and started to move away, then turned back and said, "Two? There should be three." He turned and walked away.

Nell stared at his retreating back. Chaney, Schwerner, and Goodman. They had been found; two white men from the North and one black man. Nell slowly remembered the details. A tip had led to a recently built earth dam. Their families had asked they be buried together, but at that time even the cemeteries were segregated. James Chaney had been buried alone.

What if they had all been black and no one, save the split earth fifty years later, had chosen to talk?

Nell started her car and drove to pick up her children.

SEVEN

THE RAIN HAD FINALLY passed in the night and the day was perfect and clear, one of those fall days that lulled Nell into thinking she could like this hot, humid, subtropical belt. When she was growing up, it was the winters that had to be endured, long endless days of cold and slush, but now it had changed to the summers, the heat arriving in March or April and lingering until September.

A perfect day for digging bones, Nell thought as she dropped Josh and Lizzie off at school.

Perfect in more ways than one, she considered as she parked behind several other vehicles. Nell McGraw, intrepid girl reporter, had a professional excuse for being dressed as she was: blue jeans, a T-shirt layered with an old sweatshirt, and her scruffy hiking boots. It also helped that there would be a woods teeming with graduate students, deputies, and other assorted people, rather than just her and Kate and the rictus grins of the skulls.

Nell heard the voices halfway down the path. Her timing was good; the graduate students had just finished rolling up the rain-soaked and leaf-strewn tarps she and Kate had left.

"Nell, welcome to our site," Kate called as several people turned to stare at the newcomer. Kate's greeting was followed with a flurry of introductions. Nell got the business cards of the two professors: Ellen Cohen, full professor and clearly in charge, and a much-younger assistant professor, Lynda Breeton. But none of the graduate students were as well equipped. She carefully spelled their names.

As she watched, Nell understood the real advantage of graduate students: they were young enough to do most of the actual digging.

There was a deputy from the sheriff's department, but he seemed content to leave the bones to the experts. He either didn't mind or didn't notice a reporter taking multiple pictures of the crime scene.

As she watched them carefully dig, Nell wondered about Marcus's final remark. She debated mentioning it, but wasn't sure how or if it was safe to reveal her source—an old man said there should be three bodies here.

They were very carefully extracting the second skeleton. Nell got a close-up of the chain as it lay exposed on a screen shifter. It had been cheap when new and was now rusted and corroded. She got another picture of the bullet hole and confirmation from the senior professor that it was definitely a bullet hole.

"Can this be mold?" one of the graduate students asked. He was pointing to a green stain on the pelvis bone of the second skeleton.

Kate answered, "Not likely. It might be copper staining. This fellow might have had some pennies in his pocket."

Nell watched in fascination as the shifted soil slowly proved Kate's words to be true. Out of the dirt came several coins. Four pennies, two nickels, and a dime.

After careful cleaning, the student who found them read off, "1958, 1961, 1960, 1963, 1960, 1963, and 1952."

Ellen, the senior professor, commented. "That's probably going to be some of our best evidence for dating these bones. Given the range of the coins, it's likely they were buried here sometime around 1963. The pennies are the later dates and they probably reflect the year or close to it."

The work was slow, tedious, and painstaking. Nell made herself useful by fetching water for those digging but also spent a lot of time standing around, watching the earth being slowly moved and shifted.

"Any guess as to sex, age, and race?" she asked Ellen when more of the bones were out of the ground.

"Young, healthy—until he died—male, probably African-American. I'm guessing early twenties. Both his legs were broken at the time he was killed. You can tell by the edges of the bones. Old wounds would show healing; dead bone breaks different from green bone—living bone, that is. But I'd appreciate you not writing any-thing until I've had a chance to examine them."

"Tortured and murdered," Nell said. "I'll wait for your okay."

"Definitely not natural causes. What a lonely grave this is," she said.

"Both African-American?"

"Probably. I'd have to do the measurements, check the tables to do more than guess."

"Think they tried to register to vote?" Nell said.

"Someone wanted them silent and gone." Ellen glanced at the dep-uty, then said quietly, "Do you think this will be investigated properly? Or do we dig up the bones to put them in a pauper's grave?"

"I intend to find out who these people were, and as much as I can, what happened to them. I'd like to think this will be treated se-riously … but I don't know."

"A newspaper story will make this hard to ignore."

"There will be newspaper stories," Nell promised.

One of the graduate students interrupted them. "We've gone several inches below where we found the last artifact. Should we keep going?"

Ellen said, "We've probably found what we're going to find, but a few more inches ..."

Nell cut in. "There might be three bodies here. Can you go a little deeper?"

Ellen looked at her, then said, "It's a beautiful day for digging. The earth awaits you." She waited until the graduate student conveyed the message to the others before turning to Nell and asking, "Three bodies? What makes you think that?"

"I've been asking around and was told that there were three people missing, not two."

Ellen just nodded and said, "We'll keep digging for a while. I wanted to look at the bones you took to the morgue, but they're not going anywhere."

Time passed, broken by a quick lunch of shared peanut butter sandwiches, the rest of the hours marked only by occasional conversations and the sound of soil being shifted. A few birds added their voices, but mostly the woods were silent. An expectant waiting, Nell thought. Or maybe I'm just projecting my worries onto the trees. She wished she'd been as prepared as Ellen and brought some of the paperwork piled on her desk. All she was doing was sitting on a tree stump and waiting. She paced down the trail, wondering if she was sending the graduate students on a wild goose dig.

Suddenly one of the students yelled, "I've found something! There's another one!" His excitement rippled through the site.

It didn't touch Nell. Instead she felt the perfect day had been shattered. Another person had been tortured and murdered here. Still, she joined the huddle around the dig.

The buzz from their find covered the sounds of voices coming from the trail, but finally the heavy masculine tones reached them.

Chief Whiz Brown and two of his police officers strode into the clearing.

"You got a permit for this?" he barked.

"I'm sorry, but who are you?" Ellen asked.

The sheriff's deputy, who had been sitting off to the side almost dozing, tried to quickly stand up and almost tripped instead. Attempting to balance, he said, "I'm here overseeing this." He didn't give a very forceful impression.

"Who are you?" Chief Brown shot back at Ellen.

"Ellen Cohen, professor of forensic anthropology at Louisiana State University. I was asked"—she nodded at the hapless deputy—"to help investigate this site."

"You still need a permit to be digging in a state park," he retorted.

Nell wondered who had jerked his chain. That Whiz Brown had bestirred himself to worry about permits wasn't likely. "Chief Brown," she interjected. "I'm surprised to see you here. Unless the Board of Aldermen has changed the city limits, you're beyond your jurisdiction."

He gave her a cold, flat stare. Nell stared back, refusing to look away.

He finally turned back to Ellen. "I'm closing this thing down."

"Whiz, for corn sake's, why?" the deputy asked.

"They ain't got a permit," was his reply.

"But Sheriff Hickson told them to come out here and do this. What other permit do they need?" the deputy argued.

"And why is the Chief of Police of Pelican Bay personally stepping out of his jurisdiction to handle permits?" Nell asked. She wouldn't get an answer, but she was furious that the interference was so blatant and sloppy.

"Got to have a permit to do any work in the state park," he parroted.

"Does this sudden need for a permit have anything to do with the discovery of murder victims on land the mayor granted to the state parks?" Nell threw out.

"I don't know what you're talking about," Whiz Brown answered, making it clear that he knew exactly what she was talking about.

"So the mayor sent you? Maybe you should go back and tell him you need something better than a 'permit' excuse," Nell said.

"Mayor didn't send me anywhere." He put his hand on the butt of his pistol, as if reminding himself he was armed and dangerous.

"What are you going to do, shoot us all?" Nell retorted. Then she wondered, what kind of crazy fool am I to goad an idiot with a gun? An angry fool, furious at Thom's death and now these deaths; like my anger will find some kind of justice for any of us.

They had divided the duties, the night of the accident. Sheriff Hickson himself went to tell Mrs. Thomas, Sr. about her son. The police got the duty to tell the widow. Of course Whiz Brown had ducked out of that unpleasant task. Instead he had delegated it to a young patrolman who clearly had never had to deliver news of a death before. When he got to the hospital, he stood in the doorway, his silence alone telling Nell. He hadn't a clue how to handle her shattered reaction, her disbelief and fury, and had hastily retreated from the haunted eyes of the widow. The nurses had started to put a sedative in her IV drip, but she'd ripped the needle out of her arm.

The deputy, as if to make up for his earlier imbalance, said, "Whiz, you got to talk this over with Sheriff Hickson. He tells us to shut down, we'll shut down. But right now, this ain't your jurisdiction."

"You sayin' I should let crime happen just because it ain't my jurisdiction?" Whiz Brown finally replied. It clearly took him a while to think up that answer.

"Crime?" Nell said. "You create some fictional permit to impede a murder investigation and you talk about crime? And when did you start looking into crimes out of your jurisdiction? The last time we had this argument, you took the other side."

"Look, lady, just because you run the paper doesn't mean that you can question me," he growled.

"But it means precisely that. Freedom of the press, Chief Brown, it's in the Constitution. You know, law, the thing you're supposed to uphold."

Nell's anger galvanized the rest of the workers. Two of them were still digging, to get as much out of the ground as possible, but the others had gathered behind her. Whiz Brown finally had the sense to look around and see it was him and two of his men against a deputy sheriff, about ten graduate students, and two professors from LSU, as well as the editor of the local paper.

"You need a permit to be here and if I catch you again, I'll run you in," he pronounced, then left, trailed by his officers. One, like his chief, was stony-faced, but the other looked abashed, as if he knew how foolish they looked.

Ellen muttered, "Don't laugh until they're out of earshot."

Save for the diggers, they silently listened to the thrashing steps of Whiz and his troops departing. No one spoke until the sounds of his retreat could no longer be heard.

"Let's get as much out as we can," Ellen instructed. "In the meantime, go ahead and pack up what we've already got, in case we need to make a hasty retreat." In a quieter voice to the deputy, she said, "Are we safe? Should we get out of here?"

"Well, ma'am, I can't think they'd do much more than bark," he slowly answered. "I can't think of any permit we'd need to be here. Sheriff's in court now. I'll call when he gets out. Or maybe go wait and see if he gets out sooner."

"And leave us here?" Ellen asked.

"I doubt the chief will come back today."

"That may depend on how desperate whoever sent him is for us not to investigate," Nell said.

"Whiz Brown may not be … " The deputy thought better of what he was going to say. "But he can't be fool enough to take on the sheriff's department and muck up a murder scene."

Nell peered at his name tag. "Mr. Johnston, three people have been killed here. We can't assume whoever did that won't kill again if they feel threatened."

"But this is different," Johnston argued. "These are old murders and besides … it was different back then."

"Different?" Nell said.

He sighed, then said it. "Mrs. McGraw, a lot of black people got killed back then. But we're, well, 'important.' Even Whiz Brown can't be stupid enough to think he can come out here and murder about fifteen people like us and get away with it."

"Not to mention a deputy sheriff," Kate, who had joined the conversation, added.

"You said that this land belonged to the mayor?" Ellen asked Nell.

"Used to belong to his family. They bought a huge tract back in the early sixties, still own half, but gave this part to the park system. It does make you wonder."

"You think the mayor told Whiz to come here and claim we needed a permit?" Kate asked.

"You really think Chief 'It's Not My Jurisdiction' came from a sincere concern about paperwork?" Nell replied.

"But is he hiding long-ago murders or just trying to throw a wrench in something that might prove embarrassing during a tight election?" Kate said.

"Hubert Pickings is stupid enough to do the latter," Nell conceded. That Whiz hadn't shown up until after Aaron Dupree's announcement argued for that.

"Whoever killed these poor souls has got to be old or dead," Deputy Johnston said. "This sounds like Hubert trying to flex his political muscle. Dead bodies on land his family used to own is going to just about hand the election to Aaron Dupree."

"What I need to know right now is should I pull my students out or keep going?" Ellen asked. "If you stay"—this was to Deputy Johnston—"then I'm inclined to see if we can get this skeleton out of the ground."

Kate's cell phone rang. "Hello," she answered as she stepped away from them.

"Keep digging, ma'am," Deputy Johnston told Ellen. "Soon as I can I'll call the sheriff and see if he can wrangle loose another man for out here."

"Nell," Kate said. "It's your daughter, Lizzie."

"Lizzie? How did she get your cell number?" Nell asked as she took the phone. "Lizzie, what's going on?" This was probably an "I need a ride" call, which happened more than Nell thought it should.

"Mom?"

"Yes, what's going on?" Nell asked again. She almost said "if you need a ride, too bad, it's a long wait or a long walk," but decided she didn't want her onlookers to know she had that derelict of a daughter.

"Mom, I'm okay. It's Josh."

"Josh! What's wrong?!"

"Yeah, that's right, worry about him and not me," Lizzie said, commenting on Nell's dramatic change of tone.

"I'm talking to you, so you're obviously okay," Nell replied.

"Right. For all you know I could be on my death bed and these would be my last words on this earth."

"Lizzie," Nell said, cursing the timing of her daughter's adolescent mood. "What happened to Josh?"

"He's okay. Maybe just a broken arm."

Nell didn't consider that okay. "What happened?"

"Some jerk threw a stick into his bike wheel. Good thing he was actually wearing his helmet."

"Where is Josh now?"

"Here at the ER. They're doing an x-ray. Do I have to call Grandmom?"

Nell debated, then chose what suited her. "No, you don't need to call your grandmother. I'm on my way. Can I talk to Josh?"

"He's getting an x-ray right now," Lizzie pointed out, winning Nell a few more stupid-mother-who-wasn't-listening points. "I talked to him before he went in. He told me to call Kate's cell to get to you."

Her children were alive. She could get the rest of the story in person and not use up more of Kate's minutes. "All right. Please be someplace where I can find you. I should be there in about twenty minutes or so."

"See you, Mom. Be careful. The guys that threw the stick yelled at Josh to tell his mother to back off."

"What?" Nell said, but the phone faltered and they were cut off. "Lizzie!" she yelled, but the call was lost. I'll ask when I get there, she told herself.

"Thanks." Nell handed the phone back to Kate. "Josh had a bike wreck and may have broken his arm."

There were murmurs all around hoping that he would be okay. Both Kate and Ellen promised to update Nell of anything that happened at the site.

Nell hurried down the trail, breaking into a run in the less overgrown parts.

"Goddamn them!" she cursed as she started her car. Josh could have been killed. Her anger boiled until she had to tell herself out loud to calm down or at least not let her anger affect her driving.

By the time she got to the ER, Nell was calm enough to marginally pay attention to parking in a legal spot, far enough from the entrance to cause her to run. She wasn't sure if it was worry about Josh or a way of getting rid of the still-searing anger. Thom is dead, you bastards, she thought as she pounded across the pavement, and now you want Josh. Bastards, bastards, fucking bastards.

"Be careful, you don't want to trip," someone in scrubs called to her as she ran up the steps. An ambulance was in the bay and two wheelchairs were passing on the ramp, one entering, one leaving. Nell hurried in front of the entering one.

Approaching the desk, her breathing heavy from the run, she said, "I'm looking for my son, Joshua McGraw."

As the woman flipped through papers, maddeningly reducing Josh to a name on a sheet of paper, Nell scanned the waiting room for Lizzie. She'd better be with Josh, Nell fumed, as the woman turned another page and slowly scanned it.

Another sheet was thoroughly scanned and Nell was about to start yelling when she spotted Lizzie coming down the hallway, her hand in a bag of chips, a soda tucked in the crook of her arm.

"Lizzie!" Nell called, ignoring the scanning woman. "Where's Josh?"

"Mom? You got here fast."

"I told you to wait where I could see you, damn it! Did you think the candy machine was the best place?"

"I was only gone a minute."

"You knew I was on my way. Couldn't the minute have waited?" Nell demanded.

With an angry gesture, Lizzie suddenly threw her chips and the still unopened can of soda into a trash can. "There! I'm sorry; I didn't know I should be your handmaid waiting every second for you! Making sure Josh was okay and getting him here isn't enough. God forbid I get hungry!" Lizzie ended her speech close to a wail. Nell felt ashamed as she watched tears on her daughter's face.

She has to be as scared as I am, Nell thought. Thom is just as dead for her as he is for me. Lizzie handled her raw emotions with the inexperience of a teenager.

She reached for her daughter, but Lizzie spun away.

"I'm so sorry," Nell said softly. "I … I guess sorry isn't quite enough."

Lizzie still kept her head turned away, hastily wiping the tears away.

Nell continued. "I'm sorry. I was worried about Josh and I … oh, fuck. You didn't hear that." Lizzie glanced her way. "I'm not doing a good job here. You did the right thing; you got Josh here and made sure he was going to be okay. And, well, what else is there to do while waiting around in a hospital? It's not reasonable you'd do home-work."

"I'm worried about Josh," Lizzie said in a voice cracked by tears. "About you, too. I wondered if something had happened when I couldn't get you at the newspaper or home."

The tear-stained words cut into Nell. Even if I were a perfect mother, she thought, I couldn't make up for the hurt and fear that's come into their lives. "Please, honey, I messed up, okay? Can you forgive me?"

"Okay, this time," Lizzie said, but Nell recognized the armor for what it was, a thin layer of tinfoil. The same flimsy protection she'd worn when she was an adolescent.

Nell reached for her again and Lizzie didn't pull away, instead wrapping her arms around Nell with a fervor that belied her cool words. They held the embrace, and then Lizzie said, "Did you really say 'fuck'?"

Nell kept her arm around her daughter's shoulder and her face close to Lizzie's. "Yes, I did. You now know the truth. I know those words. But that doesn't mean you can say them, particularly if there is a chance your grandmother might find out. Okay?"

"Okay."

"Let's go find Josh," Nell said.

"Okay. But can I get my drink out of the trash? I'm thirsty."

"No, you can't get it out of the trash. But you can certainly get another one. I've got change in my purse. Can we see if Josh wants something, or are you dying of thirst now?"

"Oh, yeah, I guess it wouldn't be polite of me to munch and slurp in front of him."

The woman finally finished scanning her pages. "He should be in the third slot on your left."

Josh indeed was, looking lost and pale against the white hospital sheets.

"Mom," he said weakly. "I'm going to be okay. Arm's not broke."

A doctor entered, carrying x-rays with her. "Nope, the arm's not broken. Good thing you were wearing a helmet. You're going to be a little bruised and have some ugly scabs for a while, but nothing's going to follow you into old age."

"He's all right?" Nell asked. She wanted to hear it again.

"He'll be fine. You're his mother?" the doctor asked.

"Thank God," Nell said, then answered the question. "Yes, I am."

"He can go home soon. It won't hurt him to just lie still for a while. He's probably going to be sore for a few days. Any sharp pain, anything that seems odd, come right back in. I'm not going to write a prescription for pain meds; the over-the-counter stuff should do. No aspirin, of course. Take it easy for a few days and keep wearing that helmet." With that, the doctor exited the cubicle.

"How are you feeling?" Nell asked Josh.

"I'm okay. A little sore, I guess."

Nell looked her son over. He had a scrape on his chin; the helmet hadn't protected him there. His left elbow looked like raw meat. His legs were still covered by the sheet. "Can you tell me what happened?" she asked.

Lizzie and Josh exchanged a glance, as if trying to decide how much to tell—and worry—Mom.

"I must have hit a pothole," Josh said.

"It's too late," Lizzie interjected. "I already told her about the guys throwing the stick in your spokes." She added defensively, "I had to let her know. They might have come after her next."

They're protecting me and worrying about me, Nell thought. She wondered how she could return her children to their interrupted childhood. Or if there was even a way.

"Tell me what happened. We're going to have to go to the police with this," Nell added.

Again they exchanged a look. Nell thought about demanding they tell her what they were hiding. But that could wait; she would give them a chance to tell her on their own, without heavy mother-strong-arm tactics.

"We were going home from school. Josh was riding his bike and I was a little behind him," Lizzie said.

Nell was attuned enough to her children to see the gap of information. Lizzie, walking, would have been left quickly behind by Josh on the bike. Still, she didn't interrupt.

"And this red truck comes zooming around and pulls up even with Josh's bike. Some guy hollers out, 'You Josh McGraw?' Josh, dumb bunny, answers, 'Why, yes, I am.'"

Nell suspected that Josh didn't really say that; Lizzie often made fun of the way he talked like his parents while she was taking on the speech of her peers.

Josh protested. "I just said, yeah."

"So they yell out, 'Tell your mother this is from us,' and they shove a broom handle into his wheel. Josh goes head over heels into the air. And we ended up here," Lizzie finished.

Nell decided it was time to ask a few mother questions. "What else can you tell me about the truck?"

"It was red, sort of new," Josh said.

"Bunch of junk in the back," Lizzie added. "Boards and paint, like they did that kind of stuff."

"What about the people in the truck?"

"It happened so fast, I didn't really see them," Josh said in an abashed voice, as if he'd failed miserably by not being a hero, or at least not getting a good look at the bad guys.

"Men or women?"

"Men, of course," Lizzie said.

"Young? Old?"

"Not young," Lizzie said. That could be anyone over twenty-five, Nell thought. "But not real old either."

"White?"

"Yeah. Brown scraggily hair on the one who threw the stick, and he wore a sort of dirty baseball cap," Josh offered.

That sounded like the Jones brothers to Nell. She decided the rest of the questions about the attackers could wait until they talked to the police.

"Just how did you get here?" she asked.

Lizzie jumped in. "Well, Billy Naquin just happened to drive up on his motorcycle and he had a cell phone."

That supplied the missing information. Nell was more than sure that Billy didn't just happen upon the scene, but Lizzie had been catching a forbidden ride on the back of his bike.

"So he called the ambulance. I tried to call you at work and at home. Then the ambulance showed up, and we came here and then Josh suggested I call you on Kate's cell phone. And that's the story."

Not quite. "How did you manage to keep up with Josh on his bicycle?" Nell asked directly. She had to admit that in this instance, Lizzie being on a motorcycle behind Josh had been useful, but it was still too large an infraction to go unnoticed.

"Um . . . I was walking. Some of us decided to walk for a ways."

"Walking? How were you able to keep up with Josh on a bike?"

"Well, uh, we started before he did, so he just happened to be passing us when it all happened."

"Ah, I see. You just happened to be in the same place where the hooligans attacked Josh. And it just so happened that Billy Naquin came riding up on his motorcycle at that same moment."

"Well ... yeah."

"I would be very disappointed if I were to find out you had been riding a motorcycle, something both I and your father have forbidden." Nell didn't add "and with a grunge kid three years older like Billy Naquin." She knew that might only serve to drive Lizzie into the time-honored teenage rebellion of dating someone her parents hated. "There are a few gaps in your story that make me suspicious," she continued, "but right now the important thing is that you and Josh are okay. This one time you get away with it. Next time it's three months detention."

Lizzie didn't protest, which was the final proof that she'd been on the back of the motorcycle.

"Can we go home now?" Josh asked.

"Soon," Nell said. "Lizzie, why don't you get whatever from the vending machines while I go do the paperwork that's required to get us out of here." She dug in her purse and gave Lizzie a handful of change and some single bills.

She left them with Lizzie reciting the possibilities from the drink and snack machines. Like the mercurial adolescent she was, Lizzie was now poised and mature, cheerfully taking care of her younger brother. Nell was abashed that it had taken only an apology and a candy bar to work her way back into her daughter's good graces. Vaguely she wondered if this was the kind of thing that would surface twenty years later in therapy.

The clerk was much more informed about billing procedures than where actual patients were and she gave Nell a stack of paperwork. Nell felt the familiar clench in her stomach as she calculated what this unexpected expense would do to the budget. Suddenly she felt a new stab of pain, as she realized Thom's life insurance would keep them comfortable for a long time if she was careful. I guess not having to ask your mother for money is a benefit of your being dead, Nell thought bitterly. It still left her with the fucking paperwork. She signed the final line with a savage vengeance.

After that, she found her way back to Josh and Lizzie.

They were happily sucking down sodas, with two candy wrappers spread across the bed.

"Okay, you're sprung," Nell announced. She and Lizzie had to exit the cubicle for Josh to dress. His biking shorts had been cut away, but he had his sweaty clothes from gym class in his backpack.

Nell walked slowly as they left the hospital, to save Josh from having to admit he was sore and getting stiff. As they got in the car, she said, "We do need to report this. I'd like to stop by the police station if you feel up to it." For Josh's sake, she would have just gone home, but she wanted the cops hot on the trail of the Jones boys before they arrived at an address that was all too easy to find.

Josh seemed most chagrined about being in his sweatsuit, and if he could worry about that, Nell decided he was well enough to make it through a trip to the police station.

The sky was losing light, the day leaving and night coming. Nell pulled in front of the police station as the street lights glimmered on.

"Okay, let's do this. It'll be pizza for supper when we get home," she told them, hoping a pepperoni reward would make it less of an ordeal. As expected, they didn't complain that they'd just had pizza.

The Pelican Bay Police Station wasn't a hotbed of activity. With the day people gone, only the night shift was on duty. Unfortunately, the night shift included one of the officers who had come out to the dig in the afternoon, the stony-faced one.

"Can I help you, lady?" he asked.

He also recognized her. She peered at his name tag and let him know it. "Officer Jenkins, I need to report an assault," she stated calmly.

"Yeah? No one looks too hurt," he replied, hooking his hands in his belt loops, fingers pointing at his crotch. He was young, maybe early twenties, with the arrogance that came from the muscles bulging under his uniform. He had thick, heavy lips, brown hair curling over his collar a few weeks past-due for a haircut, and a nose that wouldn't be kind to him after a few decades of drinking too much beer.

Lizzie, still in her protector role, jumped in. "Some jerk drove by my brother Josh here while he was riding his bike and threw a broom handle into the spokes. We had to take him to the emergency room."

"Some kids playing pranks?" Officer Jenkins asked. It was close to a sneer.

"No, it was some older guys in a truck," Lizzie retorted.

"Officer Jenkins, is there some reason you're not taking this seriously?" Nell asked. She had learned to ask blunt questions and was willing to use the skill when needed.

"Who said I'm not taking it seriously?" he said, openly sneering now.

"You're writing nothing down, you're not asking any questions, you immediately dismissed the incidence as a kid's prank. That gives the impression you don't take this seriously," Nell said. And you've got your hands pointing at your crotch, she thought, something you think you can get away with in front of a woman, a girl, and a boy.

"You tellin' me how to do my job, lady?"

"I have no intention of telling you how to do your job, but I can recognize when you're not doing it." Nell guessed he was a bully, used to people cowering at his uniform and belligerent manner. She added, "Whiz Brown will retire in a few months."

"What's that supposed to mean?" he demanded.

"You're taking out his humiliation at the dig today on me, but he's not going to be here much longer to protect you," Nell spelled out for him.

"Yeah, and so?" But his sneer wavered slightly.

"Do I have to call the mayor and get him down here?" Nell threw out.

"Mayor's gone home for the day."

For an answer, Nell crossed around him and picked up the phone. She punched in a number, then said into the receiver, "Hi, Hubert? This is Nell McGraw, the Editor-in-Chief of the *Pelican Bay Crier*. I'm at the police station." She paused for a moment, then said, "I'm very sorry to disturb you at home, but I'm trying to report an assault and the young officer on duty seems rather inexperienced…"

"Shit." Officer Jenkins reached for the phone from Nell.

She spun away from him and continued. "I wonder if you would come down here and have a word with his boss. I know you want to show examples of your leadership to the people of Pelican Bay."

"I'll take the report. Tell the mayor it's all a misunderstanding. Just didn't want to use the resources of the department without checking things out," he said, loud enough for everyone in the room and on the phone to hear.

"It seems to be a misunderstanding," Nell said into the phone. "I do appreciate your concern, but I don't think you need to come down here after all." She paused again and then said, "You're very kind to say that, Mr. Mayor. Give your wife my best." She put the receiver down.

Officer Jenkins retrieved a clipboard and led them into an office. He asked, "Okay, so what happened?" He was sullen but doing his job.

Nell let Lizzie and Josh tell most of the story, only occasionally prompting them or asking questions to make sure that everything was covered.

As Lizzie was repeating the description of the truck, Chief Whiz Brown came into the room.

"What's going on here?" he demanded.

Officer Jenkins looked as surprised as Nell to see his chief back on duty. He blurted out, "The mayor call you?"

"The mayor? Why would the mayor call me?" Whiz Brown asked. He might have gotten away with that, but he had to follow it with, "Can't the Chief of Police come into the station? Don't need no politicians to tell me what to do."

Clearly someone is telling him what to do, Nell thought, given his protesting too much.

Just as clearly, Whiz Brown didn't like finding Nell McGraw in his police station. "What are you doing here? Ain't made enough trouble for one day?"

"I'm trying to report an assault," Nell said, deliberately returning calm to his surliness.

"Nothin' happened out in the woods," he stated.

"Someone threw a stick into the wheels of my son's bike as he was riding home from school," Nell countered. "This has nothing to do with the dig in the woods." Or did it? The Jones brothers were the most likely offenders, but three murdered bodies were high stakes.

"Some joke?" Whiz Brown asked.

"I didn't find it funny," Nell retorted.

"No, someone joking on your son and just roughhousing too much," he restated.

Nell started to lose her temper at the pattern—don't take women and children seriously. She noted where Office Boyce Jenkins had learned his methods. "Some adult men, in a red truck, threw a broomstick into his bike spokes, shouting that it was a message to me. We just got out of the emergency room," she said in a cold voice. Much as she wanted to call him a fucking asshole, she didn't think it would get her what she wanted—nor would it be a great example for Josh and Lizzie. But she couldn't resist adding, "Or are you going to say that Government and Willow are out of your jurisdiction?"

Whiz's mouth compressed into a thin line. Speaking around her, he said, "You got the report, Boyce?"

"Yes, sir," the younger man replied.

"That's all we can do," he told Nell bluntly. "'Less you happened to get a look at their driver's license plate or something else that gives ID."

"How about a little logic, Chief Brown?" Nell retorted, trying to keep her voice the same cold neutral. "J.J. Jones is in jail and his brothers don't like it. They drive a red truck. They're not happy with me because I'm the chief witness to his drunken murder. They're trying to scare me out of testifying in hopes he'll get off. Or is it too much work for you to look at the logical suspects?"

"Well, you may not like 'em, but that don't mean they done you wrong," Chief Brown said.

"In other words, you're too lazy to investigate." Nell congratulated herself for leaving out the "fucking" in front of lazy. Ever the perfect mother example.

His lips got even thinner. "Now, I ain't sayin' we won't look into this, but your son don't look too hurt and I ain't gonna go after innocent men just 'cause you're riled."

"Maybe I should go have a chat with the Jones boys," Boyce Jenkins put in. Nell didn't think he was on her side; it seemed more likely he wanted to be a tough cop with someone and the Jones boys would do.

"And just say what?" Whiz Brown shot at him.

"Doing some police work," he answered. "Kid got hurt; we can't have that here." He clearly was imagining his picture on the front page of the paper. As Nell had pointed out, Chief Brown would be out of a job very soon. Part of him seemed to be enjoying his boss's discomfort.

"You wanna do some police work? Run a trace on every single red truck in the county. See if the Jones boys really got one. Get a list of anyone else with a grudge against Mrs. McGraw. Check the color of their trucks while you're at it."

Nell watched the power struggle between the two men. "I can't think of anyone besides the Jones boys who have a grudge against me," she said, to get them focused on something besides who could piss a greater distance.

"You sure, Mrs. McGraw?" Whiz Brown said. "You out there diggin' up nigger bones in the woods and you don't think you riled anybody up?"

"I beg your pardon, Chief Brown," Nell said, trying to keep the shock off her face that he would be so blatantly racist.

"You got no business out in the woods digging up graves. It just upsets folks."

"Who? Who does it upset?" she asked.

He finally seemed to realize what he was saying and mumbled, "Just people. You know, like people who go to the park. Don't like thinkin' about bones when they're out enjoying nature."

"So some picnickers attacked my brother?" Lizzie interjected.

Suddenly Nell wanted to get out of the police station. Whiz Brown was right about one thing: Someone was upset enough about the emergence of those forgotten bones to goad Whiz Brown into action. Someone didn't want those bones found, and that someone could be added to the list of people with a grudge against the reporter who was about to put the story on the front page.

"I need to get my children home," Nell said. To Boyce Jenkins, she added, "You'll let me know the results of your investigation."

He hooked his hands back over his belt and said, "Be glad to, Mrs. McGraw. I'll come by your home in the next few days and let you know." The look he gave her was sexual and not friendly. Another power game.

"You might do better to see me at the office. I may be staying with friends for the next few days."

"That better not end up in the paper," Whiz Brown told her.

"What better not end up in the paper?" Nell asked, her hand on Lizzie's shoulder, steering her and Josh out.

"You know. What I said."

It would have been safer to have given him that, but something in her wouldn't back down. "I don't tell lies in my paper. You didn't go off the record, Chief." She hurried Josh and Lizzie out of the station. They seemed to catch her fear, or at least her intent to get out of there with haste.

Nell didn't even let them properly get their seat belts on before pulling away.

"Those cops are jerks," Lizzie said as Nell turned onto the street.

"Think they'll really do anything?" Josh asked. He sounded tired. And hurt. There was enough pain in his voice for Nell to know this was all too serious.

"I think Officer Jenkins will be willing to throw his weight around and the Jones boys are the kind of people he'll be comfortable doing it with," Nell answered. The night was too dark, as if the moon and the stars had conspired to create deep pools of black that could hold a monster. One that would attack children.

"He's still a jerk," Lizzie said. "Are you going to call the mayor again? Tell him his top cop is a major jerk."

"The mayor?" Nell said, then remembered. She decided not to lie, even if it meant giving Lizzie and Josh a subterfuge she hadn't learned until her mid-twenties. "I didn't call the mayor. I called our house and acted like I was talking to the mayor."

"Mom!" Lizzie let out, but there was a touch of admiration in her voice that her stodgy mother could be capable of such guile.

"Besides, I know enough about the politics in this city to know there's no love lost between Mayor Pickings and Chief Brown. The mayor will never know he wasn't called, and Chief Brown won't dare bring it up." Nell did know they didn't socialize together; Whiz was more comfortable downing beers and watching sports at Ray's Bar, while the mayor liked good bourbon at the country club. But that didn't mean they weren't connected in the ways that men in power found useful.

She felt an odd stab of relief as she turned the corner that would bring them home. The street lights were shining, several houses were lit up; the black of the night seemed to lift as if this were a normal evening.

But something had sent Whiz Brown out to the dig and back into the office tonight, and someone had attacked Josh this afternoon.

Having just the Jones brothers to worry about was bad enough, but now Nell couldn't dismiss the possibility someone else might have thrown the stick.

"Do we really have to stay with Grandmom?" Josh asked from the back seat.

"Stay with Mrs. Thomas?" Nell echoed.

"You said we might be staying with friends. And she's the only one we've stayed with," he said. A broken air conditioner had driven them into the cool comfort of her in-laws' house for almost a week last summer and they'd also stayed there when they repainted the bedrooms, opting for a few nights away from the paint fumes.

Nell started to say they weren't going to do that, but she realized it might be an option. She tried to think of a friend she could call up and say, we're camping out at your house until it's safe.

There was Jane, of course, but she was in Chicago. Only a few locally came to mind, but they were Thom's friends more than hers. How would they take it if the widow McGraw, one month after her husband's death, suddenly appeared at their doorstep claiming people were after her and her children? They would take her in; Southern politeness demanded that, but they might also shake their heads behind her back and quietly make phone calls about getting her help.

Nell turned into their driveway, going more slowly than usual, letting the headlights sweep across the lawn and into the backyard. None of the shadows seemed out of place.

"Not tonight, anyway," she said as she turned off the car. Maybe I'm rationalizing, she thought, but I can't see us any safer at Mrs. Thomas's house. If they know where we live, they easily know where she lives.

"My bike!" Josh suddenly cried as he started to get out.

"It's locked to the stop sign at the corner," Lizzie informed him.

"But I don't want to leave it overnight," he argued.

"We'll get it in the morning," Nell told them. She wanted them in the house, not standing here surrounded by shadows.

"But it's just out on the street. Only the frame is locked up. I might not have much of a bike left in the morning," Josh said.

Nell started to point out that Pelican Bay was not a hotbed of crime and Josh's bike was likely to be unmolested, but she realized that argument would ring hollow to a boy who had just been assaulted; "they may have tried to kill you but your bike will be fine" wasn't persuasive.

She settled for the more realistic argument. "Look, those two idiots may still be running around. I think we're less likely to run into them in the morning. If something has to get damaged tonight, at least let it be the bike and not any of us. We'll go first thing in the morning," she assured him.

"Do we have to go to school tomorrow?" Lizzie asked as she switched on the light in the kitchen.

Nell again felt odd relief; the kitchen seemed so normal, even down to the breakfast dishes still in the sink. How could the day have changed so starkly in such little time? Even the familiar irritation surfaced, Lizzie with her seemingly unerring adolescent eye for seeking advantage in a way guaranteed to annoy her mother.

"Is there a reason you think you shouldn't go to school tomorrow?" Nell asked, hoping her voice was merely cool and not irritated.

"Well, Josh got attacked going home and so we might be safer here."

"The two of you home alone?" Nell queried. Not waiting for an answer, plus suspecting that any answer might be the one that would tip her into truly annoyed, she continued. "You'll be much safer at school than here alone. The danger wasn't school, but going there. I'll drive you and pick you up."

"What if Josh isn't feeling up to school? Wouldn't he be better off with me here?" Lizzie countered.

"He can come with me to work and hang out on the couch in the break room," Nell answered. "We're not debating this," she added tersely.

"Sure, but if we get killed tomorrow, it's your fault," Lizzie retorted.

Nell felt herself starting to lose her temper. Why did Lizzie always have to push things too far, spar with her mother when she knew it would do no good?

"I'm okay," Josh put in. "I'll be fine for school tomorrow. Got a test in math that I don't want to miss."

"Oh, right, Brother Perfect," Lizzie said, then mimicked his voice. "Don't want to miss that math test."

"I'd just have to make it up. I'd rather get it over with," Josh said.

Nell grabbed the tail of her temper. Her son's interjection gave her enough time to remember that Lizzie didn't *always* do anything, including annoy her. She'd been remarkably mature taking care of Josh. Lizzie was in the sway of surging hormones, searching for adulthood.

"We're probably all tired and hungry," she said in her best calm-and-controlled mother voice. "Why don't you two decide on a pizza and order it?"

That diverted their attention and they took the team approach to request the mega-meat pie, the one Nell usually called "heart attack by twenty-one." But tonight she made no comments about healthy eating, even going so far as to eat two whole slices herself.

Josh watched a little TV, then went to bed. He mumbled about not having slept much last night, but Nell could see that the day had taken its toll. She wandered around the house, making sure all the windows and doors were locked, then sat down and tried to read, but nothing held her interest. She realized she was listening to each car as it passed. Waiting for one to slow or stop.

How can I do this night after night, she thought as she peered through the drapes as headlights slowly made their way down the street, finally pulling into a driveway halfway down the block. Mrs. Mertz coming home from her church social. Then Nell felt a stab of anger: am I giving them more power than they could ever take? The Jones brothers were probably plopped in front of a TV wrestling match and on their second six-pack already.

This is a quiet residential neighborhood and everyone knows everyone. A strange truck will be noticed, Nell reassured herself.

When Lizzie lifted her head from the computer screen, Nell pointedly looked at her watch. Her daughter got the hint.

"Just need to send some email and then I'm going to bed," Lizzie said.

A few minutes later, Nell heard her in the bathroom. She softly cracked the door to Josh's room, wondering if he, too, was sharing her fears and wakefulness. But he was asleep, his arm flung out as if reaching for the night and the stars in the sky, his hair tousled in a way that made him look even younger and more vulnerable.

Nell softly closed his door. As she made her way back down the hall, Lizzie came out of the bathroom, her face scrubbed, smelling of toothpaste and soap.

"Good night, Mom," she said.

"Good night, Lizzie. Sleep well." Nell reached out to brush a strand of hair off her forehead. She wanted to touch her daughter, make some apology, some connection, even though she knew Lizzie could be standoffish, as if needing her mother's arms might keep her in childhood and slow her journey to being grown up.

Unexpectedly, Lizzie responded by hugging her. Maybe she knows I need it, Nell thought as she returned her daughter's embrace.

"You sleep well, too. And thanks, Mom."

"Thanks?"

"For being a good mom. Taking care of Josh and me." Then Lizzie pulled away and went into her bedroom.

A good mom? For a cynical moment, Nell decided that good mom meant letting them buy pizza packed with calories. She didn't much feel like a good mother, by any scale, except perhaps compared to a crack addict. Maybe I'm a good mother because I'm the only one she's got; if I don't love her, no other mother will. The thought was less cynical but still put a sting in her daughter's compliment. Nell had covered some court cases, watched children begging to have their drug-addicted parents back. The bond was so elemental and important; to be clung to and fought against, as Lizzie was doing.

Nell suddenly felt an overwhelming ache of loneliness. She made her way to the kitchen, hoping that its cheerful normalness would assuage her gloom. But without the voices of her children, the bright kitchen seemed barren, even mocking, the cheerful colors a place Nell could no longer enter.

She turned to confront a face in the window and startled for a moment before realizing it was her own, a wan pale moon reflected against the black glass. Her hair turned from a chestnut crown into a gray smudge in the dark reflection. How did I get so old? Nell wondered. Then she spun away from the dark mirror, pulling a strand of her hair out and holding it in her hand to assure herself that it was still a vibrant brunette, not the faded gray of the murky glass.

She listened to the night, for her children. Then she found the bottle of Scotch and poured a generous shot. The harsh taste did what she wanted it to do, pulled her into the immediacy of the burn in her throat, the taste on her tongue, then the blurring of edges. Even the mirrored image didn't seem so sharp anymore.

As she poured another glass, she wondered if this was wrong, if she should stay awake and vigilant for her children. It didn't save Thom, Nell thought. She'd been stone-cold sober that night, the perfect wife and mother for years, and nothing had saved him. She took a long swallow of the amber liquid.

Before she took another sip, she put the Scotch bottle back exactly as she found it, then returned to the kitchen, carefully avoiding the window into the darkness even as she stood in front of it, pouring the remaining Scotch into a plastic tumbler, the kind she used for water on the nightstand. She rinsed her glass, drying it instead of leaving it on the dish drain.

After putting the glass away, Nell turned out the light in the kitchen. The outside came in; all the shadows left by the streetlight were visible without the glare of inside light. She stared, but the night gave back nothing.

Nell went to her bedroom, detouring upstairs to pause and listen at both Josh's and Lizzie's doors, but she heard only a soft snore from her son, and the rustle of Lizzie turning in her sleep.

When she came to her door, she again paused. There's a ghost in there, Nell thought. I keep him at bay with the details of a day, work, the children, exhaustion at night. But her anxiety from the day's events kept her awake, and the alcohol had loosened the tight reins of control that kept her from seeing all the places Thom had been.

He lived in every inch of this house, but most especially in their bedroom. That was where she alone had seen his playful side, his passionate side, his worried and vulnerable side.

Nell turned away and went to the bathroom. She finished the Scotch in one long gulp. I'll be in bed by the time it hits me, she thought, rinsing out her mouth so the taste of mundane toothpaste wouldn't be jarring. Her routine was perfunctory; she was careful only in rinsing the glass before refilling it with water, as if that had been its purpose all along.

Again, at the bedroom door, Nell paused and considered sleeping downstairs on the couch or in the guest room. It won't banish my ghosts, she thought, slowly turning the doorknob. Maybe someday the ghosts of memory would be friendly, comforting, but now the loss was too raw, and the memories seared.

The bed was as she had left it that morning, a hasty pulling-up of the covers, halfway in between being made and left as she had rolled out of it, as if she were rebelling against something but couldn't quite bring herself to mutiny fully.

Several of her brothers had come for the funeral, and they now had sons old enough to wear the garments of a man. They had taken most of Thom's clothes. Nell kept some, the ones she occasionally wore, including a tweed jacket he had once wrapped around her shoulders on a cold night. She couldn't let go of that memory of enfolding warmth.

But still he was here; the sheets on the bed were ones that they had slept on, made love on. There was no washing that could take away those memories. Nell recalled the last time they had done so. It was a weeknight; they had sent the paper to press that day, always the busiest day of the week.

He had stripped off his clothes, and was lying under the sheet, catching up on last week's *New Yorker*. Nell had been lying beside him, wearing the old T-shirt she usually wore to bed. She remembered debating whether to roll away from him and shut her eyes and let sleep take her, or to ask him what he was reading, to talk for a few minutes before drifting off. She had rolled to him, draping her arm across his stomach, her head on his chest. They lay like that for several minutes; the only sound their breathing and the turning of pages. She remembered feeling the heat from his body, her mind wandering to the ease of their touch, him naked, her in only a T-shirt, and they could simply be together. But thinking about the absence of passion brought memories of being without the absence. Nell listened to his steady breathing, the beating of his heart; he was, as he said, "built on the slim, academic line," but she knew the power in his arms from the times he had held her fiercely. She put her hand under the sheet, trailing her fingers down his stomach, not stopping until she reached her destination.

He turned another page, but she knew him well enough to recognize the slight change in breathing. Nell often made the first move. This was one of the secrets they hid behind closed doors. She had once referred to herself as the aggressor; Thom had stuck out his chest, curled him arm muscleman fashion, and said, "No, I'm the aggressor, you're the instigator." That had become a shorthand. He would sometimes ask, "Is Ms. I in the house?" Or she would say, "I really need to meet with Mr. A soon."

But that last time, the time they didn't know would be their last, they had said little. Nell had begun a gentle massage and was rewarded with another change in the rhythm of Thom's breathing.

A stray practical thought filtered in. Tonight was a weeknight, with children to be readied for school. That gave Nell justification to skip a slow buildup. She slid down the bed and replaced her hand with her mouth. Thom gasped and the magazine fell to the floor.

It had become one of the covenants of their relationship, Nell often made the first move, but Thom rarely said no. She was safe being bold and showing her desire. It was a secret they kept from the world. Out there, she was practical, mundane; he was the talker, the social person. To see them together, few people might guess how they would change behind closed doors. Thom, leaving aside the burden of leading, allowing Nell to change from mundane to wanton, a woman who took her passion. It was a comfort and release for both of them, this reversal of roles; it increased the possibilities of who they could be.

Like that night, with Nell changing from soft cuddling to hard desire. Thom's response had been quick, a testimony to Nell's experience of his body. She alternated light teasing touches with sudden hard strokes until she was ready. Then she slid back up his body, straddling and slowly lowering herself onto him. Again, the reaction she wanted and anticipated. Thom gasped as her weight lowered and his hips began a hard rocking motion, his hands pushing under her T-shirt to find her breasts.

His explosion came quickly. He wrapped his arms around Nell in the fierce, possessive way he often did after they made love, as if to say he would never let her go. Remembering, she knew it would be one of the things she would miss most desperately, the tightness, the feeling of forever, in his arms.

He had murmured a soft apology, then confessed that instead of reading the magazine, he had been watching her undress, lingering on her breasts as she removed her bra. "They're quite lovely and I'm the only guy that gets to have my way with them," he had whispered.

After another deep breath he said, "Roll over, woman, I've got something important to take care of." He was always enough of a gentleman to make sure her pleasure equaled his. Like her, he was familiar with her body, knew just where to kiss and touch to take her both slowly, as if time were nothing and this moment was to be stayed in as long as possible, and inexorably over the edge.

Again, his arms wrapped around her, this time added to by his weight on top of her, another moment of the fleeting sense of forever. Then he had softly kissed and caressed her until she noticed that he had become aroused again. Sometimes once was enough, but other times, like a delicious gift, they just kept going.

Nell couldn't remember if they said anything. She knew she had spread her legs wide, opening herself to him. She had wanted it as much as he did. She remembered this second time had followed the usual pattern for them. He was slower and she, as if their first love making had primed her body, responded more quickly, holding him tightly, even digging her nails into his back, passionately kissing his neck, his face, his mouth, her hips thrusting, urging him on. Her orgasm had come first, her gasping and writhing had triggered his. Then they had lain together for a long time, not talking, just holding each other.

The bedroom suddenly became unbearably lonely, everything still here, still in place, only Thom missing, irrevocably gone. Nell grabbed a pillow and held it over her face, to muffle the moaning sob she couldn't contain.

Then she flung herself across the bed, face down, still hiding the sobs in the pillow. They racked through her body, the shudders of grief replacing the remembered shudders of passion.

Finally the tears subsided, and the anguish settled into a rage. A rage at herself for being weak and sneaking drinks to get through the night—and knowing she might easily do it again tomorrow. A rage at the absurd randomness that had torn apart her life. Just a few seconds would have made all the difference. To that rage, she added a fury that J.J. and his brothers would try anything, including attack her son, to avoid suffering consequences from his drunken stupidity. Another rage piled on that, at the murderers who had callously left three bodies hidden in the woods, men who had escaped justice. Those rages blended.

Nell slowly sat up. She again caught a flash of her face reflected in the dark glass of a window. It was still pale, ghost-like. But even the wavering image reflected the fury, the grim set of her lips, the furrow at her brow.

They might win, Nell thought, but it will be a fight.

She got up to wash her face, to dry away the tears and leave only the anger.

EIGHT

JOSH INSISTED ON GOING to school, even hurrying Lizzie so there was time to get his bike. Nell had to rush Josh through his inspection but allowed him to lock his bike in the bike rack at school. She would pick him up in the afternoon, but this way he could take more time with it at lunch. The bruises and scrape looked ugly, but Josh seemed okay, even oddly proud of his injuries, as if they were proof he could take it. With a final reminder she would be by to pick them up right after school, Nell headed for the office of the Crier.

As usual on school mornings, she was the first one there. But unlike usual, she locked the door behind her.

She had made her decision last night. The front page of this week's paper would be about the bones left in the woods. She used the quiet time to work on a first draft. She wanted to call Kate and get the final report on the dig but felt it was too early for long, probing questions. She would also call the morgue and the sheriff's office. They would adhere to harsh morning hours, but she wanted to have Kate's information before calling them. The more she knew, the more she would know to ask.

A little before nine, Nell heard the first set of keys in the lock. She got up and looked out of her office, both to see who it was and to let them know she was here.

"Oh! You startled me," Ina Claire said as she noticed Nell. Part of the startle might have been having the boss catch her with a half-eaten doughnut in hand.

"I'm sorry," Nell said. "I got here early and didn't want to be alone in the office with an unlocked door."

"Perfectly reasonable," Ina Claire said, not commenting on it being a significant change. She moved away from the door just as both Dolan and Pam came through it, the doughnut hastily wrapped in a napkin and stuffed in her purse.

Nell started to retreat to her office but decided to tell her staff about Josh. She wanted her outrage shared, but also to warn them. Someone might attack the paper.

"I have some disturbing news to report," she said, wishing she didn't sound so stiff. "Last evening someone threw a broom handle into the spokes of Josh's bicycle, causing him to wreck. They shouted that it was a message for me. I suspect the Jones brothers are behind it, but it could be related to the story about the skeletons in the woods."

For a moment, there was silence. Then Dolan said, as if he were the group's voice, "Attacked Josh? That's outrageous! Is he okay?"

"He's okay, a bit bruised and scraped up, but okay," Nell answered.

"You think they might come here?" Dolan asked, clearly seeing where Nell's thoughts were going.

"It's possible," Nell said. "But they might be too cowardly to do anything during the day and when they don't vastly outnumber their target."

"I swear I'm going to bring my daddy's ten gauge and keep it at my desk," Pam muttered.

Dolan managed to say "Only if you promise not to shoot any of us with it" before Nell launched into a serious no guns speech. Thom would have easily understood that Pam wasn't really going to bring a shotgun to the office; why couldn't she? Because we don't know each other well enough, Nell realized. I'm still Thom's wife, they're still Thom's employees, and we haven't gotten to Nell McGraw and her employees.

"Well, then Ina Claire is going to have to give me one of her wicked hat pins," Pam said.

"I'll even give Dolan one, if he wants," Ina Claire rejoined.

"I know it's hard to think something might happen in this perfect little town," Nell said, "but until this settles down, if you're here alone, lock the front door. Don't go by yourself to the parking lot, go in pairs. They were driving a red, dusty truck, so be on the lookout for that." She wondered if she should mention that the law might not be on their side. But she didn't know how to say it and make it credible.

"You've told the sheriff?" Ina Claire asked.

Nell noticed that she didn't mention Whiz Brown. "No, not yet. I did report it at the police station. One of the young officers said he would look into it."

There seemed to be an unspoken agreement the chief was useless. Nell wondered if it was just his well-known general lassitude or if there was some undercurrent she didn't know about.

Jacko came in then. "I've got a great tip from someone I know at the morgue! Those three skeletons from the woods? Every one of them was murdered."

Nell recognized the excitement in his voice. It was the lure of the story, although it could easily be seen as excitement at the mayhem and misfortune of others.

"Good work. How'd you get that?" Nell asked. "Anything on the record?"

"Just a friend of a friend," Jacko said. "Doesn't want her name out. Not on the record yet. But the sheriff should have something late this afternoon. Right after deadline," he added.

"Damn," Nell said softly, although it wasn't surprising. She wondered if it was just the sheriff's usual "don't upset the people" mode or if there was more in his burying the story after her deadline and into the weekend. "I can get something from the site people; there were enough grad students around there that someone can talk. Okay, do a quick outline of the stuff from the morgue, use it to call the sheriff's office and ask some questions. I've got a rough of the story and I'll incorporate whatever you can add to it. I'll query the people who were working the site. Jacko, do a quick and dirty, because I need you to make a photo list from the pictures I took at the site."

"On my way," he said as he spun into his desk and grabbed the phone.

To the rest of the office, Nell said, "We're going to put the story of the skeletons on the front page. It may ruffle a few feathers. These people were murdered. Their bodies were hidden on land that belonged to Hubert Pickings' family at the time they were killed."

"A few feathers?" Dolan said. "Kill the whole damn bird." But he had a grin on his face, as if saying full speed ahead. "Ina, give me your cooking column to look over, so our Editor-in-Chief can do the big story."

Nell nodded thanks and went back to her office. Ina Claire was a great cook but couldn't write her way out of a mixing bowl. She seemed to feel no umbrage at how rewritten she always was, took it as one of the rhythms of the paper. The task usually fell to Nell, including translating Ina Claire's dollops and dashes into useful measurements. It was very kind of Dolan, who tended to hold to traditional male spheres, to take on that task. Perhaps he also knew a paper without Ina Claire's cooking column would get more that its usual share of phone calls.

She now judged it late enough in the morning to call Kate Ryan. "Kate, this is Nell McGraw," she said as the phone was picked up on the first ring.

"Nell. How's Josh? Is he okay?"

Nell felt a prick of guilt. She hadn't really thought of Josh since dropping him off safely at school this morning. She'd left Kate worried at the dig. Nell veered close to venal sin in thinking she could have called Kate at the crack of dawn on the pretext of telling her Josh was okay. "Nothing was broken, thank goodness. Some ugly scrapes and bruises. But he insisted on going off to school today. So, all's well that ends well."

"If it's ended," Kate said.

Nell was both grateful and annoyed that Kate went beyond the polite veneer. "I don't like people attacking my children," she said, a hard rage suddenly in her voice. "He's okay now. I need to keep him okay."

"Any leads on who did it?"

"Probably the Jones boys to protest J.J. being in jail. Fucking assholes." She was finally able to put those words to use.

"Fucking slimeball assholes," Kate seconded. "Any chance it has something to do with what we pulled out of the ground?"

"Maybe," Nell admitted uneasily. "But why me? I'm not the expert who proves these people were murdered."

"But you're the one who will report it. Ellen is essentially working for the sheriff's department. She writes a report and gives it to them. They can bury it, if they choose. The only person who can put it on the front page is you."

"Maybe. But I can only put it on the front page of the *Pelican Bay Crier*. It won't take much for a story like this to break big. One leak from one grad student and it's all over the wire. They'd need to shut up a lot more people than me."

"True. But they may not be smart enough to think of that."

"That's a pleasant thought," Nell said.

"I'll help look after Josh. He can always hang out at the bike shop."

"Thanks, Kate. I do appreciate it. Be warned I'll probably take you up on that. And I might have to include Lizzie."

"The offer stands."

"What can you tell me about the bones? I'll quote you only as a source close to the investigation and not use your name," Nell said.

"I'll be glad to answer questions, but Ellen is here and she might do a better job," Kate said. Then, as if she needed to explain: "Most of the students drove back, but the morgue let us have a space to work, so Ellen spent the night here." Kate added, "On the couch."

As Kate went to get her, Nell considered how Ellen had struck her as a no-nonsense, practical woman; no makeup, her hair short. She was either the working mother of three children or a lesbian. Nell wondered if Kate's last remark was aimed at the latter supposition. Then she wondered if she was overanalyzing.

"So I get to be the anonymous source?" Ellen came on the phone.

Nell stopped wondering about Ellen's sexuality. For the questions she wanted answered, it didn't matter. "Unless you'd like to go on the record."

"Let me hide behind the cloak of anonymity. They'll know you talked to me, but I'd prefer to be able to act like I played by the rules."

"We go to press this afternoon," Nell explained. "The paper will be on everyone's doorstep tomorrow morning. I plan to make this the front page story."

"Okay, here's your scoop. There were three bodies, buried on top of each other, so whoever did this only had to dig one grave. Lazy bastards, but it made our work easier."

"How sure can you be that it was the only grave?" Nell cut in.

"Did we stumble onto a killing field? I doubt it. I had the grad students check out the area for other possible burials. Without burial vaults or coffins, the ground will usually sink in as the body decomposes. Especially three bodies. The tree probably covered up the resulting depression. I didn't see anything that made me suspect others had been buried there, but that's at best an educated guess. They were in the ground a long time and that obscures things."

"Okay, so tell me what you did find."

"Three bodies, all likely murdered. One was male, two were female. The male was the one with chains on his wrists and he was shot in the base of the skull. We found a bullet; it was a .22. They often don't have the velocity to exit the skull. That's probably what killed him, although it may have taken awhile. Both his legs were also broken."

"Damn," Nell muttered.

"Yeah, damn," Ellen echoed. "Usually a bullet to the back of the head is about as kind and gentle a murder as you can get, but I think we can rule that out. One of the women was strangled; we managed to find the fractured hyoid bone, which is a small bone in the throat that's usually the tell-tale sign of strangulation. The other woman…"

She paused long enough for Nell to prompt her. "The other woman?"

"Not quite sure how she died. Her pelvis was fractured. That sometimes happens in cases of violent sexual assault. But… by this point there's not enough evidence to prove that one way or another. Just a guess, a feeling, really on my part."

"What's your feeling from?"

"The other two were African-American. She was Caucasian. A lot of this is just… well, instinct, or my bias or whatever. Clearly these three people were together and forty years ago, white women didn't go anywhere with black men. They killed him. And punished her."

"By violently raping her."

"Or assaulting her in the groin area, maybe repeated kicking, a baseball bat."

"Gang rape," Nell said. "You think there was more than one murderer?"

"Again, just guessing. But yes, probably a lynch mob."

"And no one talked," Nell said harshly.

"Oh, I'm sure they talked, just not to anyone who would have or could have done anything about it. They may well have parties where they bragged about what they did. Like those men who bombed the church in Birmingham. That was some of the strongest evidence against them, the people they bragged to."

They were both silent, and then Ellen continued. "They were all fairly young, early to mid-twenties at most. Between the coins found in the site, the age of the tree, and the characteristics of the bones, I'd say they were killed about forty to sixty years ago, call it fifty. But like most things, that's just an educated guess. For this climate and soil conditions, they had to be in the ground at least ten years."

"Any clue who they were?"

"Three people who died at an early age. Other than that, no, not a clue. Someone had to miss them."

"It'll take research to find out. Going through paper archives can be time-consuming work. And after fifty years, even those might be hard to find," Nell said. "It's possible they were brought here from somewhere else. That whatever dusty file holds the key to their identity is hundreds or even thousands of miles from here."

"Think we'll find out who they are?"

"I'll do my damnedest," Nell replied. "People leave trails. Three young people didn't just disappear. Someone reported them missing. Perhaps someone still misses them."

"I'm going to be doing more peering and poking stuff, checking all the tables to make sure I can dot the i's and cross the t's about sex and race. Then I'll write a report for the authorities. It's just possible one of my many, many grad assistants would assume it should be forwarded to the newspaper."

Nell had to smile at her offer. "I'd appreciate any assistance your grad students could give me. For this first story, though, I'll be pretty bare bones—sorry, pun not intended. I won't go into your speculation about the cause of death for the second woman. Something along the lines of three skeletons, evidence points to homicide. I'll have a week to see if I can discover their identities. That might go a long way to proving or disproving your theories."

"You're right. The more evidence you have the better. This one could buzz louder than a rattlesnake in a hornet's nest. I'll be here playing on the computer most of the day. Call if you have any other questions."

"Thanks for all your help," Nell said. She thought about asking to speak to Kate again but couldn't think of anything to add, or any polite phone conversation way to say please help keep my son safe.

After hanging up, she turned back to her computer screen and incorporated what she'd learned from Ellen into her story. Jacko came in, only long enough to leave a sheet of paper on her desk and grab the camera. The information he got from the morgue told her nothing that Ellen hadn't already given her, but still Nell recognized Jacko had done an intrepid job of finding a good source. She had to remember to compliment him on it.

The sheriff's office had responded only that they would release a report in the afternoon and would take any questions then. The spokeswoman added that they would be limited in what they could answer, as the investigation was ongoing.

Nell suddenly thought of someone else that she should call. She hastily looked through the campaign literature and found a phone number for Marcus Fletcher.

"Good morning," he answered. Even on their short acquaintance, Nell was able to recognize his deep voice.

"Good morning, Mr. Fletcher. This is Nell McGraw from the *Pelican Bay Crier*." She again cursed herself for being so formal, but that had been her role; Thom was the informal one.

"Mrs. McGraw, how pleasant to hear from you."

"I'm afraid my call doesn't have a pleasant purpose. I'm sorry to tell you that you were right. There were three bodies. I was wondering if you had anything else you'd like to add, or if you'd like to make a comment."

"Nothing on the record. At least not yet. Being a newspaper woman yourself, I'm sure you'll understand how reluctant I am to interject myself in the story."

"At least not yet," Nell echoed. "Would you be interested in hearing what I've written so far?"

"Most interested. Can you email me the story? Just because I'm an old man doesn't mean I haven't entered the modern age. "

"Of course. But I'm on deadline, so if you have anything to add, it'll have to be soon." She took down his email address.

"I'll look forward to reading it." Then he added, "Even without a byline, I can usually tell which ones are yours."

"That could be a good thing or a bad thing," Nell replied.

"Very true. But in this case, a good thing. You're a talented writer, Mrs. McGraw. I can tell they're yours when I find very little to edit." He added a goodbye and rang off.

Flattery or the truth? Or a bit of both? She again admired him for how much he'd gotten out of her and how little he'd given in return. She emailed him the story. He was playing her, but she didn't think it was simply because he liked pulling strings; rather, he was letting her prove she deserved his trust.

Her phone buzzed and Pam said into the intercom, "Nell, there's someone here to see you." Pam's desk wasn't really far enough away to need an intercom; a projected voice could do as well, but a few years ago, Thom had decided they should be beyond yelling through the newsroom.

Before she had a chance to ask who it was, that who was at her door.

"Mrs. McGraw," Aaron Dupree said to her. "I hope you don't mind my dropping in. I was in the neighborhood."

She quelled the schoolgirl response of "you can come by anytime" and settled for a more professional "Not at all, Mr. Dupree. A newsmaker like yourself is always welcome in our office. Is there something I can do for you? Or did you just want to scope out the media?"

"A little bit of both. I've come up with some thirty-day, six-month, and one-year goals if I'm elected mayor. I thought I'd give the mighty media a chance to incorporate them into stories. Even if the stories shoot them down," he added with a self-deprecating smile.

Nell took a moment to note again how he was a handsome man, and a handsome man who had come to see her. Part of her hoped his attention was just a political ploy and he wouldn't become a complication in her life. Another part of her wished quite the opposite, that his coming by just used the election angle as a way to see her.

"Good, I've just loaded all the guns this morning," she answered.

"I am yours to take aim at, ma'am," he replied.

Nell didn't miss the possible double meaning in his words. Nor did she respond to it, save with a slight smile. Even if she knew she wanted to, and she was far from that, she was not about to openly flirt with a candidate for mayor in her workplace.

"How about a tour?" he continued. "I know this is one of the historical buildings in Pelican Bay, and it's been a long time since I've been here."

"Sometimes I think 'historical' is code for lousy plumbing," Nell said.

"And my final request, before we embark on the tour of your historical lousy plumbing: this Saturday is the gala and silent auction for the Historical Preservation Society. My sister was going to go with me, but she can't. It's going to be quite the political show; I thought a keen observer like you might enjoy it. See us pols when we don't think we have to behave."

Nell almost said "are you asking me on a date?" but she caught herself. As a reporter covering the election, she could go. As the recent widow of Thom McGraw being asked out, she should say no.

"Thank you for thinking of me, Mr. Dupree. Are you sure you want to give a reporter with loaded guns that kind of target?"

"I flatter myself to think I won't be the best target. Will you go?"

"I'll have to make arrangements for something vaguely adult to be with my kids, in a way that doesn't scream babysitting, but yes, I'll go."

"My campaign is having an envelope-stuffing party that evening. Two young and energetic hands would be welcome."

Nell calculated for a moment. Lizzie, having been dazzled by Aaron Dupree at her school assembly, would go. Josh wouldn't think it a great evening. They could always go to their grandmother's and get Nell some points for letting the grandkids come visit. She'd decide when it got to the point of having to make a decision.

"You politicians are all alike. Now I see the real reason for your offer—a slick plan to trap my children into an evening of free labor to further your political ends."

"I'm abashed at how easily you see though me."

"As long as we know the terms. Now, why don't I show you our historical plumbing?"

The building tour was perfunctory and didn't include any actual plumbing. The real purpose of his visit, beyond what had happened in her office, appeared to be for him to meet the staff without handlers at his elbow. Nell had to admit it was an astute move, to drop by and establish connections with the staff on the local paper.

Jacko came upstairs just as Aaron Dupree was listening to Ina Claire recall him being a young high school boy. He discreetly laid several print-outs of the photos on his desk, face-down, and shook

Dupree's hand with a coiled excitement Nell recognized. There were some good pictures there and he couldn't wait to show them to her.

When Ina Claire had finished her story, Aaron Dupree seemed to sense a shift in the room—or perhaps he had other places to go. He said, "I've taken enough of your time and I'm sure you've got better things to do than listen to me." The truth was he'd been doing most of the listening and her staff had been doing most of the talking, from both Ina Claire and Dolan remembering the younger Aaron Dupree to Pam discussing cleaning up the beach.

Nell walked him to the front door.

He turned to her and said, "The gala starts with cocktails, so for us to arrive properly late, I should pick you up on Saturday around seven."

"That'll be fine," Nell agreed, and Aaron Dupree gave one final wave to the still-gathered staff and headed down the stairs.

"Saturday at seven?" Dolan asked, arching an eyebrow.

"To a political function only," Nell answered. "Good Lord, Dolan, I'm not ready to … I'm not … He just had an extra ticket and all the candidates will be there." Dolan wasn't the only one who had overheard and they were all watching her. "Should I get an extra ticket and have you come along as a chaperone?" Immediately she regretted her words and quickly added, "I'm sorry. That was uncalled for. I guess I'm … touchy on this."

"It's your paper, Nell. You get to run it how you want to," Dolan said, his eyes not quite meeting hers. "And it's your life, same rule applies."

"I'm not ready for … anything other than going to an event explicitly as a reporter," she replied softly, wondering if it was as true as she wanted it to be. "And we all run this paper. I just pay the bills."

Dolan nodded, then allowed himself a slight smile. Meeting Nell's eyes, he said, "Maybe I'm a little overprotective of Thom's memory."

"I can't stop being a woman. And I'm going to have to deal with a lot of men." Nell wondered if she should remind Dolan that one night ago she went by herself to a political rally. Had he not been worried because the men she was with were black? On the other hand, none of those men had picked her up and escorted her there.

Whatever else she might have said was cut off by Carrie showing up. On seeing everyone in the newsroom and all of them watching her, the young woman mumbled, "I was off working on a story."

In your dreams, Nell thought; Carrie's puffy eyes clearly revealed what she'd been working on. "Do a quick write-up of what you've got. I have a few gaps that need to be plugged," Nell told her, although there were certainly no gaps she expected to fill with what Carrie was putatively working on. Her real purpose was to call Carrie's bluff. "Then I need you to cover the Harbor Commission meeting that starts at two this afternoon." Nell also knew that covering bureaucratic meetings was scut work Carrie despised. The Harbor Commission was going to have a fun-filled afternoon on the problem of dumping oil and trash fish in the harbor. "When you're done with the Harbor Commission, come back here. We may have last-minute chores to make sure the paper gets out."

Carrie had a habit of leaving for a meeting and not coming back to the office. It was one of the unspoken rules of the Crier: if a boring meeting ended around four, you didn't have to come back. But Carrie had pushed the rule; if she left for anything after one o'clock, she didn't return. Thom had even had to go to the extreme of talking to her about it.

Nell turned from Carrie, gave Jacko a nod, and returned to her office. He followed her in with his stack of pictures. He didn't say anything, just spread the print-outs across her desk and pointed out the pictures he thought were the best.

Nell took her time slowly studying them. Jacko did have a good eye and had picked several dramatic shots: a close-up of the skull with the bullet hole clearly showing; one of Ellen holding up a skull, her expression sober and focused, sad around her eyes. Another photo showed one of the graduate students almost prostrate on the ground, digging out a femur.

Nell took a long time looking at the pictures. I have to make this decision, don't I, she thought. In the past, even when she decided, it had never been her sole responsibility. Sometimes the best picture was obvious and if it wasn't. Thom was always there to second her or point out something she'd missed. Jacko was good, but he wasn't Thom. He didn't—and couldn't—know the town the way Thom did, or have years of shared sensibility like she and Thom had.

She finally chose the shot of the graduate student. It was dramatic, although the shot of Ellen and the skull was even more so. But the student's face was turned away from the camera and Nell's instincts told her it would be better to keep anonymity for this story. The other picture she picked was a wide view of the dig, a good shot of the site but not the best. It just showed the most turned backs or side views.

"These two," Nell finally said, and she pointed them out to Jacko. He gave her a puzzled glance.

"You've got a good eye, and the others are nice shots. But Ellen gave me a great scoop and I think she'd prefer not to have her face and name all over the paper. Yes, we could leave her name off, but it would seem odd with such a clear and distinct portrait. Although go ahead and print a couple, I think she'd love to have copies and it's a good way to say thank you. The grad student has his face away from the camera, so we don't have to name him. We're probably going to be running this story for a while, so I want to save the skull picture. And part of the story is about the land and who it belonged to, so I wanted a picture that gives a sense of location."

"And you choose the one where no one is facing the camera," Jacko observed.

"Precisely," Nell said. "And you did a great job with the source at the morgue. I got a lot of it from Ellen, but having more than one source is a very good thing—it allows cross-checking and it also covers our tracks better."

"You really think that's so necessary for this? They were murdered, but it had to be decades ago."

"Hatred strong enough to do this doesn't easily go away. I'd rather be safe." Nell paused a moment for the implications to sink in, then told Jacko, "Now get to these pictures. We've got a paper to put out."

Jacko saluted, grabbed the print-outs, and headed back to his desk.

Nell pulled up the story to reread, see if she wanted to add anything. She looked at the screen for a moment, then decided to check her email. Sometimes it was a way to avoid work, but occasionally a break from staring at the screen gave her brain time to do its subconscious sorting. Amid the usual junk email was a reply from Marcus Fletcher.

"Good, brave story. You tell it straight without losing the weight of it," he wrote. "I've taken the liberty of doing a little editing. Attached is my version. Respectfully yours, Marcus."

Nell opened his attachment. Had she more time, she would have waited. Editing is a tricky business and she had known many disappointing editors in her career. She didn't want Marcus Fletcher to be one. His praise mattered to her. In the past, all she needed was Thom telling her it was a good story. His admiration—and judgment— cancelled out everything else. Nell realized she needed those strokes; they told her she was going in the right direction and would find her path. Now she felt lost in a way she never had before. Until she'd met Thom, she'd always been the one to go it alone. Now she was alone again and she couldn't seem to remember how she'd done it before. Thom had been her equal in many ways; he meant his compliments because he also didn't withhold criticism, but even his red marks weren't there to cut her down but to push her to do better, to go a little further than she thought she could.

With a harsh shake of her head, Nell told herself she had to get a paper out. The last few issues had been mostly filler, stories taken from the wire or minor pieces, drifting ink. Dolan and Jacko had cobbled them together, doing the best they could; she was only floating in the background. This would be the first real paper with Nell in charge.

She started reading his edits. There weren't many; two typos, a query about an unclear point. A suggested rearrangement of sentences and an idea for a better opening line. He was right; every single one of them made it a better, tighter story. Nell felt a quickening, like she was again finding her path. He hadn't disappointed her and she trusted his instincts enough to believe his praise. She started to write Marcus a thank you, but didn't. He'd see the story tomorrow; somehow she knew that would be enough. She made his changes and saved the file, then read over one last time what would appear on tomorrow's front page.

A recent storm took the life of a tree, uprooting it and disturbing the ground it had stood on for several decades. Not an uncommon occurrence in an area known for hurricanes and sudden rumbling thunderstorms. But this tree, half a mile along a rarely used trail in the state park, had secrets hidden in its roots. The disturbed ground and a hiker passing by finally brought an unmarked grave into the open. The hiker, experienced in anthropology, knew enough to recognize the bones as human.

Forensic experts, taking over from the hiker's quick survey, have excavated the location. What they have found is even more disturbing than the mere sight of a human skeleton. Three bodies were piled into one grave and indications are that all three were murdered. According to several sources, two of the bodies were female, one African-American, one white; the third body was an African-American male. All were young adults, in either their late teens or early twenties. From the condition of the skeletons and coins found in the grave that were likely in the victim's clothing, experts guess that this lonely grave has remained undisturbed for close to fifty years.

The land now belongs to the state park. It was donated in 1985 by Hubert Horace Pickings, Pelican Bay's current mayor. The mayor's family held the property for over twenty years before turning it over to the state. Once part of a vast tract of woods and farmland, today it is divided into the parkland, which is left to its natural state, and land on the Tchula River that was the location of the paper mill that closed in 1992.

The sheriff's department is handling the investigation and said that as of yet they are unable to answer questions as to whether these murders could be tied to the civil rights violence during the 1960s. The inquiry is ongoing and authorities are seeking any information about the identity of the bodies or about the murders.

Nell gathered the rest of the stories. Carrie, as she suspected, didn't turn in anything related to a story she might have worked on during the morning. Dolan did get Ina Claire's cooking column into reasonable shape.

"The reason I do the business side is because I can't write," he had gruffly said as he handed it to Nell.

"No, the reason you do the business side is that you write well, you just manage better," she replied. He rewarded her with his brush-off wave of the hands and the slight pink in his face that told her he appreciated the compliment.

For the next few hours the office had a purposeful hum. Pam was starting to do more of the graphic design and she and Nell had a running dialogue as they sized things into the proper format. Ina Claire did a deli run for lunch, giving precise instructions on sandwich preparation, which resulted in something better than the usual tired roast beef or ham and cheese.

Dolan, as business manager, didn't have many direct duties in getting the paper to press but was usually around. Today he seemed more around than normal. First Nell just thought of the cliché—he like a father expecting a baby—but as she watched him help Ina Claire distribute the lunch sandwiches, she realized it would be more apt to call him a father who is watching his son put a car back together for the first time. Will it start, will it run? Nell amended her metaphor further: like a father watching his daughter put the car back together. Dolan had started out with Thom's father, and in some ways his life was more invested in the paper than hers was.

They made the deadline, with little to spare. Kane Printing knew that the Crier was going to arrive around three on Thursday afternoon. Nell let Jacko and Dolan have the honors of delivering the words and images that would turn into tomorrow's newspaper. They could send it electronically, but there was a relief in the ritual of getting in a car and going, as if the paper deserved the effort and movement.

Nell didn't retreat to her office, instead hung out in the newsroom with Pam and Ina Claire, content to simply sit and let Ina Claire give Pam cooking tips, or actually sandwich tips: special mustards, a variety of lettuces, Brie instead of cheddar.

Nell suddenly glanced at her watch. "Damn. School's out."

Just as she remembered her responsibilities, the phone rang and Pam picked it up.

"Hi, Lizzie, she left a minute ago," Pam said into the receiver. Nell quickly retrieved her purse while Pam continued. "We just put the paper to bed; she managed a bathroom break and headed out the door."

Nell's actions matched Pam's words, albeit a little off on timing.

Press day was always hectic, and Nell had been the one who usually pulled it all together. If either of them had to go on a kid errand, it was Thom more often than not. As she braked for a light turning red, Nell felt an abrupt heaviness at all the little changes, the details, routines that worked before and would no longer, all the small places that would have to change and would add up to huge changes. Time to throw out the jar of sweet pickles in the refrigerator; only Thom liked them. She felt a pang at taking one minor thing off the grocery list.

The light changed and she drove on. As she came to a stop sign, a red truck slipped through the intersection, honoring the octagonal sign with the barest of slowing. Nell watched as it drove in the direction of the school.

Her stop probably wasn't perfectly legal. As fast as she dared, she drove to where Josh and Lizzie were to be waiting. To her relief, the truck didn't turn into the schoolyard but kept on going.

"Sorry I'm late," Nell called as she pulled in beside her waiting children. Josh had his bike with him. As she got out to help stow it in the trunk, she added, "It was hectic getting the paper out and I couldn't get away sooner."

"That's okay. I got to tell half the football team that, yeah, my little brother knows better than to pick on me," Lizzie said.

"You did not," Josh rejoined, his beloved bike secure. "You just used me as a show and tell to flirt with them. Hey, I get the front, I'm the injured one," he said as they both converged at the car door.

"You can spread out in the back seat. I've got seniority."

"Accident of birth," Josh replied, but let Lizzie have the front seat.

Nell was glad to see them in their usual sparring match, teetering on the edge between affection and annoyance. She usually let them go unless things ended up too much on the annoyance side. As Josh got in, she watched him in the rearview mirror. Location made the scrape on his chin the most noticeable, but there was a bruise behind it, and Nell could also see part of the abrasion and bruises on the hurt arm.

"Do you want to go back to the office with me or to your grandmother's?" Nell asked.

"It's afternoon, can't we go home?" Lizzie whined.

"Did I mention that as an option?" Nell returned.

"I need to do some stuff on the computer," she argued.

"We have computers at the paper. You can use one of them," Nell answered, deliberately playing the dumb mother. She knew Lizzie wanted to be on the computer to check her email and chat with friends, not do the research she was implying she had to do.

"Can you drop me by the bike shop? The front tire is all messed up and I'd like to look at it before I go riding," Josh said.

Nell did another parent translation: he was going to look at Kate looking at it. "That adds another option," she said. "Paper, grandmother, or bike shop." Kate had offered, after all.

"What would I do at the paper?" Lizzie groused.

"Work on the computer, like you said you needed to. Or there's always cleaning the bathrooms."

"I guess I'll go to the bike shop."

"Yeah, the bathrooms there can be cleaned, too," Josh piped up from the back seat.

That decision made, although she suspected there would be little bathroom cleaning involved, Nell headed for the bike shop.

Halfway there, a red truck passed her. Nell almost slammed on the brakes until she noticed the writing on the side identifying it as Flanagan's Plumbing, and she recognized Mr. Flanagan and his wife riding in it. They usually took out a small ad in every paper.

They're getting to me when I'm spooked by half-the-size-of-a-gnome Mr. Flanagan and his even shorter wife, Nell thought as she let the truck pull away. How do I make this go away? If I ask the DA to go easy on J.J, then I have to worry that next time, he'll swerve into Josh or Lizzie. Or take me out and leave them with no parents. But how long do I have to watch for red trucks? As long as J.J. is in prison? Maybe just long enough for Tanya to find another boyfriend and the Jones brothers to get used to doing the work their brother used to do? She hoped the alcohol had robbed them of long memories.

The rest of the ride to the bike store was truckless, red or otherwise.

Lizzie was content to let Josh wrestle his bike out of the trunk, but Nell felt she had to help even if her son seemed not to want help, especially not from an old lady like his mother. "I've got it," he said as he tried again to lift it out, the wheel having been shifted so that it no longer caught in the trunk hinges. Nell kept a discreet hand on the back tire, guiding its protruding gears away from the finish of her car.

Josh wheeled his bike into the shop.

"Hey," Kate called out, "the brave bike warrior. What's the damage?"

"How'd you know?" Josh asked.

"Your mom and I were out digging bones in the woods when the call came. I couldn't avoid knowing," she said, as if to say it's no one's fault you were deprived of telling the tale.

"I think the front wheel is pretty messed up," Josh said.

"Hi, Kate," Nell greeted her. "Do you know my daughter … ?"

"Hey, Kate." Lizzie cut her off with an easy familiarity.

My children live lives that I'm not part of, Nell thought. Obviously Lizzie had met Kate long enough ago to be able to call her Kate instead of Ms. Ryan, which would have been the standard way Nell and Thom had trained her. But Nell didn't know when or how. That was another adjustment you made as a parent, from being in every part of your child's life to letting them go.

"Kate, how much would you hate me if I left the kids to your tender mercies and did some more paperwork at the office?" Nell asked her.

"Not at all. Lizzie can man the counter—she's cute enough to bring the boys in—and Josh and I can check out his bike. If it's after six, I'll take them to my house and we can all have fun pulling weeds out of my garden."

"Thanks, I'd appreciate that," Nell said.

"So would my garden," Kate answered as she moved from behind the counter to let Lizzie in. Kate waved goodbye, but Josh was too focused on his bike and Lizzie on watching for boys to pay attention to their mother leaving. Kate had been very kind, not only in looking after the kids but in how generous she was about it, especially in offering to keep them after the store closed. And in a way that didn't sound like babysitting.

As Nell pulled into the parking lot, she noticed Jacko and Dolan were back but Carrie's car was still missing. She managed to glance at her watch before letting the irritation build. It was only a quarter to four, so there was a good possibility that the Harbor Commission meeting was still going on.

"All quiet on the Crier front," Pam greeted Nell as she entered.

"And no ax murderers made off with my children, so we're all happy."

"Where are Lizzie and Josh?" Dolan asked. "Seems like they should be here celebrating with us."

It did, but Nell was also glad they were finding ways back into the rhythms of their lives. The staff was celebrating getting the paper out, but there was also an unspoken celebration—Nell would and could run the paper without Thom.

"Josh is more worried about his bent-up bike, but he's used to the paper getting out every week. And Lizzie is manning the bike shop counter, which I've just learned is prime boy-cruising ground. Kate Ryan at the bike shop is looking after them."

"You did a good job, Nell," Dolan said quietly, the only acknowledgement of the real celebration.

"Thanks. We can go ahead and take a slow afternoon, but by next week's edition, I want to know a lot more about those three skeletons." She was speaking most directly to Jacko, as he would be helping her with the research, but she also wanted everyone else to know, and to see what their reactions would be. "Who are they? How did they end up in that lonely grave?"

"Think we can do what the authorities can't?" Dolan asked.

Nell held his eye for a moment, but saw only a question, not a barricade. "Possibly. We can probably do a better job of searching for old newspaper stories. Three young people missing should have made news somewhere."

"You're right," Jacko said. He'd been leaning back in his chair, but he sat forward as he said that, almost reminding Nell of a hunting dog that's sighted its quarry. "But a lot of this stuff is only going to be in paper archives."

"Probably, but three bodies, two African-American, discovered in a small Mississippi town is a big enough story to get some looking through morgues in exchange for information. And even if we can't do more than the authorities, we can at least make sure the bones don't become as forgotten as their grave has been until now," Nell added.

"I'll keep looking in our own morgue," Jacko said. He stood up as if he were about to head downstairs.

"You can do that tomorrow," Nell told him. "We've already done a good day's work."

"Too big a story," he said, shaking his head. "I can look at what we have tonight, and tomorrow during business hours I'll contact other sources."

"Okay," Nell agreed. He clearly wanted to get started. "I'll take the sheriff's press conference. I don't think we'll learn anything, but someone needs to be there."

"Oh, right. You can do the archives and I'll do that," Jacko gallantly offered. They both knew the statement from the sheriff would involve at least half an hour of waiting. When he finally appeared, Sheriff Hickson would read a half page of paper in a monotone and answer any questions with "the investigation is ongoing."

"No, get thee to the basement," Nell told him.

Jacko grinned his gratitude and trotted down the stairs. He had an affinity for digging in old files, and if things were slow, he would be down there, looking over papers decades old.

"You want me to try the grandmaw network?" Pam asked.

"The grandmaw network?" Nell queried.

"My grandmother calls her friends and asks them if they remember if anyone disappeared about fifty-plus years ago," Pam explained. She added softly, "Might be the black community would remember that."

"That's a good idea," Nell said. "When the newspaper hits tomorrow, that'll get some talk going." She started to go back to her office, then turned to Pam and faltered, unsure of how to say what she wanted to say. "Let them know ... I will do what I can to make sure what happened won't be forgotten. As best this paper can, we'll write the story of those years."

Pam nodded but said nothing. Nell again turned to her office, wondering if she'd just made a liberal idiot of herself or if she'd conveyed anything close to what she wanted to.

After checking her phone messages, calling a few back, and in turn leaving messages, Nell glanced at her watch. Time to head off to the sheriff's press statement. She'd noted that Carrie still wasn't back. She threw on her jacket; the days were still warm, but the high humidity made the slight cooling of the evening chill enough to require an extra layer.

As she passed Pam's desk, Nell asked, "Can you think of any subtle way to call and see if the Harbor Commission is still meeting?"

"Not a problem. Angelita, one of my best buds from school, works there."

"Thanks, I'd appreciate that. When Carrie does get back, tell her I want her to have a write-up of what she was working on this morning, as well as the write-up from the Harbor meeting on my desk by tomorrow morning."

Pam nodded, then said, "Gran is burning up the phone lines. She didn't know anything, since we moved here in '72, but she'll be on the phone all night if I know her."

"Good. The more sources, the better," Nell told her as she headed out the door.

Getting in her car, Nell told herself this wouldn't be a waste of time. Even though she knew what the content would be, the subtext would be illuminating. One thing she might find out was whether or not the sheriff had a real interest in seeing justice done. He couldn't ignore three bodies found in the woods, especially when the editor of the paper already knew, but he could go a long way to making sure they were reburied with little notice.

The courthouse parking lot was mostly empty; it was late in the day, the tickets had been paid, the criminals were in jail, and the judges and lawyers were either home or at a local bar. As she suspected, the sheriff's press conference wasn't going to be well covered. That in itself wasn't a good sign. Three murders should have had every local TV station in attendance; they needed the visuals, even if the sheriff himself wasn't very visual.

As she walked around the courthouse to the building that housed the sheriff's department, a TV van pulled up. Nell was almost disappointed—she had been girding herself for a lone battle and now she was relegated to being a mere print journalist. She hurried up the stairs into the building. She could at least get a better seat than the TV crews.

That turned out to not be a problem, as the seats were plentiful and unfilled. Nell took one in the front row, claiming the seats beside her with her camera and notebook. A glance at her watch told her the press conference was still ten minutes away, if it started on time. She used the stretch to hastily scribble down possible questions, including the ones she knew she couldn't ask. How did these three people disappear so completely without someone in power knowing? How did the white establishment here handle the unrest of the civil rights movement and the violence it sparked? She looked at that question and realized it was one she would have to ask about the *Pelican Bay Crier*. Jacko was going to have some more things to research in the morgue.

The TV crew arrived, trailing their equipment. They took the entire front row on the other side of the aisle. Nell noticed it was only a camera crew, not a reporter. They were just going to get some footage to use—or not use—later.

Either he wanted to get home or one lone reporter and a single camera crew wasn't enough sport to keep waiting, but the sheriff appeared at the appointed time. As he hadn't changed into a bright, shiny uniform, he seemed to know this wouldn't get major coverage.

Without even looking at the camera or Nell, he propped his written statement on the podium and started reading. "The skeletonized remains of three persons were discovered in a remote area of Iberville State Park. Cause of death yet to be determined. Identity of the deceased has yet to be determined. Information concerning these persons should be given to the Sheriff's Department." He folded up the paper, paused, then added, "Any questions, I'll take them now, but the investigation is ongoing and there's not much I can say."

The TV camera crew clearly had no intention of asking questions. They'd already snapped off their bright light, leaving only the lesser lights of a government office. The room seemed smaller, diminished without the high wattage of TV.

"I have a few questions, Sheriff," Nell said.

"Miz McGraw. Good to see you out and about," he replied.

There wasn't enough warmth in his voice for Nell to believe he really was glad to see that the widow McGraw was getting on with her life. Even when she was present, the sheriff had always dealt with Thom, as if only a man should be running a newspaper. She wondered if he was employing the usual civilities or if he was subtly reminding her she was a lone woman out in the world.

Thom would have thought of something polite to say back, but Nell couldn't, so she went to her questions with only a slight nod of acknowledgement. "I've had several sources indicate there's evidence these people were murdered. Are you investigating this as a homicide?"

"Your sources are pretty quick. I haven't seen any official reports yet, so I can't comment. We're viewing this as a suspicious death and treating it accordingly."

"Is your investigation looking into the fact the property was owned by the father of the mayor at the time of the murders?"

He didn't like that question; the downturn in his heavy jowls made that clear. Nell doubted he would answer it, but, given the story was already rolling off the printing press, she wanted to ask it.

He finally replied, "As I said, we're in the early stages. So far there's no connection we know of between who owned the land and how the bodies got there."

"Are you ruling out investigating that avenue?" Nell persisted.

"We haven't ruled in or out anything."

"My sources have also indicated that two of the victims were African-American and one was white, and—"

He cut in. "Wish your sources would report back to me, so I could know this stuff."

Nell didn't suggest to him that reading the reports on his desk in a timely manner might be the crux of the problem. Instead she asked, "Is it possible that these deaths were linked to the civil rights struggles?"

Sheriff Hickson gave her a hard look, then rubbed his jaw in his hand as if trying to make the heavy jowls behave. "Look, Nell—Miz McGraw—it's late in the day. I don't have the answers to any of your questions. We can stay here and you can ask them, but nothing is going to make me have answers until I have the answers, okay? This here," he said, waving the bare half-sheet of print, "is all I got."

"When do you anticipate having more?"

"When we get it," he answered unhelpfully. "You got my phone number. You can call it as often as you like." That seemed to be his declaration that this was over.

Nell decided to throw down the gauntlet. "Sheriff, three young people were killed, almost certainly murdered, and left in a hidden grave. I will be calling you and I will be following up on this story for as long as it takes to find out who they were and if there's a way for them to finally go home. And for justice to finally be meted out."

He seemed to think for a moment, then said, "We're on the same side here. I'd be sad to put those bones back into some poor grave with no name on it. I just can't pull answers out like they do on TV."

"I understand reality, Sheriff. But it's hard not to wonder if these hidden bodies aren't tied to the violence of the civil rights era. And there may be a lot of people who'd prefer that history remain buried."

"You sayin' I might be one of them?" he challenged.

Now it was her turn to be coolly professional. "Not at all, Sheriff, but it's something the Crier will be looking into."

"Well, you won't find anything. It's not just the white folks of Tchula County that voted to re-elect me."

"I'm not on a witch hunt, Sheriff, but it's hard to see how three people could have disappeared with so little evidence in the official record. Three bodies dumped in the woods, and so far we haven't found a single missing persons report that's even remotely likely to be relevant." Nell let the heat seep into her voice; her anger at their lonely grave.

"Oh, hell, I'd hate that to be. Don't you write this down," he quickly added.

"What if it's the truth? Can you be sure some former sheriff wasn't in on this?"

"No, damn it, I can't. But it'll open all sorts of wounds. We spent all those years getting over that stuff and then all the national press will be back down here and we'll be just another stupid, bigoted Mississippi town."

"Better to let the murders go unpunished than have that happen," Nell said acerbically.

"I'm not sayin' that. Just … just, if it's gotta be, then that's that. But I'd prefer some regular old murder, one that don't reopen all that stuff."

"But we don't get a choice, do we?"

"No, ma'am, we don't. You can call my office every day. You find out something, you let me know. You think I'm not doing what I'm supposed to, you call me first before you put it on the front of the paper. Least let me get my side in."

"Fair enough, Sheriff," Nell said.

"And give some of the good stories a little play, too."

"Like the long-lost cousin who is donating a squad car?" Nell replied.

"Exactly. The good stuff about the South, like that. How family matters, that blood connection makes you do the right thing."

"Exactly," Nell echoed. "Like the Jones brothers sticking with jail-bird Junior."

"You always got to see the bad side," he chided her.

"Hard for me to miss it, given the latest turn of events," Nell retorted.

"Something happen?" he asked. He wasn't a stupid man, for all his good old boy ways, and he had caught the undertone in her voice.

"Just my son going to the emergency room because two men in a red truck threw a broom handle into his wheel, telling him it was a message for me."

"You should report it. Then we can do something about it," he admonished her.

"I did report it," Nell sharply replied. "Whiz Brown blew it off as a joke. If he or the other officer actually wrote anything down, I'll be glad to get you a copy of that report."

He had either the grace or the political sense to look abashed. "Next time something like that happens, you call me direct. Them Jones brothers are trash, just the kind of trash to go after a boy. If Whiz is too busy planning his retirement, you give us a call."

"Thank you, Sheriff," Nell said, although she knew he was doing the right thing for all the wrong reasons. The cowardly acts of the Jones brothers was bringing out his latent, and as far as Nell was concerned, little-lamented chivalry. Children and widows were to be protected by the men. "I'll be calling," she added, leaving it ambiguous.

He tipped his hat before placing it firmly on his head and heading off through a door that led back into the building, as if he were returning to his office. Nell suspected it was the quick way to where his car was parked. The TV crew was long gone, having not even stayed to hear her questions. They wanted a picture, they got a picture, it was time to go home.

Nell glanced at her watch. That wasn't a bad idea. Tomorrow would be hectic. She wondered what the reaction to the front page would be.

Her circuitous journey home first led her back to the Crier office. Carrie wasn't there, although there was a hastily scribbled note on Nell's desk to indicate the young reporter had breezed by: *"Notes from Harbor meeting jumbled, will have it written tomorrow."* Pam also left a note: *"Harbor Comm. Meeting ended at 3:30. Carrie arrived at office at 4:35. Said she didn't have time to write things up."*

Jacko was still in the basement. Nell poked her head in long enough to tell him he should go home soon. Or at least order dinner on the Crier's account. She also asked him to look for the Crier's coverage of the civil rights movement.

From there, Nell went to get her kids and go home.

NINE

WITH JOSH'S BIKE IN the shop, Nell taking them to school was a foregone conclusion. She wondered if Kate had plotted to keep the bike to prevent Josh from being an easy target.

When Nell got to the office, the door was locked and she had to flip on lights. She was relieved that Jacko wasn't still there, or so eager he'd arrived before her. She appreciated his enthusiasm and wanted to be careful not to take advantage of it. It was easy to lean on him instead of dealing with Carrie. With a sigh, Nell decided one of the things to do today would be to talk with her. She dreaded going through the long process of interviewing and hiring right now, with everything in flux, but she couldn't let the young woman's attitude seep into how she ran the paper.

With a start, Nell realized she hadn't locked the door. She crossed the newsroom to do it.

Just as she got to the door, it was shoved open.

Hubert Pickings, his face puffy and red from the walk across the town square, stood there.

"Nell, what the hell is this?" He shook the paper at her, his anger deepening the red in his face.

Nell worried he would have a heart attack right here. "It's today's paper," she answered blandly.

"We went through all that shit about the paper plant years ago." He again shook the paper as if trying to dislodge the story. "If you're going to point fingers at every place there's ever been a dead body, you'll have to point at every place in town."

"I have no knowledge of anyone ever dying in this building," Nell replied. She just couldn't feel threatened by this short, pudgy man with his balding, unruly cowlick. "And it's not dying, it's murder. Murdered and hidden for fifty years."

"You just want to hand this election to Aaron Dupree and his liberal friends," Hubert almost shouted at her.

"I want to report the facts. Is there anything I wrote that's untrue?"

That seemed to stump him. Either it was the light or his hairs were actually quivering in the effort to think. Finally he said, "Facts aren't always the truth. Why bring up all this stuff now? Why not after the election? Unless you don't want a fair election," he accused her.

Not that Nell felt he deserved an answer, but he hadn't taken this off the record, so she felt no compunction on stringing it out. "Because the bones were discovered now. We report news. Waiting until after the election would be censorship. You do believe in a free press, don't you?" She knew that really didn't have much to do with anything, but given the man had burst into her office, she felt free to throw the Constitution and the kitchen sink at him.

"Free and responsible. Bringing this up now just isn't responsible," he huffed back. "You want any more election ads from me, you'd better be more responsible, Mrs. McGraw."

"Mr. Mayor, one month of ads from one candidate is hardly going to affect the Crier," Nell pointed out. "Are you attempting to extort favorable coverage by withholding ads?" She did manage not to laugh in his face, but her words conveyed what she thought of his crudeness.

"No, nothing like that, and this is all off the record," he said, his brain seeming to finally slip into first gear.

"Off the record isn't retroactive."

He was again silent, the hairs quivering in thought. Finally he said, "Look, that mill stuff is way old news. We're working on cleaning it up, okay? And I'm not a state park kind of guy, so it's not like I've been hiking out in the woods all these years. I just want to get my side of the story in." His political sense seemed to finally have caught up with his outrage.

"I have no problem with reporting all sides of the story. I do have a problem with suppressing information. If you write an op-ed piece, I will print it. Keep it under two thousand words and I'll run it in its entirety. Your side in your own words. Is that fair enough?"

"You let me say whatever I want to say?"

"Whatever you want. Unless it's libel. I'll run it next week."

"And you'll run a follow-up story to this and say that the mill stuff is a long time ago and I didn't have anything to do with any murders?"

"I'll certainly run a follow-up story and I'll quote your response," Nell said.

He seemed to think she was agreeing with him and nodded his head. "Okay, Mrs. McGraw. It's just going to be me, right? The other candidates don't get to write anything."

"It seems only fair that I also give them a chance to air their views," Nell replied.

"But I'm the mayor, they're just candidates."

This is why I dislike the man; he's stupid and he whines, Nell thought. "Some candidates might be better off keeping their exposure to a rehearsed few seconds on TV." As she suspected, Hubert Pickings had no clue this might most directly apply to him.

"Good, good thought. I get the top billing, right?"

"You'll be the lead op-ed piece," Nell assured him. One of the pieces had to be at the top of the page; it might as well be his. Agreeing might get him out the door.

Hubert contemplated the offer. He seemed to know he hadn't quite won but wasn't sure enough how he had lost to come up with any argument. He settled for "I do appreciate your seeing it my way."

"And I appreciate your concern in civic matters," Nell answered as she opened the door, a strong hint that it was time for him to return to his mayoral duties.

Hubert couldn't think of anything to say except his standard campaign line: "Yes, indeed, you do have a friend in city hall."

Nell hoped he could talk and walk down the stairs at the same time, as that was what he was attempting to do. She firmly locked the door but took his early appearance as a harbinger of things to come. Pam wasn't going to have an easy day of it.

She settled in her office to have a good look at the actual paper. Of course, she knew what was in it, or should be in it. She wouldn't read the whole thing, but she did want to get a sense of what the average person saw when turning the pages. As she glanced through it, it felt like something was missing. Finally Nell traced it to her solitary reading. Usually both she and Thom would partake of this ritual.

She almost stopped, halfway to the end. I can't run from everything we did together, she thought. She hurried through the rest as if speed could bypass the memories. Next week it won't be so hard, I'll get used to doing it alone, Nell told herself as she put the paper down. And the week after that and the week after that.

She turned on her computer. From her email address book, she picked several of the other reporters and editors she knew well enough to ask for any leads on three missing people. Some of them would do it because they were friends, some because they would see a big story and a way to get a scoop on all the others who could only relay on the wire. She wrote a brief note, attached the story, and sent the emails.

She sent the same email, without the story, to Marcus Fletcher.

As she hit send, Nell heard a key in the front door. Reinforcements have arrived, she thought as she got up to see who it was.

"Nell?" Jacko called.

She came out of her office. "Jacko, how'd you know I was here?"

"Saw your car in the lot," he said. "Did some brilliant investigative reporting and deduced that you beat me to the office."

"Very impressive. How late did you stay last night?"

"Only until ten."

"Only? That's not getting your rest," Nell told him.

"It's not like Pelican Bay has much to offer by way of exciting night life," Jacko countered. "I was having a good time. Besides, it's easier to just do it in one long haul rather than breaking it up."

"Did you find anything?"

"No report of missing persons, at least nothing that could be linked to our trio in the woods."

"We shouldn't assume they disappeared together, or that they were reported together," Nell said.

"I didn't. And even then the only thing I uncovered was for a young woman, but she was found."

"Dead or alive?" Nell asked.

"Dead. Her husband was arrested for her murder. He reported her missing and was stupid enough to hide the knife in his workshop. Guess he thought he'd clean it up afterward. Her body was hauled up by a shrimper. Bet that was a surprise."

"An unpleasant one," Nell added. "Even a day or two in the warm waters of the Gulf would turn her into something grotesque. Was she the only one?"

"The only one remotely close to the ages we're looking for," Jacko echoed. He hesitated for a moment, then said, "There were no reports of any missing African-American adults during that time."

"None at all?"

"I couldn't find any," he said, to soften the implications.

"How long a period?"

"From 1959 to 1965."

"How many total reported missing?" Nell asked, somehow knowing he had counted.

"There were twenty-eight reported missing persons. Twenty-six were probably white."

"Probably white?" Nell asked.

"Two were black. Two kids. They were the only ones whose race was mentioned. And … in other stories, if someone was black, it was always noted. So I'm assuming if it didn't say, they were white."

"This from a paper with a reputation as a bastion of liberalness," Nell said acerbically. "What did you find on the coverage of the civil rights protests? Or do I even want to know?"

Not directly answering her, Jacko said, "I've got a stack, you can look through them. It … may not look good now, but it probably wasn't too bad for the time and place."

"Thanks, Jacko, you did good work," Nell told him. "If I'm going to examine what this town did during the civil rights struggle, it would be hypocritical to leave out the local paper."

He repeated, "It's really not too bad. No glowing descriptions of the KKK as the saviors of the flower of Southern womanhood. No N word." He picked up a stack of papers he'd placed beside his desk. "Shall I put these in your office?"

"You might as well. I'll try to get to them this weekend. What are your thoughts as to what to do next?" she asked as he transferred the pile to a corner of her desk. In unspoken agreement, she sat down at her desk and he sat across from her.

"I might as well do the quick and dirty Internet search. I don't have much hope it's the best place to find old records. But it's easy and I might just stumble over something. Then I'm hoping either the paper or Pam's grandmaw network will turn up a good lead. If that doesn't work, then I'm going to call in favors with some law officers I know and see if they'll have a gander at the old files."

"That all sounds good, but you might want to leave the official route to the sheriff. He can probably do better in getting into the old files."

"Assuming he does ask. But if I get there, I'm going afield, out of state."

"Let me know when you're at that point and we'll make the decision then," Nell instructed. "Did you know that there was a black paper? I mean, a paper for the African-American community? The *Coast Advocate*."

"Really? Does it still exist? That would be a fascinating place to look if they kept any of the old issues."

"It would. I don't know if anything exists or if we can get access, but I'll work on that."

"I'd like to help," Jacko said.

"If I get us into their archives, you can be right beside me," Nell told him.

"Okay, off to the Internet," he said, standing up.

"Oh, Jacko? The mayor already paid us a visit. Said he considered our story slanted. He claims he's going to write an op-ed piece for the next issue."

"Slanted? Do you think he has anything to do with the murders?"

"That's what I've been wondering since he left. He's not really old enough to have been anything other than on the fringes. Is it just political squawking or something else? Be careful out there."

"I will. You, too," Jacko said.

I will, Nell silently answered. And I know I'm not immortal. Jacko might be young enough to think he is.

The door opened again and Nell heard the voices of Dolan and Pam. She stuck her head out long enough to tell them about the mayor's visit, then had to repeat it for Ina Claire when she came in at the tail end of the first go-around. Nell suspected that "a friend in city hall" would be the office tag line for the day.

Ina Claire made the coffee; no one was fool enough to do it in her stead. Nell waited long enough to snag a cup before heading back to her office.

Not that much was likely to come back so soon, but Nell checked her email. In any case, it was better than trying to think of how she was going to handle Carrie. Most of it was the usual junk email. Nell quickly hit the delete button, not dwelling on the irony of advertising Viagra to a widow.

Marcus Fletcher had responded. "Talk to Penny March at the Whispering Pines. Let me know what she tells you," was his cryptic note.

Nell felt frustration, wishing he would just give information to her instead of making her—as well as Jacko—jump through hoops. But, she realized, I wouldn't just give it if I were him. He needs to know he can trust me, and one story won't do it. Will I back off, or will I keep pushing? Nell wondered if there wasn't something more, if he wasn't pushing and goading her into finding and following the story to prove that she could do it—without Thom.

She hastily grabbed her jacket, then had to slow down to thumb through the papers on her desk to find Penny March and Whispering Pines. It had once been the local hospital, but technology had outpaced the building and it was now a "long-term care facility."

On her way out, Nell told Dolan that when Carrie arrived, she could assist him in any odious task he could come up with. She didn't quite use those words, settling for something more innocuous like "the long-neglected filing," but her meaning was clear. With a mental squaring of her shoulders, she said he should tell Carrie she needed to talk to her today. Her duty done, she was out the door.

She hadn't bothered to call ahead about visiting hours, knowing she was likely to get in if she was there but could easily be put off over the phone. She gauged almost ten in the morning to be early enough to not run into lunch but late enough to be beyond the morning routines best kept from visitors, like bed pan emptying and denture brushing.

Many of the original details of the old building had been preserved, including a carved-wood reception area that wouldn't have looked out of place in a private club catering to an older generation of men. Nell was relieved to note the public areas were neat and smelled vaguely of pine cleaner, or perhaps the whispering pines that had been left to grow tall on the grounds.

The woman behind the reception desk looked as if she could have been carved out of pale, sunless wood. She had thin lips that might disappear altogether if she dared smile. She didn't risk it as Nell approached.

"Hello, I'm here to see Penny March," Nell announced.

"Miss March? Is she expecting you?" The woman accented the Miss a little too hard, as if Penny March had failed not only by getting old, but also by ageing without marrying.

"I would think so," Nell answered. She would think whatever she wanted in situations like this. Right now she was thinking it was possible Marcus had alerted Penny March to her visit.

"Visiting hours don't really start for another fifteen minutes."

"That's fine. I'll wait," Nell replied without moving, making it clear she would wait right here where the lipless woman would have to constantly be annoyed by her presence.

That seemed a greater burden than reception pay demanded. "Miss March is out on the deck."

"The deck is this way?" Nell inquired, as offering directions didn't seem part of the woman's duties.

A nod was all the response she got.

At the far end of the hall, a glass door showcasing the sun in the pines seemed close enough to the direction of the nod for Nell to feel officially sanctioned.

Her guess was correct; the door led out to a wooden deck covering the entire back of the building. On one side, engrossed in a card game, were three women and one man. Nell started toward them, but then noticed a single woman at the far corner. Although given the numbers it was likely that Penny March was among the card players, Nell crossed to the lone woman.

"It's a beautiful day, isn't it," the woman said as Nell approached. Then she added, "Is it visiting time already or did you manage to slip by the Medusa?"

"Told her I'd wait standing right in front of her. So I've managed to get in all of fifteen minutes early."

"A rule breaker. I like that in a woman."

"I'm looking for Penny March."

"How about Nickel Waltz? Quarter Tango? It does sound like something the local band should be playing, doesn't it?"

"You're Penny March?" Nell asked, guessing only the owner would be so free with her name.

"I am. In the living flesh. Or what's left of it after eighty-seven years. And you are?"

"Nell McGraw. I'm with the *Pelican Bay Crier*."

"I've been hoping you—someone like you—would come. Those poor children." The day remained bright, but her face changed abruptly as if a cloud had raced across the sun.

"Which children?" Nell asked softly. She pulled over a chair to sit down next to her.

"The ones in today's paper. The ones found in the woods."

"Do you know who they were?"

"No, I don't know who they were, but I think I know what put them there."

"Murder?" Nell queried, leaning in closer.

But Penny March, too, had to learn to trust her. "How did you find me?" she countered.

"Marcus Fletcher suggested I talk to you."

"Did he say why?"

"No, just that I needed to talk with you."

"And how is Marcus doing?

173

"He's doing well enough to run for mayor."

"Good. Then I'd best live long enough to vote. It's been a while since I've seen him. You know it just isn't done, a man of his age and skin color visiting a woman of my age and skin color. Medusa follows him around like he might steal a bed pan."

"Still?" Nell asked.

"Do you really think people outlive their bigotry?"

"I would hope that at least some people could change," Nell replied.

"Some do; some harden and pass it on. She does call him Mr. Fletcher, but I think that's only because she can't pronounce Marcus."

"And you have to live here in her power."

The old woman shook her head. "She has no power over me. Oh, she can do things like make my visitors hew to the rules, the petty chest-thumping the truly powerless have. If I care at all, it's about how sad that she does these small things. They have no effect, yet she keeps on doing them as if she has nothing else in her life."

Nell nodded, then got back to her story. "Why were those bodies left in the woods?"

"It won't seem like we're going there, but we are." Penny March turned to face Nell directly, her eyes a clear, penetrating blue. "I was born two decades before this building was built, all shiny and modern at the time. Just as well; I'm glad not to die in the place I was born. That seems fit for homes but not impersonal hospitals. Born here in Pelican Bay, grew up here, lived here, and will die here. The most adventurous thing I did was serve in the Army during the war. Korea. My father was furious I signed up before my brothers. I bring that up because that experience taught me I didn't want to be a stay-at-home baby maker.

"There weren't many careers open to women back at the time, so I took what I got and started working in the records department in the courthouse. Back then it was small enough I did a little of everything: property taxes, even traffic tickets. Anything that was a record and had to go somewhere official. In 1959, a Mr. Albert Dunning came in to head the department. Of course no one considered promoting a woman to run the place. By no one, I mean not even me.

"But Mr. Dunning was … not a nice man, and he wanted more than his station would bring. At first it was easy. He just tightened the rules without warning, which wasn't nice, but they were the rules. Any late property taxes got hit with a fee, even if they were just a day late. He waved them, of course, for the important people. I remember him saying, 'They're too busy to get it in on time. But those others have no excuse.' He let the Pickings go for two whole years once. Some people could barely scrape together the tax, let alone a penalty fee. They got more and more behind, until their property was put up for tax sale. Mr. Dunning would always notify some of the 'important' people he thought might be interested in the property. I can't prove money exchanged hands, but I know some of them never appeared in the paper. Some people claimed they never got proper notice, so that makes me even wonder if all the letters made it to the post office.

"Some people did very well with the property they acquired. Did you know Lamont Vincent? He bought the property on the other side of city hall for several hundred dollars in back taxes. It was a beautiful old house, in disrepair. He left it to rot for a few years, until a timely fire burned down what was left, just as the city was looking for more property for the office complex. He made close to thirty thousand dollars off of it.

"Jeremiah Billings. He was old and frail. And colored. They had owned that land for generations. When it was due, he was too sick to come in to pay. Mr. Flanagan, my old boss, would never have minded. "He'll get it next month," was what he'd have said. But Mr. Dunning slapped him with a penalty. It broke my heart to tell that frail old man that he owed not just the taxes but a fine on top. I remember him standing there saying, "But, Miss March, I always pay, you know I always pay." I pulled ten dollars out of my purse and gave it to him. It was all I had and didn't cover the fine. He paid me first the next month, but he was still behind, so he got another penalty. He would have caught up in the summer, when he made the harvest, but that was too many months away.

"He lost his property in February, a cold hard month for a man to be put out, everything he worked for gone." Penny March was silent, perhaps contrasting her old age to his.

Nell gave her the silence, then asked, "Do you remember who bought the property?"

"Of course I remember. Bryant Brown. I was gone by the time he sold it, but it's a stretch over where the Interstate goes through. Part of it is now Wendell Jenkins' car empire."

"Brown? Any relation to Whiz Brown, the police chief?" Nell asked.

"His father, I believe. Whiz was the family ne'er do well, but Bryant and his son Buzz could get money out of road kill opossum."

"Still, why is his name so familiar?" Nell wondered, more to herself than a real question.

But Penny March had the answer. "Because Bryant Brown managed to exit this world in an act of massive stupidity. Buzz survived, but lost a few fingers. Seemed that Bryant considered himself a tough man and was always on the lookout for ways to demonstrate it. I think that one of his disappointments in Whiz was that Whiz was either too smart—I know, that's hard to credit—or two cowardly to join in. One night Bryant and Buzz managed to catch a rather large cottonmouth and after enough bourbon, decided to have a snake toss. There aren't too many snakes that would enjoy this game and this one most surely didn't. Buzz got nipped on the hand, but Bryant was bitten in the face and there just wasn't much that medical science could do to overcome that kind of folly."

"Yes, now I remember the story," Nell said.

"It was at one of those points when Bryant was most disappointed in Whiz, so he was left out of the will, although he contested it. As far as I know, that ended the two brothers ever speaking to each other."

"So Bryant Brown got the property for back taxes and, somewhere along the line, we can presume that someone bought it for a decent amount," Nell summed up.

"Yes, that's about it. You have to understand the times, too. No white lawyer would help a black person. It would be poison to their practice."

"Especially standing up for the poor black people against some of the more powerful members of the community," Nell commented.

"We can look back now and see the wrong and the right and wonder why it wasn't so glaringly visible back then. There were consequences, harsh consequences. One young lawyer told me he'd been asked by his wife to help her maid's brother. He said that he didn't really think anything of it—it should have been simple, a phone call or two and a compromise, the brother would pay a little extra and get things settled. But this young lawyer was told by his two law partners that if he wanted to work in this county he'd never do anything like that again. He had a wife, two young kids." She was silent for a moment, then added, "It's easy to look back and judge when you don't live with what they could do to you."

"And yet you saw it was wrong," Nell said.

"I saw it … yet, my mother was ill, I had to take care of her, had to have the job. One brother killed in the war, one came back only half a man, stumbling around in life like he left his soul back on one of those bloody hills. I did … what I could. Changed a date here and there, if Mr. Dunning wasn't around. Tried to warn people. That's when I first met Marcus. He'd come in with some who couldn't read and write so well. He printed something in that newspaper he ran, so people would know. I think they organized to make sure people paid on time, took up collections here and there to help those a little behind get through. It was mostly the colored folks who lost their property. A few of the people that might be called white trash.

"Mr. Dunning caught a lot of people in the sudden enforcement, but they wised up and the change of property dried up. I can remember him coming in some days point-blank asking me if anyone was late. I think he guessed where my sympathies were, so he'd stand there behind me watching, just watching. He once or twice even tried to act like it was a day later, tried to confuse me. I stopped him once, pointing out that if I was wrong, so was today's paper, and I held a copy of the Crier under his nose.

"But after about the first few years, very few properties got behind, so they couldn't grab them that way. That's when they decided they weren't going to play by the rules anymore."

"By they, who do you mean?" Nell asked. She had been noting down the names as Penny March talked.

"'They' can be vast, can't it? Certainly Mr. Dunning; also the sheriff, Bo Tremble. I think he actually enjoyed evicting people. Judge Kellogg; he had to have some idea of what was going on, or be so willfully blind that a rattlesnake would have been a smarter judge. Those were the ones I saw, that I knew about. It's a fair guess most of the rest of the town officials had to have some idea. From about 1957-58 to about 1964, over twenty percent of the property held by the black community came into white hands—and I'd guess that to be about ninety percent of the property anyone rich and powerful wanted. No interest in the small lots next to the railroad track. How could anyone who paid attention not have known?"

Nell almost said, "like the local paper," but that was her own ghost to exhume. Instead she asked a reporter's question. "What happened in 1964?"

"Many things happened. Mr. Dunning realized I was, what did he say? 'Not dedicated to the job, verging on insubordinate.' I knew I couldn't stay. I couldn't do what he was telling me to do. I found another job, lost all my city benefits, and had to start back at year one for retirement, but I was a secretary over at Keesler, the air base in Biloxi. My mother worried about me driving over there every day, like she couldn't see her daughter behind the wheel of a car."

"What happened? What could you not do?" Nell asked.

"For the entire year in 1962, no property, at least no valuable property, came up for tax sale. So the next year, money started disappearing. A lot of people paid in cash, didn't even have bank accounts. One day I came back from lunch to find Elbert Woodling arguing with Mr. Dunning, saying he had paid his taxes, how could he owe from last year? Mr. Dunning just showed him the books and kept saying 'nothing is here, so you owe.' I stepped in and told Mr. Dunning that of course Elbert had paid; I remembered him coming in and paying. Mr. Dunning told me I probably remembered the year before. I kept arguing, but he slammed the ledger on the counter and said in his big loud voice that it wasn't written down and if he paid why hadn't I written it down? Like I took the money or something.

"Then Mr. Dunning told Elbert Woodling he owed last year's taxes, plus this year's, plus the penalty, and it was all due in thirty days. Two weeks later Elbert sold his property to the Pickings. A lot less than it was worth, but at least he got something out of it. I looked at that book when Mr. Dunning wasn't around and something had been erased and written over, not in my handwriting."

"So they were changing the records?"

"Yes, although that first time I thought perhaps I had misremembered. After all, Mr. Dunning was strict, even mean about the rules, but he hadn't deliberately lied before. But then it happened again. The land over on the other side of the harbor. It had been owned for generations by the Defouche family; they called themselves Creoles and had come from New Orleans. They always paid their taxes on time. The first time, they repaid the taxes, bringing half their family with them, including a cousin from New Orleans who was a lawyer as witnesses. I guess they thought they made their point, but their land was on the water and it stretched back up the bluff, almost to Henry Street. The next time Mr. Dunning himself made sure to take the taxes and then he turned around four months later and told them they hadn't paid. The cousin from New Orleans wasn't licensed here, so he couldn't help. They came up with the money again, but I could tell it was a struggle. I started writing everything in ink. Thought maybe if they couldn't erase it, then they couldn't pretend it didn't happen.

"Mr. Dunning hired in a new girl to help, said it was too much for just me to do, and he put her up front as much as he could to take the payments.

"It took them two years, and rumor had it a few burning crosses, but they finally got the Defouches' land."

"Who got it, do you know?" Nell asked.

"They broke it into six parcels: one each to Alderman Bobby Pearson, Alderman Jonas Becker, Sheriff Tremble, one to Mr. Dunning himself, one to something called Pelican Property, and the final one to Shelby Cruthers, a local developer. This happened shortly before I left. Mr. Cruthers let the others build nice expensive houses, to jack the property values up, then he built a big, ugly apartment building and charged rents for a waterfront place with rich neighbors. It spent a few years winding around in court until finally Hurricane Camille solved it by washing away everything except one of the houses. Then Mr. Cruthers was sued for not building to code, and for all I know that may still be winding through some court somewhere."

"What year was Camille?"

"In August of 1969. I remember one of the airmen at the base telling me they clocked the winds at two hundred and ten miles an hour before the wind vane was blown off."

"Not a good year to have beachfront property," Nell commented.

"God has a sense of irony, I always thought."

"Ms. March, you have a very good memory," Nell said.

"I always have had. It's starting to slip now, but perhaps because I have so many years to remember. You're wondering how I can recall all these people, the events of so long ago."

Nell ducked her head, her eyes on her notepad, hiding how clearly Penny March had read her thoughts. Is this a credible witness? Or someone spinning tales for attention?"

"I remember because it was important to remember," Penny March said. "I knew at the time a great injustice was being done. I could do little to stop it except bear witness and hope that someday, someone would ask for these memories." She put her hand on Nell's wrist.

Nell covered the old woman's hand with her own. "I want your memories. The past is never completely gone. Justice may be hard to find, even impossible, but this place won't escape its past."

"Many have died. Mr. Dunning built half his fine house and then collapsed of a heart attack. Never lived a day in it. I guess his widow made some money off the property."

"How could they get away with being so blatant?"

"Who was to stop them? The federal government wanted little to do with the 'Negro problem' and the rest of those in power either were part of it, scared to get involved, or made it a point to be as blind as they could be."

"Who else do you know that they deliberately changed the records on?"

"Mr. Dunning kept me in the back, me and my ink pens. There were a couple of other parcels that adjoined the Defouche land, owned by various cousins who had been given them somewhere along the way. I think there were about another three or four of those. I believe Mr. Cruthers got most of them. Then there was a good section of the bayou land that is now the Back Bay Marina. It was just some ramshackle fishing camp, but someone realized the bayou was deep enough, or could easily be made deep enough, to be navigable. Two old brothers owned it. They got drunk one night and their cabin burned down with them in it. Mr. Dunning 'discovered' they hadn't paid their taxes. No one looked very hard for any heirs and the land was passed over."

"Who got it, do you know?"

"It was that Pelican Property group. Someone ashamed enough not to want his name on the stolen property. They also took over the Jacobs farm up there. Now it's Back Bay Estates, Back Bay Country Club. That poor woman."

Nell recognized the location, of course; that was where most of the money of Tchula County ended up, especially the old money. The Country Club was considered the most posh on the Gulf Coast, with membership criteria to make sure it stayed that way. The houses averaged about 1 to 2 acres each, and access was by a winding, secluded road. The developer had taken time and money, leaving many trees intact to heighten the sense of being in a wooded glade. The homes were diverse, from Tudor to modern, and the most expensive had access to the water.

"The brothers whose house burned. Was it possible it was arson?" Nell asked.

"And murder? No, or at least not direct murder. Gary Radnor was the volunteer fire chief at the time and he'd served with my brothers, so he came by regular to check on me and my mother. He told me those men—I don't remember their name, I'm sorry, someone should, but I don't—had built a fire, been cooking fish, and got too drunk to pay attention to the blaze. He did say he thought they had some help with the drinking. The brothers scraped by with fishing, some handy work. Not much more than a few nickels to rub together. Gary said they found about four bottles of bourbon there and not the kind those men could afford. He thought, and I agree, someone gave them the liquor, knew drunk men on the water had a good chance of being dead men."

Returning to her other comment, Nell asked, "Why do you say 'that poor woman'?"

"Hattie Jacobs. Her husband Daniel was killed in an accident and she was left to run their farm by herself, with four kids, the oldest at the time I believe around fourteen. I remember her coming in, carefully straightening out her folded bills and counting out what she owed. They were blatant and they were sloppy by the time they got to her. Thought no one or nothing could stop them. Mr. Dunning told her she hadn't paid her taxes. She just calmly said that can't be right and just as calmly pulled out a receipt that showed she had. It was in ink, in my handwriting. Mr. Dunning grabbed that receipt out of her hand and tore it up.

"I was so angry I snatched it off on the floor where he'd thrown it and said she had indeed paid her taxes, he wasn't going to make a liar out of me, not with that receipt in my writing. He got mad and started yelling, told me to go to the back, this wasn't my business. I handed Hattie Jacobs her torn receipt and he grabbed it again and thrust it in his pocket. Then looked at us and told us we were both wrong, with this awful smirk on his face, saying Miss Jacobs—like her husband never existed—hadn't paid her taxes and she needed to come up with them plus the penalty in thirty days or she'd lose her property.

"She managed it once, to repay those taxes, to unfold those crumpled bills. I'm guessing her kids didn't get new shoes that winter. But they wanted her land. They'd gotten the bayou property, but they needed the land to go with it. They talked some of the local groceries out of buying eggs from her. I remember her eldest son selling eggs out on the road in front of the farm. Some of us bought as many as we could, but we couldn't make up for what the stores stopped buying. She also had a stand of Christmas trees. End of October that year, someone chopped them down. After that, she sold the farm, got nothing for it, and moved to New Orleans. Never heard what happened to her. Hers was the last deed I recorded. Those dry pieces of paper held the story of such human misery."

Penny March was silent, looking into the pine forest.

Nell glanced down at her notes, the scribbled names. Most of them would be dead by now, perhaps a few left. Even those would have gotten away with it, save for Penny March's memory. Nell knew there would be no justice, at best only a faint shade grasping them in the twilight of their life. But with the names Penny March had given her, the locations of the properties, she could coax the story from those dry pieces of paper. Not easily, she admitted, but without these guideposts, it would be an impossible maze of documents.

Nell felt angry, but she also felt eager and keyed up, the feeling she always had when she knew the story was there.

"It won't be justice," she said, again taking the old woman's hand, "but it will be remembrance. You've given me enough to find those old records, prove what you're saying, trace the few living witnesses, add their stories to yours. Those men—their past will hunt them down. Living or dead, they won't escape."

"'Their graves were tainted, bitter with bone,'" Penny March quoted. "My brother sent that to me, the last letter I got from him. It could be a line from some great poet or something scribbled by the person next to him in the trench. He's buried in Hawaii. That was why I finally went there, not for the beaches but to see a poor infantry-man's grave. Just a few memories. Some faded ink and a stone where my brother had once been."

Memories, faded ink, and a gravestone, Nell repeated to herself. That could sum up what she had of Thom. Suddenly life seemed a long stretch; she would hold the memories just as Penny March held hers, years upon years.

"Although I do seem to recall a beach or two in that trip," said a woman who joined them.

"Julia!" Penny March exclaimed. "I was beginning to think you'd gotten lost in the grocery store."

"Hello, dear," Julia said as she bent down and, amidst juggling a few grocery bags, gave Penny a solid hug. She then stood up and hoisted her bags like trophies. "It's just astonishing the lengths to which the liquor industry will go to entice people. Bad for the youth of the day, but lucky for us. Got you both hard lemonade and hard cider. Medusa only saw the lemonade and let it pass."

"Nell, this is my good friend Julia Tyne. Julia, this is Nell Mc-Graw from the *Pelican Bay Crier*."

Nell shook hands. Julia was an older woman, although younger than Penny. Nell would have guessed they were sisters if Penny hadn't introduced her as a friend. It wasn't their looks, but an easy camaraderie and intimacy that was readily apparent.

"You must think I'm some kind of rum runner, smuggling in alcohol like this," Julia said to Nell.

"But at eighty-seven, I'm old enough to drink, and enjoyment of life is more important than health. Although I firmly believe that an afternoon relaxer is more healthy than not," Penny filled in.

"Don't worry, I'm just a reporter, not the vice squad. I never reveal my sources," Nell said.

"Good to know one's friends," Julia replied. To Penny, she added, "I have your weekend all sorted out. I'll come back by and pick you up this afternoon and don't have to bring you back until sometime Monday. Karl and Lenny are coming over tonight for pizza and poker. Then on Saturday we're doing a bar crawl, over in Biloxi."

Penny broke in. "We're doing no such thing. More likely a sedate drive along the beach. Julia, dear, Nell has been interviewing me; you're going to make me sound like the most unstable of witnesses."

"Interviewing you about what?"

"A long time ago. When I worked in Pelican Bay in the records department."

"Ah. That has come to light."

"Yes, finally," Penny answered. "Poor Julia, she thought I would pass before her and she would be left to tell her secondhand version."

"You're going to bring this all out?" Julia asked Nell.

"As best I can. I want to do more research before I print the story. Others will remember, if you have. I'm going to track down those who lost properties and add their voices. Plus dig in the old records and look at the deeds of sale."

"You might compare the tax records of the taken property to those of people like the Pickings," Penny March suggested. "I know that they paid late on several occasions."

"Yes, I'll do that," Nell replied. She'd already thought of that, but it was an intelligent suggestion. "Any others that you can think of?"

"Might try the Browns. I was too grubby to take their money; Mr. Dunning always saw them himself. I think right around the time I left their little group had a falling out. Just a few things I overheard. Something about the Jacobs property being sold instead of taken for taxes. I surmised one of those in on it had bought the whole thing, when the plan had been to parcel it out."

"No honor among thieves," Julia snorted.

"Who got the Jacobs land?" Nell asked as she ruffled back through her notes.

"The Pelican Property group, so I don't really know who," Penny answered. "But that gave them the marina and the back bay property in a package, quite an attractive parcel all together."

"I can do a records search and find out who was behind Pelican Property," Nell said. Rather, Jacko could do a search, as old records were his specialty.

They were interrupted by an aide opening the door and calling out, "Lunchtime."

Nell glanced at her watch. Lunch was served at 11:15. She'd still been talking to Penny March longer than she'd thought.

"I'll go tuck these in your room, dear," Julia said to Penny. She bent down and kissed Penny, then headed off.

"You've been a great help, Ms. March," Nell told her. "You said you knew why the bodies were put in the woods. How does this connect?"

"Proof? I have none. But there was so much money involved, all that land. Three people died at the same time. Someone fought back. And died for it. Life can be brutal and it can be random, but I still hope it can't be brutal and random enough for two great evils in one place at one time, instead of just one."

"You might be right. And we may never find proof."

"Look. Please look. Put something bitter in their comfortable graves." She was silent for a moment. "Can I get you to give me a wheel? I'll wait forever for one of the aides to remember I'm out here."

"I may have other questions," Nell said as she unlocked the brakes on the wheelchair. "Is it all right if I come here again?"

"I do have such a full social schedule, but I think I might be able to work you in."

Nell pivoted at the door, to open it with her hips and gently bring the chair over the stoop. She flashed back to her mother in a wheelchair. The final month, as her mother lay dying of cancer. Nell had just graduated Columbia then, and yet she was still the single daughter, the one with the duty to come home and care for a dying woman. She had hoped that death so close would change her mother, but it hadn't, or not in the way Nell had wanted. If anything, dying made her mother more demanding, more grasping, as if she had to exert every last bit of control. She badgered Nell to call her brothers; she wanted constant attendance, a stream of people to see her, although she could stand only a few minutes before dismissing them. When told the summoned relative wouldn't be coming, her mother would bray, "Vivien would have gotten them to come." Nell didn't tell her mother she'd attempted to get Vivien to help, but Vivien had dismissed her *and* their mother, saying, "It's a waste of time for anyone to go out there. A forty-five minute drive for a two-second visit? Give her a photograph." When Nell complained about being the one her mother harangued, Vivien had also dismissed that. "She'll be dead in a few weeks; you can stand her moods that long." Vivien had hung up before Nell pointed out that Vivien couldn't stand their mother's moods for a few minutes.

"Ah, you've taken over my duty," Julia said, interrupting Nell's thoughts. "Thrown me over for a younger woman, have you?"

"Nothing of the kind. I merely wanted you to have time to safely stow the goods and me to get to lunch while it's still warm."

"She always finds an excuse," Julia said easily to Nell.

It wasn't difficult to find the lunch room; most everyone else was going in the same direction. One of the aides appeared and took over the wheelchair duty. A hasty goodbye, and Penny March was wheeled in to her lunch.

"They don't like visitors around during lunch," Julia said. "Afraid we might steal a biscuit or something."

They walked together back through the lobby. Indeed, Ms. Medusa, as Julia and Penny seemed to have labeled her, had her eyes watching for purloined bread.

"It must be hard to pass by that woman every day," Nell said once they were safely out of hearing distance.

"Oh, not really. Just one of life's little challenges. We do have to occasionally remind her that these are not inmates and she is not a prison guard. But it can also be useful to have a clear adversary who is easily vanquished."

"How long have you and Penny known each other?" Nell asked.

"Sometimes it doesn't seem that long, doesn't seem we could be so old," Julia said softly. "Penny and I have been together for a little over forty-eight years now."

"How did you meet?" Nell asked.

"I was a little wild in my youth—nothing serious, mind you, nothing at all if I'd been a boy; driving a little too fast, cussing. Judge was going to give me a fine and ten days in jail, so I piped up and asked him to give me the same chance he gave the boys and let me join the military. I didn't think he'd really do it, but he did. So there I was, signing up for the Women's Air Force. I thought I'd made a major mistake when I found out I had to wear lipstick, but I learned to like it. They decided to send a nice little Wisconsin girl to the heart of the south, so they assigned me to Keesler in Biloxi. I met Penny on my second day there."

"And you've been together ever since?" Nell asked, having finally guessed that they were more than just friends.

"Penny thought I was a little young for her, but yes, we have." Julia was silent, then added, "This was her choice. I argued. Guess I could have argued harder, but I think we both knew when it got so hard for her to walk. She said, this way I can avoid the chores but still have the fun. This isn't such a bad place, really," Julia continued, as if she had to explain to Nell. "The only really annoying person is Medusa, and she's only there eight hours a day. I can know Penny is well taken care of, that there are nurses around, that she'll get breakfast even if I sleep late."

Nell put her hand on Julia's arm. "I took care of my mother for a while, less than six weeks. It exhausted me. I can only wish my family had the wisdom to make the choice you've made."

"I guess I do explain a little too much, don't I?" Then Julia asked, "How much about Penny will be in your article?"

"I'll have to back up what she says as much as possible, but she did give me most of the story and she should get credit," Nell replied.

"Don't worry about the credit. Penny won't care," Julia said with the assurance of knowing someone for a lifetime. "I think she'd rather not be mentioned at all, certainly not by name. The important thing is people know what happened. Plus ... I worry about her. Talking to you is one thing, but her heart is weak and if she had call after call, it would be hard on her."

"A lot of money changed hands. Some of those hands might still be around," Nell said. "Do you think someone might seek revenge?"

"After she's told you? It would be pointless, wouldn't it? But then criminals aren't always the most logical people. Tell the story, but leave us out if you can. She's an old woman. Death is close. But she should die in her bed."

"Until you or Penny tells me otherwise, I won't use her name."

"Thank you." Julia stopped at her car. "If you ever get a hankering for poker and pizza, we do it just about every Friday."

"Thanks. If the stakes aren't too high, I might just take you up on it."

"Stakes are pretty high. We play strip poker." With a wave, Julia got in her car.

Nell waved back and continued to her car. As she got in, she thought, Thom and I should have had forty-eight years. She suddenly pounded the steering wheel, an overwhelming feeling of fury and despair washing over her. "Goddamn Jones!" she said through clenched teeth. She sat still, fighting back tears, fighting how fragile her control was. Any step she took could open into an abyss of grief; how long would this go on? She roughly rubbed her hands across her face, as if that could wipe away the emotions.

Maybe it's not just me, Nell thought; maybe some of my anger is for all these lives ripped so far apart. What would it be like to have you home, your land, everything you'd worked for taken from you, with no justice possible because of the color of your skin?

She took a deep breath, then another and another before she was finally able to start her car. I can get Junior Jones off the road so he won't kill anyone else in a drunken stupor, she thought. And I can tell the story of this injustice.

"Maybe it's time to ask Marcus Fletcher," Nell said aloud, willing her voice to be steady. She drove away.

TEN

Dolan reported, in his usual laconic fashion, that Carrie had assisted him with much-needed filing but he'd finally decided her talents were put to better use picking up lunch. "I ordered a tuna salad for you, I hope that's okay," he finished.

Nell wanted to thank him for both the lunch and for taking on Carrie, but the best she could do was, "Thanks for handling everything."

In the sanctuary of her office, she started writing down the story assignments. She was guessing the best lead they had on the bodies was Marcus Fletcher and what he knew. He might be able to hand everything to her. He might just point them in a likely direction. Jacko was clearly the one to send to the old records, but he could probably use help.

She debated for a while before finally deciding on how to handle things. She and Jacko would do most of the work on the twin stories of the bones and the property. She'd leave Carrie with most of the reporting on the upcoming elections. Carrie hated old records, but did pretty good interviews. Nell suddenly realized that she was facing the daunting task of a major story, with only two green reporters to help. She and Thom had an almost intuitive way of working together, and in a lot of ways he had been the one who had made them pull together as a team, from flirting with Ina Claire to boyish gruff kidding with Dolan to giving Carrie a male mentor she responded to. Somehow Nell needed to remold them into a team, and she needed to do it now. "Damn it, Thom," she muttered under her breath. "Why didn't you pass on that trick before you checked out of here."

The interruption of Carrie, returning with their lunches, did little to give her any inspiration. Nell started to grab her sandwich and go back into her office, but instead pulled a chair in front of Jacko's desk.

There were a few minutes of unadorned eating, then some talk of weekend plans. Nell wondered if her presence was damping the conversation. She often overheard some raucous laughter when people congregated to eat. Although not recently, she thought.

She finished half of her sandwich just as a lull came into the conversation. "Next week is going to be a busy week," she said. Brilliant opening, McGraw, she told herself. For a moment, she fumbled, tried to think what Thom might say, but realized she wasn't Thom. I can only be Nell, and Nell is straightforward and blunt.

She began again. "I know it's different without Thom here. It's … at times I feel like I'm in uncharted territory. We're left with the hard task of making up for all the places he was. It's probably an understatement when I say it's going to be a busy week. We've got a lot of follow-up to do on the bones discovered in the woods. I've stumbled onto something that might be a link, but is certainly a story—an explosive story—in its own right. In the late fifties, early sixties, a number of poor, mostly black, people were cheated out of their property by, at best, an unforgiving and unfairly applied tax collection, and, at worst, by outright thievery. Jacko, I have a feeling that following this property scam might lead us to the people in the woods, so I've got some records for you to go after. Carrie, we've got to still pay attention to the upcoming elections. I want you to continue to follow the candidates. You're going to have to pursue some hard questions, like how Hubert Pickings got his money."

"The bones are the big story," Carrie said testily.

"Yes, they are," Nell acknowledged. "I'm going to be blunt here. You and Jacko are pretty new at reporting. I need to use your strengths. He does good work in hunting down the details. You're a good interviewer, able to read people and get them to reveal more than they intended. If what I've found so far plays out the way it looks like it will, the bones and the property scam will blow up this election. So far the names that have benefited are Pickings, as in Hubert Pickings, and Brown, as in Whiz Brown's family. Those are big boys, and if you're questioning them about stealing property from poor black people, you're going to be playing in the big leagues."

"I get to do the follow-up?" Carrie asked.

"If you get results, you get the follow-up," Nell told her.

"You don't think I can do it, do you?" the young woman challenged.

"You have to do it, since there's no one else. It doesn't matter what I think."

Carrie was silent, then said, "Hubert Pickings is having his 'Pickings in the Park' event this weekend. How hard do I hit him there?"

Nell considered. "Pickings in the Park" was a picnic/rally in the state park, a not-so-subtle reminder that his family had donated the land. "Let's see how much Jacko and I can dig up by then. If we can show that he got the land for a song, it would be a very poetic place to confront him."

"What about Aaron Dupree?" she asked. "I know that you're going out with him on Saturday, but he's doing a meet and greet at the fishing rodeo on Sunday. What do I hit him with?"

"So far I've found nothing to link the Duprees to any of this. That doesn't mean we won't. Right now I can just suggest that you push him for his reaction to the discovery of the bodies. See how he uses the information." Then Nell added, "And I'm not going out with him on Saturday, it's a political event. He'd probably be willing to substitute you for me."

"I don't think he's interested in me," Carrie replied.

"I don't think he's interested in me, either," Nell retorted. "He wants the coverage."

"I'm sure that's all he wants," Carrie said, her meaning not quite clear enough for Nell to call her on it.

For a moment there was silence. It's my job to fill the silences now, Nell thought. "Are there any questions or concerns?" With that, she glanced around the room, taking in Pam, Dolan and Ina Claire as well as Jacko and Carrie.

"You might be poking some pretty big guns," Dolan said slowly. "Hubert didn't much like the story about the bodies, what's he going to do if you come up with a story that his family cheated to get what they got?"

"Are you suggesting I back down?" Nell challenged. "What if the Pickings family did get their property by cheating a poor black man out of it?"

"Better have good proof," Dolan said. He quickly added, "I'm not saying that to make things difficult, just ... " He trailed off.

Nell started to demand, "Just what?" but held off. Trust was a two-way street, and as she had to learn to know and trust what they would do, they also had to know and trust what she would do. Was the widow going to go off on a half-cocked crusade, an amalgam of angers, or would she be a sober reporter hunting the facts? When she could speak, she said, "Dolan has a good point. If we pursue this, we might find we've yanked the tail of a tiger. If so, we're not just going after thieves, but murderers. It's something we all need to think about."

She paused for a moment, then continued. "Right now what I have is a witness, someone who worked in the records back when this happened. She's given me enough names that we should be able to verify everything she's told me. I'm also going to trace some of those who lost their property, get their stories. Nothing goes in the paper without adequate documentation, enough to defend the Crier should anyone sue."

"Do people do that anymore?" Jacko asked. "Public figures? They're just about fair game for anything."

"It doesn't mean they can't sue," Nell said. "Nor do we want anyone to say Nell McGraw has gone mad with grief and has some crazy agenda. It's possible we'll find out that Hubert Pickings is a saint and his family gave some poor dirt farmer a nice retirement. We'll print that, too."

"That would take a lot of proof," Dolan said. He slowly added, "Okay, I'm in. I'm just worried about you Nell, about the paper. Don't think I can get another job at my age."

"You know I'm with you," Pam said. "But you knew I would be," she added.

"Hey, it's a great story," was all Jacko said.

"It's more than a great story, it's a chance to right some wrongs, fix some of the things that the older generation left for us," Carrie said, a subtle poke at Dolan's hesitancy. Nell wondered if that meant

Carrie was finally taking her out of the old fogy category, or if she was just ignoring Nell's age to make her point.

As usual, Ina Claire surprised them all. "Well, I marched in Selma. Seems this is on the same road."

Nell caught the look that took place between Dolan and Ina Claire, let the younger generation top that, it said. She was gratified when Ina Claire caught her eye and included her.

She hurried to her office and snatched a sheet of paper. "Jacko, to the courthouse. Here's a list of names and, as best I could get, dates. Go for these first, but see if you can get comparison properties. What were they selling for? Check the tax records. Were the rules strict only for some and not the others? Get what you can this afternoon. Report back to me when you're done. Carrie, you can go ahead and take the afternoon off, but I'll call you after I talk to Jacko and see what questions you might ask Mayor Pickings. And the rest of you … just carry on."

Jacko swallowed one last bite, then said, "Off to the courthouse." His excitement was palpable as he quickly gathered what he needed to take with him.

Carrie, at a more leisurely pace, corralled her purse and other necessities. "I may be doing some errands, so call me on my cell," she told Nell.

They both headed out the door, Jacko restraining himself enough to hold it for Carrie, but then he quickly bounded across the town square to his car, leaving her behind.

Lunch was over. Nell carried her half sandwich back to her office. The pile of paper on her desk was daunting, everything from bank statements to ad revenue reports to press releases from every charity, organization and business in all of Tchula County. She had to go through them and make decisions about which to run and which to toss—and do it before the event date passed. There was also a long list of phone calls to return, from the printer with scheduling questions to the organizers of the fishing rodeo to Whiz Brown. Nell stared at his name. He had called twice. He left no message other than she needed to call him back. If Nell were a betting woman she'd put her money on him reinforcing the mayor's earlier message rather than any developments on Josh's assault.

Nell developed a rhythm, a few press releases, a bite of sandwich, dialing as she finished swallowing, finishing the phone call and going back to the press releases. She hated making phone calls, usually Thom did it. She started out being methodical, taking them in order, but quickly abandoned that after the third person who felt the need to say, "Oh, I was so sorry to hear about Thom's passing." Nell sorted out those who really needed to be called back today. Then, in either a bolt of inspiration or cowardice, she sorted those into ones she personally needed to call and the ones that could be handled by someone else.

She sheepishly approached Dolan with the handful of messages. "I have neither the ability nor the patience to make all these phone calls," Nell confessed. "Don't worry, I'm not going to dump them all on you—and if you feel there's any that really should come from me, pass them back. But any of these that you can take care of, I'd appreciate."

Dolan looked up from his ledger and took the handful of messages. He looked through them before saying, "No problem, don't worry." Then he called out, "Ina, your cousin Alvin is calling from the fishing rodeo. See what he wants. Pam, can you manage the fifty calls it's going to take to get the basketball schedule?"

"Thank you, thank you, thank you," Nell chanted as she retreated to her office. In quick fashion, Dolan parceled out the messages. She overheard Ina Claire saying, "We'll give you coverage, Alvin. Don't worry, if you catch it, I'll come up with a recipe to cook it."

The only messages left were Whiz Brown and Mrs. Thomas, Sr. Nell turned to her email. Nothing there she could use to avoid those calls. But there was an email she could write.

"Mr. Fletcher, I talked to Penny March this morning. Right now Jack Evens, one of my reporters is digging in the files in the courthouse. Can you give us any assistance in tracing the identity of the bodies found in the woods?"

Nell suddenly had another idea. "In fact, I could use assistance in other areas. Both the murdered people and the property swindle are big stories and we're short-handed. Would you be interested in coming to work with us at least through these stories? The Crier can't pay much, but let me know what you'd need."

With that she hit send. She had no real idea of whether Marcus Fletcher was really a reporter or just someone who had thrown together a sheet of information, but they were short handed enough that even the latter might be a help. Nell's instincts said he could be a big asset, not just in his knowledge and connections in the African-American community, but in the way he had edited her story, she felt he would be good.

That left her mother-in-law and Whiz Brown. Being a true coward, Nell called the police chief first.

"Well, Miz McGraw, I was wonderin' when you'd call back," he greeted her.

"So have you found them yet?" Nell cut in.

His reply, "Found who yet?", made Nell wish she'd had someone to make her bet with.

"The men who assaulted my son," she testily reminded him.

"Oh, them. Well, we're still investigating."

"And what has your investigation found?" Nell questioned.

There was a silence that indicated he either didn't like the question or had no idea what the investigation had found.

Nell continued. "Have you traced the truck? Have you questioned the Jones boys? Certainly by now you should know what kind of vehicles they drive?"

He was again slow in answering. "Well, Boyce Jenkins is handling that. I'll tell him to give you a call and let you know what's going on." He hurried on, as if making sure that Nell didn't get a chance to ask another question. "Now, I'm calling about all the riled citizens who are calling up the police station worryin' about murders and the like since you ran that story. Seems to me that some old bones in the woods are causing a lot of fuss. Seems to me you ought to be just a little worried about causing this kind of stir."

"Chief Brown, I can't understand why anyone would get upset about three young people shackled, brutally murdered, and dumped in an unmarked grave. No matter what the forensic evidence, they are, as you've pointed out, just old bones in the woods." Nell almost quoted him, calling them "nigger bones," but she wasn't sure she could get the vile word out in a properly caustic fashion.

Chief Brown was again silent, only his heavy breathing on the phone. He evidently wasn't sure whether Nell was being sarcastic or agreeing with him. It seemed to finally occur to him that she had put it on the front page of the paper. "I got to keep peace in this here town, so I got to step in when I see people riling up some people."

"And just who are the 'some people'? The mayor has already been here. Who else could it be?"

"Why, just the citizens of the town. Old ladies worried about killers creeping in the middle of the night. Mothers worried about their children, letting them play in the yard…"

"Right, all the orphans, widows, puppies, and kittens," Nell cut in. "Are you threatening me, Chief Brown? Suggesting I not report the facts? Hide a few murders because they're just 'nigger bones'?" This time she did get it out, the anger rising in her voice. The man was a fool. She had to wonder if he was a dangerous fool. First he blew off the assault on her son, then was clumsily trying to bully her. Nell decided it was time to do some bullying of her own. "I've already sent the story to colleagues at NPR and the *New York Times*. This one is going national, Chief Brown. Do you want CNN and all the networks camped outside your door? Want me to pass on some of your enlightened comments? Drop a few hints about the chief of police trying to stymie the investigation? Tell them my twelve-year-old son was assaulted and you couldn't bother to look into it? It's my paper breaking the story, they'll all come to me and I'll sic them on you like young hounds on an old fox. Forget taking it easy on your way out the door, forget a peaceful retirement. After the media smears you across this town, you won't be able to get a part-time job at the bait shop, let alone the casino security job you're looking for."

"You can't do that," he sputtered.

"Want to find out? One email and we can see just how hard the media will come after you."

"Dammit," he muttered, then said, "I don't need that."

"Fine. Tell Boyce Jenkins to find the men who assaulted my son. Stay the fuck out of my reporting and if you've got an opinion, you're welcome to write a letter to the editor. Do we have an understanding, Chief Brown?" Nell almost spat out his name.

He was again silent for a moment, the only telltale sign the heavier breathing coming from the phone, then he said quietly, almost as if he didn't want anyone to overhear, "Look, this wasn't my idea and I didn't have anything to do with it. I just don't want no trouble."

"Have anything to do with what?" Nell asked.

"Whatever upset 'em. I just don't know."

"What do you know?"

But again there was silence, and this time in the background, Nell could hear other voices. Finally he came back and said in his usual voice, "I'll have Boyce get back to you as soon as he gets in. I think he's made some progress on things. We just don't want trouble here in town. I don't want any trouble." With that, he put the phone down.

Nell was left wondering how seriously to take his threat. She couldn't call it anything else. She may have used it, but the truth was she couldn't see the story fading out. Nell could walk away, stick to reporting high school football scores, but she doubted she could kill this story. And if it's going to come out, I might as well get the credit because I'll certainly get the blame, she decided.

That left one final phone call. Her mother-in-law rarely called her, almost never when Thom had been alive; they always communicated through him. Nell would have to finesse Saturday night, getting Mrs. Thomas, Sr. to agree to take Josh and Lizzie without actually admitting where she would be going.

"Hello, Nell, glad you could finally call me back," was Mrs. Thomas, Sr.'s greeting. "You certainly were the topic of conversation at my bridge club. I don't think the *Pelican Bay Crier* ever had real human bones on the front page before."

"I'm always glad to enliven your bridge club. I'll be happy to show you the pictures that I didn't print."

Nell detected as much of a sigh as Mrs. Thomas's politeness would allow. "Is it really murder, do you think? How can they tell after it's been so long?"

Nell did know her mother-in-law well enough to know she was not asking for an explanation of forensics. She wanted murder and mayhem to all be a mistake that could be taken away with just a closer examination. "Given all the evidence, it couldn't be anything but murder."

"And if it couldn't be anything save murder, you couldn't do anything but report it."

"Are you suggesting the paper ignore this story?"

"Nothing of the sort, but to play a decades old murder on the front page? Is that necessary?"

"It's a big story," Nell said, suddenly wondering if her mother-in-law was in on it, too. Pelican Bay's prominent families—could that include the McGraws? She reminded herself it was totally in character for Mrs. Thomas, Sr. to comment on the front page, particularly a page that upset her bridge club. Nell felt a trickle of anxiety as she considered it might be something more.

But Mrs. Thomas let it go, saying, "I suppose so, but if you're going to run any more stories like this please give me some warning so I'm not unfolding the paper in front of who knows whom."

"I'll do my best," was all Nell conceded. At least I didn't get into my censorship and free press speech. Mrs. Thomas was good at bringing out the pontificator in Nell.

"Now, when am I going to see my grandchildren again?" Mrs. Thomas launched into what Nell suspected was her real reason for the call. "This is some lovely fall weather we're having and it would be enjoyable to do some strolling with them."

Sometimes fate was kind. Aaron would have to do without Lizzie stuffing envelopes. "Actually, I was going to see if you could keep them for part of the weekend. It's going to be a busy one, with the elections coming up. We're trying to cover all the candidates, plus some follow-up on the murders."

"Well, the last thing I want them to be doing is digging around in the woods for some old bones," Mrs. Thomas said with some acerbity, letting Nell know her activities had been observed—and reported on. "Perhaps a nice little trip over to Ocean Springs, we can take in the Walter Anderson Museum and stroll the downtown."

"That would be quite educational for them," Nell said, meaning they'd both hate it, but learning to be polite was one of the major steps from childhood to adulthood and this would give Lizzie and Josh ample opportunity to practice.

"Good. Then I'll come by at around nine tomorrow morning," Mrs. Thomas instructed.

Another thing they would hate, getting up school early on a Saturday. But Nell was going to sell them even further down the river. "There's an event I have to cover on Saturday night. Would you be okay keeping them late or even overnight?"

"Yes, I suppose I could do that," Mrs. Thomas said slowly, as if trying to fathom why Nell was so easily giving her what she wanted. "What event are you covering?"

Damn, Nell thought, she would have to ask. Better not to lie; getting caught would only make it worse. Mrs. Thomas, Sr. could be counted on to have spies at the Historical Preservation Society. "I'm going to the Preservation Society event," Nell said.

"Oh? I wouldn't have thought that would interest you. If I'd known, I had two tickets and gave them away."

205

"It wouldn't normally interest me, but several of the mayoral candidates are going to be there and a friend with a spare ticket suggested I tag along."

"It doesn't hurt to get out more, although not so ... well, let me know if you want to go to any of their other events. I used to be on the board, so I get everything."

Nell understood what Mrs. Thomas was going to say. Not so soon after Thom's death. "Mother, I'm not going out for a relaxing evening," she replied, her voice slipping into that coolly polite tone. "I'm going because ... I'm going to have to be doing these kinds of things now. This is a close election and the Crier has to come up with our endorsements soon. I'd like to do more than just base those on press releases."

"Of course, Nell, I didn't mean to sound critical. As always, I'm delighted to have the children. I'll see you tomorrow then."

That was the end of the phone call. Nell was willing to bet that even as she put the receiver down Mrs. Thomas was speed-dialing all her Historical Preservation friends to ensure everything Nell did would be recounted in copious detail.

Maybe I should just wear a red dress and get it over with, Nell thought.

Then she realized it was time to get back to being a mother. She grabbed her purse; at least this time she would actually be out the door before Lizzie had to call.

I can't get used to this, Nell thought as she hurried to the parking lot. I keep forgetting about my children, and that's not a good thing to do with maniacs and murderers running around. And if I forget, there's no one else to remind me or do it instead.

The traffic was kind and Lizzie and Josh were just coming out as Nell pulled up. As they approached the car, Nell realized she hadn't gotten to the logistical follow-up. She couldn't drop them off at home; between attackers and Mrs. Thomas, Sr.'s disapproval, that was too daunting. But she couldn't keep dumping them on Kate.

"We're going back to the office," Nell informed them as they got in, Lizzie again peremptorily taking the front seat.

"Do we have to?" she protested.

"Yes, we have to. I can't leave yet and with everything that's going on, I'm not comfortable leaving you home alone," Nell responded.

"Can I go to the library or is my leash shorter than that?" Lizzie asked.

"Depends," Nell said as she pulled back out onto the street.

"On what?" Lizzie pushed.

"My mood and your behavior," Nell answered, but she said it lightly. Lizzie was being grumpy, but it was low-level grumpy for her, and Nell wasn't going to risk a contest of wills over going to the library. "What do you need at the library?"

"Get some books, stuff," her daughter replied.

"Josh, do you want to go to the library?"

"Oh, God, do I have to babysit him?" Lizzie said.

"I don't need you to babysit me," Josh answered from the back seat.

"Did earlier this week," was his sister's reply.

"I'm sending Josh along to spy on you and make sure you don't take a side trip on the back of any motorcycles," Nell informed Lizzie. That quelled her protest.

Nell dropped them in front of the library and watched as they entered. Although the building was across the square from the Crier's offices, she didn't want to worry about them walking unescorted across that open space. She wondered if she was being paranoid or cautious.

Then it was back to the world of press releases, phone messages, and paperwork.

She had just gotten the new press releases and messages sorted into reasonable piles when Pam interrupted her to announce a visitor.

In the time it took Pam to tell Nell that the sheriff was here to see her, he'd crossed the newsroom and was at her door.

The mayor, the chief of police, and now the sheriff of the county, Nell thought. I must be batting a thousand.

"Afternoon, Miz McGraw," he greeted her.

"Good afternoon, Sheriff. If you're here about the story in the paper, I've already heard from the mayor and Chief Brown. To save both of us time, I will repeat what I said to them. Too many people know about the bones by now; there's no way to suppress the story. My intent is to report in a fair and evenhanded manner, but I do intend to follow up."

"Mayor Pickings and Chief Brown got a problem with that?" Sheriff Hickson asked.

"They seemed to think keeping it out of the local paper would be effective in killing the story. I gather the remains being found on land the mayor's family used to own is politically embarrassing, at the very least."

"They came over here and warned you off?"

"Beat you to it, clearly," Nell retorted. "Now that you're here, why don't you tell me how the investigation is proceeding?" She motioned to the chair across from her desk.

"Mayor's dangling a possible retirement bonus in front of Whiz, so when he says jump, Whiz's already in the air 'fore he asks how high. Tight election this year and Hubert is just fool enough to think he can tell you what to do." The sheriff eased himself down in the chair. "Well, I'm not here to talk to you about the bones. I'd like to know who they are and who did it, but given how long ago it all was, I don't have much hope. May have to settle for just a proper burial. I don't have much to report yet. We're going through old missing persons records, but fifty-some years back isn't easy. Harold Reed, the assistant DA, is trying to pry loose some funds to do facial reconstruction. We do that, then I'd be more than glad to have you put in on the front page."

He continued. "I got some bad news and thought it best to deliver it in person. Junior Jones made bail. Judge reduced it, somehow his brothers managed to get it, and we had to spring him this afternoon."

"That bastard's out?" Nell demanded. "How the hell did that happen?"

"I think his wife got to the judge, went on about needing him to provide for the family, that with all his ties here he wasn't a flight risk…"

"Just a drunken murderer," Nell interjected.

"Charge is manslaughter, makes it harder to set high bail. I got to say, I think Junior had his chances, could of cleaned up if he wanted, and his promises now are just jailhouse talk. I wasn't happy to let him out."

"You know his brothers probably assaulted my son," Nell said. "As a warning to me. What do you think they might do now that he's out?"

The sheriff puzzled for a moment, then said, "They ain't forward thinking folks. He's out now, they're happy. They just might leave you alone until it gets time for the trial and they get hit with him going back in."

"That's a big comfort," Nell said sarcastically.

"I know the police here are just a tad overworked, so I'll tell my boys to keep a smart eye out for the Jones vehicles. Broken tail lights, anything; just let 'em know they're being watched. Also wanted to remind you about my cousin coming to town tomorrow and donating the funds for a new squad car. I'd sure appreciate some good coverage on that." His purpose fulfilled, the sheriff eased out of the chair.

He hadn't directly linked the two topics. Nell admitted he probably even had decent intentions in coming to tell her about Junior Jones, but he was too much of the political animal to offer a favor without implying that one should be given in return.

"I don't know, Sheriff," she said. "You're competing with the fishing rodeo and 'Pickings in the Park' tomorrow." Nell couldn't quite bring herself to give it to him on a platter. But she hastily added, "I'll be there, ready to do you justice," as she wasn't sure he would see the humor.

"I'd sure appreciate that. Tomorrow at noon, right in front of the courthouse." He stuffed his hat back on his head and shambled out of her office.

Nell again missed Thom; he would sort out the politics. She was astute enough to notice the sheriff didn't have a great deal of professional esteem for Whiz Brown, but how did the county machinations fit in with the town? Thom had always kidded that a campaign contribution of a certain amount prevented speeding tickets in Tchula County. Nell suspected there were several good ole boy networks operating; Thom would have known for sure, as he knew the unwritten rules. She did know the sheriff had fought hiring women, firmly believing it just wasn't a woman's place to strap on a gun or drive squad cars after miscreants. He'd finally relented when the sister of one of his deputies needed a job after a divorce. She had a degree in criminal justice, and perhaps that helped him see her as almost equal to men with only biceps and a high school diploma. Nell didn't believe the sheriff was on her side—whatever side that was. He would use her for his own ends, from the press coverage he wanted to feeding her select information about his political enemies. But Nell didn't know who those where or what feuds from twenty years ago might only now surface.

With Thom, she had played the role of devil's advocate. She would have said, "Why are we doing his bidding? Why show up on a Saturday to get a posed picture of a cousin handing him a check?" She got to stay on the sidelines and remain pure, while Thom did the grubby, glad-handing work. "So I play the sheriff's game, the mayor's game, the police chief's game; I just don't know the rules or how to score."

Nell glanced at her watch; it was a little past five. She was waiting for Jacko to come back, as he should have been kicked out right at five. She was hoping he either got nothing or a lot. Nell was too tired to wrestle with the conundrum of questioning Hubert Pickings with only half of what was there.

As she had guessed, Jacko returned a few minutes later. Nell left her office to greet him and was surprised to notice that Dolan, Ina Claire, and Pam were all still there. They usually left at five, especially on Friday.

"I could spend days there," Jacko announced as he put a stack of papers down on his desk.

"And you probably will," Nell told him. "What did you find?"

"I was only able to track down a few things, but so far everything agrees with your source. The one bombshell I managed to find today is that our esteemed mayor's father did get the property for $3,000. Three months earlier, it had been appraised for tax purposes at

$32,000. However, the year before, it was listed as worth $21,200. The property assessor had decided the property had increased in value by just over a third in a year, with, obviously, a similar increase in property taxes."

"Who was the assessor?" Nell asked.

"Albert Dunning."

"Was there any stated reason for the increase? New buildings? Property improvement?"

"None stated."

For a moment Nell was silent, thinking over the implications of what Jacko had found. "They used the system every way they could. If the people pay the taxes, they reassess the property and increase the taxes so they can't pay them."

"Hubert Horatio Pickings bought the land for less than a tenth of what it was appraised for," Jacko stated.

"How could he get away with that?" Pam asked.

"It was the age of Jim Crow and White Citizen Councils," Ina Claire answered. "No mass communication; lot of people didn't even have phones. People were isolated and these men were the law."

"According to some notes there was a lien on the property," Jacko said. "Pickings *père* had loaned Elbert Woodling a tractor, with the property as collateral. It appears that the sale price included payback for the tractor. Just imagine what kind of tractor $30,000 would have bought back in those days."

"Damn, they got the poor guy every way, coming and going," Dolan commented.

"That's most of what I got. It took a while to find that assessed value, but it was worth it. That's what's going to hang them. All the stuff looks legit, 'back taxes.' But then you compare it to how they were handling other properties, sudden increases in tax bills, maximum late penalties assessed if the bill was even a day late. I started on the Defouche property: they supposedly paid a day late, but I looked up a 1961 calendar and the day they supposedly paid was a Saturday, which probably means that the date was changed. They paid on a Friday, on time, but someone changed the date to make it look like they were late."

"And sloppy enough not to check the days of the week," Nell said. She added, "Great work, Jacko. It's those details that will tell the story. It was smart of you to both think of them and track them down."

"And Alberta Bonier is going to be there tomorrow catching up on some stuff and she told me I could come in if I wanted. So I'll have a couple of hours tomorrow to keep digging."

"Very good."

"Young stud sweet talking those old courthouse ladies," Dolan joshed.

"She's got a son around my age," Jacko replied, a hint of blush on his face. "And she said she hates to be there by herself."

They had all worked hard and cared enough to stay late. Time to get everyone home. Nell picked up the phone on Jacko's desk and dialed Carrie's cell number.

When the young woman answered, Nell said, "Carrie, you are to be all sweetness and light tomorrow with Hubert Pickings. Lead him on, ask him how his family got the property, dig as much as you can into the history of it; get him to go on record about it. Fawn if you have to. Ask things like how much his father bought it for, how much was it assessed for when they donated it to the park. Ask him what he knows about who owned it before them. See how much he knows. When you come in on Monday, I'll brief you on what Jacko has come up with and the questions you can ask when you change to steel and nails."

Carrie ran down some questions with Nell, then said she'd see her on Monday. Nell put the phone down and told her assembled troops, "It's late, go home, get some rest. We'll be busy next week."

Nell did as she told her staff. They were all quickly out the door and, by unspoken agreement, walked together to their cars.

Nell felt a little foolish driving only a block and a half to the library, especially as driving was the long route and walking would have been shorter, but she wanted the car as close as it could be. She parked in front.

"Hey, Mom, can we go to a cookout in the park?" Josh asked the second she walked through the door.

"Shush, Josh, you don't need to be so loud here, people might be reading," Nell said.

"No one's reading. Late Friday is the slow time here," Marion Nash, the librarian, answered. "And tonight is the cookout for our various reading clubs, and I know that Josh and Lizzie are members of at least one of them."

More in the breach, Nell thought. Both her children read a good deal, but she couldn't remember any recent outings to book clubs. Then she slowly recalled there had been a few; there just hadn't been any in the last month.

"It'd be fun, Mom. We'd like to go," Lizzie piped in.

"Who's going to be there?" Nell asked Marion Nash.

"I will, of course. Lilith, you've probably seen her on Saturdays, is already out there securing the fire pit. Robert and Marge, two of the high school English teachers, some parents. A healthy assortment of chaperones," she added, getting to Nell's real point.

I'm getting paranoid, Nell thought. Marion Nash was the daughter of Erma and Payton Nash, and Erma was one of Mrs. Thomas, Sr.'s best friends. Payton had died a few years ago and Erma's health had declined, which was what brought Marion back from the Pacific Northwest where she'd been living. I'm interrogating Marion the Librarian, as Nell had to think of her, and wondering if she would be a proper chaperone for my children. In truth they would probably be much safer with the book group than home with only Nell.

"Kate is going to bring out some of the rental bikes, so I can do some bike riding," Josh said, the icing on the cake as far as he was concerned. To placate his paranoid mother, he added, "We'll be in a group and on the trails, no one can drive by us out there."

"I don't know," Nell said. "It'd mean an entire evening when I could read what I want, get on the computer if I like, not have to muster a children-approved supper."

"That means she'll let us go," Lizzie interpreted.

"It'll be hard, but I might just manage it. Want to keep them all weekend?" Nell joked with Marion.

"Perhaps. Do they wash windows and weed gardens?"

"If you starve them long enough they might," Nell answered, then wondered if Marion would take her dark humor askance. She was the daughter of Mrs. Thomas, Sr.'s best friend, after all.

"Mom!" was Lizzie's opinion on Nell's suggestion.

"Darn, and we already bought the hot dogs," Marion replied, rewarding Nell with a quick smile.

Nell tucked that away, wondering if there was more to Marion the Librarian than she'd guessed. "How late will this shindig last?"

"We won't tempt the dreaded curfew monster. It should go no later than ten or eleven. Someone—one of the trustworthy adults—will get them home, so you really do get a free evening. They can either stay here, or if they want to change, you can drop them back by six when we close," Marion offered.

"I need to change," Lizzie decided for everyone.

Nell glanced at her watch. It was just past five thirty, which, given Lizzie's changing pace, meant they needed to move. "Okay, we'll be back here by six." Nell agreed, with a quick look at her daughter to let her know "six" was meant for her.

It was flurry of running home, helping Lizzie find the right pair of pants—"Wherever you put them" wasn't the proper answer. Then back to the library just as Marion was locking the main door. Lizzie and Josh got out of Nell's car and into Marion's, and Nell had her evening free.

I haven't had this in such a long time, she thought as she reentered the silent house. There had been a parade of people in and out, family in town for the funeral, Josh and Lizzie out of school, hovering around her as she hovered around them. A sudden death, a prominent man, attention had been paid. Her friend Jane from Chicago had stayed for a week, been a great help with everything from making space in the refrigerator for yet another casserole to listening to Nell, holding her at night when Josh and Lizzie were in bed and she felt safe in releasing her grief. They had all been a comfort. They had also been a burden. Jane, who'd lost her husband to cancer, had warned Nell that this would be the hard part—when the tumult and attention subsided, when she had to learn to be alone.

Nell had always relished her moments of solitude, Thom off with the kids and the house blessedly hers. This time was different. As before, there was the release and luxury of having only herself to pay attention to, but this time was tinged with knowing this aloneness would come more often. Josh and Lizzie would grow up and away, even now in book clubs and on bike trips. Being alone was a luxury if it was rare, and Nell had to wonder how rare it would be in the future.

Jane may have been right, but still it was good to be alone. She nibbled supper, a container of yogurt; sliced an apple and some cheese. Broke her rule and sat at the computer to eat. It's not really a broken rule if you're the ruler, Nell decided. She checked her work email. There was a reply from Marcus. "It would cause apoplexy for my pension folks for me to go back to work, although I appreciate your offer." Nell felt a stab of disappointment, but then she read, "However, I could certainly volunteer my services. The only thing I ask in return—and it may seem vain—is either a byline, if the reporting merits it, or a listing in the staff column. It's not your burden, but many years ago I wrote a few stories for the Crier during the integration of the beaches, and my name was never put to them. The closest I got to an explanation was that a black man reporting on civil rights issues would make it seem like biased reporting. If these conditions are acceptable, let me know when you'd like me to start. Also, of course, I can't do any reporting on the mayoral race, nor should I be present for any discussions about it. I will expect that you give me the same hard-nosed coverage you give all the other candidates."

Nell immediately answered. "Your services are very welcome, and your conditions, considering the history, are most mild. You are, of course, right about the mayor's race, and from our end we can promise not to take advantage of your presence in the office to gain inside information about your campaign. Can you be at the office on Monday at around nine?" She hit send.

Certainly it had been racist, seen in the light of today, and Nell was ashamed of the Crier's decision to hide the color of a reporter's skin. But it was both easy and hard to judge. In absolutes it was wrong, but for the time and place, just letting a black man be a reporter for the— and there was no other name for it—white paper, the paper of record, was a small step. Or maybe this is just my way of trying to rationalize it all, Nell thought, to lessen the burden of inherited guilt. I wonder if I'll ever have the nerve to ask Marcus what he thinks about it.

She got up from the computer. It was barely eight o'clock; no children for hours. No one to judge her if she poured two fingers of Scotch into a glass and sat out in the backyard to watch the stars.

The first sip was a comforting burn. I need not to care, not to think, Nell told herself. Not to feel. These empty moments let too much in. Nell could handle the day-by-day, what to do in the morning, how to fill the afternoon, but staring at the stretch of future was daunting. How do I take care of two fatherless children? Today and tomorrow and next year and the next? Is this the life I want? In this small town? Running Thom's paper? Or is it my paper now?

Two fingers weren't enough. Nell fetched the Scotch bottle from the kitchen and brought it with her. As she poured, she thought, is this the only comfort I have? The blurring of alcohol? Then a jolting thought: is this what J.J. was after?

"No," Nell said aloud. "There is a goddamn difference. I'm sitting in my backyard, and I'm not getting into a car until I'm stone-cold sober." J.J. might have been running from the confines of a life that would never be bigger than working at his brothers' garage, a grasping wife and kids he'd never planned for. But if his life was small and closing in on him; those were his choices. Maybe he went to the bars to relive the glory days of high school football, or to get away from his wife and squalling kids and slip into a fantasy of another life. But he'd escaped as recklessly as he had lived his life, no heed to the consequences.

Nell put the cap back on the bottle of Scotch. That, in the end, was the difference; she would pay heed to the consequences. She finished what was in her glass, letting the evening blur into cool air and bright points of light in the sky.

Only as the night turned to chill did she get up and go in, carefully washing the glass, putting the Scotch back, moving it behind some of the other liquor bottles. She brushed her teeth, gargled; hid the traces of her lapse.

She was in bed reading when she heard Josh and Lizzie return. Nell poked her head out long enough to make sure they were heading straight to bed. She said little, afraid that her words might slur tellingly. They took her claim of tiredness at face value, and then the lights were out.

Nell slid quietly into the oblivion of sleep.

ELEVEN

Josh and Lizzie were lively at breakfast, with Josh trying ardently to convince Lizzie that he and his bicycling buddy Joey had seen a bear in the woods.

"It wasn't a bear," Lizzie said. "It was probably Bigfoot or the Loch Ness Monster." Her big-sister disdain was clearly expressed on her face. "Or the result of eating five hot dogs."

"I didn't have five hot dogs!" Josh retorted.

"Okay, four and a half."

"Maybe I had four, but over the whole evening."

Nell was almost glad that Mrs. Thomas, Sr. would get to referee this fight. Josh was developing the appetite of an adolescent boy and Lizzie was developing the delicacies of an adolescent girl—having potential boyfriends watch her younger brother wolf down food was a social disaster. Clearly she was going to spend the day making Josh understand that big sisters did not take social embarrassment lightly.

Nell put a temporary halt to further retorts by saying, "You need to hurry up. Your grandmother is going to be here any minute."

"Do we really have to stay the night?" Lizzie wheedled.

"Yes, you do. I don't know how late I'm going to get home tonight, so it's better if you stay."

"Better for who," Lizzie muttered.

"Better for whom?" Nell corrected, but made no further answer. "Get packing. Unless you want me to pack for you."

That threat sent them to their rooms, and after a flurry of activity, Josh and Lizzie had overnight cases in hand just as Mrs. Thomas, Sr. pulled into the driveway.

To forestall her coming in—and seeing the breakfast dishes still on the table—Nell led her reluctant children out the door.

"Good morning, Mother," she called.

"Good morning, Nell," Mrs. Thomas answered. She got out of the car to give Josh and Lizzie a hug and to supervise the stowing of luggage. She didn't give Nell a hug, but then she rarely did, only on the necessary occasions when it would have been an obvious slight. Even from the beginning, Thom had seemed aware his mother and his wife would not be close friends. They got along, both too polite to devolve into anything less. Nell had genuinely enjoyed the company of her father-in-law, so usually he and she would pair off, and Thom attended to his mother. But those two stalwart buffers, the men in their lives, were gone. As she watched Mrs. Thomas, Sr. instruct Josh on proper trunk shutting—firm but not hard—Nell thought, we can be allies or enemies, something to be looked at in strategic light. They both wanted Josh and Lizzie to be healthy and happy, they both wanted the paper to remain viable and important. The devil is in the details, Nell reminded herself—they just weren't always in agreement about what was healthy and happy or viable and important.

"What time would you like me to come get them tomorrow?" Nell asked.

"We'll go to church, of course, and then I thought it might be nice to do luncheon at Tutweiler's while they're all dressed."

Nell didn't respond to the gauntlets which that seemingly innocuous reply threw down. She and Thom did not regularly go to church, feeling more comfortable with a tepid Protestantism that reserved church for weddings, funerals, Christmas, and Easter. They had been liberal about religion, letting Josh and Lizzie accompany friends to Catholic and Jewish services. Nor would they have said no to Muslim or Buddhist services, but those had yet to come up. Mrs. Thomas, Sr. and Thom had argued about it. After hearing about the trip to the synagogue, she'd said, "Where do you draw the line? Paganism? Satanic worship?" Thom had given her the usual reply: "There's no harm in them being exposed to a variety of beliefs. They are our children; we get to raise them our way."

Nell decided it wasn't capitulation to her mother-in-law to let her haul her grandchildren off to her church, but an example of their tenet of exploring religions.

Mrs. Thomas, Sr. came from a family with money, something she'd been chary of reminding both her husband and son about. They'd made it clear they would make it on their own—as men should. Tutweiler's was the nicest restaurant in the area, and luncheon there would equal a week's worth of groceries in Nell's budget. Nell tried to take the charitable view: Mrs. Thomas was lonely, wanted a chance to indulge, and taking her grandchildren out presented a perfect opportunity. The uncharitable view was that her mother-in-law was using her money to covertly buy them by offering things Nell could never afford.

"Why don't you give me a call after lunch"—she wouldn't say luncheon—"and I'll come by and pick them up?"

"That will be fine," Mrs. Thomas affirmed; any goodbye was lost in the starting of the engine. Josh and Lizzie waved as she pulled out of the driveway.

Nell headed back to the house, wondering if her children had been savvy enough to pack church-going clothes.

She quickly washed the breakfast dishes and wiped down the stove and table, mostly because, if Josh and Lizzie did lack a suitable wardrobe, Mrs. Thomas, Sr. might come by to help them pick out something. Suddenly she wondered if she should feel slighted she hadn't been invited to join them at Tutweiler's. It was only today that she was busy. "Maybe if I volunteered to go to church with them, I might have been invited," she groused aloud. Then she decided she probably had been left out, but she didn't really want to go to a fancy restaurant with Mrs. Thomas, Sr. and would have a better time sleeping late anyway.

The leisure from the previous night didn't linger. The possibility that Mrs. Thomas, Sr. might reappear for some vital thing Nell had neglected to pack, and the coming events of the day, left her tense. First she would be the sheriff's poodle—as close as she could, anyway, covering his selected story. Then there was the evening. To get the decision over with, Nell retreated to her bedroom to look for something suitable to wear.

They had gone to a few Mardi Gras balls and assorted other high-social events, but not often enough for Nell to have amassed a wardrobe of any great note. "Red, blue, or black," she muttered as she considered her choices. Really, blue or black. The red wouldn't do, not with its plunging neckline. That, and Thom had picked it out. She'd been trying on a demure cream thing and Thom had brought the red dress over to her. When she'd come out of the dressing room, he'd said, "You are absolutely, rivetingly hot in that." He enjoyed the attention she got wearing that dress even more than she did. Nell had muttered a complaint about the looks her cleavage was getting; Thom had merely grinned and replied, "Let them look at what they can't touch." Oddly, it had been reaffirming for Nell, quieting the little voice that whispered she was smart, not pretty. Thom, the man she most wanted to be pretty for, thought she was beautiful and was confident enough to display her for other men to envy.

Nell quickly put the red dress at the back of the closet. She couldn't wear it—not for a long time, maybe never again. The black was what she called bland black. It was suitable, but she didn't really like it; one of those hurried decisions, she had needed something full-length and had needed it that day. It was sequined and beaded and felt heavy and lumpy when Nell wore it, making her feel heavy and lumpy as well.

She looked at the blue. It was cobalt, three-quarter-length, which meant worrying about shoes and hose. This is ridiculous, Nell thought. It's not a date, just a job. Wear the blue, pick up some hose somewhere during the day, rub a rag over the black pumps, and leave it at that.

That decision made, Nell headed to the Crier. The house was too lonely, with too many memories.

As she expected, she was the only one there, but she wanted the quiet, an hour or two of having only herself to pay attention to.

Then it was time to go appease the sheriff. Nell quickly grabbed a camera and notebook in case she needed to pretend to write something down.

When she got to the courthouse, Nell noticed Jacko's car was parked on one of the side streets. He was indeed plowing through musty old records.

The sheriff was already there, in a dress uniform that had been fitted in slimmer days. But he would be fine if he remembered to suck in his stomach for the brief click of the camera. Several of his deputies were there, also in dress uniforms, including his one woman deputy.

Sheriff Hickson greeted her. Nell dutifully introduced herself to the deputies, including getting the correct spelling of their names. She'd just finished when a gleaming silver Bentley turned the corner. Nell took several strides up the courthouse steps to get a shot of both the sheriff and the car. And the female deputy.

The car stopped in front of the assembled group. A uniformed man—white, Nell noted, wondering if it was just happenstance or if the descendant of a plantation owner had made a deliberate choice—immediately jumped out of the driver's seat to open the back door. An elegant woman emerged. There were a few murmurs of confusion, but Nell immediately understood. She had just re-charged the camera and would take pictures until the battery wore out. Sheriff Hickson's rich cousin was a black woman.

"Check and mate," Nell muttered to herself as her camera caught the woman extending her hand to the sheriff.

"How do you do, Sheriff Hickson. I'm Beatrice Carver, your long-lost cousin," the woman said. Nell had to admire her aplomb—and her gumption for both setting up this situation and walking into it.

For a moment, the sheriff looked utterly perplexed. He stole a quick look at Nell, as if to say, get that camera out of here. Nell snapped the shot. Then, in a nuance that the camera couldn't capture, she saw the political creature overcome the redneck good old boy. Twenty-five percent of Tchula County was black; Sheriff Hickson smiling and happy to discover a long-lost cousin who just happened to be black could improve his support in a group that almost always voted for whoever ran against him.

He extended his hand and gave hers a hearty shake, one he made sure Nell caught on film. "Pleased to meet you, Miz Carver. Any long-lost cousin is … uh … well … is welcome here." Not giving her a chance to speak, he continued. "Now, Miz Carver, I want you to know how much the people of Tchula County 'preciate your generous gesture. Crime's a worry for folks 'round here, and a brand-new patrol car will help us do our duty. Now, I'd like to introduce you to some of the men you … the men and women you are aiding in our cause." With that, he proceeded to introduce Beatrice Carver to each and every deputy, getting a little banter going with each—anything to avoid giving her a chance to point out that a forefather of the sheriff's had raped a foremother of hers.

After Sheriff Hickson ran out of deputies, he hesitated for a moment and Nell quickly made the decision for him, coming over to introduce herself to Beatrice Carver. The sheriff glared at her as she added, "I'd love to interview you about your research and experiences in tracing your family line."

Beatrice gave Nell a smile that indicated she knew a coconspirator when she saw one. "I would be delighted," she answered.

"Might have to wait for another time," Sheriff Hickson cut in. "I want to make sure that Miz Carver gets a chance to see our office, then we got the official presenting of the check. Don't want to rush through the important stuff."

But Beatrice Carver was the patron and she could change the agenda—or at least hew to her real objective, exposing the tangled racial legacy that had led to her and a Southern sheriff being kin. "The 'important stuff' isn't so important that it will take more than an hour. It really is just handing you the check"—this to the sheriff. Then, to Nell, "After that, we can have the whole afternoon to talk."

"Perfect," Nell agreed, giving Sheriff Hickson a big smile. After all, he was the one who'd insisted she be here.

The "important stuff" took considerably less than an hour, probably closer to five minutes. It mostly consisted of Henry, the chauffeur—Nell noticed an earring in one ear and wondered if he was gay; he certainly did seem to be having a good time tossing all the expected notions on their head—getting an oversized check out of the trunk of the car. Beatrice Carver and Sheriff Hickson, remembering to suck in his stomach, posed holding the check between them long enough for both Nell and one of the deputies to take shots until the sheriff had to breathe again. Then there was the exchange of the real check, and Beatrice waved goodbye to Sheriff Hickson and tucked her arm into Nell's.

"Have you eaten or are you up for lunch?" she asked Nell. She suggested they go to the best restaurant in Pelican Bay.

Nell listed several, but the best was Tutweiler's. Well, at least I get to go, Nell thought. She followed the Bentley in her car. After a few blocks, Nell noticed another car also following. That it made no attempt to hide made her suspect Beatrice had not come with just Henry and his earring to protect her. She was proven right when they pulled into the restaurant parking lot and the second car parked next to the Bentley. Three men who would have looked more appropriate coming out of the Saint's locker room emerged.

"Should we eat here?" one of them asked Beatrice.

"Not unless this kind of food appeals to you," she replied, clearly knowing the answer.

A few suggestions from Nell headed them to the best beer and burger joint in town, with an agreement to meet later at the Crier office.

As they entered the restaurant, Nell was glad she'd decided to dress in what she called "high professional" instead of her usual khaki slacks and cotton shirt. Her dark charcoal wool pants and cream raw silk shirt should pass the Tutweiler's standard. Beatrice Carver had dressed to match her car—an elegant burgundy suit, her only jewelry a strand of pearls that had the irregularities to prove them hand-plucked from the sea, and a set of matching earrings.

Four men, all in suits, entered just behind Nell and Beatrice. It could have been simply that their long stride took them to the hostess at the same time Nell and Beatrice reached the reservation desk, and perhaps she hadn't noticed the men entering behind them. The hostess turned to them first, leaving Nell and Beatrice to wait behind them.

This is what it's like, Nell thought as the hostess bantered with the men. Is this slight just the vagaries of life or the color of skin of the woman with me?

The men were led away to a table and the hostess turned to them, saying in a polite voice, "We're busy right now. It might be a wait."

"We'll wait, then," Beatrice Carver answered in an equally cool voice.

"May I take your name?" the hostess asked.

"Nell ... Mrs. Thomas McGraw," Nell answered.

The woman looked at Nell, clearly recognizing the name but not fitting Nell's face to it.

"Junior," Nell added. I hate this kind of stuff—unless it works for me, she thought as she watched understanding cross the woman's countenance: daughter-in-law of one of the town's doyennes, now running the local paper.

"Just a moment," the hostess murmured. She disappeared, then returned and said, "Right this way."

They were led to a table Nell remembered as being saved for regulars. It was in a corner, with a view over the back bayou.

"Okay, what's your theory?" Nell asked as soon as the waiter left them. "Was the cold shoulder from your skin color, that we're 'just' woman, or because neither of us comes here very often?"

"All the above," Beatrice replied easily. "I'd peg it as minus three points for being strangers, and minus five each for the color of my skin and our sex. Hard to tell if we should also take off a point for a white and black woman being together." Then she added, "But your name opened the door."

"It's not fair those things close doors and the name of my husband opens them," Nell said. Then it came out who Thom was, who Mrs. Thomas, Sr. was, how Nell was almost cheating to use that name.

From Nell's life they went to Beatrice's. The family fortune, made first in farming then put into a bank that served colored people when the white banks wouldn't. Beatrice told Nell of her decision to search for her ancestors, the emotions she had on discovering one forefather had been a slave owner.

Nell began taking notes as the coffee was served. After the first tense moment, the service had been impeccable; evidently money and name added enough plus points to make up for the minuses of skin color and sex. I suppose that's progress, Nell thought to herself—there was a time when no black would be anything except a dishwasher for this restaurant and no woman allowed in without a man.

As they left, Nell also noticed the envious looks as Beatrice Carver got behind the wheel of the Bentley. Most of the men here would never own a car like that.

They returned to the Crier office and Nell lead Beatrice through her account, this time from the angle of a newspaper story. The sheriff probably wouldn't like what would end up on the front page, Nell thought as she wrote down Beatrice's words. But she found it a fascinating and timely story, and one with a local twist.

"That's great," Nell said as they wrapped up. "This is front page material."

"Will it cause you problems?" Beatrice asked. "My story brings up all the things that have been hidden for so long. Hidden things upset people."

"I'm a reporter. I report the news, I don't make it," Nell replied. "I'll probably get the usual crank letters to the editor, but I get those when I report the Pelican Bay Pirates lost a football game."

There was a knocking at the door. "My entourage has arrived," Beatrice noted. They both stood up, and she added, "I'd love to see a copy of the story."

They were at the door. Beatrice handed her a card with contact information.

"I'll email you a copy before I print it, to make sure I've got it right, and also send you a copy of the actual paper," Nell offered as she fumbled for her card.

And then Beatrice Carver was gone.

Nell returned to her office; a glance at her watch told her she had a little time to sort through the notes she had taken. She began a draft of the story. It was easy to write while it still was so close in her thoughts. As she saw the words gather on the page, Nell wondered if perhaps Beatrice was right: this story, the story of the bones in the woods, the story of the property theft—all hidden things that she was exposing. Nell worried if it was worth the cost—but then quickly reminded herself she didn't know what the cost would be. Perhaps, as she had so cavalierly said, just a few crank letters, and a story or even two that could go national.

She finished roughing out the draft, then left the camera on Jacko's desk to remind both of them to look through the pictures. Time to go home and get ready for the evening.

TWELVE

IF THIS WAS A real date, I'd be taking a long perfumed bath, not this hasty shower, Nell told herself. She didn't dwell on the fact she rarely took showers in the middle of the day; it usually required working in the yard in the muggy summer heat.

Nell looked at herself in the mirror, watching as her hands hooked the black frilly bra. Go ahead, tell yourself it's the only bra that really works with this dress, she thought as she stared at her breasts framed by the delicate scallops of lace. Suddenly Nell felt like she was watching someone she used to know, a past self abruptly intruding into the present. Dice had been rolled in her life, taking her back ten paces—no, sixteen years—before Thom, back when she was Naomi Nelligan primping for a date. I want this and I hate it, Nell thought. I should be at "happily ever after" instead of another round of kissing frogs and hoping for a prince.

She quickly turned from the mirror, a spray of perfume; not Thom's favorite, but one Mrs. Thomas, Sr. had given her last Christmas. After slipping on her dress, she fastened a strand of pearls around her neck. That and her wedding ring would be her only jewelry.

Nell again stared at her image in the mirror. I'm not sure who I am and I'm not sure what I want, she silently mouthed at her glass twin, one she barely recognized. I guess I'll have to trust my instincts and my experience, Nell thought as she turned away. And being around my mother-in-law's friends as chaperones.

Aaron had said he would pick her up. As Nell waited, discreetly hidden by the curtain she was watching behind, she wondered if she should have taken her own car. If it really was just business I would have, she told herself, but by now she admitted it wasn't just routine business. Instinct and experience, she reminded herself. But they didn't seem very trustworthy.

His car pulled up. He was enough of a gentleman to come to her front door. Nell felt lost, like she couldn't quite remember what she was supposed to do. Then she grabbed her purse, slowed her hasty walk to the door. This is when you need a father to ask your young man just what his intentions are, Nell mused as she stopped to take a breath before opening the door. But her father had never asked those kinds of questions of the few dates who had come to the Nelligan residence. If he talked at all, it was of sports scores or the weather, his banter only to fill the space her mother might load with her crude comments. "So, you're going out with my Naomi, huh? Her sister is the beauty queen, but that's obvious, isn't it?"

Nell opened the door. Aaron smiled at her.

"You look great," he said.

He either sees something that shouldn't be there, Nell thought, such as the animal glow of sexual desire, or else he's a skillful politician, because what I probably most resemble is a deer in the headlights of an oncoming eighteen-wheeler.

"Thank you, Mr. Dupree," Nell replied. "I must compliment you on your political skill. I've had a rushed, busy day, and have spent at most twenty minutes throwing on something that will get over the low bar of acceptability at the Preservation Society, and yet your compliment sounds as sincere as our governor promising no new taxes." Nell turned from him to lock the door and to avoid gauging his expression.

"Oh, dear," he said in mock chagrin. "Now any accolade I pay you will be treated with the high respect given our governor's stump speeches. Tell me, how do I sound sincere when I really am sincere?"

His banter got them to the car. He opened the door for Nell, handing her in. It was something Thom had done, but not as a routine; Nell had been impatient with the markers of polite Southern gentleman society. She didn't object to men opening the door for her, but she also saw no point in waiting in supposed female helplessness for them to do so. "The first person opens the door," she'd told Thom. "Or not if your mother is around and you think she might consider you a bad boy."

But this was a new man and the old rules didn't apply. Aaron got in the car and started it.

"Do you often go to Preservation Society events?" Nell asked to keep a conversation going—and to be in control of it.

"More often now that I'm running for office. But I did even before I had pretensions of political power. Both my mother and father had a strong interest in keeping the history in Pelican Bay, not letting it become overrun by so-called progress."

"Interesting," Nell commented, "considering your father's legacy of developing some of the priciest land in town."

"But he did it the right way. He didn't tear things down, save for a few farm buildings that were falling down anyway. And he didn't go for the quick and cheap cookie-cutter design. He had several different architects and told them he didn't want the houses to look alike.

He may have had critics, but I think they were jealous of his success. He had the vision and will to create one of the best places to live on the coast."

"Don't worry, I'm not asking the question as a reporter," Nell said. There was a subtle defensiveness in Aaron's voice, as if this was his weak spot and he didn't want anyone to know it.

"I didn't think you were," he said smoothly. "Otherwise I would have launched into a treatise on urban planning, creating infrastructure for the modern age, and so on."

"Good. I don't think I could manage that, going over some of these potholes."

He smiled uncertainly, as if not sure whether she was joking or not.

Nell continued. "I'm not going to promise not to ask reporter questions, but I will be fair enough to warn you beforehand." She wondered if she'd already violated her promise; just because we don't quote it doesn't mean that it doesn't get tucked away. Some had praised Dupree, Sr. as the person who'd changed Pelican Bay from a sleepy backwater fishing town, permeated with the smell of oyster shells left in the harbor marsh, to a vibrant costal town known for its artsy community, oak-shaded city square, and high-end real estate. Some cursed him for almost the same reasons. Clearly the son was defensive of the father. Thin skin? Nell wondered. Or were the whispered complaints too close to the truth? It was rumored that Dupree, Sr. had ways of making those who didn't agree with him pay. Those who opposed so much as a stoplight suddenly found themselves without invitations to the high-society Mardi Gras balls, or unable to get loans to expand a business. So far, his name was absent on the property swindles, and his development of them in the '70s and early '80s suggested he'd acquired them later. He could have paid market value and had no idea of how they'd previously changed hands.

But those rumors were old, and Nell was savvy enough to know how much the years were likely to have embellished them. History seemed to have proved Aaron's father right; his properties had brought an influx of money, from well-to-do New Orleanians seeking a weekend home to buyers in upper management in the industry of the area. Pelican Bay had an enviable tax base and citizens who were active and civic-minded.

"Just as long as you ask my opponent equally difficult questions," Aaron answered, his smile still in place and still uncertain.

"Will the current mayor be there?" Nell asked.

Aaron smiled more broadly at her subtle hint this mayor might just be current, not future. "I would expect so. The Historical Preservation Society is something no candidate can afford to ignore. Don't quote me on this, but this is both votes and money."

"And I suppose I'll have to dance with both of you to keep up the appearance of an unbiased media," Nell said.

"A reporter's life is a hard lot," Aaron said, his smile finally losing its uncertain look. "I should stop for gas."

She realized he was heading to the gas station in the center of town. "You're going to the Jones brothers' place?" she asked, wanting to be sure.

"Yes. I know they're not the cheapest, but my family has always gone there. Momma never trusted anyone but old Norbert Jones to work on her cars."

How do I tell him that I can't sit in his car at that gas station, Nell thought. Maybe blunt was best. "Junior Jones was the driver who killed my husband. It would be hard for me ... " She trailed off, no longer trusting her voice.

"My God, I'm so sorry. I should have known that," Aaron said. He turned at the next corner. He reached over and took Nell's hand, and then seemed to realize he didn't have that place in her life. He put his hand back on the steering wheel.

Nell was glad of his concern and also glad he had pulled back.

He changed the subject, chatting about the things he'd missed about Pelican Bay while out in California: the food, the uncrowded beaches; all light and easy topics. After a few minutes Nell was able to fall into his banter, telling tales of the Indiana girl learning to clean a crab. That conversation took them to the Preservation Society affair. It was at one of the older mansions in the city, with enough money in the family to be perfectly preserved. Aaron is right about this being a nexus of wealth, Nell thought as she noted the cars parked along the drive. They were new, they were expensive, and if she had come in her car, she would probably park in back.

She let Aaron be a proper gentlemen and open the door for her. The ambience of the place seemed to demand a return to a more traditional—preserved—time. He confidentially tucked her arm into the crook of his elbow.

Nell caught a glimpse of a possible future—a different life here in this small Southern town that wasn't her home, the wife of the mayor, still running the newspaper, going out on the arm of a handsome and kind and gentleman—but the image was fleeting, quickly replaced by the irregular cobblestones under her feet, the eyes that were already turned their way. Suddenly she felt as unsure as her footing.

I'm not ready for this, Nell thought as the unfamiliar high heels teetered over the cobblestoned drive.

"Nell, how nice to see you out," an older woman said. Nell recognized her as one of Mrs. Thomas's friends. She glanced at the woman's face, searching for an implied criticism—the new widow already stepping out—but saw only kindness and welcome.

I'm no better than Aaron, Nell thought, seeing my fears. I know exactly how long it's been since Thom died, but no one is keeping track.

She returned the woman's greeting, remembering her name in the nick of time. Then she and Aaron made their way through a gauntlet of small talk into the house itself.

As Nell glanced around the room, she realized the money and votes of the Preservation Society members was indeed a political magnet. The mayor was there, as were four of the five aldermen. Sheriff Hickson was there. Nell would have thought him out of place, his belly being more beer than champagne, but he was happily glad-handing his way to the bar.

Nell was handed a glass of the bubbly, and Aaron was swirled into a conversation about beach property rights. Nell ambled on without him, murmuring hellos to people she knew. She did notice all the faces were white, save for those carrying the trays of food and drink. No, Dr. Martin, Josh's pediatrician, was there, and she also saw several men and women in uniform from the local Air Force base.

"Well, Miz McGraw, good to see you all … uh … dressed up and all," was the mayor's greeting.

"Good evening, Mr. Mayor." Nell turned from the painting she'd been contemplating—mostly guessing the cost—to face him.

"Can we talk for just a moment?" His hand was already on her elbow, leading her away.

Probably better to talk to him than dance with him, Nell thought.

"Now, I wouldn't dream of telling you not to run any stories," was his preamble, "but I also know you're a fair-minded woman and … uh, whatever your personal views"—which told Nell her entrance on Aaron Dupree's arm had been noticed—"I know you'll want to keep this as fair an election as possible. And, well, about them bones. Now, you and I are reasonable and smart people and we know some old bones on property my family owned way back when doesn't mean a thing, but some people aren't that smart. Now, those bones have been out there for a long time and not in the newspaper, so all I'm asking is any more stories stay out of the newspaper for another few weeks, until after the election."

Pickings was not known for his short speeches, and he continued. "You know, people can just be superstitious and all that, and bones just gets them fussing. Now, ordinarily I wouldn't even give it a thought, but this year I've got a worthy opponent backed by the Dupree fortune. It's gonna be a close election, and it's just not fair if some old bones make the difference. Can we make a deal?"

"No." Nell was tempted to leave it at that, but politeness and political sense aside, it didn't seem fair to answer his loquaciousness with brevity. "Remember, Mr. Mayor, I'm not the only one reporting this story. It might be better to get my fair version rather than the TV tabloid treatment. They'll make it seem like you murdered those people yourself."

He had a befuddled look on his face, as if he couldn't quite think what to do next, now that Nell had done an end run around his request. "Oh, I guess that is a point. But…" He glanced around, realizing there were too many people about to argue more vehemently. He settled for, "I'd just hate to lose this election because of some old bones in the woods."

"With your record, Mr. Mayor, I doubt you have to worry about bones in the woods determining the outcome of this election," Nell replied.

"Well, yes, that is true. My years in office should count for something, now shouldn't they?"

"And as I said yesterday, you're certainly welcome to write and express your views on the bones in the woods, tell the people yourself what they mean."

"Very good point. Yes, I will write in, probably the best way to handle it. Tell the people myself just what they should think about these things."

The mayor doth protest too much, Nell thought as he was claimed by other partygoers. She would certainly be "fair" enough to print whatever he might send in—she was a cynical enough journalist to know there was no better way to keep a story going than to have someone deny it.

She noted he left his conversation with her to parley with several of the aldermen. Alfonse Gautier was the oldest one, so senile he barely made it to meetings, kept on more because he was a reliable vote for whoever talked to him last. Festus Higgins, one of the newest aldermen, seemed to be doing most of the talking. Nell wondered if he was the brains behind the mayor. Higgins had done well, owning most dry cleaners in this part of the coast. Her guess on him was he'd finally made enough money and now wanted power to go with it, but she'd only seen him a few times.

Nell wandered around, admiring the paintings and the way the mansion had been redone. She came in and out of conversations, mostly the usual on the weather, the home, safe subjects like the need to preserve historical sites without getting into the hard details of who would pay for it and who decided just what historical was.

She was surprised to see Desiree Hunter sipping champagne in front of a large brick fireplace. "I thought I had your ticket," Nell said as she approached.

"You do." Desiree immediately picked up on her underlying question. "It's not what it looks like. I didn't want to come and wasn't going to, with my kids as an excuse, but my mother thwarted my carefully laid plans. She hired a babysitter and had my dress laid out when I got home. She thinks I should get out more, her way of saying I'm a woman without a man and I need to make every effort to change that."

"And how do you feel about changing that?"

"I would have been happy to stay home, spend time with my two kids, put them to bed, and read a book."

"But you're here," Nell noted.

"Yes. Mother is good at getting what she wants. I'm living with her at her house. So … I have to balance between her wants and mine." Desiree sighed. Then, with the barest shrug of her shoulders, she added, "I'm working out of the house. Everything for Aaron's campaign is on the computer Mother bought for me, so I'm there enough in any case. She might have a point that it's good to get out. Just not solely on a man hunt."

"Your mother should know that brothers are the best chaperones. No one is ever good enough for a younger sister."

"You were the younger sister?" Desiree queried.

"The youngest. I'd still be a virgin if it were left up to my brothers."

"I hope Aaron's not that restrictive, but he's going to make sure I don't end up with someone like Frank again."

"Your ex-husband?"

"Yes," she answered, then was silent, looking into the fire as if deciding whether to say more or move on to safer topics. She turned back to Nell. "Aaron blames Frank, but I blame myself. I knew who he was when I married him. I was young enough to think I could change him. Enough love … a child, then another child, a boy this time … " She trailed off.

"But he didn't change."

"No, he didn't. I got old enough and wise enough to know he wouldn't."

"You divorced him?"

"Got the best lawyer my parents' money could buy and had enough sense to know coming home with my tail between my legs was better than another day with him." She paused again as if realizing they were at a party, not two women talking in front of a fireplace. She added in a lighter tone, "Now I just have to find the perfect Mr. Right who can take me away from home."

"Mr. Right of Pelican Bay," Nell said, matching her tone.

"Not too many of them, are there?" Desiree replied.

"I just want the one I had back," Nell said, but her tone wasn't light.

Before Desiree could make a reply, they were joined by three other people, all friends of the Duprees, all brimming with party banter. Nell nodded politely and slipped away. As she did, Desiree reached out and took her hand, a brief press.

Nell headed for the nearest waiter with a tray of champagne. Maybe that would get her back into the party mood. As she finished that glass and took another, she wondered if her comment would get back to Aaron. But it didn't matter, she decided. It was true; she wanted the one she had back. It was also true that was the one she couldn't have.

She occasionally ran into Aaron and they compared notes for a bit before he or she was claimed by someone else. He apologized on one of these occasions, but he did seem to know everyone in the room, and, save for Mayor Hubert Pickings, seemed determined to get their vote.

I like him, she decided after their third encounter. He was funny and smart and seemed able and willing to let her go her own way. He also seemed to understand she didn't want to be clearly marked as his date, and so he was attentive, but not overtly more so than to any of the other women who surrounded him. I also like his sister, Nell realized.

She made a bathroom run. She was suitably impressed with the massive marble tub, separate shower, and the black-and-silver design up to and including the toothbrush holder.

On opening the door, she was surprised to find Sheriff Hickson in the hallway. They were alone in this part of the house. Nell stepped aside to let him through.

But he didn't step aside, instead blocking her way. Either his cologne or his breath had a distinctively gin-ish smell. Nell wondered if he was going to make a pass at her in this empty hallway. He can't be that stupid, she told herself; he knows I'll put it on the front page. Drunken Law Officer Mashes Editor at Preservation Society Fund Raiser.

"Can we talk somewhere in private?" he asked her.

"There doesn't seem to be anyone around," Nell pointed out. Next to the bathroom was as private as she was going to get.

Sheriff Hickson looked over both shoulders to verify no one else was making a privy foray. "About that story and all them pictures you took today," he said in a soft voice. "You know some folks just read the headlines and they get the wrong ideas."

Who knew that the paper had such clout, Nell thought, as she could see where this conversation was going—I could topple the entire power structure of Pelican Bay with a few lines of type.

He continued. "Miz Carver is a fine lady and all that, but we're not really cousins, and I don't want people to get the idea there's a whole line of colored Hicksons somewhere on the wrong side of the track."

"So you're telling me not to run the story?" Nell queried. She almost added "until after the election," to save him the trouble.

"They might even think I've been playing around. Me, a nice proper married man and all. Some of my deputies have been ribbing me about stepping out for some brown sugar."

That he was drunk did little to ameliorate his crude remark. He moved in closer, and the gin smell was more obvious on every exhale.

"Not that I never did nothin' like that," he quickly said, seeing the cold look on Nell's face. "But you know how people talk, how they just got to believe the most bad about people."

"Like someone being so racist it changes everything when they find the color of someone's skin is different from their own?" After Nell said it, she wished they were less alone. By now someone else should have downed enough punch to feel the call of nature, but the hall remained empty.

"Like what?" he fumbled.

"Like when you thought Beatrice Carver was white you were doing everything you could to get me to give the story major play. Change the color of her skin and now you're begging me to not run it at all. Like that."

"Now, Miz McGraw, I know you're a Yankee and all that and maybe you just don't understand how things are down here—"

"I understand perfectly well, Sheriff," she cut in. Racism wasn't limited to the South; Nell could remember some of her mother's ugly comments. "You'd prefer people know you to be a bigot than risk they might have a clue white plantation owners were in the habit of raping their slaves."

"You're going to run the story, aren't you?" he said, his voice hard.

"Front page," Nell retorted. "And I don't remember you taking this conversation off the record."

There was a long, strained silence until finally the sheriff blustered, "Of course this is off the record. Can't come in here to some party and be a snoop reporter. That ain't fair."

"And accosting me at a party like this is fair? You'd be much better off sobering up and talking to me at the office."

Again, the sheriff was silent, his eyes cold and hard. Then suddenly he reared his head back and guffawed. "Damn, lady, pardon my French, but you got balls. No one, man or woman, has dared talk to me like this in about twenty years. Let's do the old back room deal. You can run the story, but take it off the front page and make sure you get in there real prominent this family connection is real old, going back 'bout a hundred years. I don't want no one thinking my Pappy was a fence jumper. My end of the deal is the Jones boys. It'd be real easy to keep them revolving through the door in traffic court. They could get tickets if they forget to use a turn signal. Every once in a while, just for fun, I might have one of my deputies follow them for a spell. That sound like a deal you can live with?"

"I certainly don't object to the Jones brothers realizing that the law does apply to them. I will print the genealogy chart as part of the article and make mention in the first paragraph or so that you're cousins many times removed." More for Beatrice Carver's sake than yours, Nell added silently. "Is that a deal you can live with?"

"That'll do. First thing Monday morning, the boys get the word about those Joneses and their traffic violations."

"First thing Monday morning, I'll write the article."

"Don't suppose I could get a look at that article?"

"Of course you can. On Friday when the paper comes out."

He gave her another stare before saying, "Okay, that's our deal. And Miz McGraw, add a little sugar to that vinegar. It'll go a long way." With that he brushed past her to the bathroom.

Nell stood in the hallway, knowing she'd made a deal with the devil. On principle, she should be appalled at what the sheriff was offering to do to the Jones brothers. If he could do it to them, he can do it to you, she told herself. Then she heard Thom's voice reminding her the difference was that the Jones boys had played fast and loose with legal niceties whereas Nell McGraw had never even shoplifted gum as a teenager. Plus they had threatened her and assaulted Josh. The principle was still shaky, but a good argument could be made for them deserving extra attention from the law in a way that would be egregious if applied to her.

Fearing she would still be in the hall when the sheriff emerged, Nell hastened back to the more peopled area.

She looked for Aaron, but he was in the center of an animated group, no doubt winning votes and, given the look on the face of a blond at his elbow, hearts. This didn't seem the time to pull him away to vent about the assumption that if you were white you "understood" about racial matters, about how things were done. Nell was also relieved she didn't have to confess to the deal she'd made with the sheriff—a little extra harassment for her least favorite criminals in exchange for writing the story she intended to write anyway. She now wished her car was parked at the servants' entrance and she could slip away into the night.

Nell grabbed another glass of champagne—after all, she wasn't driving—and let herself follow another hallway into what had once been a grand ballroom. A DJ took the spot that once might have held a chamber orchestra. Not only did she recognize all the music being played, but Nell was chagrined to realize she'd danced much of her adolescence away to these songs. They were considered rebellious at the time; now they were suitable for the Preservation Society.

She danced for a while, including one whirl around the floor with Marion Nash, the librarian, until an older gentleman tapped her shoulder, obviously feeling that it was too feminist for women to dance without a man. The gin on his breath reminded Nell of her encounter with the sheriff and she quickly pleaded breathlessness, content to watch the gyrations from the wallflower position.

That was where Aaron found her. He bowed, then asked, "May I have this dance?" Nell felt a slight thrill of anticipation as he led her out to the dance floor. The song was a slow one, and he took her hand and placed his other arm around her waist.

It's been a long time, Nell thought, since I danced with a man; last time was with Thom at a Mardi Gras party.

Aaron's cologne was subtle and his breath had not a single hint of gin. She enjoyed being in a man's embrace, but then the small things crept it. How different his hands were from Thom's; the height of his shoulder where her hand rested felt odd, out of place. Even the champagne couldn't cause Nell to relax into this dance. She felt too aware of all the ways he wasn't Thom.

I'm not ready for this, Nell knew with a heavy certainty. Even if love comes, it can't replace what has been. The clarity overcame the false giddiness from the sparkling wine. I wish I'd known this yesterday, she thought. She could have been upfront with Aaron, stated plainly that at least for a while, she could offer nothing beyond friendship. But his arms around her spelled out he wanted more than six months of handshakes good night.

"I'm sorry," Nell said as the music ended, "it's been a long time since I danced with anyone other than my husband, and I'm just not coordinated with anyone else." That wasn't true; she'd certainly danced with other men—and a few women—but always Thom was in the background, and always that last dance was with him.

"You were fine," Aaron assured her.

Nell wondered if he'd understood her implied message, but on this dance floor at this party was not the time to be more explicit.

The rest of the evening seemed a blur. She took another glass of champagne, but it only gave her a headache. She didn't return to the dance floor, citing the headache when asked.

Aaron sensed her changed state, but Nell couldn't tell if he had any clue of the real reason or if he took it to be only the headache. He fetched a glass of water for her and produced two aspirin. Then he was captured by a TV news crew. They were covering all the mayoral candidates—more likely trying to catch them sipping a drink or worse, as this was the more tabloid news team.

Nell suggested she could catch a ride home, but Aaron told her he was leaving soon. The party was winding down; he'd captured most of the votes he was likely to get. He was good on his word, and after a few required goodbyes, he was back at her side. "Probably too many candidates in the room," he said. "That'd give any reporter a headache."

"Or the politicos demanding I not run some stories." Nell proceeded to get Aaron up to speed on both the mayor's and the sheriff's requests. It was a brief version; she left out her deal with the sheriff. There are some sins you just shouldn't confess on the first date.

Aaron listened sympathetically, murmuring about politics resembling swamps: dark, murky, and full of snakes. He then added he had to put in a token protest on the story about the bones, because if he didn't then it would look like he was encouraging her to run the story for his political advantage.

"And if asked, I will testify that you made a gallant effort to postpone more articles until after the election, but I insisted on having freedom of the press. Will that keep your hands clean?"

"Clean enough for an election," Aaron agreed.

They headed for the door. They managed to arrive at the same time as Hubert Pickings. He didn't seem happy to see his rival in such proximity, and the amount of alcohol he'd consumed—his breath told a tale of bourbon—did little to turn him into an agreeable man.

"Well, Mr. Dupree. See you cozying up with the local press."

"Good evening, Pickings," Aaron said tersely.

"Think your Dupree money's gonna win you this election, don't you?"

"I think the issues and our abilities are going to win this election," he retorted.

"You're speaking like you think your little lady friend is gonna quote you," the mayor spat out.

On his face was a sheen of desperation. He had to know Aaron Dupree had a very good chance of winning. He was, Nell realized, fighting as a caged animal does—blindly, enraged, and with no hope of getting out.

"Good night, Hubert. I'll see you at our debate." Aaron took Nell by the arm and brushed past him.

"Yeah, that's right. Thom McGraw barely in his grave and already you use your dick to get an endorsement," Hubert Pickings called after them.

They both stopped and turned again to face him.

"You little runt ..." Aaron started.

Nell cut in. Using her most polite tone, putting every ounce of sugar she could into the vinegar, she said, "Excuse me, Mr. Mayor. I'm afraid I didn't catch that. I thought I heard you express a crude, sexist lie using terms suitable only for lowlife drunks. Since I know that anyone with the wisdom and experience to run the City of Pelican Bay wouldn't use such vulgar, foul terms, nor make up exaggerated and ugly stories, I'm sure I must have misheard you. Could you repeat what you just said?"

By now they were the focus of attention, with enough blue-haired Preservation dowagers at the mayor's elbow to ensure he would be not just a fool, but an utter fool, to repeat himself.

Nell was disappointed when he proved, at least in this instance, that he wasn't an utter fool.

"Uh, sorry, can't remember what I said. Somethin' like good night." One of his friends had enough sense to take him by the arm and lead him away from the throng at the door.

"That's not what—" Aaron started.

"Let's go," Nell interrupted. She whispered, "He's made a fool of himself. You don't need to do the same."

They exited the house and into the evening.

The air seemed to cool Aaron down. In a rueful tone, he said, "And I was so looking forward to being a macho turd."

"Defending the little woman?"

"Something like that. But I'm gathering the little woman can defend herself."

"When I need to."

"But can I punch him after the election?" Aaron asked.

He was bantering, but Nell recognized under it was a real urge to have gotten into a fight, or at least mark his territory. Part of her appreciated it and part of her detested it. Her headache took it to the detest side.

"The man was drunk and stupid. Can't you let it go?"

"I'm trying, but he just pisses me off."

"Beat him in the election. That ought to be close enough to fisti-cuffs."

"Not when you want blood." He opened the car door for her.

"I'm sorry, Aaron. I'm tired and have a headache and I'm not in the mood for blood."

He seemed chastened at her words and was silent. Then he said, "My mother was always after my dad to put up more of a fight, ac-cused him of being too reasonable. Guess I was listening to my mother's voice."

"And your reasonable dad ended up one of the richest and most powerful men on the coast."

"You're right. My sister said the same thing. Maybe I should lis-ten to the reasonable women around me."

"Wise choice. You can take this one home and let me sleep off my headache," Nell said, but as she did, she noticed that the cool air and being out of the confines of the crowd eased the tension of her head.

They talked little on the way home. Nell realized she was melan-choly. Aaron was a nice man, but he wasn't Thom, and being with him seemed only to bring home that she would never be with Thom again. All the coming dinners, the parties, the charity events, would be without him. Even though she'd told Aaron to blow off the may-or's comment, it rankled her, echoed the accusing voice in her head. Thom McGraw was barely in his grave. Nell knew she wasn't ready to get involved with anyone, but a physical part of her wanted to be touched. She briefly wondered what it would be like to invite Aaron in, to go to bed with him, to linger however fleetingly in the oblivion of physical passion. But the longing was quickly intermixed with the vision of taking him in the same bed she and Thom had shared for so long.

They pulled into her driveway.

"Aaron, I had a good time with you …" Nell said, her hand on the car door. Do I say it now, she wondered, or do I just open the door and worry about it the next time?

He didn't give her a chance. His answer was to wrap his arms around her and kiss her.

Nell was shocked at how quickly her body responded to him, how much she wanted this. Then the mayor's taunt, "Thom Mc-Graw barely dead in his grave," reverberated in her head and she pulled away.

"I'm honored and I'm flattered and … I can't," she said. "I'm not ready for this, I'm sorry. But … it's too soon."

"No, I'm sorry. I was out of line," Aaron said gallantly.

"I'm … ambivalent about this. Right now … I'm terribly lonely, but it's because I miss Thom. I can't want someone else yet. Someday, when I can put away things like the cheap pens he used to use without bursting into tears, I hope I'll be ready for something more."

"I understand. No, I probably don't understand. What I went through was divorce. By the time the separation was final, the love was gone. I don't want to be a cad, but I can't promise to wait around for five years, either. Keep me in your life, Nell. Let me know where you are."

"That sounds fair. I sincerely hope I can get beyond this in less than five years … but I don't know. Maybe six months, maybe longer."

He bent in and gently kissed her on the cheek. Then he was quickly out his door and around to open hers. Nell got out and walked to her front step, but said nothing. She glanced back once as she entered the house. He was waiting by the car, watching her.

After she gently pulled the door closed, she heard his car pull away. She felt both relief and loneliness. She hurried into the bedroom and flung off her dress, as if it was evidence of her betrayal. She then rushed to the bathroom, throwing water on her face, washing off the makeup, a bare bit of blush and powder and lipstick. But the face looking back at her in the mirror still showed guilt and despair.

This is too hard, she thought. I take a few steps out of my numb shell—going back to work, contemplating finding love again—and all it does is crash me into grief and guilt and an empty house with empty rooms.

Nell quickly threw on an old pair of jeans and a sweater. She felt she just couldn't be in the house right now, with the memories and without the needs of her children to force the demons away.

Where am I going, she thought as she pulled out of the driveway? She answered herself, it doesn't matter. First she headed to the beach, to drive along its moonlit length, but that held memories. Sometimes she and Thom would detour, a few extra minutes in each other's company with the waves and the sun, or the glistening water and the moon.

Someplace else, Nell thought, turning away from the shore. She found herself driving on the highway, the strip with its garish chains of fast-food restaurants and low-budget stores. This was the mecca for the newly enfranchised with driver's licenses. Besides her, the oldest person on the road was the police car that was slowly cruising along. She turned off the highway into a residential section. Its streets were quieter: cars parked, windows softly lit, an occasional blue of a TV screen visible.

But even these quiet homes with quiet lives held demons. Nell resented them, the placid existence she supposed they lived, all the horrors of life safely on television. She knew she wasn't being fair. Her house would show the same façade, the same gentle light. But alone in her car, Nell didn't have to be fair. She could be angry and scared and desolate.

Get away from the quiet houses, the ones that mirror my own; go to an unfamiliar part of town, with no memories, no glimpses of happier times. She turned down a road and then another and ended up on the old highway that used to connect Pelican Bay to other towns, but its worn two lanes had been replaced long ago by one with four lanes and then the interstate. Now it was a strip of tired donut places, auto repair shops, and bars, the tense zone between the poor white section of town and the poor black one.

The bright colors of neon beer signs alternated with the dark and shuttered businesses. There were few people on the street: several outlined in the fluorescent of the donut shop, one man in a shapeless coat pushing a shopping cart that was probably his home.

Then Nell spotted his truck. It was pulled over and parked on a side street, but there was no mistaking J.J.'s massive black truck with the Confederate flag in the back window. Nell turned and parked in front of it, staring at it in her rear-view mirror as if mesmerized.

There was still a dent in the front end, one of the headlights smashed, remains of the damage J.J. had received from the accident. That front fender had swerved into their car, crumpling the hood, sending them veering off the road head-on into the trees. One of the thick branches had come through the windshield on the passenger side—where Thom has been sitting.

How dare he be out here drinking, driving that truck, like he hadn't killed a man with it? Suddenly furious, Nell scrabbled in the glove compartment, looking for something sharp, something that could scratch or gouge. But even the usual pen wasn't there, given to Lizzie a few days before because she'd forgotten to put one in the purse she decided to use that day.

"Damn it," Nell swore aloud. She looked at her keys, debating whether to risk breaking them. "Goddamn it," she swore again. She couldn't just leave his truck in peace, as if it hadn't so horrifically invaded her life. What if he's drunk and kills someone again?

She silently got out and walked to the corner of the street. All was quiet and no one was about. There were vague noises from the bar in the middle of the block, presumably the one where J.J. was celebrating his bail and freedom. A disco beat was playing, voices raised over it. There would be a sharp increase of the noise if the door opened, Nell decided. That would have to be her warning.

She returned to the truck and knelt next to one of the tires, fumbling off the air valve in the dark. Using the tip of a key, she pressed open the valve. The hiss of air was loud and sharp in the dark. Abruptly, Nell stopped, her heart thudding. Someone must have heard, she thought. But there were no noises save for the background from the bar, a shush of wind in the trees. She opened the tire again, stopping every few seconds to listen.

I wouldn't be a good crook or a vandal, she thought as she again listened for any sound of discovery. The tire seemed little affected. I could be here all night. Her only hope was that J.J. would stay in the bar for an equally long time.

Nell let the tire hiss for a long time before pausing again, but the sidewall still felt firm to her touch.

"Goddamn it!" she suddenly let out, a wave of anger and frustration coming over her. She pounded the tire with her fist, its firmness at each impact mocking her. "You bastard," she muttered. She again jammed the key in the valve, the rush of air escaping obscuring the sound of footsteps until she felt a hand on her shoulder.

Nell jumped and whirled away, her keys still in her hand, ready to scratch and fight.

"Calm down, it's a friend." Marcus Fletcher stood before her.

"What are you doing here?" they both said at the same time.

His answer was calm. "I was down the street at Joe's Corner, having my usual two Saturday beers. I was walking home."

Nell said nothing, her brain coming up with no explanation. She finally settled for the truth. "You must think I'm crazy."

"No. But I am curious."

Suddenly it came rushing out. "It's his truck. J.J. Jones, the man who killed Thom, my husband. He just got out on bail and now he's here drinking again. I was driving around, I couldn't stay at home, my children at their grandmother's and the house is too empty. I wanted to drive someplace that didn't have memories and then I saw his truck and I couldn't just leave it . . . leave it for him to drive away in."

Marcus looked at her, then at the truck. His eyes narrowed at the Confederate flag proudly displayed in the back window. "You shouldn't be out here by yourself doing this," he said. "So why don't I help you and let's do it right." He pulled out a small pocket knife, opened it, and jabbed the blade deeply into the tire that had so frustrated Nell.

Wrenching the blade out, he proceeded to the next tire. "You just let the air out; he can fill them up again easy enough. Might be stupid enough to drive around on the rims and ruin them, but you can't always count on people being stupid when you need them to be."

He pulled the knife out of the second tire and said, "Keep a watch" as he moved to the side of the truck on the street.

Nell walked to the corner, looking both ways, but no one, save them, was about. Only by straining to hear it could she pick out the soft hissing of the tires from the other noises of the night. It hadn't been that loud, she realized; only in her head, rambling around with guilt and fury.

"All done," he said softly.

Nell rejoined him at the truck. Why am I crying, she thought, realizing that there were tears running down her face.

He clearly noticed, handed her a tissue, and then said, "Let's leave him a message." Marcus carved *"KKK = Idiots"* on the driver's door. His handiwork was crude but legible. "It should cost people to be racists and it should cost people to be drunken murderers. Now let's get out of here. Where are you parked?"

"Right here," Nell replied, trying to wipe the tears away. Relief, that's why I'm crying, she thought. And maybe guilt and frustration and anger. Four flat tires was small satisfaction. Putting him in jail wouldn't be enough.

"Okay, we need to drive far enough away from J.J.'s truck. He has the kind of temper that might take it out on anything close by."

Nell got in her car, with Marcus climbing in the passenger side. "Where to?" she asked as she turned the ignition.

"Halfway down the block. You can park in my driveway. He can't go on a rampage against every car on the block."

"Maybe I should just drop you off and go home," Nell offered.

"You're in no condition to go home alone," Marcus said. His voice was calm, even warm, as if stating a mere fact.

He pointed to a driveway and she pulled in.

"Now let's go back to Joe's, find a quiet corner. We can talk or be silent, whatever you need."

"Thanks," was all Nell said.

They walked back past the truck, the tires now satisfyingly listing, and at the corner turned the opposite way from the bar with the disco music. In the next block was Joe's, a hand-lettered sign over the door, no blinking neon beer signs in the windows, only the soft glow of light from some wall sconces and from behind the bar.

Marcus nodded to several people as he led Nell to a table in the back. Billie Holiday was playing softly in the background.

The barman brought over a beer for Marcus, presumably his standing order.

"I'll have the same," Nell said to his questioning look. When he brought the beer, it was cold, and it took away the fever she'd felt when she saw that devil truck.

"You still must think I'm crazy," she said as she sat the glass down.

"A few years back, I lost my wife. She got up one day, said she felt dizzy, and then collapsed on the kitchen floor. I called 911 right away, but it was too late. A massive heart attack. She was sixty-eight. We had a good life together. Four kids, got ourselves through Darin not coming back from Vietnam, all the other kids now adults with kids of their own. She got a number of years with the grandkids. We all got to go and she went quickly, so I can't really complain. But, no, I don't think you're crazy. I had almost fifty years of not being lonely. When it hit, it hit hard."

"It's been a month," Nell said softly.

"A month? You could be howling half-naked at the moon and I wouldn't think you'd be crazy."

"Thank you. I will, however, try and confine my insanity to misdemeanors of the clothed variety."

Marcus picked up his glass and touched it to hers. "Woman that can manage a touch of humor after a month is going to do all right. Took me almost six weeks before I got there."

"It seems so hard," Nell said softly.

"Yeah, it does and it will. It always will."

They sat in silence, listening to the music.

Marcus went to the bar and got two more beers. There was an unspoken agreement that neither of them wanted to go home, and they had achieved a communion of grief that could best be expressed in simply being together.

After a few songs, the music changed to Louis Armstrong jazz, and it changed the mood.

Nell asked, "How do you know about J.J.? You said he was the kind to rage at anything."

"Man that parks his truck with a Confederate flag in this neighborhood gets noticed. He came out of that bar one afternoon, found someone had stuck a beer car on his antenna, and he just let loose. Screamed racist drivel at a teenage boy who happened to be walking by. He might have started swinging, but about five of us came out of Joe's and I guess he was only drunk enough to take on one black boy, not five black men."

"How long ago was that?"

"A while back, probably a year or two. A few vandal things happened right after that. We couldn't prove it on him, but the suspicion was high. Someone threw a brick through the window at Joe's and people saw a black truck speeding away. I don't think anyone around here would mind if he spent a few years in prison and left us alone."

"What about his brothers?"

"None of those apples fell far from the tree. Every list we ever made of Klan members had Norbert Jones'—the father's—name on it. J.J. has the hottest temper and hangs out in the bars the most, from what I hear. But given a choice between any of them and a rattlesnake, I'd take the snake any day."

Nell told him about the probable assault on Josh.

"Two men that'd go after a young boy to get back at his widowed mother? That's lower than despicable. Don't know that I can do much, but if you give me a call, I can get five big guys from Joe's and a few other places to come around."

"Thanks, but I hope not to need it, especially as I've bartered my soul to the devil." Nell proceeded to tell him about the sheriff's consternation at finding out his rich cousin was black, his drunken confrontation with her at the bathroom, and the deal they'd made. By the time she'd finished and Marcus had added his comments, they were both laughing so hard they were almost crying.

"I'd give half the hair on my head to see the look on his white face when he caught sight of her black face," Marcus hooted.

"I won't take your hair, but I have pictures. I made sure I got several of that look. It stayed on his face for a long time."

"Page two, with one of those pictures. I'll trade that for getting you the five guys. You can trade off this story to the whole town. Get everyone to go after the Jones boys."

They finished their third beer before finally winding down.

"This is just what I needed," Nell told him.

"A little vandalism, a few tears, and some belly laughs. I have to say it's been a while since I've had this much fun. We should do it again."

"We might skip the vandalism. I'm a much better newspaper woman than I am a criminal."

With the same unspoken agreement that had held through the evening, they both stood to leave. It was only as they walked out that Nell realized she'd been the only white person in the bar. As if it matters, she thought. Maybe Josh and Lizzie will get to a place where they won't even notice.

As they came out, Marcus said, "We might want to go the other way."

Nell looked where he was looking. A group of men were leaving the disco bar, heading in the direction of J.J.'s truck. From this distance they were just a blur of shapes, their voices loud with liquor and bragging.

She and Marcus turned, going around the block the other way. As they rounded the corner that would bring them back to Marcus's house and Nell's car, they heard the sound of loud cursing, confirming that J.J. had indeed been one of the exiting men.

Nell took Marcus's arm, as if conferring some protection on both of them. They walked slowly and quietly to his house, sticking to the shadows of the street. When they got to his driveway, they both stood beside Nell's car, watching the scene over its roof, barely visible.

When J.J. started screaming, "Someone is going to pay for this," Marcus went into his house and called 911, then rejoined Nell as they watched for the arrival of the police.

"Maybe I should saunter by when the police get here and suggest that J.J.'s blood alcohol level violates his bail," Nell whispered.

"Be good if you could do that without him seeing you," Marcus softly answered.

When the police car arrived, Nell recognized one of the men as Boyce Jenkins, the officer supposedly looking into Josh's attack. He greeted J.J. as if he knew him. Nell shivered in the shadows and Marcus put an arm around her shoulders.

They watched for a long time, the police taking the report. Finally they left and J.J. went back to the bar.

"Perhaps it's time for me to turn into a pumpkin," Nell said.

"Can't imagine you accomplishing that, but you might want to get home," he answered.

Nell hugged him, then impulsively bent up and kissed him on the cheek. "Thank you," she said. "See you Monday morning."

"Monday indeed. Be safe," Marcus said.

He watched her as she drove away.

After she turned a corner, then another, she glanced at her watch. It was almost two in the morning. No wonder I'm finally tired, Nell thought as she yawned at a stop sign.

Her neighborhood was dark, save for a few night lights. She quietly closed the car door, as if making sure no neighbors would hear her late arrival and perhaps link it to an act of vandalism on the other side of town.

I'm being paranoid, she thought as she entered the house. Except, if anyone thought hard about it, I should be high on the list of suspects likely to attack J.J.'s truck. It was probably a good thing he had a habit of parking his truck with its racist symbol in a black neighborhood. That added a long—and anonymous—list of suspects.

Nell crept through the house, turning on no lights until she got to her bedroom. She hung up the dress she'd flung off. Then she got ready for bed, but lay still for only a minute. Her thoughts buzzed through her head; there were too many things to think about from this night. She got back up, still not turning on lights, and went back to the kitchen. Using the dim glow from the street, she found a glass and her bottle of Scotch. She poured a generous amount in the glass and started to put the Scotch bottle back under the counter, then changed her mind and carried it with her back to the bedroom.

THIRTEEN

NELL WAS WOKEN BY the ring of the phone. She groggily sat up, disoriented as to time and day. She glanced at her clock while the phone still rang. It was after ten. She glanced at the Scotch bottle, and then answered the phone.

"Nell. Ah, you're home," her mother-in-law greeted her.

"Yes, Mother, I'm home," Nell answered. She had the first inklings of a headache.

Mrs. Thomas, Sr. got right to her point. "Someone drove by last night at around midnight; your car wasn't in the drive."

This was guaranteed to give her a headache. "I had it around back; I was working on the engine."

"After dark?" Then Mrs. Thomas seemed to remember her daughter-in-law was not an auto mechanic. "This isn't a joke; I was concerned about you being out at all hours. Lizzie was very upset at the news coverage."

"What news coverage?" Nell demanded, sitting up in bed, which jarred her head into throbbing.

"From last night," Mrs. Thomas said, annoyingly withholding what she knew.

Nell had visions of a hidden camera catching her slashing J.J.'s tires. "What news coverage are you talking about? Why was Lizzie upset?"

"Of course, I haven't told them your car wasn't in the drive after midnight. That would only upset them further."

You bitch, Nell almost hissed. She managed to keep her voice calm enough to say, "Mother, I have no idea what you're talking about. A little more information would be helpful." Like if I should be calling a lawyer to arrange a plea bargain.

"Well, you can't blame her," her mother-in-law said frostily. "We were watching the ten o'clock news and there was that picture of you dancing with another man at the Preservation Society function. She was quite upset at seeing you that way."

Nell punched her pillow, knowing the sound wouldn't carry. "I danced with several men last night, and even some women. I neither made nor received any marriage proposals," she said tersely, suspecting that Lizzie was less upset than Mrs. Thomas, Sr.

"It was a close waltz with that man running for mayor, the handsome one. And then your car wasn't in the driveway until, who knows, just minutes ago."

"I did dance with Aaron Dupree. He's a nice man; he dropped me here at around ten in the evening. We chastely said good-night." Nell was of a generation that could call a mere kiss chastity. "Then I found I didn't want to be here alone so I met some friends. And just as chastely left them a little after midnight." She could also call only a few hours a little; it was compared to, say, a whole day.

"Oh," Mrs. Thomas said. "Well, we were worried. Where did you go?"

Nell counted a beat and skipped her first answer—"None of your damn business"—and instead answered, "Joe's Corner, over on Government."

"Joe's? On Government? Isn't that a ... colored bar?"

Did I imagine it or was she going to say something else? Nell counted another beat before saying, "I was with some African-American friends and that's their usual hangout." She decided it was best to gloss over that she had been out with a man, even with the thirty-plus years difference in their ages; she was sure Mrs. Thomas would see something salacious.

"You went out after coming home from the Preservation Society do?" Mrs. Thomas asked.

"Yes, I went out." A silence hung between them. Nell filled it. "The house felt too empty and I didn't want to be here with my memories. I just needed to be out and with people."

"At a bar?"

"Tutweiler's wasn't open at that time."

"Nell, I know it's hard, but you really do need to pull yourself together and not go off like this."

"Why? So my car can be in the driveway when your spies, I mean friends, come by to check up on me?" Nell retorted.

Mrs. Thomas was silent, then totally ignored Nell's comment and said, "Well, we've just left church and are on our way to luncheon. I did want to call and make sure everything was all right. It would be too stressful to have to worry through our time at Tutweiler's. I'll tell them you're fine. I'll have them back to your place at around two or so." With that Mrs. Thomas hung up, expressing her disapproval by giving Nell no chance for a final reply or even a coolly polite goodbye.

Nell slammed the phone down, then gingerly rolled out of bed, shambled to the bathroom, and quickly downed two aspirin. Then she added a third one, to give her headache a clue that she really wanted it gone.

After that, the first thing she did was hide the Scotch back in the cupboard, then washed, dried, and put the glass she'd used back in its usual place. Then she made toast and slathered butter on it, the aspirin already starting to gnaw at her stomach.

By the time her headache had finally subsided to a mere dull throb, Josh and Lizzie arrived home. Mrs. Thomas chose to let them off, not even getting out of the car. Nell didn't go out to greet her either.

Lizzie walked in, slammed her overnight bag down, and announced, "I can't go to school tomorrow."

Josh had followed her in and was quiet, as if to balance her noise. "Why not?" Nell asked.

That unleashed a firestorm. "Because I can't face all the kids after they got a glimpse of my mother, the hussy widow!"

"Honey, what are you talking about?" Nell tried to keep her voice calm and reasonable.

"You know what I'm talking about!" Lizzie yelled.

"No, I'm afraid I don't."

"They had it on TV last night. You dancing with that man! The TV announcer saying, 'And here is Mrs. Thomas McGraw, the recent widow of newspaperman Thom McGraw, dancing with the recently divorced Aaron Dupree, candidate for mayor.' How could you?" Lizzie let out in a wail.

This is my punishment for leaving them in the clutches of my mother-in-law for twenty-four hours, Nell thought. "He asked me to dance," she said blandly.

"And you just had to do it," Lizzie shot back.

"No, I didn't have to do it. But it was a song I like, and he's a reasonable dance partner, so I chose to do it."

"That's my point!" Lizzie screamed. "Dad hasn't been dead for a month yet and you're already dancing with other men!"

Nell decided this was not the time to point out it had been over a month. Her temper was fraying, but the last thing she wanted was to devolve into a shouting match. Let's try reasonable one more time, Nell decided, before I bring out roaring bitch. "Lizzie, honey, I can see that you're upset. I'm not out dating, nor do I have any interest in doing so. But just because your grandmother"—well, so much for fair—"thinks I should wear a black dress everywhere I go and only talk to other widows and spinsters, it doesn't mean that's what I'll do. All I did was dance with Aaron. One dance."

"In front of a TV camera, where everyone could see it," Lizzie cut in.

"I didn't notice the camera and wasn't aware they were filming. And remember, that's the skankier TV station anyway. They always sensationalize things."

"If you hadn't danced with him at all, they couldn't have filmed it!"

"Lizzie, be reasonable..."

"I am being reasonable! You're the one being a hussy!"

"Lizzie!" Nell shot back. Reasonable faded to a dim hope. "I don't appreciate that word when I've done nothing to deserve it."

"What do you think Dad would say about this?"

"He'd ask why I took a whole month before dancing with someone." Thom might well have, but Nell was aware it would do little to calm her daughter. She had to worry about calming herself first.

"Mom!" Lizzie wailed, as expected. "He'd accuse you of ... of being a slut!"

"Your father had much stricter standards for sluttish behavior than one dance in a room full of people. Like sneaking off and riding behind a boy on his motorcycle." Nell knew that Thom would probably have labeled that foolish, not sluttish, but she had sunken to trading insults with her daughter. One of us has to be the adult here, Nell realized. And Lizzie, being fourteen, made Nell look like the only qualified candidate.

"Mom! That has nothing to do with the issue here!"

Since neither being reasonable nor mean had much impact, Nell decided on the law of the land. "Look, I'm not a slut and I won't be called names in my own home. I did nothing to be ashamed of and I'm not going to be castigated, either by you or, in proxy, by Mrs. Thomas. If you want to live your life with tolerance and understanding then you'd better give a little in return. Got it?"

Lizzie fumed for a full minute. She knew by the tone of Nell's voice that she had crossed the line, but she was too lost to give in. "Fine. Do whatever you want to do. I'm out of this house when I'm eighteen!" Lizzie stomped off to her room, closing the door with a loud bang.

Josh and Nell just looked at each other. His face was expressionless, and Nell couldn't tell if he sided with her or his sister.

"I'm sorry about that," Nell said to him. "Are you upset by seeing me—on TV, no less—dancing with someone else?"

"Naw, I don't think it's that big a deal, but Grandmom and Lizzie were going at it like you were some sort of criminal. It's like me going out on a science trip and getting paired with some girl. Next time it might be another girl."

Nell decided against pointing out how far he was stretching his analogy. A random pairing wasn't the same as choosing a dance partner, and perhaps the sexual tension possible in that situation was invisible to him—twelve and more excited by sharks than girls—than it was to his older sister and his grandmother.

"Yeah, it's something like that," she said. "It doesn't really mean anything. I actually danced with several people last night, including Marion the Librarian."

"I didn't know that women could dance together."

"Oh, we do it all the time. When we get tired of waiting for some man to ask us and the music is good," Nell explained, glad they had moved on to more innocent topics and that Josh, unlike Lizzie, seemed not to have been scarred for life.

Nell took advantage of Josh being a perfect son and used the afternoon to do the yard work that hadn't been done. She let him push the mower, a task Thom usually did. It felt good to be outside; the day was a crisp, cool fall one with brilliant sunshine. The physical labor seemed to purge Nell of both her headache and the emotions left over from the last twenty-four hours. It also gave her time with Josh. The imperfect mother part of Nell didn't mind that Lizzie was alone huffing in her room.

They finished bagging the last of the raked leaves just as the sun was setting. Nell suggested they walk to the beach and watch it from there, an idea Josh happily accepted.

Have I been so inattentive, Nell thought as they walked the three blocks to the beach, that my son hangs by my side as if starving for any notice? Josh always liked to scour the shoreline for new or interesting shells and sea creatures. Usually once or twice a week, Thom would take him there and they would beach comb for an hour or so. Sometimes Nell joined them, and she remembered Josh skipping ahead, just barely in sight. Now he was walking by her side. She suspected if she reached out and took his hand, he would allow her, something in the last few years he had wiggled out of as being "too mushy."

Maybe he was just glad to have this routine back in his life. Suddenly, Nell realized he must have missed the beach, the custom of seeing it change every few days. He hadn't once asked to go, even mentioned it. Lizzie got attention because she demanded it. Josh was trying too hard to be perfect to ask for attention. I have to be better, Nell thought, be more aware of the places they've lost Thom, do a better job of making up for it. And stop bullets with my bracelets, as well as make the world safe for democracy.

But Josh seemed happy, naming the birds that flew by, even if it was mostly a litany of "seagull, seagull, seagull."

They walked on the beach until there was little light left, barely enough to get home by. When they got back, Nell noticed there were no lights on. She imagined Lizzie intoning, "It's all right, my hussy mother likes me to sit in the dark." She found her steps slowing as they got closer.

Nell asked herself the question she probably should have asked at the beginning. What was making Lizzie so upset? Other than Mrs. Thomas, Sr. egging her on. Was it her mother showing hints of sexuality? Lizzie had seemed to like Aaron when they'd met; was there some jumbled jealous crush going on here? Was it an eruption of anger and grief and this was just something to hang it on?

It was probably some tangled conjunction of all the above, plus five other things Nell didn't think of. The next question was how to handle it. Any TV mom or dad would have already solved the crisis. Of course, TV moms and dads had the advantage of being able to write in a reasonable daughter, one who could easily see the wisdom of her mother's gentle reasoning within the allotted half hour.

They entered the house and Nell began flipping on lights. Lizzie hadn't completely been a conservator of energy, however, as the overly loud sound of music, some mournful ballad, came from the closed door of her room.

Nell decided the most satisfyingly reasonable—and the most satisfyingly annoying—plan would be to just ignore her; her too-loud music and the dim house was an attempt to gain attention. She told Josh to put on some music. Then they tackled the kitchen, cleaning it up and ordering a pizza in the process. Since Lizzie was absent, she and Josh chose the toppings, including olives, which Lizzie claimed she couldn't stand.

The bustle of a rung doorbell and delivered pizza produced a crack in the door. Then the door shut again and the music got louder.

They had their pizza in front of the TV, Nell letting Josh watch his nature shows. He was a willing ally, content to be the focus of his mother's attention.

Lizzie broke down in the middle of the evening, making a stony-faced and silent run to the kitchen. Nell listened to her rustle in the refrigerator, going after the leftover pizza.

Suddenly there was a wail. "Olives! You know I hate olives! How could you be so mean?"

Nell sat for a moment, then decided that ignoring her would only make things worse. She got up and stood in the kitchen door. "You didn't seem interested in eating, and Josh and I both like olives. You can always just pick them off."

"No I can't! They make everything else taste olivey."

Nell sighed.

"I can't go to school tomorrow! I haven't had anything to eat and I can't face what everyone is going to say!"

"That's enough, Elizabeth. You're going to go to school, unless you produce a fever of over a hundred, and there's plenty of food to eat in this house. Starvation isn't a possibility."

"You hate me!" And she burst into tears. She sat the pizza down on the counter with a loud clatter.

At least she didn't throw it on the floor. "I don't hate you," Nell said, but even she heard her exasperated tone. She contemplated divvying up her children, keeping Josh and letting her mother-in-law reap what she had sown. But then possessiveness flashed in her. You're not going to get my daughter, Nell silently told Mrs. Thomas Sr.

"Honey, I don't hate you. I think you're very angry that your dad got killed. It's damned unfair. You've got a right to be furious. But you can't let anger fly all over the place and at everyone. I love you and I will always love you."

"No you don't," Lizzie replied, but it had lost its vehemence; she said it with a trembling lip.

"Unconditionally. I love you." Just not everything you do, Nell thought, but right now wasn't the moment to point out that little detail.

"Enough to order another pizza?"

"Enough to order another pizza," Nell said.

"Really?" Lizzie asked, as if unsure that her stern mother would really be so profligate.

"Really. Just remember you'll be eating the leftovers tomorrow." Unconditional love is an extra pizza.

With that, Lizzie dried her eyes. She picked up the pizza menu, studying it as if she might actually order something besides pepperoni, extra cheese, and mushrooms. With her eyes firmly fixed on the flyer, she said, "I'm sorry. I miss Dad."

"I do, too, honey. I do, too," Nell answered. She noticed the tremble reappear in Lizzie's chin and wrapped her arms around her.

For a moment Lizzie cried in her arms. Then, true to teenage form, she pulled away, wiped her eyes on her sleeve, and said, "I'm hungry."

Nell handed her the phone. This way she got not only to order the pizza, but to flirt with the high school boys who worked there.

Nell rejoined Josh in front of the TV.

He softly said, "I miss Dad, too."

"I know you do, Josh. I'll try to be …" But what could she try to be? Better about not getting lost in her grief? Better at making up for him not being here? "We all miss him. We all miss him terribly."

And Josh was a perfect enough son to reach out and take Nell's hand. He even held it until the next commercial break.

FOURTEEN

LIZZIE WAS SLUGGISH GETTING out of bed, but only her usual sluggishness. Seemingly mollified by her exclusive pepperoni and extra cheese, she didn't protest she couldn't go to school because of her hussy mother. Nell kept her calm; even, in a supreme moment of motherly cowardice, left the fussing about being late to school to Josh.

"I don't want to get in trouble because you can't get out of bed," he grumbled as Lizzie dawdled over leftover pizza for breakfast.

"Why don't you eat in the car?" Nell suggested, her hand on the door to indicate it wasn't really a request.

Her children were dropped at school just as the morning bell was ringing. Nell watched as Josh sprinted across the yard. She felt a wash of sadness, watching her son—and her daughter, too blasé to be seen actually running—and the struggles they would have. She pushed it away. It was a Monday morning and she had work to do.

Nell was the first at the Crier, but Dolan, Pam, and Jacko were soon behind her. Ina Claire entered, the door held for her by Marcus Fletcher.

"Good morning, Marcus," Nell greeted him. He gave her a small conspiratorial smile, in honor of their late-night adventures.

Nell was saved having to decide whether to introduce Marcus and explain why he was here, only to do it again when Carrie arrived, by her entering the door.

"Okay, story meeting," she called before the young woman even got to her desk.

Nell pulled up a chair in front of Jacko's desk, indicating another for Marcus. She noticed that Dolan, Ina Claire, and Pam were hanging around.

"Some of you may know Mr. Fletcher," she started out. "What you may not know is that for many years he ran a paper for the African-American community, as well as did several stories for the Crier during the integration of the beaches." She hesitated before saying, "At the time, the paper did not byline Mr. Fletcher's stories, because…" Because they were racist cowards? Because it was a capitulation to the reality of the times? "Because that was the way things were done back then," she finished lamely. "He's going to help us with the various stories that we're working on."

"Aren't you running for mayor?" Carrie asked, clearly seeing her turf threatened.

"Yes, he is, but Mr. Fletcher will be working on the stories of the bodies found in the woods," Nell said. "Obviously he can't do any of the election stories or even see them. Carrie, I want you to continue to do most of the political reporting. I think it's time to start asking our current mayor some difficult questions."

Marcus made a show of plugging his ears. Nell wasn't going to worry about it. A black man wasn't going to win, not this election, maybe not for many years. There was nothing that he could overhear that would change that.

"And I've got some good ones to ask," Jacko cut in. "The property Pickings senior bought from Elbert Woodling for $3,000 was reappraised the next time as worth only $15,000, instead of the $30,000-something Woodling had to scrape up property taxes for. From that time, in the sixties, until the early eighties, it only increased in value slightly, up to $22,000. Then suddenly, in 1984, its value shot up to $75,000, then in 1985, it again increased to $120,000, which was the value assigned to it at the time of the park donation." The look on Jacko's face reminded Nell of a hunting dog that has just brought back a prize bird.

"Okay, so what questions should I ask?" Carrie queried.

Nell managed not to sigh and said, "How did the appraised value of the property shoot up to $120,000 in a little over a year, just in time to count as a donation? How was his father able to buy property appraised at over $30,000 for only $3,000? Why was the value of the property listed as only $15,000 by the next appraisal? How can he explain what all these numbers seem to suggest—that the Pickings family used their connections to get land cheap, avoid high taxes, and still rake in a benefit when the land was donated? For starters."

"And what happened to Elbert Woodling?" Pam asked softly. "Did he 'dry up like a raisin in the sun'?"

"'What happens to a dream deferred?'" Nell responded, recognizing the quote from Langston Hughes.

"Should I ask him that?" Carrie interjected, clearly not recognizing the words.

"No, it's from a poem," Nell said. "Did you get those questions down, or do I have to repeat them?"

"No, I got most of them."

"Good work, Jacko. Great instincts to see what happened to that property," Nell told him. "Okay, Carrie, follow up with the mayor, find a chance to ask those questions and keep asking them. If he balks the first time—a good chance—hit him again when other reporters are around, especially any TV cameras to get his answer on tape. The other reporters might pick up the questions and start asking him."

"But they'll get the story."

"Only from us," Jacko said. "Alberta Bonier and I are becoming good buddies and she's agreed to be very selective about how many people can dig in the old records at any given time. Like, just one." Cat that ate the fattest canary on the block and triumphant bird dog all rolled into one.

Nell not only echoed his triumph, but also felt a surge of relief. She might have to feed Carrie questions, but Jacko was going to be good. Now, with both him and Marcus Fletcher, she had a decent chance of pulling through.

"And, Carrie, don't forget the other candidates." Nell handed her Aaron Dupree's stack of paper on his goals. "Cover them, too, and ask them both about the Pickings property and how they plan to handle the bones in the woods should they turn out to have been murdered because of the civil rights movement. Jacko, keep digging. I want to find out who Pelican Property is. Keep looking for patterns. What happened to the property after it was sold for so-called tax default? What kind of money was made? And who benefited most?"

"Yes, ma'am," Jacko said. "I've already told Ms. Bonier I'll probably be in there every day for the next two weeks."

Nell motioned for Marcus that it was safe for him to listen.

"What would you like me to focus in on?" he asked.

"The bones. Those ... children, forever twenty-something. Who were they? How did they get there? Could there be any connection between the property scams and their murders?"

Marcus nodded, then said, "I've got some ideas, but it was a long time ago and I want to make sure what I remember matches the facts. I'll look through the old records of my paper."

Nell started to ask him what he remembered, but Carrie broke in. "What are you going to be doing while we're chasing all the stories?"

Nell bristled at the young woman's implied criticism that she was shirking. "I have the story to write on the sheriff and his African-American cousin—one he doesn't want me to write—plus making sure the usuals get their due, everything from the football game" (the Pelican Bay Pirates had lost, so the story didn't need to be very long) "to fiftieth-wedding-anniversary photos. Plus fielding every phone call that'll come in about the bones being due to alien abduction, plus I'll be backing up each and every one of you on the stories you're working on."

"Plus signing all our paychecks," Dolan not too subtly reminded Carrie.

Plus worrying about my children, Nell thought. Plus J.J. Jones being out of jail, plus missing Thom.

The meeting was over. Jacko was already gathering his things. Dolan ambled back to his office. Pam was answering the phone, saying "Well, that's a very interesting theory," as if the alien callers were already dialing.

Nell briefly wondered if she could only get along with men, not women. She was locking horns with her daughter and Mrs. Thomas, Sr. as well as with Carrie. And she was getting along with Josh and Jacko. No, Ina Claire and Pam and I get along, she reminded herself. And Dolan and I have had a few tense moments.

"I should be back sometime after lunch," Marcus told her. "I'll let you know what I have then." He and Jacko both exited at the same time.

Nell returned to her office and took the phone call that Pam had been dutifully handling. It wasn't about aliens; the caller's theory was that the bones had been left in the woods from satanic rituals. The caller further added that his neighbor had a son who had dyed his hair purple and pierced his ears, a sure sign of devil worship. Knowing it was probably useless, but wanting to cling to rationality if at all possible, Nell pointed out the bones had been in the woods for over forty years, making it unlikely a purple-haired teenager had anything to do with it. Undaunted, the caller intoned that these things ran in families, and it probably had been going on for generations. As politely as she could, Nell suggested that her caller, if he had any real evidence, contact the sheriff's department. She was even helpful enough to give him the number.

The first alien call didn't come until after lunch. Nell skipped reasonable and went right to giving out the sheriff's number. She was a little less sanguine when two of the five aldermen also called about the bones. Was it just their delicate sensibilities? "Shouldn't have something that shocking on the front page," the first of them had boomed into her ear. Or was there something deeper going on? Alfonse Gautier was on the edge of senility, but that also made him old enough to have played a part in the murders. Nell felt a chill when Ina Claire pointed out that Festus Higgins had once been married to Whiz Brown's sister; she had died and he had remarried. Whiz Brown might have been left out of the will—and the family venality—but that didn't mean his sister had been. Nell left his call in the pile of to-be-called-back tomorrow.

After that, she was just waiting; she realized this as she put down a press release for the third time without getting beyond the first sentence. Jacko wouldn't be back until the records office closed, or later—he might right now be wrangling his own key. Nell wasn't sure what Carrie was up to; she had left around lunch. However, it wasn't causing her any problems, so she let that be. She was waiting for Marcus, she realized. He said he'd return sometime after lunch, and it was now far beyond that.

Nell finally bestirred herself to do parenting duty and fetched her children. With a minimum of fuss, they negotiated going to the library until Nell got off. After that she was back at the office, but Marcus still hadn't come by.

Nell wanted to know who had been so callously left in an unmarked grave. It was almost a commingling of grief. They had died young, died hard. She couldn't bring Thom back, but she could give these nameless bones rest.

If Marcus was anything like Jacko, he could be lost in his archives until tomorrow, Nell realized. Or maybe he was being a good reporter and wanted check his facts. She again glanced at her watch. It had been less than a half hour since she had dropped her children at the library. Suddenly, she decided she wasn't going to just wait around.

Getting up and grabbing her jacket, she left the office and headed across the square to the police station. She had a right to know what was happening to the investigation into Josh's assault. And she might see if she could find out anything about a certain act of vandalism that had happened over the weekend. Maybe even manage a few questions to Whiz Brown about his family ties.

Luck—she wasn't sure if it was good or bad—placed both Whiz Brown and Boyce Jenkins right inside the main entrance of the police station.

"Good afternoon, gentlemen," Nell greeted them. To start with the most legitimate topic first, she said, "I'm here about the investigation into the assault on my son Josh."

The two men looked at each other. Chief Brown remained stolidly silent. Finally Boyce Jenkins spoke up.

"Still looking into it. I hear your son is back in school, doing fine."

"So, what you're saying is that next time, when he's maimed or dead, then maybe you'll actually do some real police work."

"Listen, Miz McGraw, I know how to do police work," he said heatedly, more heatedly than a cop who dealt with an irate public should.

"You've never interviewed my son, save for the brief time I was here. Or my daughter, who was also a witness. Or Billy Naquin, a third witness." Nell didn't know that for sure, but it was a reasonable guess. "When I went to get my son's bike the following day, the broomstick was still lying in the gutter, almost twenty-four hours after I reported the crime. I used to cover the police beat, and most cops I knew would have at least tried to fingerprint it."

Boyce Jenkins looked both abashed and angry. "Look, I've been busy on other things."

It was a public enough place, with several other people milling around. Nell decided to chance it. "Yes? Like making sure that no one finds out Chief Brown's father was in the Klan and made a lot of money swindling land from poor black people?"

"That's not true!" Whiz Brown shot back. Then he added, "He wasn't in it that long! And he never took me to any meetings!"

What the guilty reveal, Nell thought. "Just took your brother. Was that why you were left out of the will?"

"No, you got it all wrong!" Whiz's face had taken on a greasy sheen of desperation. "It wasn't us. We didn't do it. We—"

"Shut up!" The voice rang across the room. Nell turned to see Alderman Festus Higgins striding over to them. His face was hard, an edge of hate showing through. Then abruptly, he changed, like a perfect chameleon, his face now a polite smiling mask. It made Nell wonder if he had any soul, or just a series of masks.

"Whiz, I've got some good news," he said. "Since you're here, Mrs. McGraw, you get to be in on it, too. We've just hired a replacement for you, Whiz. His name is Douglas Shaun, coming here from North Carolina. Quite an impressive resume, but says he wants warmer winters and better fishing. So you get to take it easy for the next few weeks. Hardest thing you'll have to do is clean out your desk."

The polite mask didn't hide his message. Nell wondered if Festus Higgins thought she was fooled. She realized it might be best if he did.

"Well, that is good news," Whiz said shakily. He had admitted something he shouldn't have, and his shaking hands meant he was scared of what the consequences might be.

"I thought so," Alderman Higgins said. His body language dismissed Whiz Brown. He turned to Nell and said, "Mrs. McGraw, I left a message for you at your office. Obviously one you haven't gotten yet."

Nell didn't disabuse him of that notion.

He continued. "What's your theory on those bones in the woods?"

She wasn't going to play his game. "I don't really have any theories, Alderman Higgins. Just a few facts. Three people were murdered, buried in a hidden grave, and, save for lightning literally striking, would never have been found." She left it at that.

"Hard to think people could be killed like that here," he said, with enough concern in his voice to make it sound like he was troubled; another mask slipping into place. "But there was a time, back in the forties and fifties, when there was gambling and smuggling going on down here. Probably some gang thing."

Nell didn't point out there was certainly gambling and most likely smuggling going on right now, but proving those two things existed didn't automatically lead to multiple bodies being dumped in the woods.

"Why don't you come to my office? I could tell you some stories, give you some ideas," he offered, his polite politician's smile firmly in place.

"I'd love to, Alderman, but I have to pick up my children. If you do have ideas, you might want to bring them to the sheriff. He's doing the investigation. I just report the facts."

Nell made her escape. As she walked back across the square, she saw Marcus entering the Crier building.

He noticed her and stood at the door, waiting until she caught up. They cut through the newsroom to Nell's office.

He pulled up a chair beside her desk. She took his cue and sat down. Placing a thick folder in the space between them, Marcus removed an old, yellowed newspaper.

He showed Nell a headline—*"Claims of Missing Interlopers False"*—and then read the brief story. "'The allegations that three so-called civil rights workers are missing have been dismissed as false by Tchula County Sheriff Bo Tremble. 'Witnesses saw them at the bus station hightailing it out of here, on their way back home. There's no cause for alarm. They were healthy enough to get on a bus. If anything happened to them, it happened back in Yankee land.' The sheriff elaborated further, saying that the false reports were an attempt to stir things up and 'their outside agitation isn't working, so they're getting desperate to make it look like things are bad down here.'"

Marcus looked up at her and placed the paper on the desk. Nell glanced at the masthead, guiltily relieved that it wasn't the *Pelican Bay Crier*. Marcus pulled out another old newspaper, but this one was a much smaller sheet. He again showed Nell the headline: *"Sheriff Claims Civil Rights Workers Left on Bus."* The story was much longer. Marcus summed it up for her. "As you know, back in those days bus stations were segregated, so I thought it was suspicious only white people noticed them leaving. I asked the porters, janitors, the people who watch, but no one noticed them. They'd been staying with some local folks and hadn't told anyone they were leaving, hadn't packed a bag, and they left everything behind but the clothes they had on. Now, it was possible they faced the choice of either getting on the bus or having something much more unpleasant happen than leaving everything behind. But three scared outsiders, no baggage, waiting at the Pelican Bay bus station, and only some unnamed witness for the sheriff notices them?"

A silence hung, letting his words sink in, and then Nell asked, "Who were they?"

In answer, Marcus pulled out another newspaper article. It was the same kind of paper as the one he'd just showed her. Nell suspected it was his paper. He pointed to a picture of several people. Moving the tip of his finger to a young man in the middle, he said, "Michael Walker. From New York City." The finger moved slightly, to a white woman. "Dora Ellischwartz. From Boston." Again the finger moved, to another woman, a petite black woman. "Ella Carr. Grew up outside McComb, a student at Jackson State."

Nell picked up the paper and closely examined the photo. It was hard to make out individual features; it was a group shot, with the caption *"Welcome given to three new arrivals from Mrs. Hattie Jacobs, Mrs. Ruth Johnson, Mr. and Mrs. John Neely, and Mr. Rufus Jackson."* The three young people Marcus had pointed out were spread among their welcoming committee. Nell read the date on the top of the paper: *"June 15, 1963."*

"What else can you tell me?" she asked softly.

"What do you know of that time?"

"The basics," she admitted. "The riot at Ole Miss on admitting James Meredith. Freedom Summer, the voter registration drive in ..."

"The summer of 1964," he supplied.

"The challenge at the Democratic Convention that same year," she added.

"I was a young man back then. Married, kids, working as a teacher at Elizabeth Keys School, the segregated one. Using my spare time—and unused talents—to put out my monthly paper for the black community. Yeah, you've got the big ones, but there were so many other things going on." He took another sheet from his folder and handed it to Nell. It was a faded purple mimeograph. She had to hold it close to the light to read it. The heading was *"Freedom Classes,"* and it had a list of several sessions, on topics ranging from how to register to vote to freedom theater. Nell noted that the address for these classes was the same as the place where she had heard Marcus speak. Under the register-to-vote class, Michael's name—just his first name—was listed.

"Mississippi had just changed its voting laws from 'read *or* interpret' to 'read *and* interpret' the state constitution. Too many blacks had learned to read, so now that had to have something more subjective as a standard. A man I knew, a PhD in history, flunked interpreting the state constitution, at least according to the eighth-grade-educated secretary who handled his registration. Forty percent of the population of Mississippi at that time was black. Five percent of them were registered to vote. So voter registration was a major focus of the groups down here, mainly NAACP and SNCC, but some others. We had to train people on what would happen when they tried, from how to read and interpret the Mississippi constitution to what to expect, what their rights were. We even had something called the Freedom Vote in the fall of 1963. It was a mock—odd term for something as serious as this—election to prove that black citizens wanted to vote, and would vote if given a chance." He paused, then continued. "I don't know if I can explain the fear, the hopelessness we had to overcome. If a black boy looked at a white woman the wrong way, he could be lynched, no consequences for his attackers. Voting, maybe even having blacks elected to office, that sounded like . . . like a revolution. That's what these three young people came to change."

"And they paid for it with their lives," Nell said.

"You and I know that. But can we ever prove those three skeletons were once these two women and this man?" His finger again rested on the picture.

"We can do our damnedest."

They both sat silently. Finally Nell said, "What else might you be able to find out about them? Would there be anyone around who remembers?"

"Always possible, although it's been a long time. There will be those who remember, like me, but who only knew them in passing. They'll be as helpful as I am," Marcus admitted ruefully, as if what they needed to know should have become emblazoned in his mind all those years ago.

"You've helped considerably," Nell pointed out. "Find out as much as you can. I'm certainly willing to go with the story on Friday about the coincidence of three civil rights workers leaving on a bus with nothing, and three sets of bones being found in the woods fifty years later. That might stir some memories. See what else you can find, especially anything that might help prove the identity of the skeletons. Also for anything that might have led to them being killed."

"Other than daring to demand equality?" Marcus queried.

"That especially. We have to keep an open mind. This might be some family grudge..."

"A white and black family," Marcus reminded her.

"Or some bizarre lover's quarrel. And, yes, white women had sex with black men, even back in those days."

"Two women and one man?" Marcus replied.

"Wife has a 'kinky' ménage-a-trois, and husband kills all three of them. Unlikely, I know, but we can't totally discount other explanations. But do most of your work on the theory their murders had something to do with the unrest of the civil rights era."

"The violence of that time," he corrected her. "Murder was the worst, but beatings, shootings, were common. Blood flowed, lots of blood."

"Let's hope no more does," Nell said.

There was another silence, then Marcus said, "This has been a long day. I was hoping to leave my so-called archives for some poor graduate student to plow through. Wasn't figuring on doing it myself. I think it's time for a brew at Joe's. You're welcome to join me."

"Me and my kids?"

"Ah, that'll be the advantage of having them grown and of drinking age."

"Maybe some other time," Nell said.

"I'll see you tomorrow then, Nell," he said as he stood to go.

She waved goodbye, made another pass at the press release that had been sitting on her desk, and after getting through it and a few more, decided to try one of those ideas that was either foolish or a brilliant leap of intuition.

Ellischwartz wasn't a common name. It was possible that anyone in the Boston area with that same name might be a family member. She got online and searched the white pages for Boston and the vicinity. She found three listings. Nell glanced at her watch; it was just after five, which meant it would be six in Boston. People might be home from work. She dialed the first name on the list. The phone rang several times, then the voicemail picked up. Nell put the receiver down; she would try the other numbers before leaving a message that sounded bizarre: "Some bones were found in the woods here and they might be related to you. Call me back."

She tried the second number. Someone who sounded much too young to have been alive fifty years ago answered. She identified herself and then said, "I'm sorry to bother you, but I'm looking for anyone who might have information on Dora Ellischwartz. This would be going back a long way, fifty years."

There was a rather long pause before the young person (and Nell couldn't quite tell if it was a high-voiced man or a low-voiced woman) replied, "Well, Ellischwartz isn't exactly a common name, but that's not familiar to me. Have you tried my cousin Derek?"

Nell admitted she didn't know Cousin Derek and was rewarded with the phone number attached to the previous voicemail.

She thanked the young person and again stared at the two numbers in front of her. Back to Cousin Derek, or on to the unknown Ellischwartz? She decided on the voicemail number, since she almost had a proper introduction to Derek. She did a quick run to the bathroom to give Derek a few more minutes to get home—or out of the facilities himself.

Nell dialed again and at the last minute, the phone was picked up. She introduced herself.

"I'm sorry, who did you say you were?" a man asked.

Nell again identified herself and repeated her request.

"Dora. I once had an aunt named Dora, but only until I was around ten or so. Never knew what happened to her."

At his words, Nell felt the excitement. How many Doras could there have been who disappeared a long time ago?

"Can you tell me anything else about her?" Nell asked.

"She was a fun aunt, kind of a free spirit. Once let all us kids skip school and took us to the zoo. But her sister, my aunt Gwen, could probably help you better than I can." He gave her Aunt Gwen's number. It didn't match the final number Nell had gotten from the directory; it was possible Aunt Gwen had married and taken another name.

Taking a deep breath to calm herself, Nell dialed the number. The phone rang and rang. Nell was about to give up when an older woman answered it.

"Please, if you're selling something, I'm not interested," the woman immediately said.

"No, I'm not selling anything," Nell affirmed. "My name is Nell McGraw and I'm the editor of a paper located on the Mississippi Gulf Coast. Did you have a sister named Dora Ellischwartz who disappeared about fifty years ago?"

For a moment, only static came over the line. Then the woman softly said, "Dora?" as if the name was so old, she could barely say it. "I had a sister, my younger sister, named Dora."

"I'm sorry. The news I have might not be easy to hear," Nell said, preparing her.

"She's been gone for too many years to count. What can be worse than that void?"

"Recently, several skeletons were found in our woods. It's possible one may belong to your sister, as well as two other civil rights workers she was with."

"Oh, my God, Dora!" the woman suddenly gasped. Nell heard the sound of tears; then the woman mumbled, "I'm sorry. I just … never thought I'd hear her name again. Please give me a moment." Nell heard the phone put down, and, in the distance, the woman blowing her nose. After another moment, she came back on the line.

Nell gave the kindest version she could of what she knew about the bones and why she suspected they might belong to Dora. When she finished, she asked, "What can you tell me about your sister?"

"I suppose you're wondering how we could have just let her disappear?" the woman replied.

Nell had, indeed, been wondering, but she could think of no way to ask. Guilt both hides and reveals.

"I was the staid one, never moved more than twenty-five miles from where I grew up," the woman began. "But Dora was the free spirit. I don't know if I can explain her in just one phone call." She hesitated, then added, "And I'm afraid you'll judge her."

"Judge her? In what way?" Nell asked.

"When she was sixteen, she hitchhiked to Cape Cod. When she returned, she was … in a family way."

"Pregnant?" Nell clarified.

"Yes. And that might be judgment number one. And judgment number two might be that she didn't keep the baby."

"She had it adopted?" Nell asked, sensing something in the woman's words.

"No, aborted. Back then it was all very hush-hush. My father wasn't about to have his youngest daughter bear a child out of wedlock."

"I make no judgment, certainly none of the kind you might be worried about," Nell told her.

"I'm telling you this so you can understand why the family didn't raise hell and high water to search for her. She went off to college at eighteen but didn't take to studying, claimed she wanted to see the world first. She managed a year in Europe, but then came back and went out to California, working as a waitress to 'get to know San Francisco,' she wrote to me. She came by to visit one time with two scruffy men and a VW Bus that didn't look like it could make it across Boston, let alone the country. She sent me postcards from places like Alaska and San Juan. We were close, at least as close as two sisters can be who live completely different lives. More than that, I didn't understand her life and she didn't understand mine.

"She came for a visit—her last one—I guess I finally know that now. It was such a hot day, in the summer of 1963. My father was very ill then. She stayed long enough to go to his funeral and then left, said she was heading for New Orleans. I did get a letter from her telling me she was working in Mississippi, trying to help blacks register to vote.

"Then I heard nothing. That wasn't so unusual; she could go months with no word, then a letter or postcard from somewhere totally unexpected. It was six months before we got truly worried. Then I spent days and days calling everyplace from the NAACP to the Citizens' Council trying to find her. All I found out was she was seen last in some place with a weird spelling."

"Tchula, with a T?" Nell asked.

"Yes, that sounds like it. I talked to law enforcement down there. They said she'd been seen getting on a bus and that was all they knew. I'd been married a few years then, had three young children, my husband was struggling to establish his practice, and there seemed nothing else I could do—except hope she would turn up. About twenty years ago, I hired a private detective, but he found nothing more than what I had as a harried housewife between bottle feedings. I had to assume she'd ended up as too many young girls ended up. I could only pray it was quick." The woman let out a wavering breath.

"Ma'am," Nell said, realizing she only knew the woman as Aunt Gwen, and that didn't seem appropriate. "Did Dora have any injuries, like broken bones, anything like that?"

"Dora? No, for all her wild tomboy ways, she always landed on her feet. She'd had her tonsils out, but that was all. Why do you ask?"

"Although we can make a reasonable guess these remains might be hers, it will be hard to positively establish identity without something more," Nell said as gently as she could.

"Ah. Of course. But I might have something better—more useful, that is, than broken bones. My husband is a dentist. He cared for Dora on several occasions. A few years ago, when he retired, he brought her file home. He'd kept it all those years, in case ... in case of something like this. We still have it. We couldn't ... just throw it away. Would that be helpful?"

"Very helpful," Nell agreed.

"It'll take me a day or so to find it ... but I suppose time isn't a factor here."

"No, but the sad fact is, if we can identify Dora, then it increases the chance the two other people who were supposed to be on the bus with her can also be identified," Nell said.

"Of course. I'll start looking tonight."

Nell got the woman's name, Gwen Kennedy (not related to those other Boston Kennedys, she added almost automatically), and contact information and promised to call her in the morning with where to send the dental records.

"Thank you, Mrs. Kennedy," she said. "I know it can't be easy to open old wounds like this."

"I can at least bury my sister before I die. That is a comfort for an old woman."

After putting the phone down, Nell sat looking out the window, the shadows of evening turning a deep blue in the dusky gold of the last sunlight. Finally she jerked herself out of her reverie and glanced at her watch. The library would close soon and she didn't want her two children out on the streets.

She quickly left the office. She was the last one, and she paused to scan the square before locking the door. The bones and the blood are old, she reminded herself, then remembered that Thom's blood wasn't old, nor was the threat from the Jones brothers.

Get my children, get home, Nell told herself. She marched across the square to the still brightly lit library.

FIFTEEN

LIZZIE PRETENDED SHE WASN'T being dropped at school by her mother, like she was adult enough to have transported without anything resembling a parent involved. Josh ruined Lizzie's pretense by waving back at Nell. For his kindness, he received a not-gentle sisterly cuff on the shoulder. Nell hoped it wasn't a sore spot.

She headed back to the Crier office, thinking about yesterday, both exultant at finding the evidence that could give answers and sad that fate had dealt such a cruel hand to a woman who, whatever her mistakes, had a zest for life and enough of a sense of right and wrong to have come to Mississippi during those times.

As usual, dropping her children at school got Nell to the office first. Gwen Kennedy's revelations had brought up a conundrum: could she trust Sheriff Hickson enough to give him dental records that might be damning? Even if he wasn't a blatant racist, or connected to the murders or to those who gained from the property scams—some major ifs—Nell still wondered if he would use it as a political football, trade favors to the highest bidder. And she doubted she had much to offer him in that currency.

Inspiration hit and she turned around, heading out of the office. She hoped Harold Reed, the Assistant DA, was an early morning man, or at least had children who adhered to school hours.

When she caught sight of him at the coffee stand just inside the courtroom lobby, Nell wondered if he wouldn't also be too much of a political animal to not use this as it best benefited him. Was she hoping that his being black would dispose him to carry the burden she wasn't willing to trust the white sheriff with? She suddenly worried this was something she should have discussed with Marcus before coming here. I have to trust someone, Nell reminded herself, unless I want to do a quick course in forensic dentistry.

She strode over to him. "Mr. Reed, may I have a word with you?" She kept her tone cool and professional.

"Of course, Mrs. McGraw. My office?"

She nodded and followed him down a long hallway, then through a walkway that led to the district attorney's offices.

Once they were settled in, he fixed her with an expectant gaze. Nell noted he was conservatively dressed: three-piece gray suit, lawyerly horn-rimmed glasses. She wondered if this style was required for a black man to have a chance at be taken for a lawyer instead of someone in need of one.

"Mr. Reed, I presume you've heard about the three skeletons that were found in the woods?"

"Yes, I have. I know you were one of the first people to see them," he said, offering her little information save that he was well aware of what was going on.

"Marcus Fletcher has been assisting the Crier recently, and, as you may or may not know, he used to publish a newspaper for the African-American community. Fifty years ago, three civil rights workers disappeared. The sheriff at the time claimed they had been seen on a bus leaving town, but according to Mr. Fletcher's sources, no one in the segregated part of the bus station saw them, and they left behind everything they owned save the clothes they were wearing."

"Very interesting. But you must know how hard it will be to establish proof of identification."

"It may not be that hard," Nell said. "That's why I've come to you. Mr. Fletcher was able to put names to those faces, from a long-ago photograph in his paper. One of the women was from Boston and had an unusual last name. Last night, I took a chance and cold-called people with that name. I was able to trace the woman's sister."

"DNA? That will be hard with just skeletonized remains that old."

"The sister married a dentist."

Harold Reed sat up straight, clearly seeing where Nell was going. "They kept records after all these years?"

"Yes. Her husband knew how important dental records could be, so he kept them, even after he retired. As her sister said on the phone last night, it wasn't something they could just throw away."

"What a damn lucky break!" he exclaimed, then added, "Sorry for the language."

"Don't worry, I've heard and said more than 'damn' in my life." Nell then added, "And I'm coming to you … because I'm leery of turning this over to the sheriff's office."

"Records can get lost so easily these days, can't they?" he said with an acerbic look. "You know what this can turn into?"

"Yes, I do. And I'm aware of how many people want this left in the past."

"I might be mangling the quote, but wasn't it Faulkner who said, 'The past is never dead. It's not even past'?" He got back to business. "How soon can you get me those records?"

"I told the woman I'd call her today with an address. She had to find them, although from our phone conversation, I'd say this is an important thing for her."

"Ask her to overnight them," Harold Reed said.

"How soon could we get a comparison?"

"Depending on what fires I can light—and I'm owed a few favors in that department—it shouldn't take long. An x-ray of the skull, compare that with the dental files. If it's a match, we have our answer."

"Who are you going to tell about this?" Nell asked.

Harold Reed thought for a minute, then said, "You know, I think I'm going to tell everyone. Once I'm sure the dental records are where they should be, I'll maneuver Buddy into a press conference—maximize the glory and play down the heat—but I think the more people know, the harder it will be to play any games."

"Half a century is a long time," Nell said, "but it doesn't mean the murderer isn't still out there."

"That is part of it, isn't it? And it's almost got to be murderers."

"Why do you say that?"

"Think about it. Three healthy young people. They had to know they weren't being led out to the woods for a picnic. If it was you or me, don't you think we would have attacked him? One person couldn't shoot us all at once. I'm not much of a betting man, but I'd bet on at least three or four and quite possibly more."

Nell slowly nodded her head. "That makes it . . . not just the blatant hatred of one person."

"Just the blatant hatred of a whole society."

With a shudder, Nell realized how right he was. Even five people, if that was the number of direct murderers, wasn't that many, but it had taken the complicity and blindness of just about every person in power at the time to allow them to get away with it.

Harold Reed was writing on a slip of paper. He finished and handed it to Nell. "Sym Luchowski, a forensic dental specialist I know over in New Orleans. Why don't you have those records sent directly to him? Just be vague about when we arranged this, so I can pretend to go through the official channels. At worse, he can make copies, just so nothing gets lost. But I think I can arrange for him to be the one to handle the comparison."

"Thank you, Mr. Reed," Nell said as they both stood up. "I think your idea about telling everyone is good, but it makes me nervous."

"Maybe they'll go after Buddy Guy instead of us."

"Or even Sheriff Hickson," Nell added.

Harold Reed gave her an enigmatic smile as he held open the door. "I'll call you as soon as Buddy has something to report."

When Nell got back to the office the rest of the staff was there, save for Carrie.

"Meeting time," Jacko called as she walked through the door.

Nell smiled at him, hastened to her office to throw off her jacket, and rejoined everyone back in the main room. "Marcus, why don't you go first?"

Like he had earlier, he laid out his papers and told their tale. It took a while, with everyone examining the fragile sheets.

"So now we know who those lonely bones might belong to," Ina Claire said softly.

"And we may well have some proof soon," Nell said, and then filled everyone in on her telephoning yesterday and her visit that morning with Harold Reed.

"Reed was a good choice," Marcus said when she finished.

"Okay, my turn," Jacko said. "Pelican Property was owned by Bo Tremble, B. Brown, Frixnel Landry, Albert Dunning, Lamont Vincent, and A.J. Smyth. It was dissolved in 1965, the year that both Brown and

Dunning died, with half of its holding distributed among the remaining principals and the other half sold to Andre Dupree."

Nell breathed a sigh of relief. It wasn't clean, but at least Aaron's father hadn't gotten his tainted land by directly stealing.

Jacko continued. "Two years later Tremble died and his widow also sold her property to Andre Dupree, so by 1967 he ended up owning most of the property surrounding the east side of the harbor, as well as the back bay property. I have the exact numbers, but they mostly make sense: no big increases either way until he developed it, put the nice houses on the lots and then made a lot of money. I did some more looking for Pickings, but it seemed whatever windfall they made was mostly from leasing the land to the paper mill. In fact, according to the gossip, it's lean pickings for the Pickings. His Honor has been trying to sell the property, but no one wants his price until it's guaranteed cleaned up. Ms. Bonier has a sister who works over at the bank and she, of course, couldn't outright say, but hinted that the Pickings accounts were going in the wrong direction."

"Guess he really needs that mayor's salary," Dolan interjected.

"What she didn't hint at, but said outright, was that about a month ago, Mr. Mayor deposited several thousand dollars cash in his account. Last week, he deposited a few more thousand in cash."

"Bribery? Hush money? Blackmail?" Nell speculated.

"Somehow I don't see Hubert smart enough to blackmail anyone, not to mention he certainly has a few things he might not want coming out lurking in his past," Dolan said.

"Bribery seems the best fit," Ina Claire said.

"He's been doing what he can to suppress the investigation, sending Whiz Brown to shut down the dig, requesting I not run the stories," Nell said. She suddenly wondered if the lack of progress on the investigation into Josh's attack could also be part of this.

"But is he doing that for himself or for someone else?" Dolan asked.

"Possibly both. His family's hands aren't very clean on the land swindle," Nell answered.

"How could that have anything to do with the bones in the woods?" Dolan asked.

"They got away with cheating people out of their land because no one here dared protest," Nell said. "What happened if outsiders came in? Willing to take on those in power? What would have happened to the property scam if, say, some reporters from the *New York Times* and a few lawyers from the Justice Department found out about it? What might they do to stop it?"

"Murder three people and bury them where they might never be found," Marcus answered.

"Maybe, but that's a long leap," Dolan pointed out.

"And one we'll probably never be able to prove," Nell admitted. "The worst of the violence was taking place upstate—Jackson, Mc-Comb, Ole Miss—not so much here on the coast. They disappeared in the fall of 1963. Chaney, Schwerner, and Goodman weren't killed until the massive voter registration drive in the spring of 1964. The killer decided they could get away with it. Clearly the sheriff at the time was in on it, or at best, in on the cover-up. The press, the one paper that bothered to report it, parroted his view and never did even the basic research Marcus did." She added, "There's no report in the Crier."

Marcus spoke up. "Certainly, if they wanted to get rid of them, they could have put them on the bus. Many people were frightened away. There may not be a link with the property scams, but isn't it odd that those two things happened here at the same time?"

"I guess," Dolan conceded, "but proof is going to be hard to find."

"Very hard," Nell agreed. "But I still want to look."

Carrie chose that moment to arrive. "Sorry I'm late," she said with no sorry in her voice.

"What's happening with the candidates?" Nell asked her as she crossed to her desk to put her jacket and purse down.

"Give me a minute, let me get settled."

"Ethics require I take a walk around the square," Marcus said, using Carrie's settling time to leave.

Nell let the silence hang, recognizing Carrie's seemingly innocent words for the battle of wills they were.

Not exactly hurrying, but not openly dawdling either, Carrie finally joined them.

"I'll repeat my question. What's going on with the candidates?" Nell said.

"Everett Evens' comment on the bones was 'evil forces have been unleashed by the ungodly behavior of the women's libbers and the homosexual agenda.'"

"Did you point out that the bones were dead before either of those was alive?" Jacko put in.

"You try talking sensibly to Evens," Carrie shot back at him.

"What about the rest of them?" Nell asked. "How did Pickings react to your questions?"

She was silent before finally admitting, "I didn't really get a chance to ask him. Only saw him long enough for him to wink at me."

"He was in his office most of the day. He had a lunch appearance at … " Nell glanced at a schedule sheet. "The Chamber of Commerce meeting, as well as speaking at the fishing rodeo in the evening. How did you miss him in all those places?"

"I was busy with other things," Carrie said, pausing a beat to think of them. "I read all that stuff Aaron Dupree wrote about his goals. I managed to catch him at his speaking engagement at the college."

"And?" Nell pushed.

"So, I didn't get a chance to come back and get to Mayor Pickings."

"If you can't do the story, I will," Nell bluntly stated.

"I can do it. I just can't barge in and ask questions strictly on your agenda."

A tense silence hung.

Nell turned to the rest of the group and said, "I think we all know what we need to be doing. Jacko, wave Marcus back in here." He did, and Nell said as Marcus rejoined them, "Jacko, go play in the court records and archives, see what else you can find. I may team you and Marcus up, since it seems we can find a lot of things that weren't reported in the mainstream press in his archives."

"My archives are a bunch of boxes up in my garage," Marcus said. "Why don't I spend the day asking some of the old timers what they remember? It'll be easier to go through all that paper with a younger and stronger back than mine." Then his eyes got a distant look and he said, "It's hard to go through all that hate again."

"I'd … find it fascinating to go through those papers," Jacko said. Nell suspected that he was going to say "I'd love to" but realized that love wasn't a good word to use when searching for hate.

"I want three major stories on the front page on Friday," Nell said. "Three skeletons were found and three people were lost. If we get the dental findings in time, it'll prove a definite link. I also want a story on the property dealings. And I want a story on the election. It's only a week away, and the revelations about Pickings and the property are going to be incendiary. Any questions?"

There were none. As people went to their various tasks, Nell said, "Carrie, can I see you?" Without waiting for a reply, Nell turned away and walked back to her office.

Again, Carrie didn't hurry, being just slow enough to be annoying without crossing to open insubordination.

Nell didn't sit, instead waited for the young woman to enter before shutting the door and perching on the edge of her desk. Carrie slouched down in the chair across from the desk.

Nell deliberately let the silence build before saying, "You are not needed here as much as you seem to think you are. Yes, we're short-handed, but Marcus Fletcher has years of experience and connections in this town that trump anything you can offer. If you can't cut it or if you don't want to work for me, then leave now. But if you keep up this insolent half-assed shit, I'll fire your butt so fast you'll barely have time to grab your purse. Is there anything that's not clear?"

Carrie was silent. Then she said, "You don't like me, do you?"

"Not especially," Nell admitted coolly, not showing her annoyance at the young woman's attempt to turn her job performance into a personal issue. "But I'm well aware it's mutual. You do your job in a competent and timely manner and like or dislike will have nothing to do with it. But if you show up late to work, leave early, stretch lunch to two hours, and claim to be working on stories with nothing to show for it, we could be the best of buddies and you'd still be out of here."

"I thought working at a small paper like this, we wouldn't have all those stupid rules."

"We don't have stupid rules," Nell retorted. "But, as you pointed out, we're a small paper, and I can't have anyone here who isn't willing to do the work. Right now, both your output and your attitude is dragging everyone down. You change or you leave. It's your choice."

"Is that all?"

"That's all I have to say."

Carrie got up, her face flushed in anger, but she said nothing. She turned to leave, then turned back, and without looking directly at Nell, said, "Mayor Pickings is having an open citizens' forum this afternoon. A number of teachers are going to be there to pressure him on the need for major repairs on the middle school building. They might be a good audience for those questions."

"Go ahead and do that, but remember you may have to ask the questions several times, push him on it."

"This evening he's appearing at the fish fry for the local food bank. I thought I'd follow up there."

"Okay, twice in one day might be good. Did you ask Aaron Dupree about the bones in the woods?"

"Yes, I did. I have the exact quote written down. He said more or less he hoped we'd find out what happened to them, but it was such a long time ago."

"Okay. Keep asking the questions."

Carrie nodded, still not looking at Nell, and exited.

Nell took a deep breath and called Gwen Kennedy. She'd found Dora's old dental records. Nell gave her the address and Gwen said she was on her way out the door to the post office. "I'd like to ... finally know," she told Nell, a trembling in her voice. It must be fifty years of accumulated grief, Nell thought as she assured the woman she'd let her know what happened as well as send copies of the stories.

Nell then busied herself with the usual flotsam and jetsam of running a paper. She finished the story about the sheriff and his cousin. Little did he know that given everything else, there would be no chance it would make the front page.

Shortly after she'd completed the ritual of picking up her children and depositing them at the library, Marcus returned to the Crier. He gently tapped at Nell's door.

As he sat down, he said, "A lot of this is no more than gossip, and old gossip at that, which means it's had years to be embellished and added to."

"Tell me what you've heard," Nell encouraged him.

"When the other three, Chaney, Schwerner, and Goodman, disappeared, there was a national hunt and publicity. So I've been wondering how these three slipped so quietly away."

"I've wondered about that myself," Nell said. "I didn't ask Dora's sister, but she told me anyway. Dora was sexually active, and had an abortion at a time when those things weren't done."

"But she was still white."

"Does the name Viola Liuzzo mean anything to you?" Nell asked.

"Familiar, can't pull it up."

"I've been doing some reading. She was a white housewife from Detroit. Five kids. She left the kids with a friend and drove down to help with the march from Selma to Montgomery. Having a car, she ferried people and ended up taking a young black man from Selma back to Montgomery. They were spotted by the Klan, who chased them, finally pulling alongside and firing into the car. They killed her and left the young man for dead. It turns out one of the Klansman was an informant for the FBI and Hoover wasn't pleased at the implications—the FBI not stopping a murder—so he ordered his agents to find out anything that would tarnish her name. When it came to trial, the defense smeared her with sexual innuendo. The first trial was a mistrial; the trigger man was tried again and acquitted."

"I do remember her now, just didn't place the name."

"And why don't we know her name, but we know King, Evers, Chaney, Schwerner, Goodman? The man she was giving a ride to survived, and there was a goddamned FBI informant in the murder car, but the best they could do to her murderers was for the feds to finally try them for violating her civil rights."

"A lot of people got away with murder back then," Marcus said.

"True. But what I'm trying to point out is that Dora Ellischwartz, like Viola Liuzzo, was judged, and found lesser, because of sex—both her gender and the hint they might be sleeping with black men."

"What about Dora's family?"

"Her sister told me she was a wanderer, a free spirit. She often wouldn't write for a few months. When enough time had passed for them to get really worried, they had no idea where she was. As her sister said, she suspected Dora had met the fate that often happens to women."

"Raped, murdered, and left to rot in some woods," Marcus said. He paused, then continued. "It seems that Ella Carr was mostly raised by her grandmother. Father a bit of what was called back in those times a ne'er-do-well. When she started getting active in civil rights, her family pulled away. They were scared. So, when she disappeared, it seems none of them wanted to make too big a fuss for fear they might be next. I didn't get as much about Michael Walker. Someone said they thought he wasn't close to his family. Had a contact who was a friend. And they were both black and that put them in the lesser category, just like Dora."

"Damn," Nell swore softly. "How do we just throw people away?"

"Two blacks and a loose white woman," Marcus answered. Then, with a shake of his head as if clearing away the past, he said, "Still got kids? If not, a beer of your choice is waiting."

"Still got them, and at the age where I can't leave them home alone long. Maybe tomorrow," Nell said, wondering if she could get Kate to keep Josh as well as Lizzie after bike maintenance class.

"I'll see you in the morning and I'll raise a glass of the suds to you this evening," Marcus said as he left her office.

Nell watched him walking Pam and Ina Claire to the parking lot. Dolan was still around; she could hear him on the phone, a soft drone coming from his front office. With a start, she realized that for the last few hours, she hadn't felt the sharp stab of missing Thom.

"Damn it, you should be here," Nell muttered. "The biggest story the Crier has ever had and you're not around for it." Emotion washed over her and she hastily stumbled to the bathroom.

I should be able to have a crying time, she thought as she washed her face, trying to get the red from her eyes before saying goodbye to Dolan and picking up her kids. Fifteen minutes in the morning, say, and get it over with for the next twenty-four hours. It's not fair to hurt this much in the middle of a work day. She splashed her face again then patted it dry.

Just as she was closing her office door, Jacko came back.

"Hey, you can just go on home," Nell told him.

"Oh, I know, but I wanted to start the rough outline for the property scam story while it's bubbling through my head. I'm a slow starter in the morning."

"Okay, don't stay too late. Get something for supper and expense it to the Crier."

"I'm not going to be here that long." Then he added, "I found out an interesting thing from someone I was talking to over in the sheriff's department. The Jones boys covered Junior's bail by putting up their garage."

"I wondered where they got the money," Nell said shortly.

"It'd be interesting to see if it's actually appraised at what they claimed it to be worth," Jacko said. "Because if it's not really enough to cover the bail …"

"That would be most interesting to find out," Nell said with a smile that didn't reach her eyes.

"It's not much," he said, "but it doesn't seem right for J.J. to be out and …"

"Thom cold in the ground," Nell finished. She was starting to hate when people wouldn't say it, would skim around Thom's death. She realized most of this was fear of saying the wrong thing. But at times she wanted to shout, "Do you think I can forget he's dead? That I don't know it every waking moment, even in my dreams?" But she didn't, and Jacko wasn't the person to start it with.

"It doesn't seem fair," Jacko said softly. Then, surprisingly, he gave her a brief hug.

Nell almost started crying again at his unexpected gesture. She took a deep breath, then said, "Thanks. Don't stay too late."

With that, she headed off to get her kids.

Josh had a huge stack of shark books waiting for the official library card. Nell proffered it to Marion, hoping no science teacher would assign research papers on sharks in the next few weeks. Just as Marion finished with Josh, Lizzie added a few books to the stack, including, Nell noted, a racy adult novel.

Nell picked it up, did one of those mother debates about whether she should censor her daughter's reading, and finally decided to take a more subtle approach. She put the book back and said, "If you want to read this, we're going to have a mother-daughter talk about the difference between fictional consequences and real life."

Lizzie gave a quick nod, not so much in agreement but because she was ostensibly getting what she wanted, yet also not getting what she really wanted, which was to sneak the book by her mother.

When they got home, Nell was relieved to note the racy novel stayed on the bottom of Lizzie's stack, and even after the required email and phone calls to friends, it stayed there. Perhaps the threat of a mother-daughter chat was enough to put her off.

When Nell was throwing together the salad, she realized she'd put four chicken breasts in the microwave to defrost. As she took them out, she thought, goddamn it, Thom. People twine in your life in so many ways and when they're gone, every place has to be unwoven and pulled apart. She stared at the extra chicken breast, then decided it would be her lunch tomorrow.

SIXTEEN

It was now routine, dropping Josh and Lizzie and then heading to the office. Before, Josh would ride his bike and Lizzie would manage a hodgepodge of cadging rides with friends, wheedling one from Thom, as he was more of a morning person than Nell, and occasionally lowering herself to taking the bus. Nell had grown accustomed to a quiet hour at home after the kids left. Thom had called it her wake-up time, when she did minor chores like bill paying or just sat at the kitchen table drinking coffee.

Maybe when they're in college, I can have that time again, Nell thought as she waved.

Back at the office, she spent a solid hour working on the story about the bones. Jacko was writing on the property dealings and Marcus would handle the three missing civil rights workers. Theirs would be intertwined stories, but he wasn't up to speed on the bones yet and she wanted him to get a front page byline. To make up for the sins of the past? As if we can make up for past transgressions, she thought. I'm giving him a byline because he's done damn good reporting.

Harold Reed called in the midst of that to say he had the official okay to compare an x-ray of the skull with the dental records of Dora Ellischwartz. The x-ray had already been sent; they were now waiting on receiving the records from Gwen Kennedy.

Just as Nell hit save, he called again to tell her that Dora Ellischwartz's records had arrived in New Orleans and that Buddy Guy, the District Attorney, was tentatively scheduling a press conference for the next morning. "But it's not been officially announced," Harold told her. "It's on only if it's a match." Harold must have called in a few favors to get things moving this quickly, Nell noted.

After hanging up, she stared at the page in front of her, knowing this would be a big story, one of the biggest in her life. But the old grief of three people lost long ago mingled with her loss, and whatever exult she felt was weighted with an inchoate sadness.

The explosiveness of these stories was brought home when Hubert Pickings burst into the newsroom while Nell, Pam, Dolan, and Ina Claire were sitting eating their lunch.

"Nell McGraw," he thundered. "Call your damn reporter off of me! How much is Aaron Dupree paying you for her to ask those questions?"

"Nothing," Nell answered, hastily putting down her sandwich, and standing so she could have the advantage of height over him.

"What the hell kind of trash are you implying about me and my family? I got a right to privacy, you know."

"The property records are public. It's not out of line to ask how your father was able to buy property appraised at over $30,000 for $3,000. Or why the appraised value changed from around $20,000 to $120,000 just in time for you to write it off as a donation," Nell said.

"Goddamn it!" His face was red and shiny with sweat despite the cool temperatures, the fly-away cowlick vibrating with either rage or the effort to think. "That has nothing to do with this election and you know it!"

"I disagree, Mr. Mayor. I think swindling a poor black person and manipulating the appraisal of your property has a lot to do with who is qualified to run this town," Nell replied, trying to keep her voice firm but calm. She didn't want him to have a heart attack in the middle of their lunch.

"Aaron Dupree must have a pretty big dick to get you to do this kind of stuff now," Hubert Pickings spat out.

"I beg your pardon," was all Nell could think to say.

"Hubert!" Ina Claire called out, packing more propriety into her voice than Nell had ever heard before. "Take your filth out of this office."

"My filth!" He turned on her. "What about the lies this woman is trying to spread about me? What about that filth?"

"I'm reporting facts, Mr. Pickings," Nell said coldly. "There might be a reasonable explanation for those facts, which you can address by answering my reporter's questions. But ... " She advanced on him so he was barely a foot away. "I'll be damned if I'll let you intimidate me into not reporting what is public record *or* let Aaron Dupree use me to win this election."

"Damn you, Nell McGraw," he blustered. "They are lies, all lies. You might want to check your boyfriend's property dealings. You'll find Dupree's hands aren't so clean."

"I don't have a boyfriend," Nell retorted. "And we're looking at all the records of that time. If you have any evidence, we'll be glad to look at it."

"You and your damn evidence. I'd like to see it myself. But I know you don't have any. You're just telling lies to spook the election."

"The public records of property transfers from fifty years ago are all lies?" Nell sardonically questioned him. "You give us proof and we'll print it."

Her taunt only caused his face to redden further. "Goddamn it, you keep this up and you're going to get your tit caught in a wringer."

"Me and Katherine Graham," Nell replied.

His beady eyes showed no comprehension, and no inclination for enlightenment. He spun on his heel and strode out of the office as fast as he could, his girth making it more like the walk of a short, angry penguin.

Mostly for Pam's sake, who had been in diapers when Watergate was making news, Nell explained. "Katherine Graham was the editor of the *Washington Post*, and John Mitchell, the Attorney General, made that same comment about her when they were investigating Nixon."

"And look how that turned out," Dolan commented. "Seems that we have ruffled some feathers."

Nell was silently gratified to hear him use "we."

Dolan got up and locked the door, saying, "At least until lunch is over. My stomach can only take so much indigestion."

After lunch, he unlocked it and an uneasy calm prevailed the rest of the day. No more blustering threats, save for one irate subscriber who claimed the paper boy deliberately aimed for his rosebush.

The calm before the storm, Nell thought as she delivered her children, this time for a change in routine, to the bike shop. Kate was willing to let them hang out, even going so far as to mention she was going to have some friends over for a cartoon marathon and Josh and Lizzie were welcome.

"You can keep them the whole week if you like," Nell responded. Josh was happy at the thought, but Lizzie answered with her usual

"Oh, Mom!" as if more than a few hours away from email was a trial too great to bear. Nell agreed she'd pluck them out of cartoon land no later than nine.

She headed back to the office, but all was calm there, even to the point of Carrie sitting at her desk typing away on the mayoral candidates.

When Marcus returned, she learned his accomplishment of the day had been to find decent pictures of the three slain young people. This time he didn't knock on Nell's open office door, just walked in and placed the photos before her.

Ella Carr was a stunningly gorgeous young woman, her delicate features fine-boned. She had chiseled cheeks and wide eyes in a heart-shaped face that wouldn't make you think she had the purpose and strength to be the one in her family to fight back. Nell looked again at the eyes, this time seeing, in their direct look, the steel the pretty face kept hidden.

Dora Ellischwartz seemed raw-boned and big compared to Ella, her face holding a wide smile that only accentuated how her mouth was a little too large. But there was also a happy, open aspect to her. Nell wondered if she was seeing it there because of what she'd learned about Dora, reading it into a woman she already knew to be a free spirit. Her hair was blond and long, in the style of the time; also in the style of the time, her eyes were outlined in mascara, but even with that, her eyes were her best feature, happy, laughing eyes that seemed to sparkle even in the black-and-white photo.

Michael Walker had a sensitive face, and his smile had a sad knowingness to it. He was slim, with sharply etched cheekbones that only seemed to highlight eyes looking off from the camera as if seeing something in the distance. He was a handsome man, Nell thought, then realized the arch of his brow reminded her of Thom. Like Thom, he seemed a man whose finest tool was his brain, not his hands.

Nell felt a bolt of sorrow course through her. For the boy who reminded her of the man she had lost and for the three of them, two girls and one boy. They were so young, only on the cusp of adulthood, walking on a short road.

"It makes them real, doesn't it," Marcus said softly. He gently placed his hand on Nell's shoulder.

"They are real. It just makes them almost too human to bear," Nell replied. Then, steadying herself, she said, "This is great work. How did you find these?"

"By asking question after question after question. One answer led to someone who knew someone who knew someone whose father had a camera who took pictures back in those days. I spend a couple of hours with his widow looking through old boxes in the attic."

"Good work. The dental records will identify Dora, but these pictures might really help with the other two."

"A good reason to spend all those hours in that dust."

Nell glanced at her watch. "Hey, guess what, I'm temporarily kidless."

"Sounds like an invitation I can't refuse. Let me hit the keyboard for a bit while I still have my sobriety, and then we can make a wild night of it."

"At least until nine, when I turn into a mom again," Nell amended.

"Which is about the bedtime for an old man like me." He headed off into the main room and took over the computer on Jacko's desk.

A little after that, Carrie placed her story on Nell's desk. "Tell me what else I might need," she said, then added, "I know you won't approve, but I did some major flirting with one of the TV guys who'll cover tomorrow's debate. He's going to ask some of those questions."

"Feel free to expense the condoms. Just make sure they're latex and not lambskin," Nell said smoothly. She was gratified with the look on Carrie's face. Probably thought I didn't know what a condom was. "Tomorrow night will be past deadline for us, but the real issue isn't so much what the mayor's answers are—unless he has something truly unusual to say—but that the questions are asked. It was a good idea to put some extra pressure on him."

"But it means the TV guys will scoop us."

"They'll get an on-camera reaction, which isn't something we can compete with anyway," Nell replied. "But this will actually work for us in the shallow waters of scooping each other. They hit him tomorrow night with the questions and get little more than headline news from it. We're on the doorstep in the morning with all the facts behind the questions. You'll get your profile raised more by having TV involved than not. Plus, in the area of public good and all that jazz, this will get the story to the public in time to help them vote. There are worse fates than merely influencing civic affairs."

"So you're not upset?"

"No, I think it was a very shrewd move on your part. This will be a good story."

"Above the fold?"

"Probably not," Nell answered honestly. "It looks like we've got positive ID for the bones—they were three civil rights workers who disappeared in the sixties. That's a major national news story. Just your luck to compete with it for the front page this week."

Her comment seemed to mollify Carrie. "I'm going to follow the mayor," she said. "He's making one more appearance at the fishing rodeo. Should I ask him again?"

"No," Nell quickly decided. "Just be there. It'll keep him sweating, and maybe he'll think he's ducked the questions until tomorrow."

"Aaron Dupree is also going to be there. He took a bunch of kids from the city recreation program out to fish on the family boat after school."

"Ask him about the ways his family seemed to benefit from the crooked land deals," Nell said. "His father picked up a lot of that land when it was resold. Interesting to see what his answer might be."

"I hate to ask him mean questions," Carrie said. "He's got my vote."

"We need to be at least in the vicinity of fair with mean questions," Nell said. "We don't want it to look like the mayor's accusations of him buying us off are true."

"I guess so. Can I come in a little late tomorrow since I'll be late tonight?"

"Yes, but be here by ten. I may need some rewriting, plus anything that you get tonight," Nell instructed her.

Carrie nodded her agreement and headed off for the land of fish.

In a revolving door worthy of a bigger newspaper, Jacko arrived as she left. At Nell's beckoning, he came into her office. She showed him the pictures.

He looked at them for a long time before finally placing them back on Nell's desk.

"Did you find anything today?" she asked.

"Nothing other than a lot of dust."

"It's like that sometimes."

"I did find out that the Jones' gas station was equal to the bail money. Sorry."

"Thanks for thinking of it and trying," Nell said, hiding her disappointment. To make sure it was completely hidden she invited Jacko along for a beer. He gladly accepted.

At least I can claim one of them as a chaperone, Nell thought as they locked up the office, although she wasn't sure which. Jacko was, she realized, about the age of the three civil rights workers when they were murdered. No wonder he'd stared so long at the pictures. Marcus, on the other hand, had that many years plus a few more on the other side of her. Let people think what they want, she decided. Maybe being seen with them would kill any rumors about her and Aaron Dupree.

Marcus led them to Joe's. They didn't talk about the stories they were working on. It was, Nell realized a few hours later, a pleasant way to spend an evening. As they left the bar, a glance at her watch told her she had time to get home and brush her teeth before getting her children.

Lizzie couldn't admit she'd enjoyed cartoons, but Josh claimed a good time. Nell was relieved to notice both of them yawning as she drove home.

Lizzie had to check her email, but there was nothing pressing enough for her to spend copious amounts of time replying. Shortly after she got off the computer, the phone rang. Lizzie snatched it up, with Nell standing by as a reminder that this was late for anything save the most essential—and brief—conversation.

"It's for you." Lizzie handed the phone to her.

"Mrs. McGraw?"

Nell didn't recognize the voice, although it sounded familiar. "Speaking."

"This is Harold Reed. I apologize for bothering you at home, but I thought you'd like to know. We've got a match. Buddy is having a press conference tomorrow at ten at his office."

"Thank you. I appreciate you calling."

That was the sum of their conversation. Nell briefly debated calling Gwen Kennedy, but it was an hour later in Boston. It would hold until morning.

SEVENTEEN

THE FIRST THING NELL did after dropping off Lizzie and Josh was go to the office and call Gwen Kennedy. She answered on the second ring, as if waiting for a phone call.

"Mrs. Kennedy? This is Nell McGraw. The dental records were a match."

There was silence on the other end, only the sound of breathing. Then Gwen Kennedy said, "I was afraid it would be and afraid it wouldn't. But after fifty years I can't believe she'll come home any way other than this."

"I'm very sorry," Nell said. "I know this isn't easy for you."

But Gwen Kennedy declined Nell's implicit invitation to talk about feelings. "What happens now? When can we … claim the remains?"

"I'm not sure. This is a murder investigation," Nell said. "They'll have to take every bit of evidence they can before releasing anything. I don't know how long that may be."

"Can it really matter after all these years?" she asked with a tired sigh in her voice.

"Can it matter? Of course it matters. Can they find the people that did this? I don't know. Even if we can identify who did it, they may well be in their graves by now," Nell admitted.

"How could anyone do that to … ?" For a moment Gwen Kennedy's feeling threatened to spill out. "Please keep me informed. If nothing else, I'd at least like to spit on their graves." With that she said goodbye.

In the time between her call and Buddy Guy's press conference, Nell worked on corralling everything that would go in the paper. It had to go to press by the afternoon. When Pam arrived, she gave her some things to lay out. Pam liked the work, and more importantly, was good at it. Nell also read over the story Carrie had left with her. It clearly showed her hurried style of writing, which was a good thing, as when she hurried she kept it closer to bare bones reporting. When Carrie spent time on a story, Nell usually edited out her writerly embellishments. And in the past, she'd had Thom to smooth any ruffled feathers.

She didn't think she'd find out much from Buddy Guy's press conference, but she wanted to be there anyway.

Despite the late notice, the conference room at the DA's office was packed with TV cameras jockeying for good angles. Nell found a place on the side, close to the front. She never quite had the temerity to ask Buddy Guy if that was his real name or if he'd taken a poll to pick what was most likely to get him elected. Rumor had it that he was a much better politician than a lawyer, with just enough sense to hire people like Harold Reed to do the real work.

Buddy Guy was of medium build, with a stomach starting to spread from middle age and a lifestyle that included too many glad-handing dinners. He had good hair, blond going silver and still thick, that he kept barely needing a haircut, as if flaunting it to the other men his age with their receding hairlines. The perfect picture of a hard-charging district attorney. Rumor also had it that he'd invested time and effort in classes on how to appear on TV.

Wanting to make sure he made all the deadlines, Buddy started the press conference on time. As Nell had guessed, he did little more than confirm what she already knew about the match. However, he did it with visuals, comparison x-rays, something for the TV cameras. He didn't give much information beyond that, claiming they were still investigating who the other two sets of bones might be. He also ducked declaring directly that all three had been murdered, merely saying, "We're looking into that." Nell wondered how he would react when she published the names and photos tomorrow in the Crier. She decided she'd wait until then to find out.

Harold Reed stayed silent in the background. Nell suspected he was there to literally lend color to the pictures of Buddy Guy. The political impact couldn't be lost on such an astute creature, of having a black man visible during the investigation of murders of civil rights workers.

Nell caught up with Harold afterward in the hallway outside his office. He was content to leave Buddy the follow-up schmoozing. Yesterday, she'd had several copies made of the photographs Marcus had found.

"Thought you might like these," she said, handing him the envelope with one set of copies in it.

He opened it up and looked.

"Ella Carr, Dora Ellischwartz, and Michael Walker," Nell said unnecessarily.

"Where did you get these?"

Nell gave him a quick rundown of Marcus's methods, with a promise that she'd have Marcus himself give Harold the exact details.

He nodded, then slipped the photos back in the envelope. He cleared his throat and said, "J.J. Jones' lawyer has put in for a continuance. He claims he needs more time to research the case."

"Damn it!" Nell burst out. "Sorry, but I don't like that bastard running around loose."

"Quite frankly, neither do I. I'll do my best to get it denied, or at least kept to a minimum. We were hoping to get it to trial next month, but this might take it into next year."

"While he runs around free on bail."

"I didn't think this would be good news."

"Is there anything I can do? Get a restraining order?"

"If he's threatened you."

"I think his brothers have, but the police have little interest in looking into it." She gave Harold a brief recap of what had happened to Josh.

He kept his professional demeanor, but Nell saw a flash of anger in his eyes as she told her tale.

"A fingerprint or two might have been helpful," he said acerbically when she'd finished. "Okay, I'll lean hard on the judge not to change the trial date. At least we're getting rid of Whiz 'Do Nothing' Brown soon."

"Soon enough?" Nell asked, but it was rhetorical. She said a quick goodbye to Harold as several other people came to claim his attention.

"Damn, damn, and damn again," she cursed softly as she made her way back to the car. The trial date had been a talisman, something she had to get past before she could go on to … she didn't even know what, but the date had loomed so large that nothing save the day-to-day plodding along seemed possible. To change it to several months later—especially with J.J. Jones out on the streets—was infuriating. Maybe Marcus and I will have to make weekly vandalism runs, Nell thought as she headed back to the Crier office.

The rest of the day was spent in a flurry of getting the paper out, everything from mundane birth announcements to checking and rechecking the facts on the main stories.

Carrie had indeed shown up at ten and added a few extra paragraphs to her story, all in her hurried style so Nell had little editing. She even volunteered to get lunch for everyone, since, with her story turned in, she had less to do than the others.

Marcus had managed to gather a few more details of the lives of the young civil rights workers. Ella was nineteen when she was killed, Dora was twenty-three, and Michael was twenty-two.

Nell read the front page stories over one more time as Dolan was standing in the door waiting to take the paper to press. With a glance at her watch—and deciding she could squeeze in the trip without endangering her children—Nell handed him the disk, than grabbed her jacket. They ended up going en masse, leaving only Ina Claire and Pam to handle the office. Dolan's car, the biggest, was used, with Jacko, Carrie, and Marcus crammed into the back seat and Nell riding shotgun with what would turn into tomorrow's newspaper cradled in her lap.

When they returned, she had to jump out of Dolan's car and into hers to get Josh and Lizzie. They both grumped at the idea of the library, so Nell brought them back to the office.

When she got there, Jacko suggested he begin work on Marcus's archives/stack of dusty old boxes. Nell gave the okay, but told him to start the next morning. Knowing Jacko, he had the energy and interest to be up all night, and Marcus had a debate this evening. Carrie left a message with Pam that she was going to the debate, so she was taking time off now. That sounded reasonable to Nell; she was content to have gotten the story she needed out of the young woman.

Jacko went back to the property records; he was too wired to sit around and rest on putting the paper to press. Nell waved him off with an admonition not to stay all night. She let everyone else out early. They would have enough to do tomorrow.

After supper, she commandeered the TV remote to watch the mayoral debate. Lizzie made noises about something she really, really wanted to watch, even pushing by pointing out they wouldn't have this problem if she had a TV in her room.

Nell suggested she save her allowance and buy one. "It'll only take about six months" ended the discussion. Lizzie grabbed the racy novel and flounced off to her room.

In the greater scheme of things, the issue of who was going to be mayor of Pelican Bay wasn't a major newsmaker. That the debate was being held on a local access cable station was evidence of this.

All four official candidates were there, with Aaron Dupree and Hubert Pickings in the center. Sensibly, Everett Evens was to the far side of Pickings, and Marcus Fletcher was on the other side, so they were as separated as they could be. Nell considered them arranged from sensible to nutcake.

The debate started off with the usual drone of what each would do if elected. Nell knew she was somewhat biased, but she thought both Marcus and Aaron made a lot of sense, having reasonable yet progressive goals. They both emphasized education, Aaron in the direction of better schools all around and Marcus focusing on bringing the children of poverty more into the mainstream. Hubert, for his part, had to claim that everything was perfect and he would keep it that way. Everett nattered away on the need to bring back the old days. The moderator managed to cut him off just as he was getting wound up on the importance of heritage; in his case, decoded to mean the Confederate flag and all it stood for.

There were three reporters, all from local TV stations, Nell noted, feeling the slight for all her print colleagues, with a professor from the local college moderating. All, save for Marcus, were white and male.

The first question was directed to all the candidates and was about their backgrounds. The men dutifully listed their educations, experience, and whatever else they thought might be impressive. Nell learned that Everett was a cousin, several times removed on his mother's side, to P.G.T. Beauregard, a Confederate general, whose name still inspired reverence among the hardcore "heritage" folks.

Hubert Pickings, jumping into the spirit of things, managed to segue from how important heritage was to wondering why "black folks just can't get beyond slavery." Nell cursed the TV questioners for not asking the obvious follow-up: why did one group of people have to totally divest themselves of that heritage—slavery, lynchings, and Jim Crow—but it was important for another group to hold on to the whitewashed side of that heritage?

Marcus managed to get in that slavery had nothing to do with the roads not being fixed in the black part of town.

Everett took advantage of a pause to get back on his heritage bandwagon. The moderator either was far too polite for his job or didn't have the skills to shut up a motor-mouth like Everett.

Nell took a bathroom break and came back in time to hear one of the TV reporters—the cutest one, she noted—ask, "Mr. Mayor, what explanation do you have for the sudden change in the value of the land you donated for a state park in 1985 from $22,000 to $120,000 in just over a year, and just in time to be the value at the time of the donation?"

Hubert Pickings looked like a man who needed twenty-four hours and five advisers to have a prayer of answering. His first try was, "I don't know what you're talking about."

The camera cut back to the reporter and Nell was gratified to notice Carrie standing behind him. From his looks, she didn't think flirting had been a terrible hardship. "Your family somehow acquired the property in the early sixties for $3,000 even though it was appraised at over $30,000. For almost the next twenty years it was appraised at around $20,000, then suddenly jumped significantly just before you donated it to the state park." Hubert, foolishly, still didn't answer, so the reporter continued. "You know, the place where the skeletons of those civil rights workers were found."

"Damn you, Nell McGraw," Hubert sputtered before thinking better of it. "You're repeating rumors and lies. I won't dignify that with an answer."

"It's public record," Marcus said quietly, his voice filling the silence.

"There are public records and there are public records," Hubert Pickings fumed nonsensically. Luckily for the audience and the spectacle, Hubert didn't have enough sense to realize that silence, as inadequate as it was, was still his best defense. He turned to Aaron. "This is your doing. Think you can win this election by repeating all these ugly things about me and my family, when your dad was out there doing worse than we ever did. At least my family never joined the Klan."

"Don't think you can tell lies about me to cover up the truth about your background," Aaron shot back.

"Damn you, Aaron Dupree! We weren't doing anything everyone else wasn't doing back then!" Hubert Pickings' face, despite the makeup he'd put on, was turning red and sweaty.

Nell would bet money that only powerful white people were doing it, but that might have qualified for "everyone" in the world of men like Hubert Pickings.

"Yeah, we got the land cheap," Hubert blustered out. "But so did a lot of people. Back then—"

Suddenly a voice out of camera range shouted, "Shut up, Hubert!" Nell thought she recognized the cold authority of Festus Higgins, but the second camera, whipping around the room, couldn't catch him.

From there the debate devolved into pandemonium. Hubert shouted, "I don't have to take this shit!"—the curse word, live on camera, no less—and stalked off.

Everett grabbed both his microphone and Hubert's abandoned one and launched into his "retribution for the sins of the world is gonna get you" speech, and he was hurling fire and brimstone at everyone from Eleanor Roosevelt to Liberace to Hillary Clinton.

The moderator, with just one microphone, was ineffectual at out-shouting Everett. Half of the room left to follow Pickings and see what else they might capture on camera. Someone finally had the bright idea to turn off the sound system to shut up Everett, but that took away the power from all the microphones. Aaron Dupree shrugged his shoulders and left the stage. As he left, the lights from the camera that illuminated the stage were turned off and Nell glimpsed Marcus's shadow making its way offstage before the program abruptly changed to a bad video of a high school track meet.

Nell clicked the TV off. She wished she'd recorded the debate. It was such a spectacular blow-up. She had to content herself with the part she'd played in the drama: her place in history—at least, the history of this small town—documented when Mayor Hubert Pickings cursed her on camera.

EIGHTEEN

WHEN SHE GOT TO the office, still school-morning early, Nell didn't take the phones off the answering machine. The blinking light told her they were already being called. They could wait until nine a.m., office hours, and more importantly when reinforcements would arrive.

As was her custom, Nell spread the newly released paper across her desk. On the top of the front page, in one of the boldest types they had ever used, was the headline *"Lost Bodies of Civil Rights Workers Found."* Below the headline were their pictures. Below that was the story, bylined by Marcus Fletcher.

> Fifty years ago, Sheriff Bo Tremble of Tchula County told those who asked that civil rights workers Ella Carr, Dora Ellischwartz, and Michael Walker had boarded a bus and gone home. In a newspaper report from the time, Sheriff Tremble was quoted as saying, "Witnesses saw them at the bus station hightailing it out of here, on their way back home. There is no cause for trouble or alarm. They're

healthy enough to get on a bus; if anything happens to them, it happened back in Yankee land." Bones found in the woods of Iberville State Park tell a different story: that the former Sheriff Tremble was at best mistaken on his claim the three safely left the area. At the time, members of the black community were suspicious, as the three had packed nothing and left everything, save for the clothes they were wearing, in the spare rooms of Rufus Jackson's and Hattie Jacob's farms where they were staying.

In a lucky break for investigators, Dora Ellischwartz's sister married a dentist, and he kept her dental records for all these years. The records proved a match for the skull believed to be hers, establishing that she, at least, never got on a bus leaving Tchula County. The other two skeletons correspond to the known physical characteristics of her two compatriots, making it likely they are the remains of Ella Carr and Michael Walker.

Carr, Ellischwartz, and Walker had all come to Mississippi to help with voter registration at a time when only five percent of blacks in the state could vote. Carr, nineteen, was a sophomore at Jackson State and had taken the semester off to contribute to the effort. Ellischwartz, twenty-three, had completed two years at Boston College and was taking time off to travel. Walker, twenty-two, was a recent graduate of Columbia University in New York City and had delayed beginning law school for a year.

As Nell again read the article, she thought Marcus had done a good job of hunting down the added details. She had gotten most of the information on Dora Ellischwartz, but it was his work that had unearthed the additional information on their short lives. And he had uncovered the pictures; young faces haunted with promises never kept. With Gwen Kennedy the only relative contacted, they had debated about revealing the names, but as Ina Claire pointed out, "After fifty years, no one can expect them to come walking through the door only to find out they won't via the newspaper." Nell was hoping that by revealing the names, others who knew them would come forward. Perhaps another sister or brother who cared enough to bury the bones.

Her story ran next to his. To keep things equal, she had also given herself a byline.

Ellen Cohen, professor of forensic anthropology at Louisiana State University, oversaw the removal of the remains of three skeletons from Iberville State Park. As Cohen said, "They didn't die an easy death." One of the victims' skulls had a bullet hole in it, with a twenty-two slug still in the brain case; another had a fractured hyoid bone, considered a classic sign of strangulation. One skeleton had both legs broken, another had a crushed pelvis; both injuries were made close to the time of death. According to Cohen, forensic anthropologists can determine whether injuries were pre-mortem or post-mortem by the condition of the bone. Rusted chains were found on one of the bodies, making it likely he was in chains when he was transported into the woods.

District Attorney Buddy Guy, in a press conference held yesterday morning, used dental records to identify one of the sets of remains as Dora Ellischwartz, a twenty-three-year-old woman from Boston. He stated that his office, as well as Sheriff Clureman Hickson, would be investigating the deaths as suspicious.

The bones were found a little over a week ago by a hiker. Lightning had struck a tree that had grown over the graves, felling the tree and, in the process, unearthing the long-hidden bodies. From the condition of the remains and the age of the tree, as well as from coins found at the grave site, experts were able to guess that the victims had died around fifty years ago. Sheriff Clureman Hickson brought in forensic specialists from LSU, in Baton Rouge, Louisiana, to aid his office with investigating the site.

Inquiries into possible missing persons from that period turned up little until one longtime civil rights activist remembered three young workers who had supposedly left on a bus, only to never be heard from again. The unusual name of one of the victims, Ellischwartz, led investigators to her sister and the dental records. DA Buddy Guy refused to speculate on the identity of the two other sets of remains, but anonymous sources admit that in all likelihood they are those of Ella Carr and Michael Walker.

Jacko and Carrie both got below the fold, but bylined. *"Mayoral Election Heats Up"* was Carrie's headline.

Polls from the campaign of current Mayor Hubert Pickings show him with a slim lead over his main challenger, Aaron Dupree. Mr. Dupree's pollsters find a similar result, but with the slight lead in his favor. With both candidates around one percentage point of each other, the results of the upcoming election are impossible to call.

Mayor Pickings is running on his signature slogan of "You've got a friend in City Hall." In a recent campaign speech, he said, "The last four years have been good to Pelican Bay, and they've been the four years I've been mayor. Four more years of me is four more years of good for Pelican Bay."

When asked about specific policy initiative, Mayor Pickings replied, "Why change what ain't broke? It's been four good years."

Aaron Dupree, when asked his reasons for running for mayor, replied, "This town is home to me. I grew up here, my family is all here. Like my father, I don't want 'good' when we can have better, or even better when we can have best. If elected, one of my main focuses will be education. I know it's a cliché, but it's true; our young people are our future. I'll lobby the school board pretty hard to get community service as one of the requirements for graduating from high school. It's important that our young people develop a sense of ownership and pride in our community. Another thing I'll do is bring city hall into the computer age. Why don't we have a good website? Why not let people apply for permits and do business with the city online? Why do we waste people's time by making them come to us for every little thing? I've developed six-week, six-month, one-year, and four-year goals for what I'd like to accomplish. Education and the Internet are just a few of the things I'd like to work on. To prove I practice what I preach, my plans are available online, or at my campaign headquarters."

When asked about the recent discovery of bones in Iberville State Park, Mr. Dupree's comment was, "While it is a sad thing for any human to have died young, we may never know who they are or what happened to them."

In answer to the same question, Mayor Pickings said, "I haven't seen the bones yet and I can't help but wonder if it's not some stupid plot to mess with this election."

Mayor Pickings was also asked about the circumstances surrounding his family's acquisition of the property that they later donated for the state park. According to property records, the mayor's father bought the land for $3,000 even though it had been appraised for over $30,000 the year before. Subsequently the value of the property was pegged at around $20,000 until just before it was donated, at which time the value shot up to $120,000. When these figures were brought to the attention of the mayor, his response was, "I don't know nothing about that. There's always lies around election time. You might ask Aaron Dupree why he's telling all these lies about me."

Asked to comment on Mayor Pickings' allegations of spreading lies, Mr. Dupree commented, "I have done no research into Mayor Pickings' background and I don't care to run that kind of campaign. I assume that my opponent is a fair and honest man."

Two other candidates are also running in this election. E. Everett Evens is campaigning on a promise to "bring things back the way they used to be, when we were a God-fearing nation, the Constitution was based on the Bible, and the homosexual agenda was stoning those sinners."

Also on the ballot is Marcus Fletcher, a longtime civil rights activist and retired teacher. When asked for his reasons for running, Mr. Fletcher replied, "Elections are a time of public discourse and my purpose here is to bring out the issues still facing the less fortunate members of Pelican Bay. It is easy to forget that children go hungry even here, and not just hungry for food, but also hungry for a good education, for a voice and a feeling of belonging to the American Dream. The words were written over two hundred years ago, but they still say it best: we are all created equal, and we all have the right to life, liberty, and the pursuit of happiness. We just need to get there."

Voting takes place on Tuesday, November 5th. All candidates agree on the importance of voting.

"Land Dealings Raise Questions" headlined Jacko's article.

Allegations have recently surfaced about irregular land deals dating from the late 1950s into the mid 1960s. According to sources still alive who remember the era, approximately 20 percent of the property owned by black citizens of Tchula County was transferred into white hands using tactics ranging from high-interest loans to property tax manipulations. A farm owned by Mr. Elbert Woodling was reappraised, raising its value from of $21,200 to

$32,000 in one year. He was unable to meet the higher property tax in a timely enough manner and was forced to sell his property to Hubert Horatio Pickings, the father of the current mayor, for $3,000. Part of this property is still owned by the Pickings family, and part of it was donated in 1985 to become Iberville State Park. Appraisal records indicate that between the original transfer of property in 1961 and the donation for the park, the value of the property went from $15,000 to $22,000, until 1984 when its value shot up to $75,000 and again, in 1985, to $120,000, at which time it was donated to the park system.

Other irregularities with property transfers also surfaced, including records with "Paid" crossed out, dates changed, entries in pencil made over clearly erased blurs. Most of the properties so marked were subsequently sold for the cost of back taxes or significantly below appraised value. One entry claimed that the taxes were paid a day late, but in that year, the date claimed for Payment Received was a Saturday, not a day the office would have been open. Had the payment been made the day before, a Friday, it would have been on time.

From there the story skipped to another page. Included in the story were photos of the changed entries, as well as photos of what some of the properties looked like today: Wendell Jenkins' big car lot, the posh Back Bay Country Club with its marina, the Coast Bank building in the middle of town, the high-priced beach property of the east side of the harbor. Jacko had done an excellent job, including running it by several lawyer friends of his as well as Denise Franklin, the lawyer the Crier used on the rare occasions legal advice was needed.

Her comment, in her typical blunt style, had been "You're going to piss people off, but it's legal."

The ringing of the phone and the clicking of the answering machine told Nell just how pissed off people were. Jacko's article had named names, all the ones to be found in the legal records, such as Bryant and Buzz Brown, Whiz's estranged relatives, the sheriff from that time, Bo Tremble, the man who ran the tax office, Albert Dunning and the properties he had accrued on his public servant's salary. It was all there, and it was all damning. Save for the murders, the statue of limitations had run out on anything illegal. Most of the men named in the article were long dead. Nell remembered Penny March's words: "their graves were tainted, bitter with bone." That was all that could be done to them, taint their graves.

She heard the sound of a key in the front door and left her office to see Pam coming in.

"Don't turn on the phones until exactly nine," Nell told her. "It's going to be hard enough answering them without starting early."

"Should I leave the door locked until then?" Pam asked.

"Might be a good idea, or at least until we get some reinforcements."

Reinforcement arrived a few minutes later.

"I couldn't get out of the parking lot before people started asking me if it was true about the mayor," Dolan said as he entered. "I told them I just do the business end, not the reporting end." Then he added, "But if we print it, by golly, then it's a fact."

That added comment put the smile back on Jacko's face. He entered right behind Dolan.

With the addition of people and the clock pointing at nine, the phone was unleashed and the doors left unlocked.

On a regular day, Pam could pretty much handle the phones herself with occasional back up from the rest of the staff. Today wasn't a regular day.

Nell quickly came up with a series of answers to the most common questions. To those whose name or family name was mentioned in the article, the standard response was that it wasn't libel if it was true. There was considerable sputtering, but only a few actually threatened a lawsuit. Other answers included "yes, we thoroughly research everything that we print," "we have no more information to release at this time," "if you want extra copies of this issue they can be purchased at …"

For the lazy journalists who wanted a hot story dictated over the phone, Nell merely referred them to the wire service. There were a few colleagues she talked to, giving them the inside story because they had done similar favors for her.

Harold Reed called around lunchtime. "Good reporting," he told her. "I can promise your front page has managed to eclipse last night's debate as a topic of conversation around here. Buddy is taking a poll right now to see which position he should take on this." He added quickly, "Don't quote me on that. I need this job until the kids are through college."

Nell promised it would remain their secret. Then they talked about the property story. "A lot of them seem unfair, but only on the borderline of illegal," she told him. "Just applying the rules a bit tighter. And even for the illegal ones, I'd guess by now the statute of limitations has long run out."

"I'm going to scour the books. There might be some federal statute about violation of civil rights we can bring up," he said.

"But how do you prosecute a grave?" Nell asked. "There are second-generation people around, like our esteemed mayor, who are going to be answering embarrassing questions, but most of those who did it are long gone."

"It makes me angry. They were so blatant and high-handed." He then changed the subject. "I talked to the judge about the request for a new trial date. Didn't get an answer, but I think he'll at least keep their chain short."

"I appreciate that. I just … want to get it over with."

"I understand. Keep me informed if anything happens. You've stirred up a major hornet's nest here."

Nell hesitated, then told him about her suspicions the killings might be linked to the property theft. "Michael Walker was going to law school. One of the properties taken belonged to a woman by the name of Hattie Jacobs, and Dora and Ella stayed with her. What if they were going to interfere?"

Harold Reed was silent for a moment. "That would get rid of the statute of limitations problem. It's a good theory. But after all this time is there any chance of finding out who did it, let alone proof?"

Nell admitted it was unlikely. He repeated his request to keep him informed if she found anything, and they rang off.

As she was getting ready to pick up Josh and Lizzie from school, she got a visit from the sheriff.

He started right off with, "Didn't trust me with the dental records or photos, did you?"

"I felt the District Attorney's office would be better able to handle them." Nell was glad she was standing up, not sitting behind her desk with the sheriff's bulk towering over her.

"Miz McGraw, I was a skinny little fifteen-year-old kid when those poor souls were killed. You can't think I had anything to do with it, can you?"

"Murder? No, I don't suspect you of that."

"Just of being a good ole boy racist enough to make Everett Evens seem like a pinko commie?"

"Not at all. No one could make Evens look like a pinko commie." They stared at each other, then Nell said, "I don't know which way the political winds blow for you. Today's front page has angered a lot of powerful people in this town."

"I don't let politics get into murder cases," he said with a steel tone to his voice.

"I'm glad to hear that, Sheriff. A change from one of your predecessors. Did you know Bo Tremble?"

"Have to tell you I didn't like reading that stuff about him. He was a good man, had a son who was slow and he spent a lot of time with that boy, never made him feel different."

"The banality of evil. Good men can do horrendous things. He had to know they never got on a bus. If he didn't murder them, he covered it up."

"I don't like to think a law man could be so lawless. Don't go saying things about people with no proof."

"With fifty years gone, what proof will there be, save for three skeletons and someone who lied about where they were?"

"Not much, likely. I respected Sheriff Tremble, started as a deputy with him. One thing I learned from him is the law is the law. And to respect the law more than any one man." He was silent, as if daring Nell to argue.

"Sheriff, I have to pick up my children."

He nodded. "Okay, brass tacks. I don't want to learn things about murders my department is investigating on the front page of the newspaper. You can tell Harold first, but you tell me second. If I gotta go put handcuffs on Bo Tremble's headstone, I won't like it, but I'll do it. You got that?"

"I can live with that, Sheriff Hickson."

"Some advice I know you don't want. Don't go around being some ballsy Yankee lady and stirring up more hornet's nests than you can slap away with your hands."

"I just report the news, I don't make it."

"Just remember messengers get shot at. Now go get your kids and you call me immediately if there's anything you think Harold Reed should know."

Nell gave him a minute to get out of the building before she headed to her car. His sheriff's car was still parked in the City Hall lot as she drove past. She wondered which speech he was giving to Mayor Hubert Pickings.

Her encounter with the sheriff had left her children waiting outside school for longer than was acceptable.

"Where were you?" Lizzie greeted her as she got in the car. "I told Janet I'd email her something the second I got home. She's probably waiting now."

Nell had expected even her children to be consumed by the front page, but they seemed wrapped up in their own world, Lizzie fretting about email she claimed was a joint homework assignment she and Janet had to have in by Monday. Josh was excited about a field trip his science class would take to Horn Island in a few weeks.

Nell listened to her children talk about their school day, the mundane details that occupied them, a far place from bones and murders. She was relieved they hadn't been affected by the front page of their . . . mother's paper. It used to be their parents' paper. Lizzie fumed about going to the library and was slightly mollified by promises she could instantaneously get on a computer at the Crier office.

When Nell returned, everyone was on the phone, both Dolan and Pam giving the same answer, one Nell had scripted earlier. Josh headed over to the library just in case he'd missed any shark books, and Lizzie bee-lined to the computer on Jacko's desk.

Just as she sat down, Jacko came back. He waved Lizzie to stay on the computer and came into Nell's office.

"Alberta Bonier had to sneak me out the back door," he told Nell. "It seems everyone whoever owned property here wants to look at the records. She finally had to claim they were doing inventory and no one was allowed in."

"Inventory in the records department?"

"She was working fast. I suggested that claiming the records were off-limits until the FBI got through with them might be a better excuse."

"Did you find anything else before you were hustled out?"

"A few more things on Pelican Property. They did most of the buying after around 1963, almost like they out-muscled the others."

"It makes sense. Wasn't the sheriff one of them? He could probably arrest anyone who underbid them."

"Most of what they bought, they later sold to Andre Dupree. They made money on it, but he got a good deal in the process. That's more or less how he got all the property for Back Bayou Estates, the Country Club, and the marina back there."

"Which is more or less how he made his fortune," Nell commented. It wasn't Aaron but his father, she reminded herself. And even the father hadn't stooped to directly cheating people out of their land, although he appeared to have benefited from those who did. Nell wondered how much the elder Dupree had known—was there really a way he couldn't have had some inkling of what was going on? But more importantly, she wondered how much the son knew. "Good work. Maybe next week, we should focus on Pelican Property and what they did."

"Might not help Aaron Dupree much in his run for mayor."

"After the way Hubert Pickings disintegrated at last night's debate, I think it would take a lot more than that to keep him from winning. Go ahead and work on that story for next week. When my daughter gets off your computer."

"I did find out something else interesting today."

"Oh?"

"But I'm not supposed to know this, so you get to figure out how to divulge the info without getting either of us in trouble."

Nell nodded for him to continue.

"I think I mentioned that Alberta Bonier has a sister who works at the bank?" Another nod from Nell kept him going. "They usually meet for lunch, and I've been in the habit of joining them. I happened to mention the Jones boys and she let slip that their garage is mortgaged to the hilt. Only if they owned it free and clear would it cover the bail."

"They lied to the sheriff?"

"Looks that way. Or they just forgot those second mortgages they took a few years ago. With a lien on the property, it no longer will work to keep Junior out of jail."

"Jacko, that's the best news I've had all day!" If it hadn't been too out of character for her, Nell would have jumped up and hugged him. "Stay here. The sheriff told me to call him earlier. I'm going to call him." She quickly grabbed the phone and dialed the number of the sheriff's department. It took her several minutes on hold, but she was finally connected to Sheriff Hickson himself. After a quick hello, she said, "Sheriff, you did check out whether the Jones brothers' garage had any liens on it before accepting it for bail, didn't you?"

"Probably not," he admitted. "Don't have the manpower to search every one of these. Why, you heard something?"

"You might want to inquire at Costal Bank."

"I might just want to do that. You want me to call when I round him up?"

"If the rumor I've heard turns out to be true, I'd appreciate having it confirmed."

"That I'll do. You stay out of trouble now, Miz McGraw." He put the receiver down.

"There is a god or a goddess," Nell told Jacko. "He didn't even ask where I got the information." That seemed like a perfect way to end the day. It was only a little after four, but Nell told everyone to go ahead and pack it in.

"I think I've answered more calls today than I did the rest of the week," Pam commented. Then she added, "But a lot of them were good, saying it was about time we told those stories."

Nell called Marcus, while Jacko contacted Carrie, to tell them the office was closed in case they might come by. According to Jacko, Carrie was working on a story about the debate, getting various reactions as well as snagging a tape of it to transcribe the comments the candidates had made. Marcus was chasing leads on where the displaced property owners might have gone, to see if any of them were still alive and willing to tell the story. "I should have something for you on Monday," he told Nell. Then he told her he was going to be at Joe's most of the evening, so if she or any of the other staff cared to join him they were welcome.

Nell pried Lizzie off the computer—with promises they were going home and she could immediately get on the computer there—and they were out the door.

Somehow Josh had found another shark book at the library. Nell waited while he checked it out.

She was relieved to find no rocks had been tossed through the windows of her house, nor dead things left on the front steps. Am I really that worried? she wondered as she opened the door. Save for the Jones brothers' clumsy attack on Josh, the hornet's nest she'd stirred seemed content to do little more than buzz angrily.

Lizzie shot past her to the computer. Josh kept her company in the kitchen, albeit with his head buried in the latest shark book. It was a quiet evening at home; they even managed to find a nature show on TV that wasn't too gory for Lizzie's sensibilities.

Shortly after she'd finally convinced Lizzie that even though it was a Friday night, she still had to get to bed before midnight, the phone rang.

So I'm finally getting a crank call, Nell thought as she picked up the receiver. With Josh and Lizzie both home, she knew they were safe.

"Nell," Sheriff Hickson said. "You gotta get down here. They fire-bombed the Crier building."

NINETEEN

"Don't open the door to anyone but me. Understand?" Nell instructed Lizzie and Josh.

"Is the Crier gone?" Josh asked, a waver in his voice.

"I don't know how bad it is yet, honey." To give him the reassurance she could, Nell said, "It's brick and stone, so it won't burn well. I'll be safe; most of the sheriff's department is there." Suddenly Nell wondered, is the firebomber on his way here? She didn't want to take Josh or Lizzie with her, but she worried about leaving them. She told herself, one look, then back here. If the firebomber was after her, he would have come to her home first. She added, "This is your chance to stay awake on a Friday night. If you see or hear anything that worries you, dial 911 immediately. I'll be back quickly."

At the door, she repeated, "I'll be back soon. Don't open the door unless it's me."

Nell rushed into the night and drove to the Crier office, parking illegally on the square. There were a number of cars, and she pulled behind the last one. Nell had little experience with fires. She was relieved there were no towering flames visible as she came around the cars.

347

She was less relieved, as she trotted across the square, to notice two fire trucks parked in front of her building, with other cars haphazardly parked around the big red trucks.

"Can't go there, ma'am." A young deputy tried to stop her.

"That's my building!" Nell told him, ducking around his outstretched arm. She added, "Sheriff Hickson called me."

Getting closer, she saw there was still smoke coming from the front of the building. Several firemen were standing around, watching the conquered beast for any signs of life.

She recognized Fire Chief Mike Zellner and ran to him. He and Thom had been fishing buddies, so she knew him from occasional dinners with the catch of the day. He was a big man, not given to talking much.

"How bad is it?" she breathlessly asked him.

"Nell," he said, turning to her. "You got lucky. Bastards threw it and ran. From the look of it, they meant to toss it through a window, but it hit the wood and bounced. Burned outside the building mostly, not in. Door caught fire, would have taken the building, but we got here in time. Water damage inside, but it was that or let it burn."

It was the most he'd ever said in one whole speech to her. "God, Mike, I thought I might get here and see flames shooting out of the top. Was anyone hurt?"

"One guy stubbed his toe getting the hose out, that's all I know of," he told her.

Sheriff Hickson found her. "Big mess," was his comment. "You'll be wading through paper for a few days."

"Who did this?" Nell asked. To soften what had sounded like a demand, she added, "Any ideas?"

"After that front page, about half the town."

"Nothing like a small suspect pool," Nell sarcastically commented. Then she asked the obvious question: "Why are you here and not the police?" This had happened within city limits.

"Got the call. Decided it'd be faster to just get moving on it." He gave Nell a sidelong look. "Besides, I suspect Whiz Brown has ceded jurisdiction over anything near the Crier building."

"Do you think he did it?" Nell asked. She hoped such a direct question might get a direct response.

"Whiz ain't got the balls, pardon my French. We did pick up J.J. a while back, so the timing is suspicious for the Jones boys, and they're stupid enough to have not gotten it through the window." Not giving Nell a chance to ask the question, he continued. "Yeah, we're running them down, ain't gonna wait for the police to give 'em a week to wash their hands. Gonna be a Jones family reunion at the jail tonight. They'd have to grow another brain to be smart enough to hide all the evidence. "

"If they didn't do it?" she queried.

"You riled the mayor. He's been comfortable all his life, but now it looks like discomfort is comin' his way. He's hard up for money; had too much fun at the casinos over in Biloxi and now he's paying for it. Now, that's a rumor, so don't you go quoting me on the front page," he said sharply.

"I only print what I can verify," Nell said.

"Can't sell the property with that polluted factory on it, only thing he can sell is being mayor. Looks like he's about to lose. Might make a man desperate. But I can't see him doing it himself and he don't have the money to hire anyone for this kind of stuff. Then, of course, there's all them other names you blazed across the front page. Might have pissed off—pardon my French—some murderers."

"My, I've been a busy girl, haven't I? But men who murdered fifty years ago probably aren't up to firebombing buildings, if they're still alive. Besides, going after me isn't going to do much about you on their trail. Assuming you are."

"Already called the FBI to consult. Doing what I can, Miz Mc-Graw, but fifty years is a long time."

"And as for the property stuff, they would have been better off burning down those files. Scaring me off won't stop others from looking. Plus the statute of limitations has passed."

"Still, when you piss people off, you just never know what you might run into."

"That almost sounds like a threat, Sheriff."

He turned to look directly at her. "Nothing of the kind, Miz Mc-Graw. Just stating a fact."

Nell was prevented from questioning him further by the arrival of Dolan. The greeting he exchanged with the sheriff told Nell that Sheriff Hickson had called him as well. Probably at the same time, since Dolan lived on the other side of town. Nell guessed the sheriff felt some man should be around. Jacko was the next to arrive. She couldn't tell if the sheriff had called him, too, or if he was plugged in enough to have this news quickly reach him.

Nell gave them the information she'd gotten from the fire chief.

"I'll stay here," Jacko volunteered. "Someone's got to guard the building."

Nell started to protest, but the sheriff added, "That's fine. I'll leave a car and one of my deputies here as well. They won't be back, but anyone could get into your building, and you don't want that."

Nell glanced at her watch. She both needed to get back to Josh and Lizzie and she needed to take care of everything. She told the circle of men around her, "My kids are home alone and I need to get back there. What else needs to be done here?"

"You go on back to your kids. We'll take care of things," the sheriff decided for them. Get the little woman home, Nell heard in his undertone.

"This is my paper and my building," Nell retorted angrily. "I can't do it all, but I'm a big part of any 'take care of things.' Understand?"

The sheriff obviously thought he was doing her a favor. The look on his face told her he didn't appreciate having his favors rejected. "Guess I'll let you handle it, then." He walked away.

Dolan cast a quick glance after him and then one at Nell. He was silent, then merely said, "Damn, I wish I could get inside and get all the insurance information."

Nell dug in her purse and found her wallet. In it was a card with the name and number of their insurance agent. "I guess we should call him tonight. We're awake, why shouldn't he be?"

Dolan took the card from Nell's hand. He'd had the most contact with the insurance people. As he dialed, Nell and Jacko walked toward the building. The door, old oak, was badly burned and would have to be replaced. Several of the windows were broken, both from the fire and the water pressure.

"Weather is supposed to clear tonight," Jacko said, following her gaze. "We can get those boarded up tomorrow."

"What a mess. What a fucking mess," Nell said.

He seemed unfazed by her cursing. "Yeah, it sure is. And this is just the outside."

"It's going to be a marathon of replacing everything from computers to copy paper to get the paper functional again." Nell felt exhausted. She half regretted her feminist streak. She could have played the little woman and been on her way home by now.

She headed back over to Mike, Jacko following. "When can we get back in?" she asked him.

"Fire seems out, but we need to check everything. You got a key? Door's gone, but you might prefer we open what's left rather than chop through."

Nell dug the key out of her purse and gave it to him.

He continued. "A few more hours. Just to make sure nothing's smoldering and no structural damage."

Dolan rejoined them. "Ten a.m. tomorrow, we have an appointment. Better to see the damage by daylight, I guess."

"Can probably get in by then," Mike told them.

They all stared at the building scarred by fire and water.

Finally Dolan said, "Who would have done this?"

"I don't know. Who have you pissed off lately with your hard driving business deals?" Nell said. She meant to relieve tension, but she was embarrassed to find herself starting to cry. It was something Thom could have pulled off, but her voice was dry and strained. She almost reached out to hold Thom's hand. But Thom wasn't there, just these men she knew only from small pieces of her life. She stumbled away, trying to gain control, hastily wiping her sleeve across her face.

The silence from the group was awkward and strained. Mike finally said, "Nell, why don't you go on home? There's not a lot you can do here now."

With a final wipe of the sleeve, Nell turned back to them. "Yeah, why don't I do that," she said, her voice barely a whisper. Taking a deep breath, she added, "I'm sorry, it's just been a rough ... few months." She was acutely aware of the smoke still heavy in the air, and that she stood outside the group of men. Everything rushed in: Thom's death, the attack on Josh, the burning of the Crier, the long-ago deaths found in the woods; they all coursed through her head. "Let me get home," she managed before she stumbled away from them.

After a few feet, she felt a hand on her elbow. Dolan, guiding her. Nell let the tears steam down. They said nothing until he had handed her into the car. "You going to be safe driving home?" he asked.

Nell nodded, then managed to say through her tears, "Yeah, I'll sit here for a bit. Thanks."

"Okay, get some rest. It'll help." He softly closed the door for her and went back to the other men.

Nell watched the scene, which was blurred by tears. She tracked Dolan until he became another vague shape. She wondered if they were shaking their heads at the little woman breaking down.

"Goddamn it!" she cursed. "I've got a fucking right to break down!" She gripped the steering wheel as tightly as she could. "Thom! Why the fuck aren't you here?"

After the outburst, she sobbed. Then, remembering her promise to get back home, she roused herself, roughly swiping the sleeve across her face. She started the car, wiped her face one final time, and pulled out.

When Nell got home, there was a big boat of a car in the driveway and every light in the house was blazing.

She felt too exhausted to go inside and face what was waiting. How in hell had Mrs. Thomas, Sr. known that Josh and Lizzie were alone? It was likely Mrs. Thomas had heard about the fire—for all Nell knew, the sheriff had called her, as she'd been a sensible little woman who'd stayed at home—and come over to make sure her grandchildren were safe.

Nell fumbled in her purse for a tissue and gave her nose a loud blow. She didn't bother checking her face in the rear-view mirror; it had to be a mess, and knowing would do little to aid her composure. Closing the car door noisily enough to give them fair warning she was back, Nell crossed the lawn—she'd had to park in front of the house instead of in the driveway.

Both the lights and her mother-in-law's countenance were blazing when Nell entered.

"Nell! How could you leave the children alone?" she demanded.

"Mother, I had to see how much damage there was."

"And leave them here? It would have been better if you'd taken them with you than left them here alone."

"I didn't know if anyone was hurt," Nell said. "I didn't want them to see that." She had covered a few fires and she knew burned bodies were a grisly sight—and smell. Her mother-in-law, without the benefit of experience, probably thought a little blood might have been the worst of it. With Josh and Lizzie there, she didn't feel like spelling out in graphic detail what they might have witnessed.

"You could have brought them with you and left them in the car."

Nell realized she could have done that—it certainly would have been preferable to this scene—but she hadn't thought of it, equating home with safety and wanting her children safe. "I didn't know how bad it would be. I didn't want them there." She wasn't going to concede Mrs. Thomas's point.

"They need to have a mother who puts them first! Who isn't more obsessed with digging old bones, rehashing old wounds, and flirting with new men!"

"Goddamn it! That's not fair!" Nell yelled back. As she'd had no control for her tears, now she had none for her anger.

"Watch your language!"

"They've heard it before. From Thom! We've got a lot more to worry about than goddamned words!"

"Yes, we do. And that's why they're coming with me," Mrs. Thomas announced imperiously.

"Coming with …? No, they're not!"

"Joshua has already been attacked. The Crier building burnt down. Are you going to keep them here until this house is burned, too?"

Nell felt frozen. There was too much truth to her mother-in-law's words for her to ignore. What if the sheriff hadn't captured the Jones brothers and they were on their way here? What if, when the morning light came and whoever had tried to burn the Crier realized they hadn't succeeded, they decided on a different method of attack? With a crushing sense of defeat, Nell realized it would be close to impossible for her to get the Crier back in shape and be with Josh and Lizzie as much as she needed to be. Sending them off with Mrs. Thomas was galling, and she wondered if it would damage her already fraught relationship with them.

She asked, "Why do you think that they'll be safer at your house than here?"

"They won't be at my house. We'll be out of town. I have no intention of staying here."

"What about school?"

"They can miss a few days. Surely the police will settle this soon." In the time waiting for Nell, Mrs. Thomas had thought her argument through.

Nell glanced away from her, with a brief thought of grabbing Josh and Lizzie by the hand, running out to her car, and driving off to … she had no idea. The best she could do would be a night or two in a hotel somewhere, and she still had to be here to take care of the Crier. It was too much, just too much. "I'll be right back," she suddenly said and ran to the bathroom.

Staring at her face in the mirror, not liking what she saw—a tired, middle-aged woman, her eyes puffy and red—Nell didn't like any of her choices, but she needed a moment out from under her mother-in-law's glare. Pride or my children's safety? She didn't want to concede to Mrs. Thomas, but even if she kept them locked up here, some maniac could still throw a firebomb in the window. She could haul them along to sort through the waterlogged remains of the Crier office, but that wasn't a guarantee they would be safe. The bomber had stuck once; he might come again. What if she was the real target? Keeping them near her would make them less safe.

I could just cash in my insurance, close the paper, and call it a day, Nell thought. But that would be giving them what they wanted. It had been a cowardly attack on an empty building in the middle of the night. No, she would fight and make what compromises she had to until they became too great. Nell filled a glass from the tap and used it to slake her thirst and help swallow her pride. She would let Mrs. Thomas have Josh and Lizzie for the weekend, and after that they'd have to see.

For form's sake, she flushed the toilet before exiting the bath-room.

"Go get packed for the weekend," she quietly told her children. "It's best if you stay with your grandmother for a few days." Then she added, in an even quieter voice, "I'm sorry. I wish … we had some better choice."

They looked at her, then at Mrs. Thomas. Lizzie started to say something, but Josh whispered, "Let's go," and they headed up to their rooms to pack.

"I want them back on Monday morning for school," Nell told Mrs. Thomas. She hadn't swallowed all her pride. "We'll take things from there. The sheriff's office has a good idea who did it, so someone will be in jail by then. Let me know where you are. I'll call tomorrow night around five, to talk to Lizzie and Josh."

"It may depend on what we're doing," Mrs. Thomas hedged, some of her pride also still undigested. "But I'll leave a message."

"Are you leaving tonight? It's late."

"No, we'll go back to my place. I alerted Dorothy, and she, her husband, and their two boys will stay tonight. We'll leave in the morning."

Dorothy was Mrs. Thomas's maid, someone she considered at her beck and call. It annoyed Nell; it was an attitude from a different era. She'd asked Dorothy once what she'd dreamed of doing as a young girl. Dorothy had answered slowly, chary at what she could reveal to the white daughter-in-law and finally saying, "The usual foolish stuff, being a singer or actress." Looking back, Nell had only proven she was a guilt-ridden Northern woman who didn't want to admit that her parents used racist words.

They waited in a tense silence until Josh and Lizzie, toting overnight bags, came down the stairs.

"Mom? What about you? You can't stay here alone," Lizzie said.

"Don't worry," Nell said. "I couldn't sleep anyway, so I'm going back to the Crier to start digging through waterlogged paper. Jacko is there, plus two deputies." Nell wasn't sure what she would do, but telling them she was staying here by herself would only worry Josh and Lizzie.

"Well, it's late," Mrs. Thomas said. "Let's get going, shall we?" She turned and headed out the kitchen door, which was closest to her car in the driveway.

Josh rushed to Nell and gave her a hug, then hurried after his grandmother. Lizzie also gave Nell a hug, holding on for a long time. "You be safe, okay, Mom?" she whispered.

"I'll be fine, honey. You take care of Josh and try to enjoy your trip."

Nell watched them from the door. Lizzie's long hug had cost her the front seat. Mrs. Thomas quickly drove away. When she could no longer see the taillights, Nell closed the door. She traversed the house, making sure everything was locked. She still had no idea what she was going to do.

As a wash of tiredness came over her, Nell decided she needed a few hours of rest, if not sleep. She grabbed the bottle of Scotch, stopped briefly at the bathroom for a perfunctory brushing of her teeth, and went upstairs to the guest bedroom. It was at the back of the house, away from the street and any window something could be thrown through. She found the travel alarm, set it just in case she dozed off, took a swig of liquor straight from the bottle, threw off her clothes, and climbed into bed.

TWENTY

Sunshine and an odd buzz woke her. Nell recognized the unaccustomed sound as the travel alarm. Glancing at it, she noted it was six in the morning. She started to lie back, but remembered Jacko had stayed the night. Someone should get there to relieve him, and she was the only someone available.

Nell rolled out of bed. As she stood up, she realized she was still tired. But I can't be tired, she told herself as she made her way to the bathroom, almost tripping over the Scotch bottle.

She took a quick shower, leaving the water cold enough to thoroughly wake herself up. She quickly dressed, remembered to remove the Scotch bottle and put it back where it belonged. After grabbing a breakfast of a banana, Nell was out the door.

When she arrived, Jacko was sitting on the front steps. He was young enough to not look as tired as he should have. A sheriff's department vehicle was parked out front, but the deputy was fast asleep in the front seat. Nell still considered that a vast improvement to the police, who were evidently fast asleep when someone firebombed a building half a block away.

"Good morning," Nell greeted Jacko. "Or is good even possible?"

"It is all relative, isn't it? The fire chief said it was okay to go in, just be careful. But I thought I'd wait for you."

"Thanks, I think." Nell gazed at the front of the building, the harsh black of ash marring its light gray façade. As far as she could tell, only she, Jacko, and the sleeping deputy were around.

"Shall we go take a look?" Nell asked.

Jacko pointed to a car entering the square. "Coffee," was all he said. The car glided to park behind the deputy, not even waking him up.

Kate got out, toting with her a cardboard tray with four cups of coffee. "Thought you could use this." She put her bundle down next to Jacko. Pointing, she said, "These two are black, one with milk, and milk and too much sugar." She handed that one to Jacko.

Nell and Kate both took the black ones.

"Expecting someone else?" Nell asked, looking at the fourth cup.

"No, wanted to make sure I brought enough. Someone can always have a second cup."

Nell was grateful for the caffeine and the kindness. She'd been too rushed to brew any before leaving home. She also appreciated that Kate didn't make small talk, seemed aware that words were of little use here. Instead, they quietly drank their coffee.

Jacko took a long sip, then stood up and started up the stairs. "I got your key back, but they left the door unlocked." He handed it to her, although Nell would never use it again.

Jacko carefully pushed the charred door open and stood aside to let Nell enter. Kate followed behind him.

Pam's desk, nearest the door, was a total ruin. Licked by flame and inundated with water, nothing could be saved. The supply closet behind her desk was also completely waterlogged.

"Too bad we just bought those boxes of copy paper," Jacko said ruefully.

"It's not like the copy machine's going anywhere except in the garbage," Nell pointed out. It lived under the window on the other side of the door from Pam's desk, the widow that the bomb had been meant to go through. It was a sad sight: the side nearest the flaming door partly melted, pools of water still in the paper trays.

Kate, practical Kate, put on a pair of work gloves she had in her pants and started clearing the area around the door.

"You don't need to do that," Nell said.

"Someone needs to. Check the rest of the building while I get this."

Dolan's office, also in the front of the building, just beyond the copy machine, had suffered considerable damage as well. His desk and computer were too waterlogged to be saved. His file cabinets were on the side of the office away from the window. Maybe all the records could be salvaged, but Nell didn't have the heart to open them to see how wet everything was.

Both Jacko's and Carrie's desks were in the main open area, about ten feet beyond Pam's location.

"A day or two out in the sun, they might dry out," Jacko said as he ran his hand over the back of his chair.

"I'm more worried about the computers than the chairs. I don't think they'll dry out in the sun." Everything was backed up on the server, but the server was kept behind Pam and was not likely to ever be used again.

"The hard drives might have survived, being in the metal cases and all," Jacko said. "I know someone who might be able to get the data off them."

Nell just nodded as she surveyed the main room. Paper was everywhere. The carpet was still a soggy mess, tracked with soot from the blaze and the feet of the firemen. The whole thing would have to be replaced.

Moving on, she looked into Ina Claire's office. It was behind Dolan's, with a smaller window overlooking the narrow walkway between the buildings. The carpet was still soggy underfoot, but her wall seemed to have protected most of her office from damage.

Nell's office, at the back of the building looked as if nothing had happened. Even the carpet seemed dry, or at least not noisily squishing underfoot.

"Guess the fire knows who's boss," Jacko commented as he glanced through her door.

"Yeah, I'm the only one who doesn't get a new computer," Nell said. Next to her office was the staff break room, and it too seemed in decent shape. "No new refrigerator or microwave either," she noted. "I wonder how downstairs fared."

"Oh, shit," Jacko exclaimed. "The morgue." He hurried downstairs and Nell followed him.

As much water as the carpet had soaked up, a lot still made it into the basement. Luck did offer a few kindnesses; the stairs opened facing the back of the building, so the old issues were kept there. The photo lab was in the far back corner, like Nell's office, and it had survived unscathed. The front of the basement was a storage space for old furniture, including the heavy and ornate desk Thom's grandfather had used. It was probably a valuable antique, but not very practical given its oversized top. Supposedly Franklin McGraw had it in the center of the main room to keep a watch on everybody and everything. Most of the stuff in that area was completely waterlogged.

The actual storage cases for the old papers were off the floor and hadn't been directly flooded, but Nell wondered what it would take to get all the moisture out in time to prevent mold and mildew from destroying the fragile old sheets.

Water was puddled in the low areas of the floor, and even the higher places had a moist sheen to them. They wandered around, as if trying to take in everything, making sure they didn't miss anything that could be fixed or saved. Nell was glad to have Jacko around. And Kate upstairs.

"I suppose we shouldn't really do anything until the insurance adjuster gets here," Nell finally said, and then headed back up the stairs. Kate had cleared a path from the front back to both Nell's office and the break room; several wastebaskets were stuffed with soggy paper. She looked up, wiping her brow.

Nell made one more circuit of the main area, again taking in what was lost and what could be saved. Then they all headed out though the blackened door.

Coming out into the fresh outdoor air made her realize that a heavy burned smell now saturated the office.

"Where did you get that coffee?" Nell asked as they retrieved the now cold cups they'd left sitting on the steps.

"Henrietta's. They opened at six," Kate answered, naming a place about six blocks away.

Nell debated whether the caffeine was worth the trip. She glanced at her watch to help make a decision. It was still hours before the insurance man would be here. "Well, we can sit on the steps or we can go get breakfast," she decided.

"I could use some food," Jacko admitted. He tapped on the deputy's window and told him where they were going. Which, Nell suspected, alerted him there would be no one around to cover up his sleeping on duty, should some higher officials chance on the scene.

Snagging a table in the back of the crowded diner, they discussed what needed to be done, making a list of things like garbage bags, fans, needed for the initial cleanup. Jacko ordered a big breakfast, Kate went for oatmeal and Nell opted for toast, the smoke lingering in her clothes didn't do much for her appetite. The waitress gave them what they really needed, a large pot of coffee left on the table.

"What will you do now?" Kate asked, her question clearly directed at Nell.

"Wait for the insurance person, try to clean up enough that we can function ..." Nell shrugged her shoulders, then took a sip of coffee.

"I meant, for you and the kids. What will you do?"

Nell picked up the coffee cup and took another sip. It wasn't a question she wanted to think about. Nor one she has an answer to.

"I'll be glad to help," Kate added. "You're all welcome to stay with me if it feels safer. Be warned, it's a blow-up bed in the living room for at least one of you."

"And at my place, too, though my offer is a sleeping bag on the floor," Jacko said.

Nell smiled. Or she hoped it was a smile; she wasn't sure her face was capable of one. "Thank you both. I'm not sure what to do just yet."

"The offer's genuine," Kate said.

"I know." Nell buried her face in her coffee cup, afraid she might cry, inappropriate in this bright breakfast place. The kindness of strangers. No, these weren't strangers, but friends. Ones she needed at this moment.

The waitress brought their food.

Nell grabbed her toast, hoping the mundane task of eating would ease her emotions. But the silence was expectant. Questions Nell had to answer hung over her.

"I don't know," she said, putting down a half-eaten piece of toast. "Somehow I can't take it in yet. Pelican Bay is supposed to be the safe, peaceful place. Where things like this don't happen."

"It's not fair, is it," Kate said softly. A statement, not a question.

"I don't want to back down. And I don't want my children hurt, and I don't know how to do both those things." After another gulp of coffee, she added, "I'm open to any suggestions."

"I wish I had some. But you're not alone. If you need someone to drive you down to the Florida Keys after this, we'll do it." Jacko nodded his agreement. "Or we can get all our friends to make a series of safe homes. Some even with real beds all around."

Nell brushed her hand over her eyes, trying to hide the tears seeping out.

Both Kate and Jacko handed her a napkin.

"Go ahead and cry," Kate said. "You've earned it."

"Or drink Scotch," Nell amended.

"Fifteen-year-old. I'll find you that bottle."

"I'll help," Jacko offered.

"You'd have to be old enough to go to a liquor store," Kate said.

Jacko looked appropriately outraged, enough that Nell had to laugh. Which, she realized as she finished her toast, was exactly what Kate had intended.

When they got back, the morning was far enough along for a smattering of people to be about. It was still too early for the insurance man and Dolan, so Nell, with an extra cup of coffee, and Kate and Jacko, perched on the front steps. Sipping the coffee, Nell wondered if the plumbing worked; she was downing a fair helping of diuretics. Or if there was anything resembling dry toilet paper in the building. She added that to the list.

The three of them were content to be quiet, as if there was too much to think about for mere talk.

Several passersby gaped at the burned building. A few had the temerity to ask Nell about it, but most seemed to consider the three people lounging on the stairs some odd grouping and most likely derelicts; none of them were well dressed. Jacko had old jeans and a T-shirt under his battered leather jacket. Kate's jeans were paint-splattered, her T-shirt so worn the letters were illegible. Nell had thrown on sweatpants and an old sweatshirt, one she wouldn't miss if it didn't make it through the day, and her yard-work jacket. Their sojourn in the building had added a layer of ash and smoke.

Dolan and the insurance adjuster had apparently met in the parking lot, as they walked together across the green. This time the five of them traversed the same route Nell had covered earlier. She let Dolan do most of the talking, occasionally adding in a detail or pointing out anything they'd seemed to miss, including Thom's grandfather's desk. Her motive was venal; she was hoping the replacement cost might help cover the real necessities that had to be replaced.

The insurance adjuster, she couldn't remember his name, said little, as if not wanting to admit that his company was actually responsible for covering any of this.

While they were conferring and had no further need of her, Nell found an ATM and withdrew several hundred dollars. She gave the money to Jacko and sent him off to get the things they would need to begin cleaning up. Kate returned to the inside, saying she'd continue making a path until she had to leave to open the bike shop.

Nell told Dolan, "You don't need to hang around. Handling the insurance mess is going to be enough of a good deed to get you into heaven."

"I'm going to stay for a bit, but I did promise my brother I'd help with his wife's surprise birthday this afternoon. I put in some calls this morning, got a carpenter friend of mine to come out and at least board up the windows and the door. We can't get any real workmen out here until Monday unless we want to pay overtime insurance won't cover."

"Thanks for arranging the carpenter," Nell said. "I need to figure out how to work around things anyway. Monday is soon enough. I think I'll spend today trying to get enough of the mess cleared out so we can function."

"You going to try and put out a paper this week?" he asked.

For an answer, Nell said, "Should I just stick to reporting high school football scores?" She wondered what her staff would do. Would they still want to work here? Dolan was her bellwether.

He was silent for a moment; then he said, "Can't say I like this. But neither Thomas nor Thom would have backed down, why should you?"

"Thanks, Dolan," Nell said softly. "The sheriff thinks it might be the Jones brothers. Revenge on me for pulling J.J.'s bail."

Dolan snorted. "Best place for that piece of trash is in jail." He paused and then added, "I knew Thom since he was ten years old. Still hard ... to think he's gone."

A truck that clearly said workmen pulled in front of the building. Dolan called out a greeting and then gave the two men the not so grand tour.

"We're just going to throw up plywood today," the older one told Nell, more she suspected as a courtesy to her as owner, than for any real input on her part. "Get you covered up enough to keep through the weekend."

A little while later Jacko returned, having even been smart enough to pick up an ice chest, and sodas and water. The electricity had been shut off last night, so anything left in the refrigerator would be lukewarm. After some debate, they turned the breakers back on, but the fire hadn't burned near any of the electrical supply. The plywood on the window cut out much of the light in the front area and if they were going to accomplish anything, they had to see.

Kate snagged a bottle of water on her way out, waving off Nell's thanks with an offhand "Karma. I have to make up for a wicked youth."

Dolan stayed until his carpenter friends were finished. He took several of his more important files with him when he left, saying he was going to spread them across his carport to dry.

Ina Claire also came by, bringing a plate of snacks. Her comment was, "Of course, we'll put out a paper. You just can't let people like this win."

Breakfast seemed a long time ago. Nell and Jacko took a break and devoured a good half of what Ina Claire brought while sitting on the steps and chatting with her.

After she left, they got back to work. Nell was glad the workmen had rigged a plywood door to replace the destroyed one. She could shut it and keep out the idly curious and their unwelcome stares.

Jacko was working in the basement and Nell was trying to clear Pam's desk when someone knocked on the plywood, then carefully pushed it open.

Nell looked up to see Aaron Dupree. "Nell, I heard. My God, what a mess," he said as he stepped in.

Nell found herself flustered at his presence. She was sweaty, dirty, and covered in soot from head to toe. "Aaron, this can't be on your campaign trail."

"It seemed an important detour. How bad is it?"

Nell gave him the rundown: the incendiary device hadn't done the damage it intended. She mentioned that the sheriff suspected the Jones brothers and they might be in custody by now. Although she was starting to have a nagging worry about that, as she had heard nothing from the sheriff. He might be punishing her for not being the good little woman when he wanted to be the big strong man.

Aaron listened quietly, then looked around. He started to pick up some of the accumulated trash sacks to take out back, but Nell told him, "Don't you dare, you're clean and in nice clothes. Everything here is covered in ash."

He conceded her point as he looked as his hands, blackened just from picking up the bag. Nell directed him to the break room which had a sink and soap. "What are you going to do?" he asked as he washed his hands. "How long before you can get the paper going again?"

"I intend to get one out this week," Nell informed him.

"Nell, don't you think you're pushing yourself too hard?" he said quietly. "You've been through . . . a lot recently."

"Damn it, I know! But I can't just stop," Nell said, again feeling the tinge of overwhelmedness that had hit her so forcefully last night. "I can't . . . let things defeat me."

"Not defeat. I can't see you doing that. But slow down and take care of yourself."

Nell was embarrassed to find she was sniffling again.

Aaron quickly dried his hands then put his arms around her. Nell started to pull away, to protest she was filthy, but he shushed her—"The town has a few dry cleaners"—and pulled her closer.

For a moment, Nell felt stiff; then she relaxed into the comfort of his arms, of having someone who cared enough to hold her. It was what she had wanted so desperately last night, to just feel Thom's arms around her.

They were interrupted by Jacko coming back up the stairs. Nell awkwardly pulled away, as if she were doing more than just being in his embrace. She handed him a paper towel so he could wipe off the worst of the soot.

He asked Jacko a few questions about the damage downstairs, easing the discomfort Nell felt. She wasn't even sure why—at being weak? Or was she still too recent a widow to be in the arms of a new man, even if it was little more than a hug for comfort. Maybe I'm emotionally exhausted, she thought.

Aaron offered, "My father probably knows every contractor in town. It's hard for him to talk, but I know he wants to be useful and he can certainly be useful to both me and you in that area. I'll be here Monday morning with names of people who'll do things right—especially for any friend of the Dupree family." He added as he slipped through the plywood door, "I'd rather be here with you picking up dirty trash sacks than discussing the business climate with the Chamber of Commerce."

She and Jacko took another break, finishing the rest of Ina Claire's snacks. Nell told Jacko he could leave anytime he wished, but he insisted on staying. They worked for another few solid hours; the back alley acquired a stack of garbage bags. Jacko brought his car around front and loaded up the computers to take to his friend. One of the purchases he'd made was a number of fans, which they placed both upstairs and downstairs. They would be left on overnight, doing whatever could be done to hasten the drying.

Nell thanked Jacko profusely as she put the shiny new key into the rough padlock on the plywood door.

He shrugged it off with the comment, "Good exercise." But even he was showing his tiredness as he went down the steps to his car.

Nell certainly felt hers as she dragged herself across the square to where her car was parked. She had just enough energy and initiative to rummage in the truck and take out the roll of paper towels she kept there, placing several over her seat to keep the soot transfer to a minimum.

One advantage of not having children home was she could strip off her clothes in the laundry room and then walk naked to the bathroom. She allowed herself a long soaking bath, including washing her hair twice.

After the bath, Nell poured herself two fingers of Scotch and took a few sips while debating whether or not to call the sheriff.

She finally decided to do it, reminding herself to try for honey, not vinegar, this time. But her debate was for naught. The sheriff wasn't around and none of the three people the phone call was routed through had any information.

"Damn you," Nell muttered as she put the phone down and took another long sip of Scotch. "I knew there was a reason I don't trust you."

Mrs. Thomas, Sr. had left the briefest message possible giving Nell their whereabouts. Nell called exactly at five, but no one was in the room. She called again at five fifteen, and this time was rewarded with Lizzie answering the phone and sounding as if she missed her. Nell spent a good half hour talking to both her and Josh. She told them a little about cleaning up the office, emphasizing the good news: the building was fine, just needed some new windows and a door.

After that, Nell settled in with her Scotch and a book and mostly managed to read, interrupted only occasionally with worries about the paper, her children. Missing Thom. That night, she again slept in the guest bedroom, again making sure all the doors and windows were locked and leaving lights on downstairs.

TWENTY-ONE

NELL SPENT MOST OF Sunday continuing the cleanup. Jacko showed up just after noon. Nell was relieved he was sensible enough to have caught up on his sleep. Between them, they managed to create something resembling a workspace. Jacko could share Nell's office; Pam and Carrie could take over the break room. Ina Claire's office was more or less usable, so she could stay there. Nell wasn't sure what do to with Dolan, but he could help make that decision on Monday. They had cleared out most of the damaged area, leaving it free to be worked on. The prosaic back door to the building would now be their main entrance—cement stairs and a metal door leading to the narrow alley that ran behind the Crier.

Jacko told her his computer friend was already working on data retrieval and had offered to help with purchasing and setting up the new computers.

Kate again came by before opening the bike shop, bringing several friends with her. They helped Jacko carry the heavier things out of the basement. Even the deputy put his brawny arms to work. The few things that could be saved were left out front to dry in the sun for a few hours; the rest was put in back for the garbage.

When Nell got home that evening, she completed her same circuit: clothes off in the laundry room and straight into the tub. She had still heard nothing from the sheriff, but vowed she wouldn't call him.

Mrs. Thomas phoned a little later to tell her they were back in town, but suggested that Josh and Lizzie stay with her for a while. Nell was so tired—and already comfortable ensconced in baggy sweatpants—so she almost gave in. But she was missing her children and didn't want to concede to her mother-in-law again.

Her effort in throwing on respectable cloths and dragging herself out of the house was suitably rewarded with the glee of Lizzie and Josh greeting her. She dutifully thanked Mrs. Thomas, including prompting Lizzie to also say thank you. Josh fell into line without a similar hint. Nell had her victory in the happiness of her children at being with her.

"Please be careful," Mrs. Thomas admonished as her farewell.

"You too, Mother," Nell answered, then packed her kids in the car and headed home.

Lizzie, of course, went straight to the computer. Josh, unable to check his email, gave Nell a rundown of what they did. They'd spent the night over at a B&B in Bay St. Louis; he'd been forced to tag along behind Lizzie and his grandmother while they wandered through the shops in the revived downtown area. Josh didn't say it outright, but it didn't sound like something he'd enjoy. Nell refereed the computer, letting Josh get his chance. She was tired enough that she left them watching TV—with instructions it went off at ten and they head for bed—and she turned in. As she was drifting off to sleep, she was gratified to hear the TV go off and footsteps head upstairs. They must be glad to be back if they were being this obedient.

"Mom?" Lizzie tapped at her door.

"Come in, honey," Nell told her.

Lizzie entered and sat on the edge of the bed. Softly she said, "I'm scared."

Nell sat up and put an arm around her daughter. "It is scary, but keep in mind they attacked an empty building, late at night. These men are cowards."

"It's not just that," Lizzie rushed in, overtopping Nell's words. "I thought I saw that truck. We were walking down the street, looking in windows, and I saw a red truck slowly coming our way. So I pretended like I really wanted to look in that store and hustled Josh and Grandmom in."

"Was it them?" Nell asked softly.

"I don't know," Lizzie said, almost crying. "When I looked out again, I didn't see anything. But it was a red truck, kind of small and dirty, and there were two guys in it."

Nell felt a trickle of worry. If the sheriff had picked up the Jones brothers, what were they doing stalking her children? She gently questioned Lizzie, but she'd seen the red truck only once and could offer no more details.

"I kept pretending I wanted to go in shops and look around," Lizzie said. "It annoyed Josh and made Grandmom think I'm turning into a proper lady. But I wanted to keep us off the streets. Did I do the right thing? Maybe if I watched longer, I could have got a license plate number."

"You did the right thing," Nell reassured her. "Your safety is most important."

"Thanks, Mom," Lizzie said, giving Nell a big hug. "I know you'll make it okay."

How do I make it okay, Nell thought as she listened to her daughter cross the hall to her bedroom. How can I possibly carry that burden? The only answer she had: you have to.

Nell slept restlessly; any sound or noise from the street woke her. She was almost relieved when the alarm clock went off and she could officially get up.

The kids wanted to see the Crier, so Nell hurried them to have enough time before school. She drove by instead of bringing them inside. That was bad enough; they were both quiet and somber on the way to school.

Back at the Crier, Nell used the back door. Wanting as little traffic as possible to come through the burned area, she made up a sign for the main door asking people to please come around back. From there she headed to the police station. She demanded to see Whiz Brown, barely waiting for the desk sergeant to announce her before marching into his office.

"Good morning, Chief," Nell said, ignoring the seat and remaining standing. "Someone tried to burn down my building Friday night, and despite it being half a block away, the sheriff's office handled the call."

"What are you talking about?" Whiz said, his eyes shifting downward in a way that told Nell he knew exactly what she was talking about.

"It's kind of odd, don't you think, that someone could drive right by the police station, throw a firebomb through one of my windows, and you didn't even notice." Then Nell threw out, "How much did you get paid to ignore that, Whiz? Enough to hire a good lawyer?"

She'd expected him to sputter and deny it, but instead he turned gray and looked down. She let the words hang, forcing him to respond. "I didn't get paid nothing," he finally said.

"Then what were you threatened with?" Nell pushed.

His head jerked up. There was a scared look in his eyes, but he looked away again. Without taking his eyes from the floor, he mumbled, "Nothing. Just nothing. Sorry about your building, but sometimes things just happened. Police can't be everywhere."

Nell leaned over his desk so he couldn't avoid seeing her, then said, "I'll find out. If they know, I can know."

His head again jerked up. "Just let me retire and get out of here." It sounded as if he was pleading with her.

"My son was attacked, my building burned. I can't just let it go," Nell told him in a harsh whisper.

He suddenly looked at her, and in a matching whisper said, "Forget the murders; forget the property stuff. That's what they want." Then he was silent, again looking at the floor.

"Who? Who wants?" Nell demanded. He didn't answer, just shook his head. Then Nell asked, "Was it your father? Did he murder them?"

The look he gave her went beyond fear to despair. But still he said nothing, until he finally whispered, "You got to get out of here."

"Who are they?" Nell demanded again, but for an answer he got up and left his office, still not looking at her.

Nell stared at his empty chair, still rocking from him hurling out of it. Then she left, wondering what—or who—had so spooked Whiz Brown.

When she got back to the Crier office, Dolan was there. Nell gave him a rundown of the arrangements she and Jacko had made, adding that they didn't know what to do with him.

"Neither does my wife," Dolan said. "Maybe I can share the office with Ina for a while. I suspect that I'll be doing a lot of running around."

Nell gave Dolan full authority to pick out paint and carpet colors, ruling out only hot pink and lime green.

"Nope, not a hot pink guy. You don't have to worry."

Aaron was true to his word and joined them with a handful of business cards, telling them to be sure to mention that the Duprees had recommended them. As Dolan was starting to make phone calls, he pulled Nell aside and asked if they could meet for lunch sometime that week. "Today, even," he offered.

"Probably not today," Nell admitted. "Can we play it by ear? It's going to be a busy week."

"Are you still trying to get a paper out?"

When she said yes, he shook his head, again cautioning her about pushing it too much.

Then Jacko, Pam, Marcus, and Ina Claire all arrived. Nell hastily told Aaron she'd try to fit him in.

"Thanks, I'd like that," he said and then exchanged both hellos and goodbyes with the new arrivals and was out the door.

Jacko gave everyone the tour, explaining the temporary arrangements. Carrie arrived just as he finished and he did it all over again. Then Nell gathered everyone in her office for a meeting. They all agreed to getting out a paper that week, as if some gauntlet had been thrown down.

"I intend to follow up on the stories that might have provoked this attack," Nell told them. "If you're not comfortable, I'm not going to make anyone stay. Feel free to talk to me privately later," she added, knowing the group might make people feel pressured.

"What's a paper without a little adventure?" Dolan commented.

Jacko explained about the computers, Dolan about the repairs on the big room. After that, they all spent the morning figuring out everything from who needed pens to how to run a few more phone lines to the temporary desks.

Marcus and Jacko decided to sort through the archives Marcus had saved. Dolan was out procuring office supplies, and Carrie had asked to either work at home or be out following the mayoral candidates. Nell had suggested she also do a quick rundown on all the other races, a brief who-and-what for the issue that would be the last one printed before the election. Even though the mayoral contest was the main one, there were still some people interested in who would be dog catcher for the upper seventh ward.

Pam appeared at Nell's door. "There is"—she glanced down at a business card—"someone named Cornelius Larkin here to see you."

Nell questioned Pam with her eyes, aware her visitor was only a wall away. Pam nodded he seemed okay, just a stranger. Nell gave another nod and Pam went to get him.

A tall, older man entered Nell's office, his hair a distinguished silver and black. Nell stood to greet him, noting he was well dressed in a conservative gray suit.

"Ms. McGraw?" he said, extending his hand.

"Mr. Larkin, how can I help you?" Nell sat, indicating a seat for him. She glanced surreptitiously at his card, wondering what a lawyer from New York wanted with her as they sat down.

He looked around the office, then said, "It looks like you've had some problems here."

"Someone tried to throw a firebomb through our front window," Nell stated.

"My God. Do they still do things like that?" he said, clearly taken aback.

"I'm afraid they do. As we found out the hard way."

"Was it because of what you reported about the murders?" He had a deep, rich voice, one Nell guessed could mesmerize a courtroom.

"That's possible, but so far no one's writing their grievances on the wall."

He nodded slowly, then cleared his throat. "I'm here about Michael Walker," he announced. He hesitated, then continued. "Michael and I were … very close friends. We were going to change the world together … both going to law school. Then he didn't come home. I went without him, maybe pushing the world just a little bit in the direction I wanted it to go." He broke off. "I'm sorry, I don't mean to take too much of your time. I just wanted to find out what … as much as there is to know."

Nell told the story, everything she knew so far. Cornelius Larkin listened intently, asking an occasional question.

When she finished, he said, "Thank you. I know it may seem foolish for me to have come this far for … for what I could read in the paper."

Nell could tell he was keeping a tight rein on his emotions. "Did you come by yourself?" She was hoping he had family with him. She noticed a ring on his left finger. "Is your wife with you?"

"My wife?" He glanced at the ring and said hurriedly, "No, I never married."

Then Nell understood. "You loved Michael, didn't you," she said softly. She wanted to ask, does it stop hurting after fifty years?

"Yes, I did. Michael couldn't hide who he was. His family had little use for that and turned away from him. I thought together we could be enough. But … as a 'friend,' I could only ask so many questions after he disappeared. I had no legal standing, and if I were to reveal … how much he meant to me, I don't think that would have helped."

"I'm very sorry, Mr. Larkin," Nell said. Now she understood his emotions. He had held this grief in silence for so long. She wanted to find out about Michael and he needed to talk, so she asked questions.

They had met at Columbia, "about the only two black faces on campus, so it was easy to spot each other." Their common background also bound them together; they were both the sons of families that had fled north for the promise of better jobs and freedom from Jim Crow. "Used to hang out together in the jazz clubs of the Village, young, spending our last fifty cents on beer, and happy. Once we had to walk all the way from 8th Street back to Columbia." He started to explain the distance, but Nell told him she had gone to Columbia J School and knew just how long a walk—half of Manhattan—that would be.

They talked for over an hour. He did once again say, "I don't want to take too much of your time," but Nell told him she had nothing to do that was more important. Finally he said, "I would like to … take Michael home. The only home he had was with me. I know that might take time and effort; I'm not 'family,' after all. I didn't really come all this way to give you my life story, but to enlist your help."

"Of course, I'll do everything I can," Nell assured him. Then she asked, "Did Michael ever talk to you about anything illegal going on here?"

"Plenty of illegal things: denying people the right to vote, intimidation, unequal enforcement of the law. I'm guessing you mean something other than the 'usual' ones of the time. I had an older brother who was a lawyer also—he passed about two years ago—and I know Michael asked if he could do some research into property law."

It wasn't a smoking gun, but it was the first concrete indication of a link between the murders and the property theft. But he could remember little more—phone calls were expensive back then, there was no email—so while Michael was away they'd communicated mostly by letter, and neither of them had been given to putting much on paper. "We always thought we'd have a lifetime to tell each other about that year."

Nell again promised she would keep him informed and do what she could to get the remains released to him. He gave Nell an additional card, writing on this one his home and cell numbers.

She sat silently after he left. For most people murder and death was something they read about in a paper, but for some it was a lifetime of always carrying the loss. Cornelius Larkin had cared deeply for a man who'd been gone for so long; cared enough to fight to take home the fifty-year-old bones.

I'll miss Thom that long, Nell realized. Even if she found love, found someone else to hold her through the rest of the nights of her life, he would still be someone who was there and then gone, always empty where he should have been.

She felt a sudden anger at the murderers, that they had so callously caused such long anguish. "No, damn it, you're not going to scare me off," she muttered under her breath.

She picked up the phone and called the sheriff. This time she reached him.

"Got some bad news for you, Miz McGraw," he greeted her. "Seems the Jones boys had a weekend fishing trip planned and Junior going back to jail wasn't enough to interfere. They loaded up the boat with a couple of cases of beer and headed out a little before sunset on Friday. By the time they were out by Ship Island, they'd had probably a six-pack or two, and between that and it being dark, they weren't navigating too good. Coast Guard had to pull them off a sandbar at around three in the morning. Talked to the skipper of the cutter just a bit ago. It's confirmation of their alibi."

"Thank you for calling and letting me know," Nell said, forgetting honey and packing in the vinegar. She debated telling him about Lizzie's red truck, but if the Jones boys had been aground in the Gulf, it couldn't have been them. She didn't need the sheriff to tell her that.

"So what now, Sheriff?" she asked. "Got any other leads?"

"Since you've pissed off 'bout half the town, it'll take us a while to interview the suspect pool," he informed her.

"So, in other words, you're not going to do anything," she threw at him.

"I got two deputies checking to see if anyone sold the stuff used for the firebomb, got another one canvassing the area to see if anyone heard or saw anything. So far they haven't found nothing useful, but we'll keep trying. You get any ideas, you let me know." With that he put the phone down.

Nell had to do a children run, again dropping them off at the library.

She returned just as Marcus and Jacko were entering, Jacko looking eager and interested and Marcus just the opposite.

"You should see the source material he has stored above his garage," Jacko let out.

"Boxes and boxes and more boxes, all jumbled together, some with no dates on them, others with just 'misc' scribbled on one side," Marcus added, their state giving a hint to his tiredness.

"Did you find anything?" Nell asked,

"Not yet," Marcus answered. "But I know we kept enemies lists—things like who was in the Klan, who had roughed up black folks.

There wasn't much law back then you could report white-on-black crime to, but we tried to warn each other. Now we'll have to find the right box—and that'll take some doing with all the years jumbled, but it'll be interesting to look at those old notes and compare them with the people who benefited from the property thievery."

"That could be very interesting," Nell said, "but let's not get our hopes high. It's likely those rich and powerful enough to get the land kept their hands clean. They joined the White Citizens' Council and let others burn crosses."

"True, but we did our best to keep track of those who joined those groups, too. Most of them had black maids or other workers—who do you think raised their children? They didn't stop talking about cross burnings because Mammy came into the room," Marcus told her. "Back then it was hard to fight openly, but we wanted to know who to short on a pound of shrimp and who to be fair with. The Defouches over on the harbor were threatened repeatedly with burning crosses. Seems I recall one got burned on a woman's lawn after she tried to register to vote." Even his tiredness couldn't keep the anger out of his voice.

"That's what the two of you can do tomorrow," Nell said, emphasizing "tomorrow" for Jacko's sake. "See what you can find. I don't know how much we can print; we might be on shaky legal ground. Property transfers are public record, but this isn't."

"Understood. Remember, I used to do a newspaper too," Marcus said. "But I don't want to let this go without overturning any and every stone."

Nell told them about Cornelius Larkin, including the request on property law Michael Walker had put to his lawyer brother. She didn't tell them about finding out that grief lasts as long as life.

"I've tracked down someone willing to claim Ella Carr," Marcus said. "Says he's her nephew." There was a hint of distaste in his voice. "He asked if I could get him in touch with the TV people to make a movie about her. Wondered how much money he might make from it."

"What did you tell him?" Nell asked.

"That I'm just an old news reporter. Don't know TV at all." He cleared his throat, then said, "I was left with the impression if he couldn't sell her story for enough money to make a profit, he would have little interest in paying for a funeral." He just shook his head slowly.

"Maybe someone else will claim her," Jacko said.

Marcus lingered in Nell's office letting Jacko update Ina Claire and Pam. "I didn't want to say it in front of the boy, but I got a disturbing phone call last night. It was late, almost midnight. A male voice, white, told me I'd have a comfortable retirement if I didn't start stirring up that old race shit—those are the words he used. And if I didn't stay away from the Crier, that they might not ever find my bones."

"Damn it, what are they so scared of?" Nell said. "You think it was just an empty warning or really threatening?"

"You never know how crazy the crazy people are going to be," he said. "If they think we might find something to link them to the murders, then the threat isn't so empty."

"They murdered once, they can murder again," Nell said grimly. "But these have to be men now in at least their late sixties if not older."

"And what old man wants to retire to jail?"

"Should we back down?"

"You might consider it. You're young, got kids. I'm not. I'm an old man, my wife is gone, my kids grown up and away. I can sit in

Joe's, drink beer for the rest of my days, or I can try to find justice for three kids buried and left lonely for too long."

"I'm not going to back down," Nell said, adding, "but I may act like I am, to throw them off."

"Okay, but you be careful. Let us old coots take the risks."

Dolan returned and needed help in unloading his illegally parked car.

In a break Marcus told her he had traced one of the people who had their property taken. "Hattie Jacobs; she now lives over in New Orleans. I'll try to get over there in the next few days." He gave Nell her address. "Sorry, I couldn't get a phone number."

Nell said it might be better to talk in person. She wanted to go with him, but didn't think she could manage it this week.

It took them until after five thirty to get everything Dolan had bought sorted, parceled out and stored away. With a glance at her watch, Nell sent everyone home.

Nell hurried to the library to get her children before closing time. For a second, she thought she glimpsed a red truck behind her, but whatever she thought she saw, it was gone.

Supper slumming, Nell hadn't been to the grocery store in much too long to feed two growing kids. They had sandwiches and orange slices (there were only two oranges, so she had to allot them out) and landed in front of the TV to eat.

A little after nine, the phone rang. Mindful of the threat Marcus had received, Nell got to it before Lizzie.

But it was Marcus himself calling. "I'm sorry to bother you, but I'm being followed." There was static on the line; he was calling on his cell phone. "I drove to Joe's because it was sprinkling and as I got back in my car, another vehicle suddenly started up behind me. Not liking that, I went a few blocks out of my way and they never left my tail."

Nell broke in. "Go to the sheriff. Go somewhere safe!"

"If they really wanted to kill me, they could have done so by now. The only thing I have they want is what's stored in those boxes. I've got an almost full tank of gas, so I'm going to take them on a merry chase. Meet Jacko at my house—spare key is under the fake dog turd at the back of the garage. Load up everything you can find and hide it somewhere. I'll keep them busy for at least an hour or so."

"Your safety is more important than those boxes!" Nell told him.

"I'll do my best to be safe. But there's no safety without justice. I told you, I'm an old man and some things are more important to me than a few more years in this world."

"Marcus, you can't—"

"Shush, yes I can. Don't argue, my battery is wearing down. I'll lead them for an hour or so, then do as you suggested and head for the sheriff's office or something. Okay?"

Nell heard a weird braying sound in the background. "What is that?"

"Their horn. It plays the first notes of 'Dixie.' Now get to packing and hauling, woman."

"Be safe, damn it," Nell told him, but he was off the line. Barely putting the phone down, she dialed Jacko's number. He answered on the first ring. She gave him a quick version of Marcus's request and he agreed to meet her at the house.

When she hung up, she found Josh and Lizzie looking at her with questions in their eyes. "I've got to run out," she told them. "I should be back in an hour or so. Don't open the door to anyone. Including your grandmother," she added, before cool and polite kicked in.

"You'll be home soon?" Lizzie questioned.

"Yes, an hour or two at most. Go on to bed."

"Wake us when you get back," Lizzie instructed her.

"I will, honey," Nell said. She gave them both quick hugs and then was out the door, pausing only long enough to make sure Lizzie locked the door behind her.

Nell sped over to Marcus's place, the quiet, even placid, neighborhood helping to calm her worries. It didn't feel like anything bad could happen here. Jacko's car pulled in behind hers. They both parked in the driveway, close to the boxes. Nell quickly got out and located the fake pile of dog shit. She picked it up, took out the key, and threw the plastic at Jacko. He dropped it before realizing it was fake. Nell opened the door, then let Jacko lead.

The boxes were stored in the crawl space over the garage, save for the first round that Jacko and Marcus had brought down already. They had to work in relays, Jacko crawling back and pushing the boxes to Nell, Nell moved them next to the ladder. When that space was full, Nell went down to the floor, and Jacko, hooking one leg in the rungs of the ladder, handed them to her. It was hard, physical work and Nell could see how it had tired Marcus, even going at a less relentless pace.

After getting the boxes down, they loaded them into their cars, packing both vehicles full, including the front seats. Jacko said he'd counted about thirty.

They stood in the driveway, panting. Nell glanced at her watch; it had been a little over two hours since Marcus had called her. "Let's get out of here," she told Jacko.

He backed out, then let her out and followed. At the corner, Nell stopped, waiting for traffic to clear. A big black truck, one that looked like J.J's except she knew he was in jail, turned in front of her. She watched it in her rearview mirror. It slowed, halfway down the block, then stopped, parking across the street from Marcus's house. She waited, but no one moved.

Don't be paranoid, Nell told herself. Just someone going home. Two men got out, both white; out of place in this neighborhood. They stood watching her unmoving car. Nell quickly pulled out and turned onto the main street. Marcus wasn't home, so if that was their intent, they were out of luck. If they wanted his papers, it was too late. But she was worried enough to take the next corner and then turn onto the street that would cross Marcus's street. She drove slowly as she went past his corner. The big truck was still parked there, with no sign of the two men. The street seemed quiet and safe. Then she heard a faint tinkle of breaking glass and, from the corner of her vision, saw a quick blossom of orange flame.

Nell's cell phone was in her purse, on the floor wedged behind one of the boxes. Rather than dig for it, she sped up, turning at the next street and jerking to a halt at Joe's Corner. She rushed in with Jacko following her. "Call 911! There's a fire at Marcus Fletcher's house!"

At her words, three men jumped up and immediately headed outside. The bartender picked up the phone and called. When he put down the phone, he told Nell, "Watch my place. I've got to see if Marcus is all right!"

"He's not there," Nell told him, stopping him from running out the door. She quickly explained what had happened, including that they'd retrieved Marcus's papers. Just as she finished her explanation, the wail of a fire truck grew loud, then suddenly cut off as it reached its destination.

"Let me go look," Jacko said, and he slipped out. Nell waited inside, near a window where she could watch their cars and the cargo in them.

Jacko returned in a few minutes. The black truck was no longer there.

"Shit!" Nell let out. "I hope he's safe. I hope to hell he's safe."

"Should we tell the police about the truck?" Jacko asked.

Suddenly Nell wondered if the police already knew; if they were in on it. Could she trust the sheriff? This is what it had been like when black people knew they would get no justice from any white lawman. "What do we really know? I saw a black truck, or maybe dark blue. Didn't get the make, forget a license plate number. Two white men got out. I only saw them in my mirror and they were half a block away."

Jacko could add little to that, but he said, "Let's try the anonymous call trick." He went to the pay phone at the bar, dialed the police station, and said, "I don't want to get involved, but I saw a big black truck, with two white men in it, parked just outside when the house on Calhoun Street caught on fire." He added, "Sorry, that's all I know," and put the receiver down.

Nell gave the bartender business cards and asked him to call if he heard from Marcus.

Then she headed home, taking extra corners to make sure no one was behind them. Jacko followed, and she motioned him into the house. She wanted to see if Marcus had called, and if he hadn't, to call him. She pulled her cell phone out. No call. Then she went upstairs to check on Josh and Lizzie. They both were still awake, although they'd dutifully gone to bed. With a kiss and hug for each, Nell assured them she was okay.

She went downstairs and tried Marcus's cell phone. Voicemail. She and Jacko brewed a pot of coffee and she kept trying his phone for the next two hours, but all she got was the voicemail. Jacko suggested that Marcus might have headed home and was now busy with the fire. His cell battery might be dead, and with no house, he had no landline or place to recharge his cell. Nell finally gave in and called the sheriff's office, giving them a quick rundown of what had happened and the make and model of Marcus's car. After that there was nothing to do. Jacko was slim enough she could give him a T-shirt and sweatpants of hers to crash in. While he was in the bathroom, she hastily changed the sheets in the guest bedroom.

They said a weary good night, and then Nell crawled into bed.

TWENTY-TWO

NELL GLANCED AT THE clock. Its green numbers had changed enough to show she had dozed, though her waking proved it wouldn't be a night with real sleep. She listened carefully, wondering if she had been awoken by something other than tension and worry.

She strained, listening, but heard no sounds out of the usual. Just as she started to relax, willing herself a few more hours of sleep, the phone rang. Nell quickly grabbed it, to still its ringing from waking anyone else.

"Who is it?" she said, preparing herself for whatever a call this late could mean.

"Nell, I'm terribly sorry for waking you."

It was Marcus. Nell felt relief flood through her at the sound of his voice. "I was awake," she quickly informed him.

"Not on account of me, I hope," he gallantly offered.

"Of course on account of you. Where are you? Are you okay?"

"I'm fine. I'm somewhere in the wilds of Mississippi, around Poplarville. That was the last exit sign I noticed. As a teacher I did a lot of driving kids to athletic games, spelling bees, you name it. The Negro schools weren't located on the main drags, so I learned a lot of back roads. Took those boys following me on a merry chase. Shook them just a bit ago. But I was so busy with my eyes on the road, I didn't keep my eyes on the gas gauge."

"You ran out of gas?" Nell couldn't believe this awful night could have such a prosaic ending. She almost started laughing, but managed to turn it to a cough instead.

"Sitting on the side of I-59 with the night critters," Marcus said. "Interested in being a knight errant and rescuing me?"

"Much better than sleeping and worrying." Then Nell remembered the fire. "Do you want the bad news now or later?"

"How bad? Who's hurt?"

"No one. But ... I'm sorry, they burned your house."

He was silent. Then he hissed out a terse, "Damn. Damn them." Another pause, and he said, "Before you got there?"

"No, after. We got everything." She then added, "All the boxes, that is." He'd lost everything else.

"I'm glad you got the boxes. I hope there's something there, something to hang the sons and the fathers."

"And the daughters. Hate is equal opportunity," Nell added.

"This battery's not going to last much longer and I can't recharge it." Marcus quickly gave her directions. As a final comment, he muttered, "I needed to redecorate anyway ... damn them."

Nell swung out of bed as she hung up. No one else was awake. As she dressed, she debated waking Jacko. Both of them couldn't go, and Nell wasn't about to leave Josh and Lizzie alone. She halfway hoped he would solve the debate by waking, and she also hoped she could use his sleeping as her reason to be the one to go.

Holding her shoes in her hand, she eased out of her bedroom. Let them sleep, Nell decided. She was awake and perfectly capable of driving to get Marcus. She hastily scribbled two notes, one for Jacko with a more complete rundown of what she was doing and one for her kids that she had to cover a story. She slipped the note for Jacko under his door and left the one for her kids on the kitchen table. She and Thom had both gone off frequently enough at odd hours that this wouldn't seem too out of place to them.

Nell slipped out of the house. It was black night, with shadows, but dawn was close; it would be daylight by the time she got back. Nell hastily shifted some of the boxes out of her car to free the passenger seat.

At this pre-dawn hour, traffic was light. I-10, the conduit for the coast with its casinos, still had cars, but after Nell exited, she only occasionally saw another vehicle. It seemed to be just her and the small area illuminated by her headlights.

Nell glanced to her watch. It had been forty-five minutes since Marcus had called. She noticed the dark was beginning to turn a dense gray. She slowed; Marcus would be on the other side and she'd have to pass him, go to the next exit, and turn around, but she wanted him to see her and know his wait was almost over.

There were no trees separating the two sides of the highway, but it was still dark enough that Nell had to carefully scan the far lane for any sign of him. She slowed even further as another minute ticked away on the dashboard clock.

Suddenly, Nell felt apprehension. What if they'd found Marcus stranded by the side of the road? What would happen to an inconvenient old man in the dark of the night?

She crested another rise and still saw no sign of him. She admonished her fears, told herself to be sensible; they couldn't spirit his stranded car away.

"It can't be daylight soon enough," she muttered aloud as she came to the top of another rise in the road.

Then she saw him. Sensibly, he had a flashlight and was slowly blinking it on and off. She couldn't make out more than a murky shape, a man and a flashlight next to it. But the slow, deliberate way he moved told her it was Marcus. Nell slowed even further, flashing her headlights in answer.

He saw her and his flashlight blinked rapidly, as if saying, "Glad you could make it."

She slowed and pulled to the shoulder, scanning the median to see if there was the remotest chance she could drive through the grass. There was a ditch in the center, too deep to risk her sedate family car. On to the next exit, then, Nell decided. But she pulled to a halt, wanting to shout at least a hello across the divide.

Suddenly looming out of the darkness, a truck appeared on Marcus's side. Nell felt a sharp stab of fear. It's just a truck, she told herself, but her brain interpreted what her instincts knew. This truck had no lights on, like a hunter stalking prey in the pre-dawn.

"Goddamn you!" Nell shouted, twisting the steering wheel of her car so it pointed directly where Marcus was. She hit her headlights to high beams, throwing a harsh, starkly shadowed light on the scene.

The truck slowed, and whatever last hope she had that they were good Samaritans disappeared as it swerved at Marcus. He jumped out of the way as the truck sideswiped his car. It stopped, and Nell saw the two men wearing ski masks get out.

She pounded on her car horn, making sure they knew there were witnesses.

Marcus flung the flashlight away and was running for the woods. But the attackers quickly closed the distance.

Nell shoved open her car door, still leaning on the horn. Her immediate impulse was to run across the road, to fight. But she hesitated—what were her chances against two men armed with what looked like a baseball bat?

She saw an arm arc up and then come down. Marcus crumpled to the ground.

"I've called the police!" she shouted. "They're a minute away!"

The arm was raised again, but hesitated at her words.

Damn it! Nell silently cursed. Why don't I have a gun? She frantically punched 911 on her cell phone. Her fingers slipped and fumbled.

She looked again at the median separating them, the deep ditch in the middle. She was tempted to roar her car over it anyway. It was at least some kind of a weapon.

"I can see their lights now!" she shouted.

The second blow didn't land. Instead, the two men scrambled back to their truck. They hadn't even turned off the engine.

They were a black ghost against the gray dawn. Then they were gone.

Nell sprinted across the highway, jumping the ditch in a leap she thought she had left behind in her twenties.

Marcus lay on the wet grass at the edge of the woods. He wasn't moving.

"Goddamn it, old man, you're not going to die like this!" Nell shouted, more to the gods than to him.

But she thought she heard a weak answer, a murmured "Yes, ma'am."

Nell hastily bent down beside him. Blood was pouring from a head wound. "You'll be okay," she said gently, willing the anger out of her voice. She had failed Thom; she hadn't kept him alive. She couldn't let it happen again.

She quickly dialed 911, this time looking at the numbers.

The call was brief; someone needed immediate medical attention, the location.

"You just take it easy, I'm going to take care of you," Nell assured Marcus.

"Um … Nurse Nell," he muttered.

"I took care of my mother while she died of cancer, I can take care of you. Now save your breath. Back in a minute." Nell ran to his car, looking for anything she could use as a bandage and to cover him up. She found an old towel thrown in the back seat, but that was all.

Nurse Nell indeed, she thought as she trotted back. At least I'm wearing a fairly new sports bra, she thought as she pulled off her T-shirt.

She covered him with the towel and very gently pressed the T-shirt against the bleeding. She didn't want to risk hurting him more. He groaned softly.

"Don't go into shock on me, okay? You've got a hard head and you're going to be fine." Nell gently eased her other arm under his head; she wanted to elevate it to help staunch the flow of blood. She slowly lowered herself beside him, so she was next to him. It probably looked odd, but she could keep him warm with her body, keep the pressure on his wound, and also cradle his head so it was off the ground.

"You're going to be okay," Nell softly told him. "You just concentrate on taking care of yourself."

His eyelids fluttered; he opened the one eye that wasn't covered with blood for a quick glance at her. "In the old days, they used to kill black men for doing less with a white woman," was his comment.

"This is a new day."

"Too bad I got such a headache." Then his one good eye closed and he was quiet.

Nell heard the faint wail of a siren.

"You're going to be okay," she told him as it grew louder. She cocked her head up and was now able to see the flashing lights.

The ambulance jerked to a stop next to Marcus's car.

"Over here," Nell called. The light was still gray and dense. There was a light fog rolling in from the woods.

The two attendants quickly responded to her voice. The seemed unfazed by the sight of her without a shirt on.

"He was attacked and hit in the head. I think that's his only injury," Nell told them.

As they got close, Nell saw that one of the EMTs was a black man, the other a white woman. She helped them move Marcus onto the stretcher. He groaned as he was moved but said little. His silence worried her.

The woman EMT handed her the bloody T-shirt back.

A highway patrol car joined them. Unlike the EMTs, the two young, crew-cut men did stare at her. Nell used the T-shirt to wipe off the blood she had gotten on herself. But the shirt was too bloody to do much more than smear it around. She hoped the troopers would realize she'd taken off the T-shirt and wasn't just traipsing around in her bra.

To avert their stares, Nell loosely held the shirt in front of her chest. Even so, they did spend most of the time staring at her upper body as she was telling them what had happened.

As she finished, she realized they weren't unkind, just young and unsure how to react to a half-dressed woman telling them of a ghost truck that stopped in the night and attacked an old man. She hadn't used the words "ghost truck" but she might as well have. A dark truck. Not enough light to get the make and model, let alone a license plate. Two men? Could she even be sure they were men? No, not in any rational way. Two people, medium build, wearing ski masks. She thought they were white, but she couldn't be sure. And she didn't know if she thought they were white because she thought they were the Jones brothers or if she'd registered their hands as light.

But why would the Jones brothers attack Marcus? They were after her. They seemed to have become her universal boogeyman.

The patrol men asked if she could identify them if they pulled over dark trucks. Nell admitted she couldn't. They would have taken off the masks by now, probably thrown them and whatever they had used to strike with into some patch of woods.

She felt a flare of anger as she pictured them sitting calmly drinking morning coffee, congratulating themselves on getting away with it.

Other cars had pulled over, gawkers trying to see what was going on. And to stare at my chest, Nell thought cynically.

The ambulance carrying Marcus left. Nell could think of little more to tell the young patrol men. One of them offered her his jacket, but she declined. An old sweatshirt, used for a windshield rag, lived in the trunk of her car. She hoped it was still there and that Lizzie or Josh hadn't purloined it for another purpose.

One of the patrolmen walked her back across the median, even going so far as to help her across the ditch. It was light enough Nell noticed his blush as he pulled her up and got a good view of her cleavage.

He even helped her move several of the boxes still in the trunk to find the sweatshirt. Smeared with grease and dirt as it was, Nell was relieved to put in on. The day was chilly enough that the patrolman had gotten not only cleavage, but erect nipples.

I should be a reporter, Nell thought as she realized she wasn't sure of the highway troopers' names. The one who had walked her to her car was Merton; his last name, she assumed. But I'm too tired to be a reporter, she realized. She slid into the driver's seat. Her car had been running the whole time. Good thing my tank was almost full. One of the patrolmen was arranging for Marcus's car to be towed. They wanted to check it for fingerprints on the off-chance that the attackers had touched it.

Checking her rearview mirror, Nell pulled back onto the road. She was tired, and the drive home was a long way. The coursing adrenaline and anger that had brought her here were gone, replaced by bone weariness beyond the physical.

What if I didn't save Marcus either?

TWENTY-THREE

The ALARM CLOCK WAS jarring; Nell had had little sleep, barely an hour. She was more jarred at hearing Jacko's voice in the hall; then she remembered last night. When she had gotten back, no one was up. It had seemed so improbable that the house could be quiet and serene, as if nothing had happened.

She hastily got out of bed and threw on a robe, not wanting Jacko to share too many worrisome details about last night's adventure. Plus she had to come up with how to add her own story to his account of the burning of Marcus's house.

When she rounded the corner on them, Jacko and Josh were talking about sharks.

"Good morning," Nell said, trying to cover her worry. "I see you've noticed our overnight guest." She gave Jacko a towel and a spare toothbrush and told him if he hurried he could get in and out before Lizzie noticed anyone else was in front of her to use the bathroom.

Nell quickly took her own shower, needing to do a more thorough job of getting the night's sweat, blood, and worry off. After she got out, she called the hospital where Marcus had been taken. They could tell her little except he was being transferred to Biloxi Regional and should be there shortly.

Nell tried to remember if Dolan had had Marcus fill out the usual forms, including who to contact in case of an emergency. She wondered if his friends at Joe's Corner, with the fire and him missing, had already contacted someone.

Lizzie didn't learn that Jacko was in the house until she started down the stairs in her ratty old bathrobe. Seeing him, she hurried back to her room to get dressed, something that helped them get out the door in good time. Then they had the car dilemma; Nell's back seat was jammed with boxes. Jacko solved things by rearranging the boxes to free up the front seat of his car. Lizzie was happy to ride to school with a cute older guy. Josh got Nell's front seat.

After dropping her kids off, they both pulled into the alley behind the Crier. Nell's arms were already tired at the thought of moving all those boxes again. However, Jacko did most of it, delegating to Nell the problem of where to put everything. It was more work, but the only sensible place was the upstairs conference room. It was little used. Dolan had spread out his paperwork to dry, but there was plenty of room to stack the boxes.

Dolan, Ina Claire, and Pam arrived in time to see the final box head up the stairs.

After legally reparking their cars, Nell and Jacko each explained what had happened.

"You let me sleep through it?" was Jacko's comment on her early morning adventure.

"Marcus? They did that to Marcus?" Pam shouted in outrage. "They burned his house down and then they assaulted him?"

"How is he doing?" Ina Claire asked. It was the worry they all had.

"He's being transferred from the small hospital up there to Biloxi Regional. That's all I know right now. I'm going to call and see if I can get an update." She didn't add her fears about the silence she had watched come over him as they lay in the wet grass.

And she still had a paper to run. "Meanwhile, Dolan, can you clear a space upstairs for Jacko to sort through that stuff? Let's find out what those men so badly wanted to burn."

It was early, but Nell called Joe's Corner while Dolan was looking for the sheet with Marcus's info. Everything had been moved out of his office, so he couldn't be sure whether it had been ruined in the fire or was at his house drying in his rec room.

"Yeah, Joe here," a tired voice answered.

"Hi, this is Nell McGraw. I'm calling about Marcus Fletcher."

"You heard about his house? Poor bastard, what a thing to do to an old man."

Nell had to tell Joe they had done more harm to an old man. "I'd like to contact his family, tell them what happened."

"I served with his son in the Marines. One of the last people to see him alive. Marcus and his wife took me in like a son, helped me get my life back together. 'Lost one son and gained one,' he told me. I'm part family. I was about to call his kids."

Nell was relieved to pass the duty on to him. Her head felt tired and thick and she didn't feel she could find the words.

After that she called the sheriff's department, but other than acknowledging the report from the highway patrol, they had nothing to add. She called the police station, not that she had much hope they would do anything. They took down the info and promised a vague "will be on the lookout for suspicious characters." Nell could only hope they were competent enough to notice two men wearing ski masks driving around at night without lights on.

She was tired, angry, and frustrated. Two men had tried to kill Marcus and destroy the information he had. Their actions had been quick and sure, not those of men old enough to have committed the murders. The next generation of hate? Her frustration was little helped by the noise of the workmen in the main room. They were ripping up the carpet, replacing windows, and doing any repair that required making significant noise.

She finally got up and shut her door. She left a note telling people to come in, as she usually only shut the door when she needed to work on something or to talk to someone in private. Just as she sat back at her desk, the phone rang.

"*Pelican Bay Crier*, Nell McGraw," she answered.

For a moment, there was just silence. Then a voice whispered, "I didn't do it. They're going to tell you I did, but I didn't."

It took Nell a moment to recognize the harsh undertone as Whiz Brown. "Did what, Chief Brown?"

"My daddy didn't have nothing to do with it neither. Yeah, he knew, but knowing is not the same as doing."

Nell heard the fear in the man's voice. "I can help you, but you have to tell me what's going on."

"Don't let them say we did it. They gave me five hundred dollars to call out my men on Friday night, to say some kids were messing around on the beach, but that's all I did, I swear. Didn't know what was going to happen. My daddy just took the pictures, but he never pulled the trigger. You leave me out of this. Anyone asks, this call never happened."

"I believe you," Nell said to reassure him, although she didn't know what to believe. "What pictures are you talking about?"

"You leave me out, got that? Frieda Connor. Somewhere in her attic." With that, he hung up abruptly.

There was a brief knock on her door and Jacko entered. He had dust on his nose and several sheets of old paper in his hand. And an excited look on his face. He handed her the first sheet. In faded handwriting it was titled *"Loan Sharks"* with a subheading *"don't take money or help from these men, costs too much."* Nell skimmed down the list, recognizing no names until she got to the second to last. H.H. Pickings. She guessed it referred to the father of the mayor, given the age of the document. The next sheet, in the same handwriting, was titled *"Loose Men"* with a subtitle that said *"keep your wives and daughters away from these bastards."* Bryant Brown was on this list, as was Bo Tremble with a notation beside his name—*"two children"*—which Nell guessed to mean that he had fathered two children out of wedlock, probably by rape. The last list was *"Klan Members"* in a different handwriting. As before, most of the names were unfamiliar to her. Reese Allen, Wayne Calvin, George Bessmer, Delbert Barnett, Frederick Connor—she paused at that one—Bryant Brown, Norbert Jones; two she did recognize. The Jones boys had a heritage of hate. But they'd gained nothing in the land swindles, and Norbert Jones was long dead and beyond any prosecution. Much as she wanted it to be them, a nice tidy package of criminals, it didn't make sense that the Jones brothers would go after Marcus. There were about twenty names in all, with one scratched out and a notation next to it reading, *"died in a car accident, the fool."*

Nell looked up at Jacko. "Good work. There may or may not be a story here—there is a story here," she amended, "but I don't think we can label people as members of the KKK on the basis of one sheet of paper."

"No," Jacko said quickly, "but we can research the names, see where that takes us. Some of these might have ended up in jail or someplace else that's public record. I'll keep digging and see what I can find."

He left the lists on Nell's desk. Whiz Brown had mentioned Frieda Connor and now she had a list alleging someone named Frederick Connor was a member of the Klan. Nell grabbed her phone book and looked for a listing for Connor. After a round of calling, she found an R. Connor over on Lancelot Lane, one of the tacky subdivisions on the east side of town. Maybe Frederick went by Rick. She dialed the number. After about seven rings, the phone was answered by a woman.

"Can I speak to Frieda Connor?" Nell asked.

"Who's calling?" The voice sounded suspicious and guarded.

"My name is Nell McGraw and I'm with the *Pelican Bay Crier.*"

"You're the paper lady," the voice said. "Bet you're calling about my stepdad and his Klan stuff."

Nell was nonplussed it had come out so easily. "I'm looking into that allegation."

"My mom passed away about two weeks ago," the woman said. "I'm over here goin' through her stuff, pitching most of it."

"Where is your stepfather?" Nell asked.

"I don't keep up with that bastard. He could of died for all I know. Last I heard was the nursing home out past the trailer park on 90."

"I've heard a rumor your mother had some pictures from that era."

"She might of. Lot of boxes. You're welcome to go through any you want to."

"When would it be convenient for me to come over?" Nell asked.

"I'm here now. Got a lot of stuff out on the street already for garbage pick-up tomorrow."

"I'll be there in about half an hour," Nell decided.

This could be an exercise in frustration, Nell realized as she got up. Even if Whiz, in his desperation, had told the truth, there was no guarantee she would find anything. Even if she did, no promise it would tell them anything more than they already knew. She asked Jacko if he could pick up Lizzie and Josh in around an hour.

Nell told Pam and Ina Claire where she was going and headed out the door.

When she got to Lancelot Lane, the house was easy to spot; the one with piles of old boxes out front.

Nell found a woman about her age in the kitchen, and she introduced herself.

"I'm Angie Pitts." The woman hastily brushed a hand off on her pants and shook with Nell. "Most of the stuff from the attic's already on the curb. Been sitting up there for decades and if we didn't use it in that time, no reason to think we might ever."

"Ms. Pitts," Nell said, "are you sure you're comfortable with what I might find? Things that, well, make your family look bad?"

"Just don't bring my name into it, that's all I ask." With a harsh laugh, she added, "You can't make them look worse than they were." She pulled up a sleeve and showed Nell a series of scars on her inner elbow. "See this here? Stepdaddy thought he'd teach me a lesson 'bout cleaning my room. Used his cigarette to do it. I got other scars, too." She savagely threw a plate into the trash pile, shattering it. "Momma shouldn't of married him, but she did. Stuck by him till a while back when he shoved her head into the toilet and us kids got together and kidnapped her. Put her in this house. Thought we got her safe, but he came crawling back and next thing he was living here. He stroked out a couple of years ago and we finally got some peace in the family."

"I'm very sorry, Ms. Pitts," Nell said. "That was a horrible way to grow up."

"Call me Angie. Not fancy enough for the 'Ms.' stuff. You drag that bastard through whatever mud you feel like."

"If I find anything, I'll let you know before I decide what to do with it," Nell told her.

"Don't need to ask. Like I say, just don't mention my name. I don't know if I want to know what other crap he did. Bastard." She shattered another plate. As if answering a question Nell had asked, she said, "Yeah, should be saving these plates, at least give 'em to the thrift shop, but I was forced to eat everything off these plates. Didn't eat the spinach quick enough for him, he'd do things like shave soap onto the plate and force us to eat that. Teach us we could be eating stuff that really tasted bad, he told us. Once made my brother eat cockroaches." Another plate shattered. "You know he messed with us girls. Never had no kids 'cause of him."

"That's evil," Nell said. "No one should treat children that way."

"You got it. Now you know why I don't give a damn what you write about him."

Nell could think of little to say to the woman's volcanic anger. There were no words that, in a brief encounter in a tired kitchen, could matter a damn against the years of damage. Nell excused herself and headed to the curb to start looking.

She wasn't dressed for sitting on a lawn and digging through dusty old boxes, but there wasn't time to go home.

Most of the boxes had little of interest: old clothes, bank statements from the fifties, old magazines. There were several boxes of Confederate memorabilia, and others that held stacks of blatantly racist material, proof of his Klan membership. Nell was getting discouraged. She was through about two-thirds of them and had found nothing of real interest. She opened the next box and found stacks of letters. She started to pass on that box until she noticed the letters in one of the stacks were addressed to a woman named Alma Smyth. One of the names from Pelican Property was A.J. Smyth. Nell took that stack out and searched through the others, but found nothing else. A glance at her watch told her she would have to hurry to get a brief glimpse of the rest of the stuff. She opened another box, deciding Jacko wouldn't leave the Crier building anytime soon, and Josh and Lizzie could hang out there until she got done.

In the bottom of the next carton, Nell found a beaten-up old metal lock box. She tried to jimmy it open, but couldn't. It looked like it would hold things like insurance papers or deeds, papers once considered important. She set it aside and moved on to the next pile. And the next pile. When she finally finished with the last few piles, all that remained was the locked metal box. The sun was setting, and despite her exertion, Nell was getting chilly.

She picked up the metal box and headed back to the house, to see if Angie Pitts knew anything about it.

But when Nell showed it to her, she shook her head and said she'd never seen it before. Nell asked her permission to break it open.

"It's trash, ain't it?" was her answer. Then she called out, "Len? You want to come break open something for the paper lady?"

A man around Angie Pitts' age joined them in the kitchen. He said nothing, just picked up the box and examined it. Then he took a screwdriver off his belt and used it to pry the lid open. Without looking in the box, he handed it back to Nell.

She set it down on a small cleared space on the counter and pushed the broken lid out of the way. A black cloth covered the contents of the box. Nell lifted it aside.

"Oh, my God!" she exclaimed and let the cloth fall back.

Her reaction garnered the attention of Len and Angie. He picked up the cloth and looked.

They had found the pictures Whiz Brown's father had taken. Steeling herself with a deep breath, Nell looked again at the image confronting her. She recognized Michael, Ella, and Dora, but only barely. They were surrounded by about ten men, several of them holding guns or clubs. Michael's wrists were chained and his face bruised and puffy. Both of the women had been stripped to the waist, their breasts exposed. The background was outside, in a wooded area.

"That what you were looking for?" Angie Pitts asked. She seemed less upset than Nell, but perhaps her life made her more blasé about human cruelty.

"This is what I'm looking for," Nell confirmed. "Can you recognize any of the men?"

Angie studied the photo, then stabbed her finger at a man in the back. "That's old Fred, I'd say. Stepdad." None of the other faces were familiar to her. Len even looked, but he hadn't grown up in the area.

There were other pictures underneath the top one, but Nell didn't feel up to looking at them. This one told her enough.

She thanked Angie and left her to their task of trying to destroy the memories with the plates.

As she had guessed, Jacko's car was still in the lot. Nell clutched the box to her chest as if both protecting it and keeping it held down, like a creature with fangs.

Lizzie and Josh were on Carrie's computer playing a game. They saw her long enough to know their mother was alive and well, and then Nell went to her office.

She set the box on her desk, unsure of what to do next. Her impulse was to hunt down Harold Reed and hand it to him. But, this late, he might be hard to find, and she was enough of a reporter to want to see—no matter how horrible—the photos. The one picture she had seen was too brutal, but there might be one she could use in the paper, to bring the horror of it home in a way words couldn't.

Putting the box in a drawer, she went upstairs and asked Jacko if there was an update on Marcus. He was in intensive care, in critical condition, and he hadn't woken up yet. Then he asked her if she'd found anything.

"Come to my office," Nell said and left without waiting for him.

She put the box on her desk as he caught up with her. Wordlessly, she lifted the black cloth. She didn't take the photos out of the box, instead keeping them contained there, flipping them up one by one. She tried to avert her glance from the fear and desperation in the eyes of Michael Walker, Ella Carr, and Dora Ellischwartz.

Like game hunters, they had taken pictures of their trophies. Both the woman had been raped; Ella Carr had a distant, vacant look in her eyes, as if she were already leaving the body she knew would not exist much longer. Dora Ellischwartz was still fighting, tears and anger on her face, a silent scream coming from her mouth. There was a shot of Michael on his knees, back to the camera, one leg clearly broken. One of the men had the barrel of a pistol pressed against the base of his skull. The next picture showed him lying on the ground, blood coming from the gunshot wound.

The final picture in the box was of the three of them tossed into the grave, with only the feet of the murderers visible. Nell gave a start when she realized one of the sets of feet were small. A young boy? Had someone brought his son along?

She closed the box and said to Jacko, "I'm going to call Harold Reed. And I'm going to ask a big favor of you." She nodded her head in the direction of Josh and Lizzie. "Can you take them this evening? Pizza and a movie?" Nell dug in her purse for enough money to cover all three of them.

Jacko agreed. Nell suggested another night in their guest bedroom; that way, she could more easily update him when she got home. Plus she didn't mind having an adult male around. She out-and-out lied to her children and told them she had paperwork to do and was sending them off with Jacko. A movie and pizza was enough of an enticement.

Nell called Harold Reed at home. She simply told him she had to talk to him and could he come to the Crier office. Those pictures felt too dangerous to move. Then she sat and waited.

When he arrived, Nell quickly told him what had led her to the photos—leaving out Whiz Brown's part in it—and opened the box. She didn't look at them. He was silent a long time, looking at the pictures slowly and carefully. When he finally finished, he looked up at her and asked, "Any idea who these people are?"

Nell told him about Frederick Conner, how his stepdaughter had identified him. "He must know who the rest of them are."

"Yeah, but is he going to tell us?"

"Marcus would know," Nell said. "This was a small town back then."

They stared at each other, leaving it unspoken that Marcus might never look at these pictures.

"That could work for us and against us," Harold said. Pointing a finger at the pictures, he added, "It's not likely any of these men is going to be helpful."

"Hattie Jacobs," Nell remembered. "Marcus traced her. She's living over in New Orleans. According to him, she had a cross burned on her lawn. She might recognize a few of these men."

"She might. A long shot."

"Is it all right if I talk to her?" Nell asked. Even if Hattie Jacobs couldn't recognize anyone, she could still tell the story of what had happened to her. The DA's office might not be interested in something they couldn't prosecute, but Nell wanted to call the past to account.

"That's okay. Just let me know if she has anything useful to say. Can I take these?" he asked, although it was clearly not a real question.

Nell hesitated. "I'll need one to show Hattie Jacobs. And I want to run one of them in the paper."

"That might be hard to look at."

"I want them to look. All those silent people who let this happen," Nell said vehemently. "Consider this—if I print a picture, someone might come forward who recognizes these men."

"True. But it happened a long time ago," Harold pointed out.

"Not long enough. They firebombed my building and Marcus's house. They were hunting him and now he's in a coma," Nell said.

"Which ones do you want?"

She took the first one, for its group shot. And the one with the gun at Michael Walker's head. It was brutal, but it wasn't the obscene gore of the dead bodies, or the horror of the sexual assaults. Nell took the two pictures and hid them in the back of one of her file cabinets, then locked it.

Harold picked up the box and they silently left the building.

Nell felt heavy and tired as she headed home. She was halfway there before turning to drive by Marcus's house, with a lost sense that he might be coming home. But the house was black and empty, most of the garage burned to the ground, the house itself licked by flames. She stopped briefly by Joe's to see if they had heard anything. The bartender sadly shook his head no.

"Call me if…" Nell said. She was afraid her voice might break.

She got back in her car and went home. Jacko, Lizzie, and Josh had beat her there, by enough to have thrown popcorn in the microwave.

Nell sat with them, managing a few handfuls, but despite not having eaten since lunch, she had no appetite. She gave Jacko a brief rundown of her meeting with Harold Reed. After that, she begged off, not even bothering with a motherly admonishment of lights out by ten p.m.

Jacko got them to bed around then anyway by going to bed himself. Nell heard their shushed whispers and the squeak of the guest bedroom door as it shut. Her last thought as she drifted off to sleep was please give an old man a few more years of sipping beer at Joe's Corner.

TWENTY-FOUR

With Jacko around, Lizzie was on her best behavior. Both she and Josh were ready for school with no hurrying from Nell. Jacko was even gallant enough to drive them. I must look as tired as I feel, Nell thought.

She lingered over her coffee. The die had been cast. Those pictures changed everything. It could be easy, it could be hard, but they would find those people. It rankled her that a young boy had been there. Teaching the young to hate. Then Nell wondered, could it have been a woman? No, women should somehow be better than that. But Frieda Connor had stood by her man, whether he was beating her or another woman. Maybe she'd followed him even there. Had she turned her head, Nell wondered, as Dora and Ella were violated? Or had she enjoyed it? Or had she suffered the night before and was relieved it wasn't her this time?

Nell put her coffee cup in the sink and left for work. It would be a long day.

When she got there, she found out it would be more than long.

Harold Reed was waiting for her. "He never woke up," he said softly. "It's murder now."

Nell flared, "He shouldn't be dead! He shouldn't be..." She felt as if she'd been hit with a body blow, a fresh jolt of the shattering from the night Thom died. She hadn't saved him either. Grief and fury concatenated, turning into a rage that had no words and that she could not stop. She suddenly slammed her fist against the wall. She was utterly out of control, lost in a frenzy of anger and anguish.

As she raised her fist to strike again, someone grabbed her arm. Someone else pulled her away from the wall, holding her tightly. She struggled, then collapsed, wracking sobs coursing through her. Nell realized Jacko was holding her; Harold Reed had grabbed her arm, although his grip had changed to one of comfort rather than restraint. Pam was in front of her with a box of tissues.

Nell grabbed a handful of them and wiped her face. When she finally felt able to speak, she said, "I'm sorry. That was... I'm just sorry." She took several breaths, wiping the still-oozing tears. "I won't do it again. Just as long as no one else..." She again sobbed into the ball of tissues. Then, gaining control, she said, "I'm okay. Well, not, but... will hold it together."

They released her but stood close, as if they might be needed again. With another few breaths, she was able to keep her voice close to steady. "Tell me what you know," she asked.

"Not much at this point. We hope we get forensics from his house," Harold said.

"Men in ski masks aren't a very helpful description," Nell said harshly.

"We're going on the theory that the men who torched his house are connected to the ones who killed him, so there might be something there that will provide the link."

"To the arson," Nell pointed out, the bitterness still in her voice. "It won't prove they murdered him, especially as the ones who burned his house couldn't be the ones following him." As she said it, she felt chilled. It had to mean this wasn't a final bit of violence from the past, one or two madmen hanging on. What happened to Marcus had to have been plotted and planned, and suddenly Nell felt small and vulnerable.

"If we get them for one thing, we have a better chance to get them for another."

"I heard their horn over his cell phone. Bastards played 'Dixie' with it," Nell remembered.

Harold just nodded.

After he left, Nell again apologized for her breakdown. She retreated to the bathroom to scrub the red off her face. Then she got a cup of coffee and went to her office. She sat at her desk and stared out the window.

Ina Claire and Dolan arrived; Jacko met them at the door and gave them the news. Nell didn't hear the words, just a short, cheery greeting as they came in, then the tone changing, voices hushed, an underhiss of sorrow and outrage.

You killed an old man but you didn't save yourselves, she silently cursed the murderers, fury coursing through her. We have Marcus's files; if we can't find a witness to name the faces in the picture, we can dredge through those documents, take the names found there, get old yearbooks, old photos from the Crier morgue, wedding shots, and painstakingly match the faces with the people. They would not escape.

Suddenly Nell decided she couldn't sit and listen to workmen pound all day. Looking through her desk, she found the address for Hattie Jacobs in New Orleans. It was in Marcus's handwriting.

She remembered to take the photo out of her filing cabinet; only the group shot, not the one of Michael's execution. The faces were the same, and it would only add to the horror.

"I'm going to New Orleans," she told her staff. They were all assembled in the break room, Pam's temporary office. Jacko again agreed to pick up Josh and Lizzie if Nell didn't get back in time. He even offered to mind them should she stay overnight.

She thanked him, then headed for her car. She stopped by home long enough to get directions and throw a few things in an overnight bag, even though she intended to be back that evening.

It was an hour-and-a-half drive from Pelican Bay to New Orleans. Nell made good time, late enough to miss the morning rush. She knew she might not find Hattie Jacobs. She could have moved, died—or just not be at home.

Nell and Thom had come to New Orleans a number of times, including more or less keeping their vow of one romantic weekend a year sans kids, so she was familiar with the more beaten paths. The address for Hattie Jacobs was on a street Nell recognized, and, according to her map, it was just a few blocks out of the French Quarter. But as Nell turned onto Ursulines, she recognized this was a part of New Orleans the tourists didn't see. Crossing over Rampart from the official boundaries of the Quarter changed the neighborhood. The houses were the Creole cottages of the historic area, but time and money for upkeep was sporadic; some well-kept houses sat next to ones boarded up and abandoned.

Nell drove slowly, looking for Hattie's address, aware she was out of place. Spying the number she was looking for, Nell pulled over. As she walked up the steps to the front door, she noticed the neighbors watching her. She nodded a bare greeting at them and knocked on the door.

One of the women on the opposite porch called out, "She stepped out, be back shortly."

Nell thought about asking if a woman named Hattie Jacobs did indeed live there, but that would tell them she was a stranger and put her into the suspect category of government agent, law, or health, hunting down an old woman.

Nell thanked the woman and said causally, "I'll be back after a few other errands, then." She got in her car and drove off, remembering a little coffee shop she and Thom had chanced on, outside the Quarter where parking would be kinder. She took a few wrong turns but finally found the right street and, in the next block, the coffee shop. But walking in brought back memories of being with Thom, so Nell got her coffee to go and wandered around, gazing at the windows of the shops along the street but with no real notice of what was in them. What a double-edged sword memory is, Nell thought. How many times will I get hit with remembering the things Thom and I used to do? In Pelican Bay she couldn't avoid places they had been together, but this city should be large enough not to ambush her with recollections that cut so sharply. She discarded her half-drunk coffee and got back in her car, then slowly made her way back to Hattie Jacobs' block. There were no memories of Thom there.

Just Marcus Fletcher, she thought, glancing at his handwriting on the address.

She again pulled in front. Clouds now covered the sun and the added chill had driven the stoop sitters inside. Nell remained in her car, trying to decide if it had been "a little while" enough for her to knock again.

She noticed a woman walking in her direction. As the woman got closer, Nell saw she was older, her shoulders stooped, wearing a cloth coat that looked like it had seen a number of winters and carrying two small grocery sacks. Nell watched her as she turned and made her way up the steps to the door.

Nell got out of her car. When she got to the foot of the stairs, she said, "Excuse me, but are you Hattie Jacobs?" The woman turned to her, and she added, "My name is Nell McGraw and I'm a reporter with the *Pelican Bay Crier*," to give the woman access to her name and a clue to her purpose there.

"Pelican Bay?" the woman said slowly.

"Yes, it's a small town over on the Gulf—"

The woman cut her off. "I know where Pelican Bay is."

"Are you Mrs. Jacobs?" Nell asked again.

"Yes, I am. What can I do for you?"

"I'd like to talk to you about some things that happened a long time ago."

Hattie Jacobs hesitated before saying, "You'd better come in then."

Nell followed her into the house. It was neat and well kept, the furniture old, a mix of colors and styles, as if Hattie had collected them slowly along the way.

"I'm making tea. Would you like some?" she asked. "Help take the chill off."

"Yes, thank you." Nell sat down on the couch while Hattie Jacobs carried her sacks back to the kitchen. From her briefcase, Nell took out the most recent copy of the *Pelican Bay Crier*, with its stories about the murders and the property theft. She left the photo where it was; it wasn't something she could show without being sure Hattie was ready to see it.

Hattie returned with two steaming cups and a small tray with milk, lemons, honey, and sugar on it. Nell added some milk and honey.

"This is the most recent edition of the paper," Nell said, handing it to her. "The two stories—"

But Hattie Jacobs cut her off by gasping, "Oh, my God! Michael. And Ella and Dora. These are the pictures that Rufus took."

"Rufus?" Nell prompted.

"Yes, Rufus Jackson. Farm just down from mine. Michael stayed with him, and Ella and Dora stayed with me." She looked at Nell and said, "They're dead, aren't they."

"I'm sorry, yes, they are." Nell could have let her read the story, but instead she told it, leading Hattie through finding the bones to establishing the identity of Dora Ellischwartz.

When she finished, Hattie asked, "May I keep this?" referring to the paper.

"Yes, of course."

"Something to remember them by," the old woman said softly. "I liked both Ella and Dora. But Michael … he was a friend. I knew he didn't just leave."

"Tell me about them."

Hattie stared at the photographs, her hands tracing their faces, then said, "Dora was the fun, laughing one. She'd come home and say, 'let's have a party,' and we'd put sugar on bread for cake, and she'd plug in that radio of hers, find some music and have us all dancing, spin my kids around the room until they were dizzy.

"Ella was quiet, a little too serious; she and Dora really balanced each other that way. She'd be reading a book until Dora took her by the hand and said, 'c'mon, you have to dance,' and Ella would pretend to be annoyed, but she was the best dancer once she let loose and got going.

"Michael. Michael and I used to sit on the porch and talk. Sometimes we wouldn't talk, but just be silent with each other and it was an easy time. Sitting watching the sun set. The others worked hard, but Michael...Michael gave me hope. Hope things would change, that my children would live in a different world. Promised me one day I'd come visit him in New York and he'd walk me down Broadway."

Then she was silent, as if remembering all the promises and the ways they had been broken.

Nell gave her a moment, then gently prompted, "What happened with your farm? How did they get it away?"

"They said I didn't pay my taxes," Hattie said, her voice hard. The words came slowly; the years hadn't taken the bitterness away.

"But you did," Nell said, adding, "I tracked down Penny March, the clerk, and she remembered. They changed the records."

"They did, they changed them. Told me I had to pay or I'd forfeit. But I had no money to pay again."

"And that was what happened? They foreclosed with the taxes?"

"No, they would've, but Mr. Dupree bought my property. I never really knew, wasn't the place for a woman like me to ask, but I think they were fighting, each getting greedy. Mr. Dupree waited until he knew I had no choice: I would lose it for nothing or take whatever he gave me. Did the same thing with my land, the bayou camp, and the bay beach. We each got hit for taxes we'd already paid, then he came around and bought the property just before it would have been taken. We got something, he got the land."

Andre Dupree. Nell had been hoping his hands were no dirtier than buying property that had been stolen by others. That would be painful enough to tell Aaron, but could the son ever forgive her for opening old wounds to find his father wielding the knife?

Nell took out a map of Tchula County and spread it over the coffee table. "Can you point out what was yours?"

Hattie did. Her land was most of what had turned into the posh Country Club and part of Back Bay Estates, with the other properties she had mentioned becoming the rest of it and the Marina. Andre Dupree had not only stolen from the poor and the powerless, but he had cheated his partners by buying the land before they could take it.

"According to the records we looked at, your land was bought by something called Pelican Property," Nell said.

"I remember the name, but it was Dupree that came out and offered the deal. He was the one who gave me the money."

"How did you know him?"

"Saw him around, his name in the paper. He was always polite, pretended to be nice. Even when he helped burn the cross, he wasn't as bad as the rest of them."

"Burned the cross?" Nell said, taken aback, still able to be shocked.

"Michael told me they couldn't take away my property, that we could fight. One last piece of hope he gave me. I had even tried to register to vote, thought the world was going to change. Then Michael was gone and I had to sell the land.

"I'd gone to the courthouse to register, then I went by the tax office to inform Mr. Dunning I was going to protest, gave him an affidavit Michael got a lawyer friend of his to draw up.

"Two nights later there were seven of them on my front lawn, wearing those starched sheets their wives had ironed, burning a cross. Telling me Michael and Ella and Dora were gone."

"If they were hooded, how could you tell who they were?" Nell asked.

"Ever recognized someone by their voice? The way they walk? Every Negro in Tchula County knew what Sheriff Tremble's voice sounded like, cigarette harsh. Also his deputy, Reese Allen. Recognized

Bessmer the undertaker with his big, pale hands. The greasy mechanic's fingernails, with a high voice, was Norbert Jones. And Dupree had a soft cough, always covered his mouth with his hand. Even when he had a hood on."

"Do you think these were the men who murdered Michael, Dora, and Ella?"

"They knew they were gone and not coming back," Hattie Jacobs told her. "How else could they know that?"

"Maybe people talked," Nell suggested.

"Dora and Ella left my house in the morning. They didn't come back that evening. Instead, these men and their burning cross, and the way they told us we could never hope again."

"The timing is damning," Nell noted.

"But an old woman like me isn't going to be enough to do much to them," Hattie said, her voice weary and resigned.

"Your say-so alone, probably not. But we've found other evidence." Hattie looked at her.

Nell continued. "They took pictures. Men like this also mistreat their daughters, and those daughters, when they grow up, don't hide the family secrets. Right now we just have photos, but no names. I brought one of them with me. It's not something easy to look at, but it would be a great help if you could identify any of the men."

Hattie slowly nodded her head and Nell took the damning photo from her briefcase. When she first saw it, the old woman stiffened, then hugged herself tightly, looking at the image without touching it. She spent several minutes gazing at the photograph. Then she recited to Nell, "Sheriff Tremble with that shotgun, Norbert Jones right next to Dora, he ran the gas place in town; Albert Dunning with the club, Reese Allen, sheriff's deputy, with the pistol, Bruce—I think his last name was Goodman—bag boy at the grocery, Rick

Connor, the high hair in back, he did odd jobs, never held one long, and Barnett, Delwin Barnett, he drove a garbage truck." She was able to name seven of the ten men there.

"Thank you, Mrs. Jacobs," Nell said as she put the photo back into her briefcase. "There is no statute of limitations on murder. You may be contacted by the District Attorney's office. Although these photos might be damning enough."

"A few twilight years of justice. Most of them already in their graves by now."

Nell couldn't argue. The men in the photo had fifty years of freedom. "What happened after you were forced to sell your land?"

"I had family over here. Came to live with my cousin Bessie till I found a place of my own. Hard with four kids used to the open spaces of a farm. I got work as a maid in a hotel. Some days I'd dream I was back on the farm, then wake up to this city and cleaning other people's trash." She was silent, then said very softly, "I still occasionally dream I'm back there, wide open green space and the time mine to make my day."

"I'm very sorry, Mrs. Jacobs," Nell said. Those feeble words were all she could say.

"Hattie. Just call me Hattie. At least they didn't get away with it forever. Twilight justice is better than none." After a pause, she said, "Would you like more tea? Mine's gone cold and the day is too chilly for that." She didn't wait for Nell's reply, but picked up the cups and went back to the kitchen. From there she said, "My son Emmett is going to come by and fix some of these drafty doors, but his wife broke her arm and he's got to do all the chores she used to do."

"Probably a good thing for him to find out how hard woman work," Nell answered. "You said you had four children? What happened to them after they left the farm?"

Hattie replied with a question. "You have any children?"

"Yes, two. Lizzie, my daughter, is on the verge of teenage angst and Josh, my son, who's twelve, is still more interested in sharks and searching for shells on the beach than girls."

"Josh and Lizzie. Family names?" She brought in two steaming cups of tea.

"Elizabeth came from my older sister, Margaret Elizabeth. She … did a lot of raising me. And Josh is just Joshua. My husband Thom was named for his father and he insisted no one else carry that burden," Nell said quickly, busying herself with her tea.

Hattie caught the past tense. "Was?"

"Was. Thom was killed by a drunk driver," Nell said. "About a month ago." She wondered why she added that.

Hattie reached over and took Nell's hand. She held it silently, then softly said, "Daniel, my husband, was killed by a tractor. White boy going too fast. It tipped over, caught Daniel under it. He lingered for about a week." Again she was silent.

"How did you do it? It's hard enough with two children for me. But how did you go on?" Nell was no longer a reporter, and her questions had nothing to do with any story she would write.

"I had to. I just had to," Hattie answered slowly. "That's how I went on. We had almost made another life when we got the farm taken away." She paused. "I lost two of them."

"Your children?" Nell asked, almost a whisper.

"Daniel, named after his father. He wanted to fight, to rip that cross down with his bare hands. Anger caught him just growing into a man. It had no place to go. Left the farm he was going to take over someday to go sleep on piled blankets on the floor of his cousins' room. He started getting into trouble with the law, then more trouble. He's … up at Angola now. Don't know whether to hope I'm still alive when he gets out or hope I'm gone and don't have to hear the gunshot and wonder if it's him—shooting or being shot."

"What happened to the other child?"

"Daisy looked for love too easy. I was working too much, just not enough to get enough money. She got pregnant at sixteen. Three kids by the time she was twenty. Too many different men. One gave her AIDS. She's been gone fifteen years now."

Two more lives, Nell thought. Consequences have consequences that travel far. Maybe their fate would have been the same if Hattie Jacobs had kept her property, or it would have been different. Nell tightened the pressure on the woman's hand.

"I am so sorry. There aren't words…"

"Love your children, love them hard and well." Hattie took a sip of her tea, then, as if the lost Daniel and Daisy were too hard to leave unleavened, she said, "Emmett and Rosa have done well. Both made it through college and now Rosa is going to law school at night. Emmett married a real good woman; they helped raise Daisy's children after she passed, plus two of their own. His wife's a nurse; he works over in the juvenile court, assessing the kids that come through. They're both doing all right."

All right despite everything, Nell thought. She worried enough about Josh and Lizzie, but they slept in their own beds in their own house. Those comforts only seem small when you have them.

She spent another hour with Hattie, mostly talking of the safe things, what had changed in Pelican Bay and what hadn't, about Josh and his beach rambles. But the edges of the other times cut too many places to avoid them; the beaches were still segregated when Hattie left. Hattie's sons and daughters couldn't have gone to the same school as Thom McGraw, even walked on the same beach.

Nell thanked Hattie for her hospitality. She wanted to thank her for her courage. But she could find no words.

"What happens now?" Hattie asked her.

"I'll talk to Harold Reed, the assistant DA, and tell him what you've told me. He gets to search for these men and bring those still alive to trial. You might talk to a lawyer about bringing a civil suit for your property. I don't know enough about the law, but given everything, you should get at least a decent settlement."

"Money won't buy my farm back. Or the life I should have had."

"No, it won't. But it's one less way they get away with it."

Hattie stood on the porch watching Nell drive away. She stood there until Nell turned a corner and could no longer see the house.

Traffic was heavier on the way out. Nell was glad for the distraction of driving on the packed interstate. She needed a slice of the ordinary to pad her away from all the horrors today had accumulated.

Nell made it back to Pelican Bay a little after five. There was a stack of messages on her desk. She didn't even bother looking through them. She picked up the phone, called Harold Reed, and told him what Hattie Jacobs told her. Harold had updates for her, too. There was black paint on Marcus's car that appeared to be from another vehicle.

As Nell put the phone down, she felt a twinge of relief. Whatever else his sins—and they were many—at least Andre Dupree, confined to a wheelchair and barely able to speak, couldn't be responsible for these current firebombings and murders.

There were two messages from Aaron in the pile on her desk, one asking about lunch today and the second about lunch tomorrow. Nell looked at them. The last thing she wanted to do now was face him. Finding out the truth about his father would be shattering. My choice is either to be a blatant coward or do it myself, Nell thought.

Nell called Carrie to see how much she had. It felt necessary to focus on routine tasks. Carrie had two stories, a rundown of the elections and coverage of the debate. She had a couple of good quotes of Mayor Pickings sputtering about suing the Crier, the reporter who had asked the question, and everyone in the room. Nell told her she needed the stories by ten in the morning and earlier was better. The trip to New Orleans may have been productive as solace for her broken soul, but it had also left her behind.

Still ignoring the telephone messages, she went upstairs to find Jacko. "Pelican Properties. Can you get together everything you found out about them?" Nell wanted to check on if a number of their names were also the names Hattie had revealed. "And Jacko … do you want to do the obit for Marcus or should I?"

"I've already worked on one," he admitted. "It felt like something I needed to do."

"Thank you," Nell said, secretly glad it had helped him work though his sorrow, because doing it would have only made hers worse. "Mention that he worked for the Crier before, covering the desegregation of the beaches but the paper didn't give him a byline because of the attitudes of the times. Don't sugarcoat it to make it look like anything other than the cowardly act it was."

They stayed late that evening, Jacko working on his stories, Nell on hers, as well as the myriad other details that required her attention. Jacko's computer friend joined them, bringing in a replacement server. At first Nell took him to be about a sixteen-year-old boy, but on second look decided he was a she and probably in her twenties. She seemed to know what she was doing, her rates were reasonable, and that was enough for Nell. Josh and Lizzie remained more or less content continuing their computer game. Jacko did a burger run and full stomachs kept them going for a while.

When they were getting ready to leave, he handed her what he had on Pelican Property. Nell started to put it in a desk drawer, but then decided, given how busy everything would be tomorrow—and she was going to have to talk to Aaron soon—to take it with her. She also took the stack of letters from Alma Smyth to Frieda Connor. Then she gathered her children and headed home.

TWENTY-FIVE

When they got home, Josh and especially Lizzie seemed to not notice they were later than usual and were determined to get their customary TV and computer time. It took three strong hints to get Josh to turn off the TV. She had to threaten Lizzie with pulling the plug to get her off the computer.

"But, Mom, I had to get this stuff done tonight!"

As Lizzie kept typing, Nell made the unwelcome parental suggestion of getting up early to take care of it.

"Mom!" She didn't even look at Nell as she said it, keeping her eyes on the computer screen.

"Daughter!" Nell replied, then, reaching the end of her patience, she hit the off button on the monitor. That got Lizzie's attention. "I'm getting ready for bed. When I get out of the bathroom I expect the computer to still be off. Understand?"

Lizzie didn't agree, but Nell headed for the bathroom. Another moment and she would be screaming at her daughter, spilling her anger in the wrong direction. Nell still wasn't sure what would be on the front page. Marcus's murder. She wanted more than an ephemeral newspaper to offer him. She was tempted to go with the election and the loss of Marcus and leave the murders and property theft for later. But she knew with the pictures and Hattie's identification, the murders would soon blow open, and these were her stories. They had cost far too much, she wouldn't let someone else have the headlines.

She finished in the bathroom, and Lizzie was still on the computer. Seeing her mother, Lizzie frantically typed a few extra lines as she was standing up. She didn't even bother to properly shut the computer down, just hit the power button.

"I couldn't get to it because we had to stay late at your office," Lizzie fumed, then ran past Nell and up the stairs to her room.

How many more years do I have to put up with this, Nell wondered. She retreated to her room, although suspicious rustlings told her Lizzie was dawdling through her bedtime routine. But Nell heard no footsteps on the stairs, so at least she wasn't getting back on the computer. She turned on the bedside lamp, deciding she would read a little of her homework before snuggling in.

Pelican Property had been incorporated in 1961, and had dissolved by 1965. For a business, a short time. It fed Nell's suspicion it had been more of a shell than real. Looking over the property transactions, she noticed in late 1963 and the first six months of 1964, Pelican regularly turned the properties over to Andre Dupree. While Pelican made profit on the transactions, it was nothing to retire on, especially for a group of six. When it dissolved, it held only the property near the harbor; the rest had been sold to Dupree. He soon bought half of that, and Nell was betting with a little more title searching, they might find out he eventually got the rest of it.

Nell looked at the list of owners, Bo Tremble, B. Brown, Frixnel Landry, Albert Dunning, Lamont Vincent, and A.J. Smyth. Hattie had named both Tremble and Dunning in the picture, and Whiz had indicated his father was the photographer. That meant that three of the six owners had something to do with the murder of Michael, Dora and Ella. Maybe it was just coincidence, but if A.J. Smyth was Alma Smyth, she seemed out of place among this group of powerful men. If they were the same, that would make it four of six.

Nell untied the string holding together the stack of letters from Alma J. Smyth to Frieda Connor. The first one was dated September 19, 1953. Skimming over it, it seemed mostly a discussion of which boys they were dating and who had the best prospects.

Nell started on the second one when she heard a stealthy footstep. As they were going down the stairs not up them, that significantly limited the suspects. She gave the late night wanderer a minute or so, in case it was a relatively innocent run for a glass of milk. Instead, she heard the distinct beep of a computer being turned on.

Putting the letter aside, Nell got out of bed. As quietly as she could, she moved to the entrance of the living room. The room was dark save for the bluish screen of the computer. Showing no mercy, Nell slipped her hand over the main light switch. The lights blazed on, capturing the culprit.

It was Josh. He blinked several times then said sheepishly, "I couldn't remember how big Great White Sharks get and it was bugging me."

Lizzie was awake enough to hear voices and she came trotting downstairs.

Nell considered roaring, "get back to bed now," but decided a compromise might get everyone tucked in more quickly than a battle would. She put on hot water for instant hot chocolate and gave them each exactly ten minutes on the computer.

Twenty-two minutes later, her children were again heading up the stairs. Nell didn't bother with the letters, but turned out the light and pulled the covers up.

The next morning in the hurried routine of getting her children up and out, Nell almost left all her homework sitting beside the bed.

Nell was relieved to discover Jacko and Pam had done most of the basic layout of the paper yesterday while she was gone. Pam, also, thanks to Jacko's tech friend and an advance on the insurance money, had a nice new computer; no more file-your-nails delays while waiting for images to load. "Click the mouse and it's there," Pam marveled.

Nell was in the middle of looking over Carrie's stories when Sheriff Hickson barged in. Without an invitation, he leaned in her doorway.

"Got a story for you, Miz McGraw."

Nell almost wanted to scream, "Keep it until next week and get the fuck out of my office." She just had to think of a more polite way to say it.

"Hostage situation goin' on right now."

That would be a story for this sleepy town, although his attitude told Nell there was more, or probably less, to this than his words were saying.

"I hope it's a hostage situation on deadline," Nell said. "I'm in the middle of getting out the paper."

"One Beauregard Lee is holed up in a house in the middle of town, holding Mrs. Hufflenutter hostage."

"What's Lee want?" Nell asked, reluctantly grabbing a notepad and camera.

"Not sure yet, no communications have been established. Want to ride with me to the scene?" He was already walking away. She followed.

Nell shot Pam a questioning look. "I'll need you in about an hour," the young woman told her. Nell grabbed Carrie's story and a red pen; she might get the final edits in while standing around. The sheriff was already halfway out the door and she hustled to follow him. As if knowing she couldn't resist the bait, his cruiser was parked directly in front of the building.

"How serious is the situation?" Nell asked as she slid into the passenger seat.

"Don't rightly know, just got the word," he answered as he started his car.

Nell put on her seat belt, noticing the sheriff didn't bother. "How did you find out about it?" She was determined to get a few questions in before they got there.

"Got a call," was his laconic answer. Then, as if he knew she'd keep asking questions, he put the siren on and they wailed the ten blocks it took them to get there.

It was a residential street of older houses, with trees grown to maturity. The house they stopped in front of was set back from the road, its faded green paint echoed by the green hedges and shrubs of the front lawn, grown to almost house-height.

Other cars were there. Nell noticed that despite its being in town and theoretically the jurisdiction of the police, only the sheriff's men were on the scene.

"Okay, you've dragged me here," Nell said in the silence from the siren. "Want to tell me what it's all about?"

"Got a call. A dangerous situation. Thought it should be covered by the newspaper."

"Why the sheriff's department and not the town police?" Nell pushed.

"We took the call. Thought it better to come here than wait around." He opened his door and got out, avoiding further questions.

Nell followed. They were almost directly in front of the house, as were the others milling around. Several neighbors had come out to watch. Clearly the danger level wasn't great; otherwise they would have cleared the block. While she couldn't claim to know every resident in Pelican Bay, the names the sheriff had mentioned didn't sound familiar.

"Please don't hurt him," a youngish man was saying. "He's only hungry."

An older woman, with enough of a resemblance to be his mother, had her own take on it. "Shouldn't oughta ever open that cage door. Just shouldn't oughta."

"What cage door was left open?" Nell asked as she edged closer.

But before she got an answer, the door to the house opened and one of the young deputies ran out carrying a cat. The older woman flung herself at him, grabbing the cat out of the deputy's arms as he came down the steps. She almost threw him off balance, and for a tottering moment it looked like woman, cat, and man might end up rolling in the yard. But the deputy righted himself and the cat was transferred, much as a flour sack would have been. The expression on the cat's face showed it was not brimming over with gratitude to its rescuers.

Nell snapped a picture of the disgruntled cat in the woman's clutches. Turning to the sheriff, she said, "That, I take it, is Mrs. Huf-flenutter. You don't by any chance know the correct spelling of the feline's name?"

The sheriff didn't answer.

Nell continued. "And just who, or should I say what, is Beauregard Lee?"

The young man answered, "A bicolored rock python."

"'O best beloved.'" Nell couldn't resist.

Seeing Nell as an ally—"ally" seemed to be anyone not openly hostile—he animatedly continued. "He's really a beautiful creature. After I played with him this morning I guess the cage lock hadn't caught, and he got out. Mom found her cat on the top of the bookshelf with Beauie following her every move. She panicked and called the sheriff."

Hearing her son's version, his mother had to get her own in. "Mrs. Huffie only survived because she's smart enough to climb up. That critter of yours was about to have her and me for lunch!"

"Ma, Beauie is only six feet long; he couldn't even get around you more than once. Worst he could do is crack a rib."

Those words were not a great comfort to his mother, neither the thought of only a cracked rib nor the implication about the thickness of her waist.

Leaving the family feud to go its way, Nell turned back to the sheriff. He was talking to the brave deputy who had rescued the cat.

"Didn't see the snake, didn't want to," the young man was saying.

"Just as well. We can probably let the young fella hunt it down," the sheriff replied.

"You brought me out here to the middle of a Rudyard Kipling story?" Nell demanded. She had a moment of picturing the sheriff's already robust nose being stretched like that of the Elephant's Child. It wasn't a pretty thought.

"Well, we got a mostly happy ending, but even you gotta admit a big snake running around town is a story."

Nell briefly considered telling him it was only a medium-size snake and would therefore be in the second section, but she decided her first crack was enough. Silently, she even conceded he was more or less right. At about any other time, this would have been an interesting story for a small town's local paper.

"Okay, Sheriff, let's get a picture. Do you want to be holding a phone for the more realistic shot, or would you like to be more dramatic and pointing a gun in the direction of the dastardly snake?"

The sheriff reached a compromise pose, holding the radio from his car, with his hand resting on his gun. Nell dutifully took several shots. The next time it could really be a man with a gun and she didn't want to give up her exclusive privileges. Not for something like mere morals and journalistic standards.

His heroic pose captured, the sheriff didn't seem to feel a need to linger in an area with a big snake on the loose. After giving his deputies instructions to shoot if the snake made a break, he escorted Nell back to his cruiser.

Most of the town streets were now one way, so they headed back by a different route.

As the sheriff pulled to a halt at a stop sign, more to answer his radio than to obey the law, Nell noticed they were at the corner with the Jones brothers' gas station.

She sat up when she noticed a big, dark truck in the back bay. Another car was parked across the entrance, as if they wanted to make sure the truck was as hidden as could be.

Nell had to see if the truck had a dent on the front fender.

"Where are you … ?" the sheriff said as she got out of his car.

"A dark truck," Nell answered as she strode across the street. She wanted a quick look. If it was the truck, by tomorrow all traces of the attack might be gone.

But there was no way to sneak into the garage, and although she was sliding behind the parked car in front of the truck before anyone noticed her, it wasn't lost on the Jones boys that Nell McGraw, with a camera in hand, was investigating their truck.

"Hey! You can't go there!" someone shouted.

"Stop me," Nell muttered to herself as she rounded the back end of the truck. It was parked front end in, and the passenger side was next to the wall, making it difficult to glimpse the front right fender.

"What do you think you're doing, lady?" one of them shouted.

"Get out of there now!" the other added.

They sounded nervous. The driver's window was open; Nell put her arm in and leaned on the horn. It blared the first few bars of Dixie.

"Goddamn it!" came another shouted curse.

Nell hurried on her circuit of the truck, squeezing in between the wall and the front bumper. It was the only way to get to the fender.

The Jones brothers were coming after her. They were large men with big beer bellies and they couldn't slide around to follow her as Nell edged around the front of the truck to the tight space on the passenger side.

"You're trespassing! We got a right to shoot you!"

Nell glanced up. She hadn't thought the Jones brothers would do much more than haul her bodily off the property. You idiot, she chastised herself. They might be murderers and they might just be stupid enough to shoot her in broad daylight.

Nell looked down at the fender. It was scraped and dented, a few flecks of the same dark green color of Marcus's car in the gouge.

Nell looked up again at the Jones brothers and was relieved there wasn't a gun pointing at her. She was less relieved that the older of the brothers was opening a cabinet in the office. They wouldn't be gunless for long.

To go back the way she came would take her straight to the brother now grunting and straining to follow her narrow path. But the space between the wall and the truck was a tight fit and she couldn't cover the distance quicker than brother number one could get the gun.

If you can't go around, you have to go over, Nell decided as she heaved herself up and into the bed of the truck.

"Fucking shit," came from brother number two, accompanied by a ripping sound. He seemed to have wedged himself in and was now attempting to tear himself out.

But brother number one had retrieved the gun. He pointed it at Nell.

She threw herself into the bed of the truck just as he pulled the trigger. A loud boom echoed in the tight space and Nell found herself showered with plaster from the bullet hitting the wall.

"What the hell you doin'? Don't fuckin' shoot his truck!" shouted another voice, one Nell recognized from her whining phone calls. Tanya was standing by her man's truck.

"Put that damn gun down." For once in her life, Nell was happy to hear the sheriff. She was less happy when he added, "Nell Mc-Graw, you are under arrest for trespassing and disturbing the peace. Now get out of that truck."

Nell slowly peered out from the bed of the truck, worried that despite the sheriff being a witness, brother number one might still pull the trigger.

"Get on out of there," the sheriff demanded.

"If he puts the gun down," Nell bargained.

"Put that gun away and do it now," the sheriff demanded.

A quick glance at the sheriff told Nell he had drawn his revolver. The possibility of being shot was enough to make brother number one lower the gun and, with a curt nod from the sheriff, to put in on the ground.

"Get out of there and off this property now," the sheriff boomed at Nell.

She reluctantly lowered herself over the tailgate of the truck, keeping her eyes on brother number one and his all-too-close gun.

He didn't move. But the sheriff did. As soon as Nell was clear of the truck, he grabbed her by the shoulders, spun her around so she was braced against the car in front of the bay, and with an efficiency she didn't appreciate, pulled one arm behind her back, slapping a handcuff first on one hand and then on the other.

"Don't you ever try any crap like this again, little lady," he told her as he marched her away from the garage and toward his cruiser. He had her arm in a painful grip and was almost dragging her at a hurried pace.

"Trespassing, what the hell is this?" Nell fumed as she caught her breath.

"You just come with me," he said, giving her a good jerk on the arm to keep her in line.

Nell suddenly wondered what she'd gotten into. Was the sheriff part of this murderous mess? And smart enough, unlike the Jones brothers, to see it would not be a wise idea to take her out in the middle of town? Handcuffed as she was, all the sheriff needed to do was find an out-of-the-way place with a few feet of water and let her drown. Or bury her in an unmarked grave.

"I'm due back at the paper," Nell said. "They'll wonder when I don't show up."

"Just get in the car," he told her in an angry voice. He opened the front door and shoved her in.

Nell landed uncomfortably on her hands and barely had time to swing her legs in before the sheriff slammed the door.

He quickly strode to his side. Nell was used to the slow, southern, almost stereotypical sheriff, not this purposeful and capable man. He started the car, not bothering with anything like a seat belt before hitting the gas. He was quickly over the speed limit. Nell found herself thrown back against her hands, catching a finger in a painful way.

"You murdering bastard!" Nell spewed at him. "That was the truck, but you knew that, didn't you? What's in this for you? A little money for your self-respect and sworn duty to uphold the law?"

"You be quiet now," he told her.

Nell had no intention of being quiet. "You make Whiz Brown look like a model lawman. Were you the one who beat an old man's brains out? Now what, do you really think you're big and strong enough to take a handcuffed woman somewhere and dump her?" Forget vinegar; Nell was now putting acid in her voice.

He took a corner, throwing her against the door.

"Goddamn you, just goddamn you!" Nell spit out as she attempted to right herself.

He jammed on the brakes, pulling to the side of the road. As he did so, he put an arm in front of Nell to keep her from slamming into the dashboard. Nell found one of his hands on her breast, but he held just long enough to brace her. She hoped it had been unintentional.

"Just hold your goddamn horses, excuse my French—"

"Fuck your French!"

"You keep this up and I will haul you into jail, Nell McGraw." He grabbed her chin in his meaty fingers and forced her to face him. "Now I know you probably think I'm the stupidest lawman this side of the Mississippi, but even I ain't stupid enough to take on them viper Jones boys with just a newspaper lady for backup."

He let go of her chin then took the radio out. "Now, if you can manage not to cuss for the next few minutes, I might even take the handcuffs off. They would'a been stupid enough to shoot the both of us if I hadn't hustled you out of there and acted like I didn't give a damn about the truck."

"Do you think there's any chance it'll still be there?" Nell asked as she tried to wiggle into a comfortable position.

"Delbert and Melbert Jones ain't a full set of teeth. They probably think I'm hauling you off to the hoosegow, so the idea it might be smart to drive that truck into the swamp hasn't occurred to them." He added, "Tanya might be smart enough, but it's more than even odds they didn't tell her if they're using J.J.'s truck for shit. She don't know, she ain't gonna think of it."

He got on the radio. "Got a truck that needs a go-over at the Jones' garage. Can y'all spare me a few cars?" After a few more calls and responses, he started his cruiser, pulling a U turn. He stopped again as he noticed Nell was still in handcuffs. Pulling the key off his belt, he said, "We got no proof of anything. The Jones boys are stupid, but they ain't been this criminal yet. You keep that in mind. I'm gonna turn you loose. You sit in this car, you stay in this car, and you stay out of my way. Got it?"

"Got it," Nell answered as she turned her back to him so he could undo the handcuffs.

After letting her go, the sheriff put the car into gear again. He drove to the corner, then stopped there. They couldn't see the garage, but they could see the street and the next corner.

Nell rubbed her wrists, then asked, "Why would the Jones brothers attack Marcus?"

"Don't know that they did."

"But that's the truck," Nell countered.

"Maybe. But that doesn't mean they were driving it. Maybe they lent it out, maybe it's not Junior's truck, only one like it. Maybe they're just doing a favor for a friend—a stupid favor, fixing his truck without asking too many questions."

Two sheriff's department vehicles came to the far corner. The sheriff started his car again. "And Mrs. McGraw, if them idiot Jones boys start shooting, you be smart enough to duck down, okay?"

Another department car fell in behind them as they turned the corner. As if on cue, the four cars all converged at the garage at once. As they got closer, Nell craned her neck and saw the truck was still there.

"Stay here," the sheriff told her one last time.

She watched as the sheriff and his deputies, including the one woman on the force, moved in. Confronted by seven law officers, the Jones brothers were amazingly docile. Or the true cowards they were.

Nell managed to be enough of a reporter to take pictures, but she did so through the window of the car, not the best angle. But she wasn't going to get out.

The Jones brothers were quickly handcuffed; it took less effort for them than it had taken for the sheriff to cuff Nell. The closed sign was put on the door and two of the deputies remained with the truck until it could be impounded.

When the sheriff returned to drive Nell back to the Crier offices, she merely asked, "Do you think they did it?"

"Maybe, maybe not," he replied.

As Nell watched him she realized she had no idea who to trust. If the Jones boys were involved, would he protect them? Or let them take the blame so others could escape?

He said little more before he dropped Nell off. She rubbed her wrists as she watched him drive away.

Nell immediately started banging out the story. The election might not even make it on the front page. She then called her printer and said they might be late on the front page, but everything else would be on time. As expected, they grumbled, named a price Nell could live with, and agreed they could probably do it if they had everything in by seven. She was hoping she could get something more from the sheriff, though it didn't seem likely the Jones would confess on deadline.

Nell finished writing and glanced up to see Aaron Dupree standing in her doorway. She wondered how long he had been there.

"I'm sorry, I didn't get back until late yesterday evening," she stumbled out. "And today the paper goes to press, so I didn't think I'd have time for lunch."

"I didn't think you'd have time either, but you have to eat." He held up a paper sack. "I got a turkey on sourdough and a tuna salad on whole wheat from Café Bayou. Your choice."

Nell was touched by his thoughtfulness and guilty as hell about the bombshell she was going to drop in his life.

"So can you squeeze in fifteen minutes for me? Even if it's just lunch at your desk?"

"You're very considerate. And you've gone to a lot of trouble for fifteen minutes."

"Trying to bribe you with a turkey sandwich to give me the paper's endorsement," he said. "You're pushing yourself pretty hard these days. Someone should take care of you."

Nell motioned him to sit down, clearing a space on her desk for the food. She desperately wanted to avoid what she was going to have to tell him. But it's not kindness to delay a blow that has to fall, and it was too cruel for him to read about it in tomorrow's paper.

"Thank you. You're being very kind. And I'm afraid we've stumbled onto some things about your father's property dealings that ... aren't going to do much to repay that kindness."

Aaron stopped unwrapping one of the sandwiches and looked at her. "What kinds of things? I don't think it's much of a secret that he was a hard-nosed businessman."

"It goes beyond just hard-nosed." Nell plunged into it, telling Aaron about Pelican Properties and how quickly it had transferred the ill-gotten property to his father. "All the land used for Back Bay Estates, the country club, and the marina were taken using the property tax scam."

At her words, his face became increasingly closed. He didn't touch the food as he listened. When she finished, he said, "He couldn't have known" with a sharp finality.

As gently as she could, Nell pointed out the obvious. "Aaron, he couldn't have not known. Some of the deals were no more than months apart. It's very possible he didn't know the exact details and wasn't in on it directly, but—"

"But what?" he demanded.

Nell had hoped he would see where it led instead of forcing her to say it. "But more than anyone, certainly the principals of Pelican Property, he gained from the transfers. I traced one of the women who lost her property and she claimed that Andre Dupree was acting for Pelican Property—its name was on the paperwork, but he made the deal."

"And you believe the word of one old, uneducated black woman…" He trailed off.

"It's not just her word—and she seemed pretty educated to me—but the accumulation of the evidence. I'm sorry, Aaron. I wish we hadn't found this."

"Then lose it. If you can find it, you can lose it."

"I can't hide the truth," Nell told him softly.

"You're going to report this?"

She repeated, "I can't hide the truth."

"Damn it, Nell, it's not truth anymore. It's history now. So a few people made bad deals with their land. That happens all the time. And this happened a long time ago."

Nell didn't know if his defensive statements were from the shock of finding out and with time he would work his way to seeing the weight and importance of what had happened, or if he so needed to believe in the honesty and integrity of his father that his rationalizations would become an impenetrable wall. "I'm very sorry," she said again, hoping he would know she really was. "I know this is hard for you to hear. But, Aaron—and I'm not saying your father had anything to do with it—these property thefts led almost directly to the murder of the three civil rights workers."

"Nice of you. My father is just a thief, and only hung around with murderers."

"I can't change the past," Nell said quietly.

"But you can put it on the front page."

"I'm sorry, Aaron," she said again. "I wanted you to know before…"

He sat silently, then he suddenly bolted up and said, "I've got to leave. I need to think about this."

"I'm sorry," Nell tried to say again, but he was out the door. Now it was her turn to sit silently, wondering if she would ever see him again, wondering if she was doing the right thing. Then she remembered the haunted look that had passed over Hattie Jacobs' face. "No, I can't change the past," she said softly to herself. She took the uneaten sandwiches to the break room, giving them to Pam and Jacko.

She went back to her office and again just sat. Then she couldn't stand staring at the wall, so she began looking over her desk for anything to distract her. She tried willing the phone to ring, for Harold Reed to call back so she could forge ahead with the murder story. Or for the sheriff to call and say that the Jones boys did it, to keep her demons all in one neat package. Or for Aaron to call back and … and what? Say he understood why she was doing what she was doing? Was that even possible? But the phone didn't ring.

She picked up the letters from Alma Smyth and started reading the next one, but it was just another listing of the young men she had an interest in or who were interested in her. Nell stumbled over the name of Bo Tremble as a possible suitor, but he was quickly dismissed. She skimmed the next letter but it was more of the same. Then she started flipping through the envelopes, glancing at the postmarks to see if she could find anything close to the dates of Pelican Property and Alma Smyth's part in it. Nell suddenly stopped flipping; her brain registered that something had changed. She paged back through the envelopes to see if she could discern any differences. It was the return address. The handwriting was the same, but the name and address had changed. Alma J. Smyth had married. Starting in 1959, her name was Alma J. Dupree.

"Oh, God, no," Nell said aloud as she stared at the envelope. Alma Smyth was already Alma Dupree when she had used her maiden name as one of the owners of Pelican Property. This brought Andre Dupree closer to the murders. Hattie Jacobs had said he was one of the men burning the cross on her lawn, one of the men who had told her Michael, Dora, and Ella would never return. Just because he hadn't been present at the murders—or in the pictures—didn't mean he wasn't an accessory.

Now her phone chose to ring. Nell snatched it up, hoping it was Harold Reed. She had to share this monstrous information with someone else.

Her caller was Alma Dupree, almost as if willed into being by the ghosts of her past. "I think we have some things we need to talk about," she informed Nell. "Can you please come over here?"

Nell was completely flustered at having the damning letters on her desk and now the woman herself on the phone. "Mrs. Dupree. It might be hard for me to get away ..."

"Please. This is very important. I'll be here all afternoon waiting for you. We're at 12 Wisteria."

The phone went dead before Nell could think of anything else to say.

Before she had gathered her thoughts, it rang again. This time she cautiously picked it up. Harold Reed.

"It's about time," she barked at him. Then immediately added, "I'm sorry, it's just that a lot has happened in the last few hours." As coherently as she could, she explained what she had learned about Pelican Property and its all-too-close connection to the Dupree empire, ending with, "And now she wants me to come over there and talk to her."

Aaron had obviously told his mother what Nell had revealed.

"But this was before you made the connection between Alma Smyth and Alma Dupree?" Harold asked. "Are you going to see her?"

"How can I, knowing what I know?" Nell answered.

"Would you consider wearing a wire?" he asked.

"A wire? Haven't I destroyed their lives enough without another betrayal?"

"This is murder, Nell," he reminded her. "And murder not just in the past, but from here and now."

"I know," Nell admitted. The innocence of the son wouldn't mitigate the guilt of the father, much as she wanted to spare Aaron another blow. Nell also desperately wanted one more chance to meet Marcus for beers at Joe's. She made her decision. "Tell me what I need to do."

Harold asked her to get to his office as soon as she could. He'd set things up on his end.

Nell found Dolan, who had just returned from purchasing new office furniture. She told him they were holding the front page; Pam already had one on her computer, the safe one with the election rundown and Marcus's obituary. If Nell didn't get back, or if they got behind, he should go ahead with that one. As explanation, she told him she had to go to the DA's office and might be there for a while.

Harold was waiting for her when she arrived, immediately rushing her into a small office. "We're working to verify the identifications Hattie Jacobs made, but so far all we've got are tombstones. Someone from back then is still alive enough to have ordered the murder of Marcus Fletcher and the attack on your building. I want that person," he told Nell.

"But Andre Dupree is confined to a wheelchair, barely able to talk," Nell said.

"That doesn't mean he couldn't orchestrate events. Or that he was going to sit and watch everything he worked for in his life be taken from him and his family."

"You may get nothing more than Alma Dupree offering me tea and telling me that I've upset her son and maybe I could consider not printing whatever it was he found so disagreeable."

"We might well get that, but she asked to talk to you, so she might be offering some kind of deal which we can use as leverage. She may let something slip. You're more likely to get anything than any of us. The minute we go in, they're going to be barricaded behind a wall of lawyers," Harold explained. "I don't think you're in danger. She may be just a little old lady offering you tea and a small bribe on behalf of her husband."

The door to the office opened and the woman deputy came in, carrying the wire.

"Are you willing to do this?" he asked Nell directly. It was her last chance to say no.

"I'm ready," she affirmed.

Harold stepped out, and the woman deputy put the wire on Nell. Good thing it's winter, she thought; the bulky sweater she was wearing was a much better concealment than a light T-shirt.

Back in the parking lot, sitting in her car, Nell suddenly thought, I can't be playing cops and robbers, doing bizarre things like wearing a wire to talk to the mother of a man I … I saw hints of possibility in. And whatever happens—such as Mrs. Dupree asking me if my intentions towards her son are honorable—I'll have an audience for it.

Wisteria Lane was located in the vast tract of property Andre Dupree had developed. It was in the secluded part; only people going here would travel this far back.

The house itself was a mansion, with a sweeping view into the bay and a lawn that could only be kept at its level of perfection by constant attention and the sweat of hired help. Nell hoped the wire could transmit the distance covered by this immense lawn. In this neighborhood, it wouldn't take long for a neighbor to spot an out-of-place blue van. Nell had a picture of someone calling the cops on the cops. She slowly drove up the long driveway, looking at the house almost as if in a dream. In some other world, she might be coming here to meet Aaron's mother as a possible daughter-in-law. A world that was gone.

Nell parked her car, not recently washed, and she noted how out of place it looked in front of the huge house.

She rang the doorbell and was surprised when Alma Dupree herself answered. Nell would have expected at least a maid, if not a formal butler. The woman's bearing was regal and her face showed faint echoes of the beauty she must have been when she was younger. The clothes she was wearing were tasteful and expensive, set off by subdued but equally expensive jewelry. She was tall, around Nell's height, her back still erect and proud.

"I'm Nell McGraw," Nell said.

"Thank you for honoring my request. Please come in." Alma Dupree didn't introduce herself, as if it was obvious who she was. "Let's go back to the sun porch; Andre doesn't like it when he can't see me."

She led Nell through a large formal living room with antique furniture that looked more for show than sitting. Nell's guess was proven correct in the next room, furnished with deep leather couches and chairs, still expensive but looking like someone occasionally sat in them rather than just walking by. From there they crossed a dining room, with a table that could easily sit twelve and a chandelier that probably cost more than Nell's car when it was new. The kitchen was all marble-topped counters, the copper-bottom pots and pans gleaming as if they were never used. The help sweated inside as well as outside. Alma Dupree then led her into an enclosed porch with wide windows and several skylights. The room was lush with plants, small trees that reached almost to the tall ceiling.

Hattie Jacobs' farm had bought a lot. From what Nell could see, happiness wasn't included in the deal.

Seated in one corner was a hunched old man Nell assumed to be Andre Dupree. His resemblance to his son was faint, lost in disease and age. Looped under his nose was a line going to an oxygen tank. His head barely turned when they entered and he made no attempt to speak; the only sound was the labored hiss of his breathing.

"Please sit down," Alma Dupree told Nell, though it came out as an instruction. "Would you like coffee or tea?"

Nell dutifully sat. Even on the so-called porch, the furniture was far better than anything she had in her house. Or probably ever would have.

The offer of coffee or tea was the thinnest veil, put on to convey this was a polite visit. Alma sat down across from Nell and said, "I hear you're making claims we cheated people out of their property."

She was blunt. Nell answered her bluntly. "The records were obviously changed. Entries crossed over, making it seem like people who had paid their property tax were delinquent."

"Then that should have been between them and the tax office. Why drag us into it?"

"Because you bought a great deal of the property taken from people," Nell told her.

"That's not true," Alma Dupree retorted. "Andre bought most of his holdings from a group of white men, some development company called ... oh, I forget what it was called."

She said it easily, the lie, as if it had been repeated enough to become truth.

"Pelican Property," Nell supplied. "Owned by five men and one woman. Tell me, Mrs. Dupree, what was your maiden name?"

She stared at Nell for several seconds, then covered by saying, "What does that have to do with anything?"

Nell revised her guess about Alma Dupree. She had assumed she'd been a dutiful wife of the time, little aware of what her husband was doing, or, even if she was aware, powerless to do more than find rationalizations for her silence and obeisance. Maybe those were both true, but also present was the fierceness of a woman who would do anything to protect her family.

"It was probably a clever ploy for the time," Nell mused. "The law would never take a hard look at what the men who controlled Pelican Bay were doing to make their money."

"What are you implying?"

"One of the owners of Pelican Property was Alma Smyth, spelled with a *Y*, which was your maiden name," Nell said. Then she added, "Your husband was hiding behind your skirts, Mrs. Dupree."

"You don't know what you're talking about," she retorted coldly.

"I'm sorry, but I do. You were very powerful back then, but in the passing years things have changed. A harsh glance from the Dupree family can no longer rewrite history."

Alma Dupree sat up straight and stared at Nell. "You don't understand, do you? If they wanted to keep their land, they could have kept it. They just weren't strong enough. That's not my fault."

"It's not your fault you took advantage of a system that would never believe a black person over a white one? That there was no law or even moral decency to stop you?" Nell threw back at her.

"If you fight hard enough you win. They didn't fight hard enough," she said dismissively.

"They didn't have your weapons, all the power packed into the bigotry and hate of the era."

"Please, spare me your politically correct view of history."

"I will. Let's see if you can *fight* hard enough to stop the onslaught of both press and legal action coming your way," Nell told her, suspecting she wouldn't much like a battle of true equals.

Alma Dupree tried another track. "Do you know what this will do to us? To Aaron? To Desiree? To our grandchildren? Why punish them?"

"Because the children and the grandchildren of the people you stole from are still suffering. They could have started their lives with the wealth from their land, but instead they started with nothing. Why did they deserve to be punished?"

"You are determined to go ahead with your vendetta, aren't you? I was prepared to make you a generous offer."

"Restitution to those you cheated?" Nell shot back.

Alma Dupree started coldly at her. "We can make your life very difficult, Mrs. McGraw." Whatever façade she had managed until now was gone, her face showing arctic fury.

"The Jones brothers are in jail," Nell lied. "Who else do you get to hunt people down and then bludgeon to death?"

"First you accuse me of theft and now murder? I don't understand what Aaron ever saw in you."

Fight ice with fire, Nell thought. She said, "Buzz Brown wasn't as careful as you wanted him to be. We found the pictures of Michael Walker, Dora Ellischwartz, and Ella Carr being murdered. You're in one of them."

The expression that crossed Alma Dupree's face was electric. Nell was in the room with a trapped animal. She'd been guessing when she'd claimed Alma Dupree was there, the small feet at the edge of one photo.

"I will not spend one minute of time in jail for the murder of stupid interlopers! Don't think you can threaten me." All masks and pretense were gone.

"Killing Marcus did you no good. His files helped, but the photos—like those of goddamned trophy hunters—will damn you."

"He was an old man, he didn't have much longer to live," was how she dismissed his murder.

"And you're an old woman, you won't be in jail nearly long enough," Nell spat back at her.

For an answer, Alma Dupree stood, jerked opened the drawer of an end table, and took out a pistol. She leveled it at Nell. "And who do you think you're going to tell?"

From his corner, Andre Dupree tried to say something that sounded like "*no*." A long raspy cry.

"Shut up! You never had the courage to do what needed to be done," Alma Dupree told him. To Nell she said, "We all made a pact that those who benefited had to take responsibility for doing what was required. Those troublemakers had to go, but poor Andre couldn't stand to do it, so I had to be there instead. I did it then and I can do it now."

Alma Dupree was the cold-blooded killer in the family, not Andre. Nell could only look at her hand and the gun in it. Keep her talking, she told herself; you have an audience and they might get here in time. "Shooting me isn't going to do any good. The Jones brothers will talk, to save themselves from being executed."

"Please, you don't think I was stupid enough to deal directly with those idiots. Their father was smarter. He married a dumb woman and got dumb children as a result. I had to give them instructions for every single step. Used a cheap, throw-away cell phone to text them instructions. Like lending their boat and driver's license to some friends so the Coast Guard would think they were aground at certain crucial times. To get their cousins to help when they needed to do two things at the same time."

"So they point to someone else, who points to you."

"You really do underestimate me. Hubert Pickings received several thousand dollars to take a sealed envelope to them. He didn't know who left it and the Jones brothers never knew who it was from. The cell phone could not be traced to me. All that mattered to them was that there was money in those envelopes."

Andre Dupree again let out his raspy cry, rocking the wheelchair in a useless attempt to move. His wife ignored him.

"You're going to shoot me in the sun room of your house and think you can get away with it?" Nell questioned. She was desperately looking for a way out, or a weapon she could use. But there was nothing faster than Alma Dupree's finger on the trigger.

"An old woman like me a murderer? No one will believe that. The gun went off accidentally. I left you here to go make coffee. You must have picked it up and it went off."

Nell heard a step in the next room and then Desiree walked in. "Mother, I heard voices and … oh, my God, what's going on?" She stared at the gun. Then looked at Nell.

"Your mother is going to murder me," Nell told her. And the people on the other end of the wire. It was little consolation Alma Dupree wouldn't get away with it.

"Mother! Put the gun down. This is crazy!"

"Desiree, please leave. This doesn't concern you."

Desiree looked from her mother to Nell, then back again. She seemed to waver, as if she was going to obey her mother. Then she said, "Mother, no. Nothing is worth this."

"Think about it, Mrs. Dupree. Back then, you were a young woman. There were a number of men there, now dead, whom you can blame. But if you pull that trigger, in front of your husband and daughter, you'll never get away with it," Nell told her.

"Desiree, please leave. Let me do what I have to do!"

"But you can't…" her daughter started.

"I can! With your help, if you say the gun fired accidentally, we'll get away with it. No one will doubt the two of us."

"Mom, please, no," Desiree said, but her voice was weak.

The daughter has the choice to turn in her mother, Nell thought. Or to cover up, go along with the story about an accident. Nell took the only chance she had. "You can't get away with it." Turning to Desiree, she said, "I'm wearing a wire. Everything said here is being recorded. If you go along with her, you'll become an accessory to murder. You're a young-enough woman to spend a long time in prison."

Desiree looked from her mother to Nell, a growing horror in her eyes.

"Don't listen to her!" Alma Dupree instructed her daughter. "She's bluffing. Nothing has to change. Just do as I say."

Desiree cast one more anguished look at her mother, then slowly crossed to Nell. "No, this has to stop." She was now standing too close to Nell for her mother to get a clean shot. "I can't…" And then Desiree broke down sobbing, but she didn't move.

"It's over, Mrs. Dupree," Nell said quietly.

Sirens sounded in the distance, coming for them.

Alma Dupree looked frantically from her daughter to Nell. Then she spat out, "You'd better hope there is a heaven and a hell, because you'll get no justice in this lifetime." Her eyes were blazing with anger. She turned to her husband. He seemed to know what she would do; he let out his strangled cry one more time. She aimed the gun at him and pulled the trigger. His chest exploded with red. She then put the gun in her mouth. Desiree screamed an animal sound. But Alma Dupree was not going to jail. For one horrific second, the scream was cut off by the retort of the pistol. Then there was just Desiree's anguished wail.

Nell grabbed her and pulled her out of the room, away from the blood and bodies.

They stood in the sun, in the cold sunlight, Desiree sobbing in her arms. The sirens wailed to a crescendo, followed by an abrupt silence filled with shouts and pounding feet.

TWENTY-SIX

NELL SAT BEFORE THE fireplace, reading the paper that had just come out. She had skipped this routine last week, being too close to the deaths of the elder Duprees to read about it again. She'd been enough of a reporter to call in the story to Jacko, leaving it up to him, Dolan, and Pam to make the final arrangements for that week's front page.

She'd let everyone go home after lunch. Now she was in her house, alone. Josh, bundled up in as many sweaters and sleeping bags as Nell could foist off on him, was on his island camping trip, and Lizzie was sleeping over at a friend's. She hadn't told them she'd had a gun pointed at her head, held by a woman who would have pulled the trigger. Alma Dupree was beyond prosecution, leaving both Nell and Desiree with some control over what stayed quiet. Nell told herself she was keeping things back for Josh and Lizzie. She acknowledged Desiree had probably saved her life, and she owed her. For now it seemed the right decision; Josh and Lizzie had recently had days go by without the haunted look from after Thom died. They were getting on with their lives, venturing out instead of hovering near home and the mother who was left them. That had Nell alone in the house, with a fire and the paper to keep her company. And a glass of Scotch.

The headline should have been *"The Election That Wasn't."* Instead it was *"Mayoral Race in Confusion."* Aaron Dupree had pulled out, making the statement he could no longer live in Pelican Bay. Nell had seen him a few times since then, mostly across crowded rooms. They never spoke. He had looked at her once, first with anger on his face and then a sad, wistful expression, as if there was a place he'd briefly dreamed of that had included her. Then the anger had closed in. He'd left for California two days ago. Both he and Desiree had agreed they would sell all the Dupree property they still held. Nell had to be cynical enough to wonder if it was the memories or if the sale would create another legal hurdle for anyone seeking redress.

One of the new police chief's duties upon taking office was to arrest Mayor Hubert Pickings. His family had been one of those Pelican Property had outmaneuvered. They thought they could get the bayou property, now the Marina, for just the cost of back taxes, but by putting a little money up front, Andre Dupree had beaten them. Mayor Pickings, deprived of what he considered his rightful heritage, had made up for it by taking any consideration people might want give the mayor. Confronted about the cash-filled envelopes and instructions to do a few errands, he had sputtered, "How was I to know it was illegal?" Harold Reed, at hearing that, had just shaken his head and asked, "How could he think it wasn't?" Whiz Brown, the bagman for the deals, had taken a few Valium and gotten calm enough to rat on the mayor and get a plea bargain for himself. He also told everything he knew about his father's involvement. He didn't know much—he wasn't the favored son—but enough to confirm where the money he'd gotten none of came from.

That meant of the four candidates for mayor, one was murdered, one in jail, one gone, and Everett Evens, the remaining one, too crazy for consideration. In what had seemed improbable a week ago, the candidate with the most votes was Marcus Fletcher. He had received a groundswell of sympathy and pulled it out by a slim margin of twenty-six. One of those votes had been Nell's. Somewhere she imagined him saying, "Not too bad for a dead man." The aldermen were debating what they were going to do.

She had done a long follow-up on the murders of Michael, Dora, and Ella. The story had gone national, and Nell managed a byline in several papers she'd once dreamed of having her name in. Thom would have been so proud. She felt a hard, empty ache he wasn't there to share it with. Or even Marcus, to celebrate over beers at Joe's. She'd sent copies of the paper to Gwen Kennedy in Boston, along with a list of graves she could spit on. She had also sent copies to Hattie Jacobs. Twilight years of justice. Only three were still alive; Frederick Connor probably would never get out of his nursing home to face prosecution, but Reese Allen, the man who'd placed his pistol to Michael Walker's head, was still hale and hearty. "Healthy enough that he might live to face meeting his maker early" was Buddy Guy's quote at the press conference. The ironically named Bruce Goodman was also alive enough to prosecute. He claimed to have found God, although not enough to have confessed to his sins, and was running one of those churches Nell considered a temple of hate.

Tanya Jones had called yesterday. The judge had turned down J.J.'s request for a delay. She'd sobbed, "What'll I do without him?" Nell had answered, "You'll do the same thing I'm doing, only J.J. will be coming back in ten to fifteen. Thom never will." Then she'd slammed down the phone.

Nell glanced at the editorial she had written for this week's issue. Her mother-in-law had already called her twice about it; the first call had been arctic, and the next one had dropped the temperature by a few hundred degrees. But Nell had read too many issues of the Crier from that time and she couldn't be hypocritical enough to expose others' sins without looking at those she had inherited.

Thom's grandfather had written, "While we strongly condemn those who use violence to further their ends, can a real solution be imposed by people who don't live here, haven't grown up here, and won't see their children grow up here? They come in, and then leave without knowing what the consequences will ultimately be." And in another editorial, "Society changes slowly. Attempting to impose sweeping social change, especially change that isn't seen as universally desired, is a long process. Those that agitate for change should ask themselves how well they might like to have their whole way of living upended by those who claim to know what is best."

Nell had flinched at its tepid liberal tone. Change comes slowly, but what happens to those whose lives are lost while waiting for change? Pelican Bay had finally desegregated its schools in 1969. That had merited only a few paragraphs in a back section of what was now her paper.

Would I have been any better, Nell wondered, taken out of this time and placed back there? Would I have had the clarity of vision—and the courage—to see the monstrous injustice? How locked are we in our own times? Thom's grandfather, and even his father—who was already the managing editor at the paper—were they good men or bad? Part of Nell wanted to know, to be able to tell her children they were wrong or they were right. Dolan had showed her a picture with "nigger lover" spray-painted on the front of the building, a result of one of the editorials suggesting that "Negroes have the same right to vote as anyone else." The best she could call them was flawed men caught in flawed times.

She had used Marcus's words to end the editorial. "The original American Revolution gave us the ideas of life, liberty, and the pursuit of happiness, and that we are all created equal. The civil rights movement, requiring risk of life and limb equal to that of the original revolutionaries, brought America several long steps closer to those ideals. We are still walking that road. Perhaps our children or their children will indeed be able to judge a person by the 'content of his character' itself and nothing else."

Nell put the paper down, watching the flames for a moment. She threw an extra log on, then poured herself another two fingers and picked up the paper again. She was suddenly reluctant to stop reading it. After she put the paper down, there would just be an empty house. She only had a bottle of Scotch to keep the ghosts away.

She took another sip, cold in spite of the fire, and again started to read the paper.

EPILOGUE

HATTIE JACOBS STOOD AT her window, watching the three women get out of their two cars. They had been easy to spot, out of place on the block. The newspaper woman had called, asking if they could come by.

As they entered, the cold wind of February came with them.

Hattie motioned them to sit, but she didn't offer coffee or tea. Part of it was pride; they had taken enough from her. Part of it was shame; she had no milk or honey, and it would be a few days before she had the money to again buy any.

"Mrs. Jacobs," Nell McGraw said, "this is Desiree Hunter…"

The pale white woman extended her hand. She was tentative, as if Hattie might not be willing to shake with her.

Hattie took her hand, but said nothing.

"… and this is Samantha Dumas," Nell continued, introducing the other woman.

Samantha Dumas was a black woman, a lawyer. There was an awkward silence as they seated themselves.

Finally, Desiree Hunter said in a voice barely above a whisper, "Mrs. Jacobs, I'm very sorry for what my family did to you. I know an apology ... isn't much."

Still Hattie was silent. It wasn't much. It wouldn't get Daniel out of prison or Daisy out of her grave.

Desiree faltered and Samantha Dumas took over. "The reason we're here, Mrs. Jacobs, is to attempt restitution. Mrs. Hunter is aware of what her father did. It wasn't fair and it wasn't right. Mrs. Hunter is offering half of the proceeds of the sale of her part of that property. She is making this offer to get this taken care of without years of litigation, years that would probably benefit lawyers more than anyone else."

"Like yourself?" Hattie asked. She wondered if this African-American woman had been brought in to convince her this was fair, on the assumption that Hattie would trust her just because of the color of her skin.

"Yes, like myself. Except most of them will be white men."

"Mrs. Jacobs," Desiree said in her timid voice, "I have two little girls. I ... need to take care of them. My parents' estate is all I have to do that with."

Hattie kept her silence, although she was tempted to tell this young woman all she'd had to care for her children was scrubbing floors on her hands and knees.

"It will mean you'll have a good amount of money soon. Legal action could take years," Samantha, the lawyer, said.

"Is this a fair deal?" Hattie turned to Nell and asked her directly. She wanted to hear what Nell would say, not necessarily take it as guidance.

"What's fair?" Nell asked softly. Then she said, "You can fight, and you might do better, but it's realistic a lot will go to lawyers. And it will take years."

"Under the circumstances, Mrs. Jacobs," Samantha said, "this is not a bad deal. Mrs. Hunter has initiated this offer—rare enough in itself, and she's giving you as much as she's getting. The choice is sign now and get a check soon, or go to court and fight for a long time with the chance you may not do as well and could even lose, given the statutes of limitation."

Or not even be still alive, Hattie added silently. She thought of fighting. Because she could. Finally, she could strike back at Mr. Andre Dupree, at his grave, at his children.

But she was tired. She had fought her whole life, fighting every day to vacuum another hotel floor, empty someone else's trash; fighting the bitterness of being a maid instead of a woman who owned property and had no clock to bend to, save that of the land. Hattie knew she would sign, but she couldn't say that yet; she wanted to hold on to this bit of time when she finally had power. The money would help Rosa get though law school, give Emmett a new car to replace the one he could barely afford to fix. It could help her grandchildren go to college so they would never have to clean up after anyone. Honey and milk when she wanted them.

Then Desiree Hunter said softly, "I know you must think me a hypocrite for keeping for myself what my father didn't allow you and your children. I probably am. But I have to take care of my children."

Hattie did think she was a hypocrite, a woman of such privilege that making a living with her back and hands and knees was a foreign idea. But she was also a mother with children to take care of. She was the only one in her family to attempt recompense.

"Do I have to sign right now or can I look these papers over?" Hattie asked. "My daughter Rosa is in law school."

"The sooner we get this taken care of, the sooner we can put this behind us," Samantha Dumas said.

"My life isn't long enough to put this behind me," Hattie told the young lawyer.

"It's been fifty years," Nell said. "If Mrs. Jacobs wants some time, she should have it."

"Of course," said Samantha Dumas. "Here's my card. Please call me as soon as you've made a decision."

"Please take my offer," Desiree Hunter said as she again shook Hattie Jacobs' hand. "It's all ... for my children. To take away their sin. Original sin; all the children of the South should know what it is. Our parents teach us to hate before we're old enough to know how hatred poisons the soul."

"I can't absolve sins," was all Hattie said to her.

Nell hung back as the other two women returned to their car, the wind of winter blowing their hair in their eyes.

"You think I should take it," Hattie said, not even a question.

"Would you find any consolation in fighting them? Desiree can only offer funds from her part of the estate. The Duprees have another child, a son, and you could fight to get part of his."

"I'm an old woman, Mrs. McGraw. I will take her offer." Hattie tried to keep the resignation away.

"Do you feel bought off by the Duprees once again?"

"It's a better deal this time," Hattie said bitterly. "Still, only money. It won't buy back a single day of those years. I can't call up Michael and tell him I'm going to fly up to New York and visit him. Or see Ella and Dora dance again, this time at a party with real cake instead of sugar on bread."

"No, it won't buy back a single day."

For a moment, they were silent.

Nell said, "He went to jail, the man who killed my husband. Maximum sentence."

"Was it a comfort?"

"Not enough."

Hattie caught the disconsolate look that passed over the newspaper woman's face. "The man that hit my Daniel was white. Nothing happened to him."

"Hell isn't enough," Nell said.

They said goodbye. Hattie wondered if they'd ever see each other again. They made soft promises: if Hattie wanted to return to Pelican Bay and see what had become of her property, or if Nell got back to New Orleans again.

Hattie stood on the porch watching her drive away. Then she retreated to her kitchen, the warmest room in the house, and made herself tea with a little half-slice of lemon still left.

It was cold, getting so cold these days.

THE END

ACKNOWLEDGMENTS

No one writes a book alone, except for the staring-at-the-screen part and turning down invitations to do fun things. Below is my long list, with hopes that my less-than-always-perfect brain hasn't left anyone out.

I need to thank all the people at Midnight Ink for letting an old(er) writer try a new trick. Terri Bischoff for accepting the book, Sandy Sullivan for her painstaking editing (but all mistakes are mine, trust me on that), Katie Mickschl for publicity, and the people there whose names I don't know but who have done their best for this book.

I also need to thank my writing community, those who have encouraged me or at least not told me I was insane to write a different series. Especially Greg Herren, Ellen Hart, Gillian Rodger, Carsen Taite, Anne Laughlin, Ali, Vali, V. K. Powell, Shelley Thrasher, Nathan Burgoine, Jeffrey Ricker, Rob Brynes, Fay Jacobs, Mary Griggs, Lindy Cameron, Felice Picano, and everyone who trekked out to Treme for the pitcher of Cosmos party or bought a round of drinks at the bar—another book is another reason to celebrate, right, Rob, I mean, y'all? Also some fab book people: Susan Larsen, Candice Huber, Connie Ward, Chris Smith, Paul Willis, all the booksellers, literary festival folks, and librarians. I especially want to thank Jessie Chandler for help above and beyond the call of duty with connections.

While this book is a work of fiction, I have tried to hew as closely as I could to the realities of the history that's part of the plot. Many conversations happened, from brief ones in the street to longer ones; there are too many to name, but thank you all: Neely, Robin, D.J., Nicky, Elizabeth, Doris, and others. A number of books helped guide my way as well, also too many to name, but especially *Freedom's Daughters: The Unsung Heroines of the Civil Rights Movement from 1830 to 1970* by Lynne Olson, *Eyes on the Prize: America's Civil Rights Years, 1954–1965* by Juan Williams, and *Beaches, Blood, and Ballots: A Black Doctor's Civil Rights Struggle* by Gilbert R. Mason M.D. and James Paterson Smith.

I also need to thank my day-job folks for being supportive of my quirky writing life, especially those who keep things running while I'm away: Allison, Joey, Narquis, and Lauran. Also Reginald, Noel, Dr. Ron, Jeannette, Josh, and Mark for their help and support. Everyone in the Prevention Department for making me look like I know what I'm doing, and the rest of the staff for being the kind, caring people you are.

Finally, the cats, because cats notice if they don't get thanked, and Spouse B for learning to make Sazeracs.

ABOUT THE AUTHOR

R. Jean Reid lives and works in New Orleans. She grew up on the Mississippi Gulf coast. *Roots of Murder* is the first book in the Nell McGraw series. As J. M. Redmann, she is the author of the award-winning Micky Knight mystery series.